BILL

OF THE

DEAD

Book 2

EVERYDAY HORRORS

RICK GUALTIERI

Cover by Mallory Rock at www.rocksolidbookdesign.com

Published by Freewill Press
Freewill-press.com

ISBN: 9781652735403

Contents

Dedication & Acknowledgements

For all those awesome people who returned after the roller coaster that was the Tome of Bill, proving to me this nerdy vampire still has plenty of life in him. You guys make stories like this possible.

Special thanks to my awesome team of beta readers – Ruby, Rachel, Anthony, David H., Walter, Pete, Kieren, David, Nick, Jeff, Lynn, Mark, Hezzy, and Stephen. You went above and beyond to point out all the parts of the early drafts that were good, less good, and what needed to be staked and buried for all eternity.

An additional big shout out of thanks to my awesome Patreon supporters – Caprice, David, Hasteur, Lee, Michael L, Michael S, Nick, Nicole, Pheonixblue, Shari, Simon, and Tina. You guys help make all of this possible.

BRAND NEW DAY, SAME SHIT

O n the scale of shit that sucked, few things were less gratifying than having one's own face slammed forcibly into a brick wall.

Crunch!

Oh wait, I almost forgot about a swift kick to the balls. Yep, that definitely topped a broken nose. *Ugh, my aching nuts!*

I slumped to the ground, knowing I couldn't afford to stay down, despite wanting to do nothing more than curl up in a fetal ball and cry for my mother. Problem was, I had a feeling the pair of human shit stains laying into me weren't finished, not by a long shot. I was simply one more stop on their merry murder spree, as they sought to paint the streets of New York red with the blood of their victims.

Someone needed to stop them, and that someone had to be me.

Okay, perhaps that's being a bit melodramatic. The two fuckheads in question, one old the other young, were both freshly minted vampires – no more than a few weeks turned. That made them dangerous, sure, but it wasn't like Godzilla and Ghidorah had washed ashore to level downtown Manhattan.

Besides, it's not like I was chopped liver, even if my scrotum currently felt like it.

"That's enough fun," the older of the two said, a near-geriatric vamp with faded tattoos up and down his wrinkled yet still meaty arms. "Let's drain this shitbox and get out of here."

Powerful hands dragged me to my feet and spun me around – adding momentum to what I'd already been preparing to do.

In human terms, this would've been no contest. The one who'd grabbed me – a shaven ape with a massive beer gut and swastikas inked on both arms – was the sort of goon who'd probably be turned away at a Hell's Angels gathering for being too scary looking.

Under normal circumstances, someone like me – all of five ten, wearing glasses, and a bit soft around the middle – would have to be crazy to tangle with this dickhead, unless they were a secret ninja or some shit like that.

I wasn't.

However, being a secret vampire was almost as good.

"Drain this, fucker," I snapped, clonking the younger of the two in the face with a backhand.

Fat Hitler went flying a good ten feet to land flat on his prodigious ass in a dirty mud puddle.

The older one, a guy who looked like he probably considered solitary at Rikers Island to be a relaxing weekend, bared his fangs at me.

"What the fuck?" he snarled, sounding about as surprised as I'd hoped he'd be.

"Sorry, did I forget to introduce myself?" I replied. "I'm the Freewill."

"Freewill? You some kind of hippie queer?"

Oh yeah, I needed to remember the vast majority of vamps these days, nearly *all* of whom were no more than a few weeks old, had no idea what a Freewill was.

Not helping was that I'd skipped my well-rehearsed opening speech the second I laid eyes on these assholes. Most vamps I'd managed to track down so far had been given a choice. The ones who weren't completely drunk on their own power were offered a chance to join the new coven I was forming, the primary rule of which was simple – don't slaughter people like fucking cattle.

These guys, though, got shunted to the *other* option within about a second of seeing them – the one reserved for feral, blood-crazy vamps, or assholes who were obviously irredeemable pricks.

In this case, the decision was an easy one.

I'd caught scent of them in the middle of my patrol and then tracked them to one of New York City's innumerable construction sites, where they'd been in the process of finishing off a security guard. It was too late for him, sadly. They'd not only drained the poor sap but had taken the time to stomp his skull into paste. On the upside, at least there was little chance of him rising again after that. One less vamp for me to worry about.

The dickheaded duo kept on pummeling the already quite dead guy, cackling like it was the funniest thing in the world, until the younger of the two suggested they find a woman next.

It didn't take much eavesdropping with my supercharged ears to realize they were enjoying the fuck out of the depraved shit they'd already done and still planned to do. Needless to say, there wasn't a lot of soul searching necessary before deciding on my course of action.

Which was probably stupid as fuck on my part.

Five years ago, this would've been a piece of cake, especially after I'd finally mastered the beast inside of me – a hell spawn of an evil spirit I called Dr. Death. I'd have splattered these fuckers across the sidewalk like so much paint. Now, though, we were in the same boat. My powers had only recently returned – thanks to the cataclysmically stupid actions of my idiot friend Dave, who somehow thought it was a good idea to hawk hand cream infected with vampire DNA. Combined with a little psycho named Gan, who'd managed to unleash magic on the world again, and you had the perfect recipe to turn my life into a shit soufflé.

Anyway, I was strong, fast, and tough, but no more than either of these baboons, and they had the advantage of looking like they knew how to handle themselves in a brawl.

Case in point, Gramps stepped in and took a swing at me, his arm moving like lightning. Fortunately, my reflexes were up to the task and I was able to block him, if just barely. Vampire he might've been but, judging by the look of surprise on his face, I felt safe in assuming that he was used to guys like me folding faster than a piece of origami.

That was the one beauty of being undead. In the normal world, size mattered. The big could bully the small. But vamp powers were the great equalizer. They could turn a peewee into a powerhouse, size be damned.

That was good for me. Not only did it save my face from being caved in, but it left me an opening to even the odds in this fight – and maybe even a bit more.

See, I wasn't just making up some bullshit superhero name when I'd called myself the Freewill. It's what I am, a rare breed of vampire – with abilities above and beyond the normal undead rabble. And one of those abilities harkened back to what Gramps here had threatened to do when he thought me still human.

Had they followed through and tried to drain me, it would've ended pretty badly, not just for me but for them, too. Vamp blood was toxic to most other vampires – the result kinda like eating potato salad that had been sitting in the sun for three weeks. However, *most* was the operative

4

word there. Not only could I drink that shit down like a cold margarita in Tijuana, but doing so would temporarily grant me the strength of the other vampire as well. With younger vamps like these that didn't mean much, but it would almost certainly be enough to turn the tide in my favor.

Of course, that assumed I could actually sink my teeth into one of them first.

Fangs bared, I stepped in before the old bastard could shove me away, only to be steamrolled from my flank by his buddy.

"No one touches Duke!"

Good to know he cared for the old guy. Mind you, that didn't help me much as I was sent tumbling end over end until finally skidding to a halt against a dumpster, sending a small shower of crud falling onto my face.

By the time I rubbed the gunk out of my eyes, both meatheads were headed toward me again, looking none too pleased. It was nice to see the intervening years at least hadn't robbed me of my ability to piss off other vamps. Speaking of abilities, though...

Yo, Dr. Death. Not to be a worrywart, but if you wanted to maybe come out and play, I have some fresh assholes for you to kill.

There came nary a peep from my subconscious or the beast residing within it. True, we weren't quite at life or death yet, but there'd been nothing but radio silence from my inner demon ever since he'd taken up residence again upon my revamping. It was starting to make me nervous – him somewhere in my mind, likely plotting some insidious scheme that would leave him in charge and me little more than a drooling vegetable locked away in a tiny corner of my own brain.

"Think you're tough, you little shitbag?" Fat Hitler said, hocking a generous loogie onto my chest. Ewww. "I used to eat little pricks like you for breakfast, and that was before. Now, we are so much more."

I debated my best course of action, knowing they'd be upon me before I could even hope to get back up. "You used to eat little pricks? What's the matter? Couldn't handle the big ones?"

Veins stood out on the fat fuck's forehead as his face contorted with rage. Oh yeah. That's the thing about tough guys. They loved to dish it out but had absolutely no ability to take it. Even less so if you dared insult their fragile masculinity.

Forget the meek. That's why the *geeks* shall inherit the Earth. We spend all day talking shit to one another, like how hard we banged each other's moms. It builds up a tolerance for bullshit.

Of course, pissing off two death row inmate wannabes was one thing. Capitalizing on it was quite another.

Before junior could pop a blood vessel, though, the one called Duke actually laughed, but not in a "this guy is hilarious" sort of way. "Don't let him get under your skin, boy. Little asshole knows he's fucked. Just trying to talk big before we shitstomp him. Ain't that right, pipsqueak?"

I shrugged. "Doesn't hurt to try."

"You got balls, kid. I'll give you that much," he replied. "Why not join us instead? I don't know what you're trying to prove by attacking us out here, but these streets can be ours for the taking."

"Yeah, I know. I heard what you two were planning."

"That? Who cares about a couple of bitches? None of that shit matters anymore. We take what we want, bite who we want, and fuck who we want. There's a new order coming, one that's rising like an angry tempest." He gestured to the black armband around his elbow, similar to the one adorning his large buddy. *Interesting*. "And there ain't nobody who can stop us."

I was just about to say he was wrong, that he'd met Mr. Nobody himself. However, before I could so much as tell him to eat a bag of heroin-laced dicks, someone else spoke up, catching us all by surprise.

"You know, I really can't stand men like you," a female voice said from somewhere in the shadows behind them, "but maybe you're right. There *is* a new order. Too bad neither of you are going to be a part of it."

Both goons spun toward where the voice had come from, blocking my view, but that was fine. I was far more interested in capitalizing on the distraction anyway.

As Fat Hitler stepped away to confront whoever had crashed our private party, I scrambled to my feet, almost slipping on the garbage slicked pavement. Regardless, up was up. That's what mattered. But what mattered more was the fact that Duke had left his ample flank unguarded.

Leaping onto his back, I forced his head to the side and buried my fangs in his jugular. Hot blood gushed down my throat, hitting my stomach like a pipe bomb.

Heat bloomed against my insides and his strength instantly became mine. Fortunately, that was all that transferred to me, which was good because I had no interest in being a fucking skinhead slime ball. Taking one out, on the other hand, would likely be doing the world a service.

I snapped Duke's right arm at the elbow, my strength now roughly double his, then reached into the inner pocket of my jacket and pulled out a stake. Well, okay, it was more a sawed-off broom handle, but whatever. It was the thought that counted, and right then mine was focused on ramming it through this motherfucker's back with everything I had in me.

Oddly enough, he didn't take it with grace and dignity – screaming like a little girl who'd gotten her pigtails pulled during recess. There was a sort of karmic justice in that.

A second or two later there came a flash of light from the wound I'd made, and then Duke ignited from the inside out, turning to dust before my eyes and coating the alleyway with yet another layer of garbage.

The bloody broom handle clattered to the ground, but I was already turning my attention toward the end of the alleyway where Duke's buddy was ... also in the process of disintegrating?

He blew apart into ash, revealing a smaller figure standing behind him in the gloom. Whoever she was, she'd apparently impaled him with the business end of a crowbar. *Ouch*.

That wasn't exactly an act that could be carried out easily by just anyone, especially since the vamp in question had been carrying enough extra mass around the middle to cushion a car crash.

I took a tentative step forward, remaining on guard. Anyone who could do that to a three-hundred plus pound biker vamp was nobody to mess with. My nose worked overtime as I tried to focus on her, but it was for naught. All I could smell was trash and vamp dust. And believe me, I had little interest in getting a noseful of either.

It was hard to get a handle on my somewhat timely savior, standing in a defensive crouch as she was. But if I had to guess I'd say she was about five foot seven, almost my height, but much more leanly built. She was wearing jeans and sneakers with her upper half clad in an oversized hoodie.

The hood itself left her face in shadow, but that shouldn't have mattered dick-all to me. The upside of vampire senses was that — while it didn't do shit for my fucking nearsightedness — it allowed me to see in perfect darkness. Nevertheless, the top portion of her face remained obscured, telling me she was likely wearing a mask or some other sort of covering.

Definitely interesting. It kinda reminded me of that time I'd taken Tom's stupid advice to play vampire vigilante. Not one of my finer moments, although I had no way of knowing whether this woman was doing the same or simply had an overdeveloped BDSM fetish.

Rather than ratchet up the already thick tension, I decided to relax my gait. This person was likely trying to figure out whether I was friend or foe, but I'd sure as shit make that an easy decision if I came across as a swaggering asshole. "Thanks. I appreciate the assist."

She grinned beneath the hood, giving me a momentary glimpse of fangs. At least that explained how she'd been able to impale one of the bad guys.

"Didn't do it to save you," she replied, "but you're welcome anyway. That is, unless you're looking to cause the kind of trouble they were."

"In case you hadn't noticed, I was fighting those fuckers, too."

"Why?"

"Same reason you were, I'm assuming. Because they were out here to put the hurt on people who don't deserve it."

"And you're not?" Her tone was defiant, but she relaxed her stance a bit, giving me a slightly better view of her face. From the nose down I got a hint of light brown skin. Above that, nothing but a black void. Definitely some kind of mask.

"I could ask you the same thing." Yeah, this back and forth shit talk was about as productive as you might think. So, before we devolved to flipping each other the bird, I changed tactics. "Listen, I know what you are."

"You do, do you?"

"Yeah. You're a vampire. I know because I'm one, too."

"You realize how that sounds, right?"

I shrugged. "And yet here we are. But I also know that we don't have to be like the movies tell us. I mean the good ones, not the boring ass mopey films where they sit around pining for Brad Pitt. Anyway, what I mean is we have a choice. We don't have to be heartless killers."

"Says the guy who just stabbed a..."

"Murderous assholes don't count, okay?"

"And who gets to decide whether someone deserves it or not?"

Goddamn, this was rapidly getting annoying. I wasn't about to stand there and take a Batman morality lesson from some chick who'd just ganked one of the vamps I'd been after.

I started toward her, slowly and with my hands out in the open. "Maybe we got off on the wrong foot here. Can we try this again? My name's Bill."

"I thought you told these cabrónes it was Freewill."

"That's more *what* I am. It's ... a vampire thing. Kind of a long story, but I'd be happy to tell you more if you want." I took a look around, noting the still very dead security guard. "But maybe somewhere else, if that's okay."

A grin passed over her lips. "Is this your way of asking me out?"

"Not quite. What I'm offering you is a chance to join my coven."

"Aren't covens...?"

"No. We had the idea first. Witches stole it. Trust me on that one. The point is, I'm out here looking for people who've been vampirized."

"Is that even a word?"

"Do I look like a fucking lit professor? Who cares? You know what I mean."

"Fine. But why make me this offer and not them?" she asked, sounding genuinely curious.

"Because they were assholes."

"I'll give you that one," she replied, inclining her head. "Okay, I'll tell you what. Fucking up that puto's shit put me in a good mood. I'll humor you. What's the deal with this coven thing that ain't got nothing to do with witches?"

"Protection, for everyone. Left to their own devices, most vamps aren't going to have the willpower to rein themselves in. Others simply won't give a shit. This way, we can maybe keep each other from turning into murderous monsters."

"And how's that going to work? Last I checked, we still gotta eat."

"True, but it can be controlled, made less chaotic. Working together, we can make sure we stay fed without turning entire neighborhoods into all you can eat buffets."

As I approached, I saw I was right. Black fabric covered the top of her face from the bridge of her nose up. No eyeholes, but that didn't mean anything. I'd once gotten one of those grim reaper costumes for Halloween, the kind with the see-through cheesecloth. This was probably something similar.

"Not disagreeing." She put a hand on her hip, not exactly relaxed, but looking less likely to ninja strike me. "But you said protection for everyone. So far this sounds like a one-sided deal."

"It's not. We'll have each other's backs, but also keep each other in check – which we'll need to do if we want to survive. Because how long do you think it'll be before someone somewhere has enough of the bloodshed and decides to pull their head out of their ass and hunt us down? The system is designed for both sides, human and vamp."

Gah! I sounded like a recruitment poster for the assholes who'd previously run things. Hell, maybe that was closer to the truth than I cared to admit. Who was to say the originators of the old coven system, started God-knows how many thousands of years ago, didn't originally have good intentions?

Holy shit! Was I setting things up now only so some future asshole could label himself Alexander the Great 2.0 and cause history to repeat itself?

I pushed that thought away. That was a worry for another epoch. With any luck, by then I could simply point a photon torpedo their way and be done with it. But, for now, all I was doing was letting myself get distracted.

"So what do you think, Miss..." I let the statement hang as I held out my hand to her.

She tentatively reached out and took hold of it. "Save the miss crap. You can call me Char."

I raised an eyebrow. "Char? What kind of name is...?"

Before I could finish that statement, her hand clamped down on mine like a vise. *What the?* She twisted and – despite me being boosted on vamp blood – flung me effortlessly over her shoulder into a pile of trash.

"It's a nice offer, Bill Freewill, but I'm more of a solo act."

The throw was a solid one, no doubt there, but for someone with vampire endurance it was far more bruising to my ego than anything. I scrambled back to my feet in the space of seconds. "My name's not Bill Freewill, it's..."

The words died in my throat at the sight of the empty alley before me. Son of a... How fucking stupid could I be to let my guard down like that?

No matter. The blood rush I'd gotten from Duke was still in effect. I could easily catch her scent and track her down again.

In theory anyway.

I lifted my nose and took a sniff. Then I held my breath and listened for the sound of retreating footsteps – coming up empty in both cases.

It was as if she'd simply vanished into thin air, leaving me standing there all alone like the idiot that I was.

BARK WORSE THAN HIS BITE

"You're the only one who can do this," I muttered to myself as I stepped into my apartment, echoing the words Christy had spoken to me weeks ago, when this crap had just been getting started. What a crock of shit. I really needed to stop listening when people went off on inspirational monologues. Those almost never ended in my favor.

I flipped on the light switch, noting the silence. A long shower was just what the doctor ordered, followed by sweeping up the trail of garbage and vampire dust I was no doubt tracking in the door.

Talk about a weird-ass night. First, undead neo-Nazi dickheads, then some masked Houdini vamp with a supervillain name and a chip on her shoulder. The news liked to call the events of five years ago the Strange Days, but a part of me wondered whether this new age didn't have potential to be even more bizarre.

On the upside, two obvious threats had been removed from the streets. That should've been enough for me. Pity that vamp hunting wasn't all that glamourous, not to mention the pay kinda sucked. Speaking of which, I could afford maybe a quick nap when this was all said and done, but that was all. After that, it was back to work. I'd taken a contract to migrate a client's database to a new platform. It was a boring as fuck project, but I'd ignored it for the better part of the week. It was probably time to get my ass in gear before the product manager started bitching.

I stopped in the living room to consider how easy it was to sink back into my old mindset. Here I was thinking about programming when I'd dusted two people tonight ... or one anyway, and just barely at that. Mind you, they'd been assholes, so it's not like I should feel too bad about it.

Regardless, Christy's words from weeks back kept repeating in my head that these new vamps were all victims, so they at least deserved a chance before we shanked them.

The problem was, not everyone handled becoming undead as well as others. The vast majority became drunk on their new power, giving in to their feral side – and that wasn't even counting those who'd been bad eggs to start. If anything, it was turning out to be more difficult than expected to find those willing to listen to reason.

And what did I do when I did find them? Recruited them into a coven, of course. What a joke. Much as I'd rued the old days with its frat-boy like vamp covens, it turned out there'd been a good reason for it. Only vamps could keep other vamps in check. Without such a system in place, it would only be a matter of time before we either ended up in some *28 Days Later* nightmare scenario, or some yahoo called in the National Guard and decided it was open season on anyone, living or not, stupid enough to be out after dark.

Talk about a karmic kick to the nuts.

I'd worked so hard to bring down the old regime, only to realize I had no other choice than to rebuild it again from the ground up. Hah. My old coven master Night Razor, AKA Jeff, was probably looking up at me from Hell and laughing his ass off.

My only hope was to maybe get lucky and get it all running again in a less assholish way. I had no interest in reestablishing a system in which younger vamps became little more than playthings to the older, more powerful...

The sound of footsteps heading up the stairs caught the attention of my supercharged ears, causing me to drop that train of thought and glance back toward the door.

Most of the building's residents would just barely be getting up for work at this hour, much less coming home – barring walks of shame of course. Ugh, not a pleasant thought. The tenants who lived here were mostly good, hard-working folks, but not a lot of lookers in the bunch.

The footsteps continued up, their pace increasing. Considering the stillness of the apartment around me, I guessed that it was likely one of my roommates, or at least the one with legs.

Despite both me and Christy insisting that he wasn't even remotely ready for field work, Tom had insisted on going out and patrolling for vamps, too. As the new Icon, it was sort of hard to tell him no. Problem was, even if he hadn't recently returned from the dead in a body not his own, he still treated the whole thing like he was living in a comic book – the only upside being that he sucked at it so far. To date, his record had been a lot of early AM catcalls with zero vamp encounters to speak of. Regardless, until he figured out how to control his newfound powers, it was risky for him to be wandering the city streets alone late at night – not that he actually was alone, sorta anyway.

Glen – our other roommate – had been more than happy to keep him company. The little slime-ball was ecstatic to accompany the Icon on patrol, despite being about as adept at it as Tom. In short, they pretty much wandered the streets together – Glen sticking to the alleyways and gutters since he was the equivalent of a living Jell-O mold – not accomplishing much, but also not getting into too much trouble.

So then why the frantic footsteps now?

That question was answered by the *crunch* of a key being jammed into the lock, followed by a muttered curse of, "come on, you stupid fucking hand," then some more fumbling around until the deadbolt finally disengaged.

My breath involuntarily caught in my throat as Tom stepped into the apartment a second or two later. I couldn't help it, still not entirely used to the fact that he now inhabited Sheila's body – the former Icon, as well as my ex. Every time he walked through the door, I found myself reminded of an earlier time when she and I...

"Outta the way," he cried in her voice. "Full bladder coming through."

And then he'd speak, instantly shattering the momentary illusion.

"Um, where's Glen?" I asked, as he darted past.

"Bringing up the rear. Should be here in a few. Can't talk, need to piss!"

He raced into the bathroom, slamming the door shut behind him.

Sadly, awesome as vampire senses could be, there were some horrific downsides, too, such as clearly hearing him pee, followed by a sigh of relief and, "Oh, that is so fucking good."

I left the door open for Glen and headed for the fridge – hoping none of the downstairs neighbors picked that moment to pop their heads out and notice him. It was probably only a matter of time before that happened, and when it did ... fucked if I knew.

Despite being moderately well-suited to rounding up vamps, I wasn't nearly strong enough to compel humans. The only way that was happening was if I was amped up on vamp blood, which was easier said than done these days as there were only two other vampires in existence older than me, both of whom were currently MIA.

I heard the melodic sound of the toilet flushing just as I pulled a plastic container from the refrigerator. Pig's blood. Not my favorite, but workable for us vamps, even if the folks down at the Asian market charged me extra to buy it by the bucketful, no questions asked. It was highway robbery, but that's what happened when there suddenly became demand for an item nobody previously gave a shit about. Gotta love capitalism.

I popped it open and took a sip as Tom stepped out, adjusting the crotch of his pants. "That is so much better," he said with a sigh, looking at me. "Oh, for Christ's sake. Put that shit in a cup or something."

"Nobody offered you any. And you do know that there's these things called restrooms, right? This isn't the only toilet in Brooklyn."

"Dude, I already explained it to you. I don't know which one to use."

"I believe the socially acceptable norm these days is to use the restroom of the gender you identify as."

"Fuck that shit," he replied, his tone and mannerisms coming from my former girlfriend's mouth – still weird after almost a month. "Guys freak out whenever I try, and it's not like I can even use a fucking urinal anymore."

"Well, you could if you got creative."

"Bite me, asshole."

"All right, then use the ladies' room."

"I can't."

"Why not?" I asked, stepping out of our kitchen nook. "You go in, do your business, then leave."

"It's not that simple." He fixed me with a stare, the eyes Sheila's but the semi-crazed expression firmly Tom's. "First of all, there's always a line, which sucks. I mean, what the fuck are they doing in there, synchronized shitting?"

Eww. There was an image I was never getting out of my head again.

"But that's not the worst of it," he continued. "Chicks *know*."

"What do you mean, chicks know?"

"I thought it would be rad as hell stepping into the *forbidden zone*, but it's not that easy, man. It's like women's intuition or something. Nobody says anything, but they don't have to. I can see it in their eyes. They know I'm an imposter."

"Pretty sure you're imagining that."

"I wish I was. But I'm telling you, it's like deep down they all have bonedar."

"Bonedar?"

"Yeah. Boner sense."

"Pretty sure that's not a problem for you anymore."

He nodded sadly. "Don't remind me."

Amusing as it was to give him shit about his lack of junk, something that seemed to annoy him to no end, I changed the subject, despite knowing what I'd hear. "Any luck tonight?"

"Not a peep. It's like the undead are purposely avoiding me."

"Yeah, uh huh. I'm sure that's why..."

"But we still managed to score big."

"What do you mean?"

"*Bark.*"

I spun back toward the apartment door ... and almost ended up shitting a brick. "What the fuck?!"

"Isn't it awesome?" Tom replied, stepping past me and giving the abomination a pat on its freakish head.

Awesome wasn't even remotely the word that came to mind. The thing standing in the doorway of our apartment resembled a large, raggedy looking dog. It looked like maybe some kind of Irish Setter mix, but mixed with what? Its coat was a filthy mess, but that was nothing compared to the big bulging eyes staring from its head, as if they were getting ready to pop out of its skull.

"Bark," it repeated.

I glanced back at Tom. "What the hell is that?"

Almost as if in response, the dog-thing opened its mouth, far wider than a normal dog should be able. It vomited forth a viscous goo – the yellowish sludge continuing to pour out until it spread across the entirety of our entranceway.

Then an even stranger thing happened. Those bulging eyes in its head pulled back in, leaving gaping holes where they'd been, as eyeball after eyeball fell out of its mouth into the rapidly growing pile of slime on the floor.

When it was finally finished, the *dog* collapsed like a deflated balloon while the eyeballs in the sludge pile all turned my way and blinked.

"Glen?"

"Isn't it great, Freewill?" he replied, sounding way too excited for my own personal sanity.

"Yeah," Tom said, stepping to my side. "Glen and I were discussing how much it sucked that he has to hide out in public."

I glanced between him and the dog ... err ... corpse lying on the floor. "Not really seeing how this fixes any of that."

"Well, we were talking about finding him a disguise. And I swear, it was like fate was listening, because not five minutes later we found a dead dog in an alleyway."

I held up a hand. "You do realize that one, that's gross as fuck, and two, it's not even remotely inconspicuous. Oh, and did I mention how gross it is?"

"Twice," Glen replied, his responses bubbling to the surface of his pliable body. "But it's fine, trust me. It was a minor issue to remove the major organs, and I think after a bit of practice I'll be able to..."

"What? Horrify everyone who sees you into a coma? That's the worst fucking dog disguise since Invader Zim, not to mention it's disgusting as..."

The phone rang, interrupting what was almost certain to be an extremely long rant on my part. All I could do was stare blankly at it for a few moments. It was way too early for the telemarketers to start and I was far too freaked out to process anything else.

It wasn't until the third ring that I finally snapped out of it.

"You," I said to Tom, "close the door before someone sees ... *any* of this shit. And you, um, move that thing somewhere else for now, preferably the garbage can." I picked up the receiver, feeling my left eye beginning to twitch. "Yeah?"

"Oh, thank goodness," Christy said from the other end. "You weren't picking up your cell."

"Sorry," I replied numbly. "Battery must've died while I was chasing vamps tonight." Off to the side, Tom and Glen were conversing over the dog corpse like it was the most normal thing in the world. "Listen, Christy, can I call you back later? Things are a bit weird right..."

"That's why I'm calling. You need to get over here. If you leave now, you should be able to make it before the sun rises."

As much as I was in favor of an early morning booty call, the situation in my living room was the poster child for killing the mood. Not to mention, the fact that I'd said her name out loud meant there was no way I was escaping without Tom in tow.

"Maybe we can catch up later," I said. "I need to hop in the shower and there's a bit of a ... situation here that I need to..."

"It's not as big as the situation here," she replied, cutting me off. "Trust me."

Glancing back at the dead mutt currently serving as the apartment's doormat, I sincerely doubted that. However, I also wasn't in favor of ticking her off, and not just because she could blow a hole through me big enough to step through. "Okay, fine. What's up?"

"It's Sally."

"What about her? Is she okay?"

"That remains to be seen. Her cocoon is starting to crack. I think she's about to wake up."

BEHOLD THIS
LUMP OF ROCK!

S ure enough, Tom was quick to join me as we hopped in my car – recently outfitted with heavily tinted windows for obvious reasons.

Glen wanted to join us, too, claiming his new disguise made him one hundred percent inconspicuous, but I ixnayed that as his meat suit was about as invisible as Drax the Destroyer in *Infinity War*. There was also the fact that it was still really fucking gross.

Along the way, I filled Tom in on the night's adventures, including my run-in with Char.

"That's fucking awesome," he said, completely missing the point. "She's already got a code name."

"Less awesome is that we apparently have a nutjob running around the city, dousing herself in manticore venom..."

"Manticore venom?"

"Yeah, it's some shit Gan used once. Kills a vamp's scent."

"Where the fuck did this chick get that?"

"No idea, but it doesn't matter, not if she thinks she can run around doing whatever the hell she wants."

"Not unless she's going all Dark Knight on the bad guys. Hell, you should put her on the payroll."

"We'll see. I'm not quite convinced she's Justice League material yet."

We made it to Christy's with maybe five minutes to spare until the sun peeked out over the buildings, meaning that by the time I found a parking spot I had to make a mad dash for cover. *Note to self: time to once again stockpile ski masks and high SPF sunblock.*

Fortunately, I made it to the foyer of her building before anyone had need to vacuum me up. Tom, being a cock, strolled up to the front entrance at a leisurely pace, stopping halfway to put a pair of sunglasses on. He might've been a hell of a lot cuter in his new body, but at his core he was still an asshole.

He stepped past me with a shit-eating grin. "Looks like it's going to be a nice day."

"Eat a bag of dicks."

"Excuse me?" a voice from further inside replied.

We both turned to find an elderly lady on her way out. She was giving me, in particular, the stink-eye.

"Um..."

Tom immediately started making exaggerated sniffling noises, burying his face in his hands. "And to think. All I wanted was to visit my beloved daughter, but instead I have to deal with this brute's sexual harassment."

The old lady's eyes narrowed even more.

"She's ... just kidding around."

Tom, meanwhile, continued to pile it on. "I cook and I clean, and this is the thanks I get."

I grabbed hold of his arm so as to drag him toward the stairs with me, but then pulled my hand back with a cry as his faith aura momentarily sparked.

"Shit!" Tom quickly wheeled back toward the woman. "Err, I have a new camera. Still trying to figure out how to keep the flash from going off. You have a good day now. Bye!"

We, along with my freshly singed hand, beat a quick retreat up the stairs before she could say anything further.

"What the fuck was that?" I hissed once we'd put a floor or two between us.

"Just fucking with you, man. Did you see the look on her face?"

"Not that, dumbass. Your aura. You can't do that in front of people."

He shrugged. "I didn't. I still don't have any fucking idea how it even works. It's not like Sheila left me an instruction manual."

"You need to be more careful."

"I don't know how."

"Try."

"It's not that simple. Sometimes it just happens, like getting a boner when you're fifteen. You could be minding your own business in PE class, when suddenly *boing!*"

"Thanks for the visual."

Fortunately, my hand had mostly healed by the time we made it up to Christy's floor, one of the few perks of being an immortal beast of the night.

I spared a quick glance toward her neighbor's apartment, still vacant as far as I was aware. The prior occupant had lost her life to a group of deranged yahoos hellbent on returning magic to the world after a five year absence. In the end, they'd succeeded, albeit not in the way they'd imagined, resulting in the reason we were here today, amongst the other crazy shit we were still dealing with.

Christy was already waiting at her door for us, which at least served to pull my head back into the here and now.

"Thank goodness," she said. "I was afraid you weren't going to make it in time."

I wasn't sure whether she was talking about Sally or beating the sun, but before I could ask, my goddaughter appeared from behind her.

"Daddy!"

Tina stepped around her mother and practically flung herself into Tom's arms, almost knocking him off balance and into me – which wouldn't have been pleasant had his aura decided to get a boner again.

"Oof! Watch Daddy's bad arm, sweetheart."

"Sorry."

Technically, it wasn't his bad arm, so much as it had been Sheila's – nerve damage she'd suffered at my hands thanks to an insane prophecy that had nearly killed us both. It wasn't something I was particularly proud of. But this was neither the time nor the place for unpleasant memories.

He picked Tina up and we both stepped inside, where she turned toward me. "Hey, Uncle Bill!"

"Hey, Cat. How are you doing?"

"I'm good. You should see all the things I can do with my magic now."

Tom frowned. "It's Cheetara, dude. How many times do I have to tell you?" He smiled at his daughter. "If he calls you that again, you have my permission to blast him."

"Really?" Her eyes opened wide in that excited way only small children could get when offered the opportunity to abuse their power.

"No, *not* really," Christy admonished. "What did I teach you about magic?"

"Not inside the house," Tina replied, a tiny bit of petulance in her voice.

"And?"

"And not to use it against anyone."

"Unless they deserve it," Tom was quick to add, stepping away as Christy narrowed her eyes. "What? You never know when some asshole is gonna need a fireball smackdown."

I glanced at Tina from over his shoulder, waiting for a reaction. "You know, your daddy just said a naughty word."

She shrugged, momentarily looking wiser than her five years suggested. "I know, but Daddy doesn't have any money."

"That's a good point. I'm the Freewill, while he's the freeloader."

I wasn't sure Tina fully understood what I meant, but she giggled anyway.

Tom put her down and grinned. "Not for long. I'm working on something."

"I already told you," Christy replied, "if you need money, I'm happy to..."

"No way. That's all for you and Cheetara."

"Yes, but it was from *your* life insurance."

"Which makes it that much sweeter." Tom grinned even wider. "Like I said, don't worry about me. I have something in the works."

"Oh?" I asked with a raised eyebrow.

"Yep. And, unlike you, I won't have to resort to sucking guys off in an alleyway."

"Tom!" Christy chastised.

"Mommy, why does Uncle Bill suck..."

"You never mind that, honey. Your father's just being silly. Why don't you go in your room and play?"

"Okay, when are we leaving for..."

"No daycare today. Mommy, daddy, and Uncle Bill have ... stuff to do."

"We'll play later," Tom told her as she skipped to her room. "You can throw lightning bolts at me if you want." When I raised a questioning eyebrow at his rather insane offer, he added, "What? I'm the Icon. Isn't magic supposed to, I dunno, bounce right off me?"

"Yeah, when your powers work."

"Guess that's one way to find out."

He kinda had a point there, even if it was in a batshit sort of way.

Once Tina left the room, Christy threw him a glare. "What did I tell you about watching your language around her?"

"Come on. I'm pretty sure her friends already say worse."

"She's five."

"Okay, fine, but in another year or so they definitely will. Hell, I remember some of the shit Bill and me used to say. Remember that song we wrote about Mrs. Blussy and her big hairy..."

"I hate to interrupt this stroll down memory lane," I said, turning to Christy, "but didn't you say something about Sally waking up?"

She nodded. "Sorry. It's been a distracting morning. Follow me."

I looked around. Christy's place was smaller than mine, with only two bedrooms. When last I'd been here, maybe a week back, she'd cordoned off an area of her room for Sally's *cocoon*, not wanting to leave it in the living room.

True, it was a bit of a mood killer, but then – between hunting rogue vamps and dealing with Tom – there hadn't been much opportunity for alone time lately. And that wasn't even counting the fact that Christy had her hands full trying to teach restraint to Tina, a little girl who supposedly possessed enough power to make short work of Gandalf, Merlin, and Dumbledore all at once.

But instead of heading toward her bedroom, Christy instead led us to a door in the far wall of her living room, one that hadn't been there a few days ago.

"That's new."

She turned toward me, a hint of sadness in her eyes. "After what happened to Mrs. McDavish, I realized it might be dangerous to let anyone else move in next door. So, I talked to the landlord and they agreed to let me take over her lease."

"And what exactly do they think happened to her?"

"Heart attack." She shook her head. "It's not right, but at least it gives her family some closure."

"Cool," Tom said, with his typical blissful ignorance. "If her place is free, maybe I can move..."

"I didn't say it was free," Christy interrupted, perhaps a bit more harshly than she'd intended.

Though it had been three weeks, I knew she was still coming to terms with what had happened, in more ways than one. Sure, she was grateful that Tina could finally get to know her father, but the fact that Tom now inhabited my ex's body was taking a bit more time. Truth be told, it was strange for me, too, but living with him day in and day out had actually made it easier to balance the two. One only had to listen to him for a short while to reconcile that it was Tom's brain in her body. That, and the fact that he considered himself still very much in the running for Christy's affections.

Yeah, safe to say I'd somehow found myself in an even more fucked up love triangle than I had five years ago.

"I also realized," Christy continued, dragging me from my weird-ass reverie, "that I needed some extra space, preferably close by, where I could properly instruct Tina in the ways of our craft."

She stepped to the door – in the same spot, I noted, where a vampire strike team had broken into her place from the neighboring apartment – and waved her hand in front of it, a soft yellowish glow suffusing both.

"You know, they make these things called keys," Tom said.

"A key wouldn't disarm the wards and, believe me, you want them disarmed."

Neither of us cared to question her on that. I, for one, had experienced firsthand what Magi wards could do to unwanted visitors.

She opened the door and led the way in. It took me all of a second and a half to realize that, even had she wanted Tom to move in, this space was no longer suited for those who cared for the comforts of home.

For starters, gone was most of the furniture, and what was left had been pushed off to the side. Even the kitchen appliances had been removed.

"I see you favor an open floor plan."

My joke fell flat as it became obvious that open it might be, but empty it was not.

Tables full of bowls, beakers, and jars stood off to one side – a miniature alchemy lab if my gaming instincts were correct. Bookshelves filled to the brim with heavy tomes lined another wall. Call me crazy, but I had a feeling those weren't suggestions from the local book club.

In the center of it all, several concentric circles had been embedded into the floor. Magic was almost certainly afoot, because I had a feeling building maintenance wasn't responsible for what looked like iron, brass, and then finally a silver circle inlaid into the floorboards.

Strange Tiki-like torches stood at the four corners of the outermost circle – metal pylons topped with what appeared to be glowing gems of differing colors.

However, freaky as all that shit was, it was what sat in the middle of the innermost circle, the silver one, that caught my eye.

Surrounded by a shimmering globe of purplish energy lay Sally, or the rocky shell containing her body. She'd been placed atop what appeared to be a coffee table of all things, perhaps the most mundane item in the room. But that's where normal took a detour.

While attempting to stop Gan, the three-hundred-year-old psycho responsible for the return of magic, Sally had gotten caught in the crossfire between a bunch of angry mages and something else – something mean, green, and powerful enough to tear down the gates sealing off our reality from whatever lay beyond.

The end result hadn't been pretty. We all thought Sally had been instantly killed, flash fried like a chicken nugget in hot oil. If anything, she'd looked like one of those statues you might see in the ruins of Pompeii. However, unlike the residents of that unfortunate Vesuvius-based town, Sally wasn't actually dead. Somehow, she was still alive, trapped inside her own rocky effigy.

Or at least that was how she had looked back then.

In the weeks since, the crust – for lack of a saner term – surrounding her body had begun to thicken and rise, as if it were the yeast in Satan's bake shop. When last I'd seen her, you could just barely make out her features in the hard exterior. Now, though, she looked less like a memorial to herself and more like a clumsy artist's attempt to recreate

Gumby from solid granite. I could still make out a torso, limbs, and where her head hopefully was, but it was all featureless and formless.

It was also moving ever so slightly.

"Holy shit! Are you seeing this?"

"That's why I called you over," Christy said, sounding far calmer than I felt. "I'm not sure what's going on. I can't even sense her in there anymore. My magic stopped being able to penetrate that shell a couple days ago."

I turned to her. "Why didn't you say anything?"

She inclined her head and smiled meekly. "Sorry. I didn't want to worry you until I knew more."

Not really the answer I wanted to hear, but I guess I couldn't blame her. For all of Christy's magical training, I had a feeling this fell outside even her wheelhouse.

"She looks like a giant turd," Tom said.

I glanced at him and sighed. "Definitely the wrong word to use."

"Oh crap, I forgot. Sorry, man. I meant, she looks like a giant piece of shit."

"Better ... kinda." I turned back toward the mass that hopefully was still Sally, taking note of the energy that was enveloping her. "Any reason for the light show?"

"It's a modification of that time dilation spell I used on you," Christy explained. "Relative to us, only a few minutes have passed for her since I called you." When I raised an eyebrow, she added, "I heard a crackling noise and saw she was starting to move. So I activated it as quickly as I could and then called you. I figured it might be best if she woke up surrounded by friendly faces."

Left unsaid was the other side of the equation. If she woke up ... different, she'd hopefully be surrounded by people who could contain her.

Thoughts like that weren't really helping my mood, but there wasn't much that could be done about it. "Are we expecting anyone else?"

Christy shook her head. "I couldn't get through to Kelly, so it's just us."

Too bad. Another witch might've been useful to have around right then, but oh well. We'd have to make do with the portion of our posse present and accounted for.

"Is she ... okay inside of that thing?" Tom asked, sounding doubtful.

Christy shot us a look that said she had no idea, cluing me in that I was right regarding her full motivation for calling us. Either way, she wasn't playing it stupid by leaving herself as the only person standing between an unknown and her daughter.

All at once, I was glad Tom and his cockblocking self were there, too. Though he was a long way from being even close to Sheila's ballpark, he'd still inherited her mantle. He was the Icon, imbued with faith magic – power that existed to nullify things evil and impure ... or simply misunderstood, as in my case.

Mind you, that assumed he could get his shit to work, which so far he'd mostly proven less than competent at.

Regardless, between the three of us we could hopefully handle this.

And if we couldn't, then at least I'd be spared from having to go out again and get my ass kicked by vampire newbs. Glass half full and all that.

"All right," I said, somehow taking charge despite knowing dick when it came to magic. "Let's spread out. Just to be safe."

"Good idea," Christy replied. "Once we're in place I'll drop the spell and..."

"Hope for the best?"

Her response was a tight smile.

It was really all we had to go on at this juncture.

BIRDS OF PRAY

Christy took a moment to tell Tina to stay in her room – as if we could really force the issue if the tyke decided otherwise – then we got in position for whatever was going to happen.

It didn't take long.

The moment she dropped her time spell, the air rang out with a sound that could best be described as hundreds of pieces of chalk being snapped all at once.

It was hard to describe my emotions, seeing the strange rocky cocoon start to move more violently, as if someone – or *something* – were trying to break free from within. I desperately hoped Sally was okay, but also knew to temper those feelings in case whatever arose was no longer her.

A memory popped into my head, me and Tom watching *Swamp Thing* in my living room as kids. The bad guy had just taken the serum which had created the titular character, assuming it would make him super awesome. But instead he'd ended up looking like his mother had taken up pig fucking as a hobby.

Hopefully Sally would fare better, but who could say? We were far off the map with this one. I was used to dealing with vampires, wizards, and Sasquatches, not unseen entities that could rip holes in reality and shoot green lightning out of their dicks.

Okay, I hadn't actually seen that last part, but you get my point.

The rocky crust surrounding Sally began to crumble, falling away in thick chunks.

A smell, not unlike that of burning charcoal, filled the air, to which Tom remarked, "Anyone else in the mood for a burger when we're done here?"

In response, I chucked one of the slabs that had fallen off Sally his way, just barely missing him.

"Are you two finished playing?" Christy snapped.

"Sorry," I said, forcing myself to once again focus on Sally.

All in all, what came next was a bit anticlimactic. No burst of light, no explosion, no fiery halo followed by Sally rising up out of the ashes and declaring herself the embodiment of the Phoenix Force ... even if that would've been insanely cool.

In the end, the cocoon simply split down the middle and crumbled away. A small cloud of dust rose up, and then I saw movement from within, catching sight of a grime-covered foot. Five toes, that was a good sign. A crud-encrusted hand reached up, revealing the right number of grasping fingers. So far so good. No sign of any pig monsters.

Come on, be okay.

Sally, or whatever she now was, began to cough violently, a deep wet rattle that caused me to instinctively step forward.

"No, Bill, wait!" Christy cried, but I was already on the move.

I reached down to help her, and immediately recoiled as I finally got a good look at what lay before me. I beheld a human shaped body, but it was like staring into the void. Where there should have been skin, black viscous tar covered the creature from head to toe.

"What the fuck?" Tom cried as it began to rise.

"Sally?" I whispered, throwing caution to the wind and putting a hand on her – it's – shoulder.

The thing that had once been Sally scrambled away at my touch, leaving my fist covered in thick black gunk. It fell to the floor, crab walking away from me until it was backed into a corner. There, it waved one tar encrusted hand out in front of itself, as if warding us off.

"What the hell happened to her?" I asked, unable to do more than stare.

"Everyone calm down," Christy ordered. Then, slowly, she stepped toward the strange entity that had once been my partner in crime.

"Be careful."

"I've got this," she told me in a tone that suggested she really didn't. Then she turned once again to face the newly birthed creature. "It's okay. It's us."

If Sally heard or understood her, she showed no indication. Instead, she continued to wave her hands out in front of her, while hocking up even more of that greasy black goo.

"I knew I should've brought my sword," Tom said, wide-eyed.

I turned and shot him a glare. "Really?"

"Dude, look at her. She's like the fucking tar monster from Scooby Doo."

Okay. He sorta had a point there. "I was thinking more like the thing that killed Tasha Yar."

"Yeah, but that episode sucked."

"Do either of you mind?" Christy hissed.

"Sorry," I replied. "I tend to blather when I'm freaking out."

"Pussy," Tom whispered under his breath.

Oh, he was so lucky I wasn't under an Icon-killing prophecy anymore.

No. Our banter could wait. We had more important things to worry about.

I refocused on Sally, still huddled in the corner. There was no telling what was going through her mind, or if she even had a mind anymore. But then she reached a hand toward her mouth and wiped away a thick swath of gunk — revealing black-stained lips, teeth, and a tongue.

"Wuh," it groaned.

"The fuck?" Tom cried, sounding seriously freaked out. "Its name is Wuh?!"

"Shut up."

"Both of you shut up," Christy ordered, once more turning to face the Sally thing. "It's okay. I'm here."

"W... what," it croaked, the word sounding almost like human speech.

"That's what we want to know," Tom replied. "Exactly what the fuck are you?"

"Not helping," I hissed.

The tar creature made a choked coughing sound, then spat out another wad of black goo before trying again.

"I said... What the fuck is going on?!"

If Sally's strange appearance had caused Tom and I to hesitate, the sound of her not even remotely strange voice rooted us to our spots. Fortunately, we weren't the only ones in the room.

"It's us," Christy repeated. "Don't be afraid."

"What was that?" Sally replied, wiping more of that tar-like gunk away. "Hold on, I can't hear shit with this crap in my ears."

And all at once, her panicked behavior made sense. She hadn't awoken as some mindless beast. She'd simply been encased in enough grossness to have no idea what was going on.

It was probably a good thing she couldn't hear us that well because I'm pretty sure we all let out a collective sigh of relief.

The spell broken, both Tom and I stepped forward, but Christy turned to him and pointed. "Go get me a couple of towels from the linen closet." She glanced back at Sally then added, "The ones from the left side."

I raised an eyebrow as Tom went to do as he was told, to which she smiled sheepishly.

"The ones on the right are new."

While this went on, Sally continued to wipe the thick black gunk from her eyes and ears. Finally, she blinked several times and focused on us, her green eyes looking extra big and bright against the muck covering nearly every square inch of her.

"Bill? Christy?"

"It's us," I said, barely able to contain the grin on my face.

"I'm gonna go out on a limb and assume we made it out of that hell hole," she replied, continuing to spit out more of that disgusting crap.

Oh yeah. It made sense that the last thing she'd remember was still being down in the Source chamber. She'd only been gone a few weeks, but it felt like we had a lifetime to catch up on. "We did."

"Glad to hear it. So, riddle me this..." She began to push herself to her feet, her body so utterly coated in that thick black paste that it could've been a second skin. "Where the hell are we? What's this crap covering me? And did I manage to kill that little cunt?"

Christy and I shared a quick glance. She wasn't going to like at least one of those answers.

"And don't lie to me, Bill. We've already been down that road."

"Gotcha," I replied. "So, in order: Christy's place, no idea, and ... Gan survived and managed to kidnap Ed, too. And before you ask, no, we have no idea where either of them are now."

Sally spat out more black gunk. "Fuck! Never send a nine-millimeter to do a forty-four's job. What about everyone else? Is Tina..."

"She's fine," Christy said, "and can't wait to see her Aunt Sally again."

That brought the semblance of a tar-stained grin to Sally's face.

"Speaking of which," I replied. "How do you feel? I mean, after ... um ... being in that thing."

Sally stepped back and leaned against the wall, likely ruining the paint in the process. "My head is pounding, and I have a feeling I'm going to need to brush my teeth about a thousand times to get the taste of this shit out, but otherwise I feel surprisingly..."

She trailed off as Tom walked back in carrying an armful of multi-colored towels.

"Those are the ones for the beach," Christy chided. "Oh, never mind. They'll do."

Sally appeared hesitant for a moment, but then said, "I'm glad to see you made it out, too."

"Yep. Good as new," Tom replied. "Tits and all."

"Excuse me?"

He smirked as he approached her. "No offense, but you look like you've been battered and double-dipped in shit."

Sally glanced my way. "She hit her head or something?"

"It's ... kind of a long story."

"And a fascinating one I'm sure." She took one of the towels from Tom. "But maybe it can wait until I've cleaned up a bit. Is it safe to assume I look as gross as I feel?"

"You probably wouldn't be wrong."

Thankfully, the bathroom facilities in the neighboring apartment hadn't been part of whatever renovations Christy had made to the rest of it. It saved us from having to shuffle Sally around and possibly be seen by Tina before she could clean herself up. It would also give us a bit of a buffer in case we discovered that things weren't entirely normal beneath all that crap covering her.

"What if she doesn't have skin anymore?" Tom asked, echoing that concern, "Or what if that shit is her skin now?"

"Not helping," I replied, leading him back into Christy's apartment, but leaving the door open behind us in case we were needed.

Christy stepped into her bedroom to retrieve the clothing we'd had the foresight to fetch from Sally's place a while back, leaving Tom and me alone in the living room.

"So what now?" he asked.

"We wait. TV?"

"Works for me. Just none of those morning shows. Good Morning America makes my vag itch."

I glanced at him as I sat down and picked up the remote. "You did not just say that."

"What? The whole package has changed. Time to update my vernacular."

"Yeah, I guess you should probably stop telling everyone to suck your cock."

Tina's voice immediately chimed in from her room. "You said a bad word!"

Grrr! I stood and dropped a couple bucks into the rapidly filling swear jar on Christy's counter. At this rate, I'd be funding a trip to Disney World in no time.

When I returned, Tom shook his head, knocking some of his shoulder-length blond hair into his face. "Anyway, not happening. You don't mess with the classics. Although I really should change this hair."

"Put it up in a ponytail," I offered, flipping on the TV.

"That would feel too much like a man bun. Fuck that shit."

I waited for Tina to scold him but, of course, she didn't. Fucking A. "Fine, then cut it off."

"I was thinking about it, but I'm not sure I want one of those dyke cuts."

This time, a different voice responded – Christy's. "What did I tell you about your language?!"

"Sorry," Tom called out. "I meant ... um, one of those dork cuts."

"You are so full of shit," I said with a chuckle. He might not be filling up the swear jar, but his critic was a wee bit harsher than mine. Then, raising my voice, I added, "And before you say anything, I already put extra money in the jar."

"Thanks, Uncle Bill."

Okay, time to nip this in the bud.

"Hold on a sec," I told Tom, raising the volume on the TV. I swear, I was the one with super vampiric hearing, yet it seemed everyone else was doing the eavesdropping. "All right, that's better."

Rather than thank me, he plucked the remote from my hand. "Change this shit, dude. The news is for..."

"...in a statement released last night, acting Police Commissioner Robert Valente confirmed that the NYPD had recently hired a special consultant, although he declined to specify the reasons behind it. Social media, however, has been abuzz with talk that it's to help the department deal with the series of strange occurrences that have plagued the city over the last few weeks..."

Wait a sec. *Valente*. Why did that name sound vaguely familiar?

Because I knew him.

"What was that?"

"What was what?" Tom replied.

That's when I realized he hadn't said anything. I'd answered my own unspoken question in my head. Awfully convenient of my subconscious. Okay, so I knew him. But from where?

However, if my memories had any insight into that, they weren't sharing. Nevertheless, the rest of the report had caught my ear. "Leave it."

"Why?"

"Just do it, moron."

Tom let out a huff and put the remote down. On the screen, the news had cut to an on the street interview. The reporter was speaking to a well-dressed man with movie star good looks. We're talking tall, dirty blond hair, square jaw, all of that. The only thing out of place was what appeared to be a handlebar mustache, of all things. Annoyingly enough, though, where that look would've turned most guys into an instant tool, this fucker somehow managed to pull it off.

"I'm here today with the city's designated special consultant, Matthias Falcon. Mr. Falcon, if you don't mind..."

"Mentor Falcon," the man replied in a crisp British accent, somehow managing to make himself sound even cooler with just two words. Needless to say, I already disliked the guy.

"Excuse me?"

"I prefer to be addressed by my official title, if you don't mind," he replied to the reporter, somehow sounding both smarmy and dashing all in the same sentence.

"Very well, *Mentor* Falcon. Can you tell us..."

"Mentor," I repeated. "I think this guy's a mage."

"Or at least he plays one on TV," Tom replied, raising his voice to be heard above the television, where this Falcon guy was busy explaining that he was here to consult on special cases, the specifics of which he was not at liberty to discuss.

"Hold on," Christy said, stepping out of her bedroom with a handful of clothes. "Did I hear that right?"

"Yeah. The NYPD are apparently hiring dipshits with stupid names..."

"Not that." She stared at the TV and her eyes opened wide in what I was certain was recognition. Oh yeah, this guy was definitely a Magi ... but hopefully not of the ex-boyfriend variety. "What's he doing here?"

Or maybe that's exactly what he was.

"My colleagues and I have been keeping tabs on the somewhat ... interesting events of the past few weeks. They recently dispatched me here to investigate, in conjunction with your city's finest, of course."

"In your opinion," the reporter continued, "are the residents of this city in any...?"

This Falcon guy, however, responded like a pro, stepping in before she could even utter whatever sensationalistic buzzword was about to come out of her mouth. "I can assure you, there's no reason to fret." He chuckled, sounding both dismissive and debonair. "I'm here merely to assess the situation, nothing more."

"But, what if...?"

"Trust me, you and the citizens of this fine city are in the most capable of hands."

He walked away, ignoring further questions from the reporter. The interview obviously over, she handed the reins back to the folks in the studio, who proceeded to change gears to the newest diet craze sweeping the city.

"So who's the douchebag?" Tom asked, drawing nary a peep from Tina's room.

"What he said."

Christy took the remote and turned off the TV, a quizzical look upon her face. "Matthias Falcon."

"Yeah, we kinda got that part. Safe to assume he's a wizard?"

She nodded. "The Falcon family is well known in Magi circles. Old world, very influential in Europe. Their ancestral estate houses both the Falcon Academy as well as the Falcon Archives."

Tom and I shared a glance, then he asked, "So ... is that like the Bat Cave?"

Christy started to shake her head, but then inclined it instead. "Not entirely."

"Spill," I said.

"The Falcon Academy is, or was anyway, the most prestigious institute of magic in Europe. They've trained mages for centuries. I was lucky enough to spend a semester there right after high school."

"Oh?"

"Harry sent me ... to work on my mind magic."

My left eye twitched at the mention of Harry Decker, the late unlamented dickhead wizard who'd originally sicced Christy on me. The only pleasant memory I had of him was being present when he'd died – both times, the first by Gan, the second by me and Sally.

Speaking of which... "Not to change the subject, but should she be alone in there?"

"She's taking a shower," Christy replied. "I have a feeling it's going to take a while to get all of that ... residue off."

Once upon a time, I'd have remarked that she definitely shouldn't be alone then. However, considering I was currently dating the resident witch in the room, I couldn't help but think such a comment would cause me nothing but pain.

I pushed that thought, along with Harry Decker, out of my head, turning back to this Falcon person and the fact that his family apparently owned a real world version of Hogwarts. "Okay, so what else can you tell us about this guy and his falcon cave?"

"Like I said, they're well known in Magi circles, quite famous actually. Their archives supposedly contain copies of every major magical tome ever written, but it's all kept under tight lock and key. I didn't see much of it when I was over there. You needed to be at least grand mentor rank to get past security, or have written permission from one."

"Oh, yeah," Tom said, snapping his fingers. "I remember you telling me. Didn't you say you couldn't even take a picture of the place?"

Christy nodded, smiling as if the memory were an amusing one. "I almost forgot about that. The wards around the entrance were crazy. I just wanted a photo but ended up turning my camera to dust instead. Too bad for me it was actually..."

"Harry's Nikon," Tom finished for her, causing them both to laugh.

I couldn't help the sharp stab of jealousy that knotted in my gut, even if I knew it was stupid. Christy and Tom had been engaged, back before he died and then became a woman. So of course it would make sense that she'd have told him stuff she hadn't told me yet. Even so, it kinda twisted my panties into a bunch.

"That's all fine and dandy," I said, interrupting their shared chuckle, "but I'm gonna go out on a limb here and assume enrollment dropped off a cliff about five years ago, along with applications for wizard library cards."

"Maybe," Christy remarked.

"What do you mean, maybe?"

"It's just hearsay, nothing more. After all, most of the communication in the Magi community broke down when the Source was extinguished. There were no more magic mirrors, no communing circles, nothing."

I was tempted to point out this wonderful invention called Google Hangouts, but figured that would just get me yelled at.

"But I heard through the grapevine a while back that the academy had remained open despite everything. According to the rumor mill, it was something of an oasis in Europe, sheltering displaced Magi while at the same time continuing to further the study of magic, at least from a theoretical point of view."

"And that would do what exactly?" Tom asked. "Without magic, all you're left with are a bunch of dorks waving twigs around. You can see the same shit at any Harry Potter convention."

Christy narrowed her eyes at him, which I didn't pretend to not enjoy. "There's more to it than that. There's preservation of our craft, our way of life, making sure the old ways don't die. Just because we don't need horses to get across town these days doesn't mean there's no point in learning to ride one."

"While waving a stick around and shouting accio Uber!"

Christy laid into him again, which should've been amusing, but something about this was gnawing away in the back of my mind – like a part of my subconscious that refused to let it go.

I shook my head to clear it, just as I realized what it was that was bothering me. "What about preparing for the day when magic returned?"

"Excuse me?"

"Exactly what I just said. What if they weren't teaching magic just for shits and giggles? What if they were keeping their skills fresh for the day it all came back?"

The look on Christy's face told me she knew what I was getting at. Sadly, that still left one clueless warm body in the room.

"Huh. Pretty good guess on their part," Tom replied. "Those are some motherfuckers who should play the lottery."

"Unless it wasn't a guess."

Christy tented her fingers beneath her chin. She didn't seem happy by what I was implying, but I could tell she was thinking about it. "The Falcon family's reputation in the Magi community has always been above reproach."

"I seem to recall the First Coven saying the same thing, over and over again, yet still being backstabbing assholes."

"Point taken." She didn't sound happy about it, though.

"Listen. Nobody's being judge and jury here. All I'm saying is it's worth looking into. And it's not like we have tons of other leads as to where Gan is or where she's got Ed stashed."

"Don't remind me," she said, her eyes downcast.

"Hey, it's not your fault."

In the days following Ed's disappearance, Christy had tried her best to scry his location. The problem was, we all knew it was likely a turd hunt. Gan was both smart and well versed in the types of sigils needed to keep prying mage eyes out of her business.

Needless to say, we'd come up emptyhanded despite multiple attempts.

"I know," Christy said after a moment, even if her eyes didn't seem to agree with her words.

"But maybe this is our chance to change our luck," I continued. "Think about it. If this Falcon fucker and his family – try saying that three times fast – were maybe in cahoots with Gan, or even knew someone who was..."

"It's just Matthias."

"Huh?"

"It's like I said. Communication broke down in the Magi community, but I still heard things. Matthias's parents and siblings were supposedly among those who heeded the White Mother's call to arms. They were down there when everything went to hell."

Oh. "I'm gonna assume this story doesn't end with them learning the error of their ways."

Christy shook her head. "As far as I'm aware, they didn't make it."

"But not this Matt guy?"

"I don't know. He either managed to make it out, or maybe he wasn't there in the first place. All I can say for sure is he's obviously still alive."

Tom leaned forward. "Unless he's not. Maybe he's actually dead but with someone else possessing his body."

Christy and I both stopped to stare at him.

"What? It happened to me."

"Safe to say, we're all hoping you're a unique case."

He smiled. "I like to think I am."

I ignored him and faced Christy again. "So, what do you think? We find this Falcon guy and..."

"Beat a confession out of him?" Tom offered.

Though a part of me was almost hoping it came to that – something about this guy made the idea of punching him sound real tempting – I was forced to play the part of the adult ... for now anyway. "Ask him," I corrected.

"Yeah, I guess that could work, too."

Christy appeared to think it over for a few seconds until she finally nodded. "You're right. We should ask. At the very least, we can make him aware that we're active in the city. I'll reach out and see if I can set up a..."

"Um, guys? Anyone out there?" Sally interrupted, calling to us from the other apartment. "I don't mean to alarm any of you, but there's something weird going on."

I wasn't sure what could freak out a woman who'd just spent the better part of a month sealed in magical granite, but I doubted it was anything good.

THE NEW GREEN DEAL

The three of us raced back to the other apartment to find the bathroom door ajar and a good amount of steam escaping – hopefully regular shower steam and not some freaky magical shit.

Although, knowing my luck, I wasn't about to place any bets.

As we approached, Tom held an arm out in front of me. "Hold up."

"Something wrong?"

Instead of answering, he flashed me a shit-eating grin and called out, "Are you dressed yet? Because if not, I'm happy to give you a hand, being that I'm a woman and all."

"Seriously?"

"Just trying to protect her modesty from the small-dicked losers in the room."

Christy, fortunately, chose to ignore his dumbassery. "I brought some clothes for you."

A thankfully human looking hand reached out from the steam obscured doorway. "Awesome. Pass them over."

Christy stepped past us and gave her the small bundle.

"Thanks," Sally replied from inside the bathroom. "Just give me a second... Really? Out of my entire closet, you chose this? Never mind. Whatever."

She definitely sounded like Sally, although the pitch of her voice was a bit off ... slightly higher than it should've been, although maybe that was just me remembering it through the haze of all the shit that had gone down over the last month.

A few minutes passed, then Sally stepped out, causing us all to gasp. She was dressed in slacks and a simple pullover shirt, but it wasn't her outfit which was causing us all to stand there slack-jawed.

"Holy Lorna Dane, Batman," Tom said.

Sally was staring at her hands, a look of confusion etched upon her face.

Oh my god, her face!

"What the hell is going on?" she asked, glancing up at us and no doubt noticing we looked as kerfuffled as her. "Tell me. W-what do I look like?"

"Huh?" I replied, tongue-tied. "You mean you didn't check?"

"That black shit got all over the mirror ... and pretty much everything else. And it wasn't until I finished toweling off that I risked looking down at myself and saw this." She indicated her arms and the flawless skin now covering them.

"You look okay, I guess," Tom said before turning Christy's way. "She's got nothing on you, babe." Then, a moment later, he flashed me a quick thumbs up and mouthed, "Piece of ass."

God, what an idiot.

He wasn't wrong, though.

"She's been ... rejuvenated," Christy said, her eyes wide.

"Okay, out of the way. I need a mirror." Sally stormed past us, pausing for only a moment to give Tom some confused side-eye.

Needless to say, we followed her back into Christy's apartment.

It was utterly amazing. She looked the same, maybe better, than she had when I'd first met her. Though over fifty, Sally had been a vampire for roughly thirty years, meaning physically she'd had the appearance of a woman in her early twenties ... and what an appearance it had been.

Hot as molten steel, she'd had an attitude to match back then. But, with the Source's destruction, so too had ended her eternal youth. Her body had instantly aged to match her years, appearing as a middle-aged woman. She'd still been cougar material, don't get me wrong, even if she'd traded in her slinky evening wear for more sensible attire in the years since.

Now, though, it was as if the last five years had been erased – with two minor exceptions.

"What the hell happened to my hair?!" Sally cried, once she reached the mirror in Christy's bathroom. "And my eyes!"

She stepped back out and faced us, finger pointed at her head. "This is *not* normal."

I couldn't argue. Her hair, light blond with colored highlights when we'd first met, was actually more a dirty blond naturally – something she'd adopted as she'd settled into her mature life. Now, though, it was a rich green, the same shade you might see adorning the trees in a forest.

Even so, it wasn't anything to lose her shit over. Hell, you could walk into the beauty aisle of any Target and probably find the same shade of hair dye. We no longer lived in an age where people felt limited to blond, brunette, or redhead.

That said, her eyes were a different story. Before, they'd been green, but now they were what one might call advanced green. It was as if her pupils and irises had either merged together or were now the exact same shade. That was a look one might need to go a bit further for. At the very least, we were in custom contact lens territory now.

Combined, this new look gave her an exotic feel as she stared back at us, like she was a budget alien from the original Star Trek – albeit the hot kind that Kirk would end up banging by the end.

"Quick," Tom said, sticking a hand in front of her face. "How many fingers am I holding up?"

Sally raised an eyebrow, along with a single digit. "More than I am."

He turned back toward the rest of us. "Her eyesight seems to be okay."

"Thanks," I said, "that helps."

Not daunted in the least, he raised an eyebrow. "So, is she some sort of vampire again?"

"Why would you think that?" In truth, though, his guess was probably as good as anything I had to offer up.

"Oh, I don't know. Maybe because she looks the way she used to."

That was ... actually not a bad point. Even so... "I ... don't think it works like that."

"It doesn't," Sally stated, although she still reached up and touched her teeth, as if checking for fangs. "No. This feels ... different."

"How so?"

"I don't know. It just does." She took a deep breath, no doubt trying to get herself under control. "Seriously, Bill, what the hell happened to me down there?"

"Aside from you getting zapped? No fucking idea."

"Ooh, you said a bad word!" Tina came strolling out of her room, the grin on her face suggesting she was thoroughly enjoying driving me to the poor house. But then she stopped when she saw Sally. She furrowed her brows for a moment, but then recognition dawned on her face. "Aunt Sally?"

For the first time since awakening, a smile appeared on Sally's face, and for a moment it was as if the weirdness was forgotten. "Hey, Kiddo."

Tina opened her eyes wide and smiled. "Oh my goodness! You're so pretty!"

Leave it to a little kid to defuse a weird situation.

"Why thank you." Sally bent low and held her arms out. "Did you miss me? Because I really missed you."

"You bet!" Tina cried, running forward and throwing herself into the offered hug.

Five years ago, we would've likely been far more cautious about something like this, innocent as it seemed, but all of us – even Christy – were still adjusting to the fact that the world we'd left behind was ours once again. It was a lesson we'd need to relearn and probably quickly. However, at that moment we were all a bit too overjoyed that Sally was okay to even realize that much.

Problem was, after what she'd been through, okay most certainly did not equal *normal*.

Sally had no sooner scooped Tina up in her arms when what could only be described as a shockwave of energy exploded from her body – sending the rest of us tumbling away like bowling pins.

It's kind of funny how the world seems to slow down when you're getting the shit blasted out of you. Obviously, that's more karmic hilarity than hah hah funny. Either way, it was like a solid wave of air slammed into me, blowing me off my feet. There was no flash of power, no fiery explosion, and definitely no warning. It was like I was standing there one moment, then being clotheslined by Andre the Giant's ghost the next.

My feet flew off the ground and I was given a split second to study the patterns on Christy's ceiling. *Hmm, there's a small crack in the plaster. She really oughta have the super fix that.*

There came a momentary flash of white light from somewhere off in my periphery, then time resumed its normal course and I came crashing down on top of, and through, Christy's coffee table to land in a bed of splintered wood and shattered glass. *Ouch.*

It wasn't a bad hit, but it was enough to knock the wind out of me.

"That tickled!"

Cat!

Fortunately, my vampire stamina was up to the task. The ... whatever the fuck that was, hadn't exactly been pleasant, but it was a far cry from being enough to finish me off.

I sat up to see Sally and Tina at the epicenter of it all – a look of confused horror on Sally's face, while my goddaughter continued to giggle as if someone had just told a fart joke.

The inviso-blast, for lack of anything even remotely better to call it, had apparently arced out in a three-hundred and sixty degree circle from them, as evidenced by the shattered curio, broken bathroom door, and general disarray all around the apartment.

"W ... what ... the?"

Oh crap, Christy!

I turned my head, thankful to see her landing spot had been a bit more cushioned – the couch as opposed to the table. Regardless, she'd been caught as unprepared as the rest of us, and she didn't have undead healing at her disposal.

There was a dazed look on her face and her nose was bleeding, but the fact that she was rising was a good sign.

"Are you okay?"

She nodded, her eyes beginning to clear.

"Oh no, Mommy!"

I turned toward my goddaughter, still in Sally's arms. "It's okay, Cat. It's just a nosebleed. Why don't you ... go into the bathroom and run a washcloth under some cold water for your mom?"

I had no idea if that would actually do anything, but that had been my mother's go-to medical advice when I'd been a kid.

Sally put her down, so she could do as she was told, then stepped over to where we were still pulling ourselves up, shock evident on her face. "What the hell was that? Are you guys...?"

"Yeah, don't fucking ask if I'm alive or anything."

We all turned to find Tom extracting himself from the remains of the writing desk he'd slammed into. His hands were covered in scratches and a cut on his forehead was dripping blood.

"Oh shit, are you okay?"

He narrowed his eyes at me. "Your concern is touching."

"But how? I saw your shield..."

"Me, too," Tom replied, limping over. "Didn't do shit."

That was worrying. There wasn't much that could penetrate faith magic. On the other hand, Tom's mastery of his powers left a lot to be desired, so perhaps it was best not to jump to conclusions until we knew more.

Before any of us could say anything to that point, Tina came back and handed her mother the washcloth.

"Mind getting one of those for your old man?" Tom asked, wiping his forehead. It wasn't a bad cut, thankfully, little more than a scratch.

"Okay, Daddy."

"Daddy?" Sally asked as Tina ran back to the bathroom.

"You ... might've missed a few things," I replied. "I'll catch you up later."

Christy nodded, then said, her voice slightly muffled by the washcloth, "More importantly, what was that? It came out of nowhere. I didn't even sense it until it hit me."

"And who did it come from? Cat or Sally?"

"How many times do I have to tell you, dude, it's Cheetara." Tom gingerly touched his forehead. "Ow. That really stings."

"Oh, stop being a big baby. You know you can heal that, right?"

He flipped me the finger. "Yeah, soon as I fucking figure out how to."

"Okay, enough," Christy snapped. "We have plenty of bandages in the medicine cabinet. That'll do for now." She glanced around at us. "It doesn't look like anyone was hurt too badly."

"Tom's ego notwithstanding."

"Eat a bigger bag of dicks than usual."

"Hold on," Sally said. "Tom?" She turned to face him, her strange eyes open wide. "That's you ... in there? You've gotta be kidding me."

I nodded. "Like I said, you missed a bit."

"All right, enough of that. Focus, people!" Christy fixed us all with a glare, made somewhat less effective by her still dripping nose. Nevertheless, Tom and I both shut our traps as she addressed Sally. "Did you do that?"

Rather than answer, she pointed a finger at Tom. "Before I say anything else, let me just be clear that if you *ever* follow me into the ladies' room, I will make it a point to test just how bulletproof you are." Then, with a heavy sigh, Sally turned her attention back toward Christy. "Honestly, I don't know. I want to say no, I really do. But when I picked Tina up..."

"What?" Christy prodded, just as her daughter returned.

"Oh, you felt it too, Aunt Sally?" Tina asked conversationally, handing a wet washcloth to her father.

"What did you feel, honey?" Christy asked.

"I dunno. It felt all funny."

Ah, gotta love five year olds and their ability to describe things in adequate detail.

"Is that funny, hah hah," Tom asked, "or funny as in show me on the doll where the bad woman touched you?"

"I liked you better when you were still dead," Sally grumbled, before returning to the point at hand. "If she felt the same thing I did, then it was a tingle, almost like a minor static shock."

Tina nodded. "Yeah, that's what it was. It tickled."

"And then?" Christy asked.

"And that's it. The next thing I knew you were all flying through the air."

Okay, that wasn't particularly helpful. God, I so hated mysteries, especially ones that sucker-punched me in the face. Those were the worst. But when in doubt, the only thing I could do was the same thing I did for any programming problem – hit it from multiple angles until I found something that worked. "Tina, did you do this?"

"Don't go accusing my daughter, dickhead."

"I'm not accusing her, I'm asking a question. Occam's Razor, dumbass. Ask the simple stuff first." Tina opened her mouth, but I already had my wallet out. "Here's a ten spot for the jar. That should buy me until the end of this conversation."

She looked down at the money and grinned, showing there was at least one trait she'd inherited from her dad.

"So did you?"

She shrugged in response. "I don't know."

"You don't know?"

"I don't think so. I wasn't trying to use my magic."

Okay, not surprising, but it was worth a shot. I glanced at Sally next.

"Unless you've got some cash for me, too, it's the same answer as before."

"Only if you're planning on dusting off your g-string and taking up pole dancing again."

"Mommy, what's a g-string?"

Oh shit! In the space of a second I'd forgotten the tyke was in the room. That was probably not going to win me any brownie points.

"Never you mind, sweetie," Christy said, flashing me a look. "Why don't you go play in your room?"

"But I want to stay out here and see what else happens."

"*Now*, Christina."

Tina glanced at her father, no doubt quickly adapting to the tried and true method of playing parents off against each other. Sadly for her, he was as big a pussy as ever. There was no help to be had there.

With a huff, she turned and went back into her room.

"And close the door," Christy called after her. Then, when it was shut, she added, "And no magic!"

"I'll take warnings I never expected to give my kid for a thousand, Alex," Tom muttered under his breath.

"Same," Christy said, "or at least not yet. I swear, I have enough wards in her bedroom to keep an entire coven contained and it's just barely enough."

"I take it she's got talent," Sally replied.

"You have no idea."

I turned to her, "Remember what I told you before you got the spa treatment from hell?"

Sally nodded. "That she conjured a fireball in your apartment?"

"Yeah, well that's the tip of the iceberg. She's pretty much a mega-Magi."

"Oh, or Magitron," Tom said, "leader of the Decepticonjurers."

Sally shook her head. "I can't even begin to tell you how weird it is to hear those words coming out of that mouth."

I offered my agreement then said, "Okay, Tina's out of the room. Let's get back to what we were talking about."

Tom smiled. "G-strings?"

"Are you sure you couldn't have put someone smarter in her body instead?" Sally asked.

I shrugged. "It's not like we had a waiting list."

"Enough," Christy stated, again taking charge. "I have an idea."

I turned to her. "Oh?"

"Yes. I need you all to focus here. More importantly..." She stood up then gestured toward me and Tom. "I need you two to brace yourselves."

She placed the washcloth to the side and began to glow, her body suffused with yellowish energy.

"Any reason for the...?"

Before I could finish, however, she stepped in, fully charged, and grabbed hold of Sally.

What the fuck?!

GESTATING THE OBVIOUS

I wasn't quite back to a point in my life where I was jumping at every shadow, but I knew Christy well enough that when she threw out a warning, I fucking made it a point to duck and cover.

Sadly, I was apparently alone in my insight because Tom stayed rooted to his spot even as I hit the deck.

"So, is something supposed to happen?" he asked after a moment.

"I ... guess not." Christy raised an eyebrow Sally's way. "Are you feeling anything?"

"Now that you mention it, I am kinda hungry. Not a lot of lunch options when you're encased in solid rock."

"I mean..."

"Relax, I know what you meant. There's nothing. Not like when I picked up the kiddo."

"No tingling?"

"Nope."

"Maybe you two, should, y'know," Tom offered, "get a bit closer."

Sally narrowed her eyes. "I swear, if the next words out of your mouth have anything to do with us making out, I will..."

He held up his hands. "Chill out. I wasn't going to." Then he glanced my way and gave me a look that suggested, yes, he actually was. God, what a moron.

Christy let go of Sally's arm and backed away. "Sorry. I figured it was something to try."

I pulled myself off the floor and put a hand on her shoulder. "It was a good idea, although maybe a bit more warning next time."

In the space of a second, Tom was there to slap my hand away. "Trust me, she doesn't feel any tingles with you either."

"Really?"

"Hell yeah," he replied. "Besides, everyone knows same sex relationships are the in thing these days. Who am I to argue?"

Christy glared at him, her eyes lighting up an angry red for a moment. "Can you behave yourself? Or do I need to ask you to..."

"Speaking of leaving," Sally interrupted. "That's my cue. All of this is ... really fucking overwhelming, if we're being completely honest, but I'm thinking the best place for me to deal with it is back home."

"I'm not sure that's a good idea," Christy said. "We still have no idea what happened to you or what caused that kinetic discharge."

Credit where credit's due. That was a lot better than calling it an inviso-blast.

Sally nodded. "I get what you're saying. Believe me, nobody is more aware than I am that something weird is going on. But I need some time to decompress, take all of this in. I'm kind of running on pure adrenaline here. I mean, I may seem calm, but..."

"It's okay," I replied. "If anyone in this whole wide world gets it, it's the people in this room."

She gave me a look of gratitude, an expression that was pretty rare for her back when last she'd worn that face. But that had also been a different her.

She'd been a vampire in those days, possessed by a spirit from beyond which had made her stronger, faster, and eternally young, but at the cost of turning her into a bloodthirsty killer. After it had been purged from her system and she'd returned to the way nature had intended, the Sally who remained still had an edge to her, but it was more from experience than some voice in her head driving her to violence. Since then, she'd changed, become a good friend to me and Christy and an excellent auntie to Tina.

She was once again in possession of her youthful hotness, through some means none of us obviously understood, but she definitely wasn't a vampire. That by itself was enough to put me at least partially at ease – albeit I wasn't stupid enough to simply assume all was back to normal, not with the changes that had been wrought to her.

Also, the fact that Christy's living room had been thoroughly trashed was a bit of a clue there, too.

At the same time, I remembered my first day as a vamp. Despite everything, even knowing that I was now a monster, all I'd wanted to do was go back home. Home was a safe place, a place to heal, a place to think. And, unlike me, Sally didn't have dipshit roommates waiting to set her on fire, which really only helped her argument.

"I'll stay by my phone," she said, perhaps sensing our hesitation. "Only order takeout, et cetera. At least for now."

Christy no doubt realized her only other recourse was to hold Sally prisoner against her will, which – crazy pulse of invisible energy aside – I couldn't say was really warranted.

There was also the fact she had a small child present. The rest of us could take a proverbial punch, but putting Tina in the line of fire was a different matter entirely.

"Okay," she said at last. "I guess it doesn't matter much if you're here or there. I'll start doing some research, see what I can find, if there's any tests we can run."

"Try Kelly again," I suggested. "Maybe you guys can brainstorm this together."

"Good idea."

Amazingly enough, Tom picked that moment to try and be the voice of reason. "I'm not the only one who realizes how batshit this is, right? I mean, she just woke up after being trapped inside a giant dildo, looks completely different than when she went in, and almost blasted the shit out of us right here where we're standing. So now we're all like, okay, go home, order some Dominos, and chill? It's not just me who sees the crazy here, right?"

I shrugged. "When you put it that way..."

Sally, however, ever the one to be a step ahead of the rest of us, was ready for him. Maybe she'd had time to think this over while in the shower.

"Trust me, you're not the only one. But this isn't my first rodeo. I've done weird before. I don't know what this is or what happened to me, but I know we'll figure it out. That said..." She gestured to the apartment around us. "...I have a big place with no neighbors, putting some distance between me and people in general, including that little girl in there. Crazy as it sounds, going home might be the safest thing for me to do because I really don't want to hurt anyone." She stepped forward and put a hand on Tom's shoulder. "But that could easily change if you piss me off. Get my meaning?"

Tom was quick to back away. "Crystal clear. There's no place like home."

"I thought so."

"Be careful and don't do anything to cause yourself undo stress."

"Yes, mom," Sally replied with a grin as Tom and I finished straightening up as best we could.

Christy, no doubt realizing she'd said and done all she could for the moment, turned to me. "I'm going to see if I can get in touch with Matthias and arrange for a meeting. At the very least, make him aware that we're friendlies."

"Speak for yourself," Tom said. "That guy gave me douche chills."

"Who's Matthias?" Sally asked.

I pulled out my keys. "I'll fill you in on the way."

"Oh?"

"Yeah, my car's outside. I'll give you a ride. Christy said no stress, which rules the New York subway system out."

Sally seemed to consider this for a moment, but then she nodded. "Okay. I seem to have left my MetroCard in my other outfit anyway. But shouldn't you, y'know, slather up? Looks like the sun's out. Not exactly vamp-friendly weather."

I let out a laugh, right before remembering I hadn't told her yet about my revamping. "How did you know I was a..."

"Observation, Sherlock. Down below, when you were fighting that little bitch, you were moving a lot faster than you normally do. That, and you got sliced up a bit when you went through that coffee table a little while ago, yet nobody said a peep about it. And now look at you."

I reached up and touched my face, feeling nothing but unbroken skin, which wasn't exactly surprising.

"Vamp healing, gotta love it," she said.

"True. Although it's hell on the sunbathing."

"Like you even know what a tan is. Okay, go and get yourself ready. I want to get back to my place and enjoy the peace and quiet while I can."

"Oh yeah. Speaking of which..."

"So, let me get this straight," Sally said from the passenger seat. "You've actually been recruiting vamps for a new Village Coven?"

"Technically I haven't named it yet."

"Whatever the fuck. Who cares? What I'm far more interested in is why you decided my building would be the perfect place to house them."

The annoyed tone of her voice aside, I had a feeling we both knew this was small talk, nothing more because, once again, everything had changed.

In a way, it would've almost been easier had Sally popped out of her shell a rampaging monster. It wouldn't have been ideal, don't get me wrong. But there was a certain simplicity in dealing with things like that.

Awesome as it was to have her back, and in a way that didn't require us to shoot her in the face multiple times, there was also the unease of once again having more questions than answers.

And that wasn't even counting all the other crap weighing down my already overburdened brain.

Tom, for example, had stayed behind, purportedly to get in some quality time with Tina, but I couldn't help but feel a stab of jealousy. Though Christy's feelings for him seemed to be up in the air, I knew his weren't. The fact that he'd known about her time at this so-called Falcon Academy and I hadn't, well, it was a petty thing to be annoyed about, but I was nevertheless. Whereas she and I were still working up to wherever our relationship was headed, Christy and Tom had actually made it to the point where they'd been planning a life together ... before it had all gone to Hell anyway.

As for us now, well, with him back in the picture, I couldn't help but think our relationship status was stuck in neutral.

The funny thing was, that was probably for the best, for now. Much as had been the case five years ago, when we'd been trying to save the world, girlfriend woes should've been the least of my worries. Doubly so because of who I was currently sitting next to and the seeming impossibility of her actually being okay, in a human sense.

I wasn't exactly a theologian, but I wasn't a base moron either. Sally had taken a bolt of energy from some insanely powerful thing that had been trying to break through to our world, an entity Gan had apparently both summoned and made a deal with. I wasn't quite ready to say the g-word yet, but I had an inkling as to both Gan's arrogance and ambition. She didn't seem the type to bother striking a bargain with some minor pissant spirit.

Even had she not somehow blasted us all across the room, it would've been the height of stupidity to assume Sally had eaten that much power, and all she'd gotten out of the deal was a facelift and a new do.

"Seriously, Bill? You couldn't have put them somewhere else?"

Her question snapped me back to the here and now. "What choice did I have? All the old safe houses are gone.

Hell, even that one we shared with those Howard Beach assholes was bulldozed a few years back."

"Good riddance to a bad shit-hole."

"Not arguing, but the only other property left from those days is the Office. Call me crazy, but I figured the folks running your nonprofit might object to sharing space with a bunch of bloodthirsty land sharks."

"True enough," she admitted, staring out the tinted windows as we slowly navigated the packed city streets. "Although, there is one place you conveniently forgot to mention, a building with your name on the lease that you actually have fucking permission to use."

Huh. Barely an hour back in her old body and already some of the attitude was starting to return. Guess someone was feeling better. "I have tenants to worry about, whereas you..."

"Enjoy my privacy?"

"I was going to say are used to cohabitating with vampires."

"Yes, once upon a time and with a disciplined coven." I glanced at her out of the corner of my eye, to which she amended, "Fine, a mostly undisciplined pack of assholes. Not my fault Night Razor was more interested in keeping his dick wet than running a tight ship. Even so, everyone knew their place on the food chain."

"I've been trying to work on that part."

"And while we're on the subject, how the fuck are there even any vampires to worry about? I thought Ed was the only one who could..."

"Dave," I replied deadpan. "That hand cream he was hawking, it had dormant vampire venom in it. When Gan turned the power back on again..."

"It became a lot less dormant," she surmised, shaking her head in disbelief. "Please tell me you at least killed his stupid ass."

I shrugged. "He's actually down in Columbia right now, making them change the formula and organizing a recall ... hopefully."

"Hopefully?"

"He's been a bit ... remiss in answering his phone since he left."

"Why am I not surprised to hear one of your dipshit friends is responsible for ass-fucking the world?"

"At least no one can claim we're underachievers."

"That's debatable."

"Says the woman who just woke up from a three week power nap."

"Hey, at least I can't complain I didn't get plenty of beauty sleep." She pulled down the sun visor and opened the mirror in it. As she gazed at her own reflection, I saw the barest hint of a smile cross her face.

"Happy to be back?" I asked, realizing full well there was a double meaning to my words.

"You want the truth or the politically correct answer?"

"Save the fluff for Twitter."

"Fine by me. So, here's the deal. I fully expected to die down there – no ifs, ands, or buts. Don't get me wrong, I didn't want to. But, oddly enough, I was kinda okay with it. My friends were there with me. I was able to save your butt one last time, and I even got to plug that little psycho at point blank range. What I'm saying is, as far as endings go, that wouldn't have been a bad one."

"I dunno, I always favored growing old and becoming a burden to my loved ones."

"As if you're not already," she said with a chuckle. "But in all seriousness, I don't. Hell, it terrifies me."

"Growing old?"

She nodded.

We stopped at a red light, watching as scores of angry New Yorkers took their sweet time crossing the street in front of us. "I thought you were okay with things, I mean after we beat Calibra and all."

She stared out the front window, watching the people walk by. "I thought I was. But that feeling of balancing the scales only lasts so long. After a while, it all recedes into nothing more than a bad memory. Then you're left with the reality of aches and pains you never noticed before, all while seeing new lines on your face that weren't there yesterday." She shook her head. "I know I'm the last one who should be allowed to complain. If anything, I got off easy. Besides, scared or not, I was pretty sure I had plenty of good years left ... or I did before those assholes kidnapped me. Truth of the matter is, they hurt me pretty bad, made me realize my own mortality."

"I know, but you still managed to..."

"Trust me, I had no intention of dying like that, chained up there like a dog. But still..."

She touched the side of her head. When we'd finally rescued her, most of her hair had been gone, leaving only raw burnt flesh from whatever they'd done to her. Now, though, it was a vision of perfection, albeit really green perfection.

"Some scars you don't heal so easily from, Bill, especially once you get older." She let out a mirthless laugh. "I know how vain that sounds now, but down there I was running on nothing but fear and adrenaline. So, I guess what I'm saying is..."

"You wanted to go out in a blaze of glory?"

71

"If it meant saving your dumb ass? Yeah, I guess so."

"That's sweet, in a disturbing sort of way."

"You're welcome. But then I got zapped."

"Trust me, I noticed. It was ... not a good moment for me, seeing what happened to you."

"Probably better than it was for me."

I couldn't argue that one. "So, all of that stuff was going through your head when it ... happened?"

"Partially."

"Oh?"

"It sounds funny now, but in that last second, just as those Magi were turning on me, the only thing going through my head was that I was way too old to be doing stupid shit like that." She let out another laugh. "That, and the old me – the person I used to be – would've been quick enough to dodge it all."

I turned onto her street, the gears in my head spinning like crazy. "Really? That's what you were thinking."

"I know, it's pretty pathetic. So much for that bullshit about my life flashing before my eyes."

"Not that. Think about it. Might it be too far of a stretch to say that in your last moments, you sort of ... wished for the old you back?"

Sally was a bright bulb, one of the brightest I'd ever met. She turned my way, her alien looking eyes opening wide in a way that told me she was coming to the same conclusion. "Are you being serious?"

"Yeah. It sounds crazy, but what else do we have to go on?"

"So you think I ended up like this because I subconsciously wanted it?"

"Maybe, minus all the green anyway. But yeah. It kinda makes sense, sorta. Remember, Gan was behind this. She somehow cut a deal with whatever that thing was. Maybe that was her price. She wheeled and dealed to get magic back into the world and in return maybe it agreed to grant her a wish, like some sort of fucked-up Aladdin."

"So you're saying that thing was a genie?"

"Not even remotely. I'm saying, I have no fucking clue what it was. But I know Gan, and there's no way she'd do anything for anyone unless there was some benefit for her."

Sally appeared to consider this. "What do you think she would've wished for?"

"I don't care to speculate, but I have a feeling it would've involved me at her side, busy updating my Facebook profile to indicate we were in a relationship."

She grimaced. "I can't believe I'm saying this, Bill, but if that's the case, then I'm kind of glad I was there to take that bullet for you."

I couldn't help but laugh. "Me, too."

"... Dave would've asked for cash, no doubt there, and Tom, well, he'd have probably wished for his old body back but with a three foot dick."

Sally held up a hand as we reached the door of her building, thankfully at an angle that shaded us from the sun. "I get the point. You really didn't need to elaborate on the stupid ass shit your friends would wish for. Trust me, I don't need that last image in my frontal lobe."

"Just trying to explain how things could've ended up otherwise."

"Safe to say, as usual, I was the best choice for the job."

She reached a hand into her pocket then rolled her eyes, no doubt remembering she didn't have her keys.

"Allow me." I stepped past her and opened the door. "They broke the lock when they kidnapped you. I didn't get around to fixing it. Figured there was no reason to, not with the place..."

"Infested with vampires?"

I stepped inside, grateful to be out of the daylight. "Infested is such a strong word, although I appreciate your faith in my recruitment abilities. Hopefully we can do right by this bunch."

"We?"

"Well, this is your home, and you ... kinda sorta know this shit a lot better than me."

"Both are true."

"Not that I'm asking you to do anything. But maybe I could bug you for some tips here and there. I mean, I know you're busy and..."

"*Was* busy," she replied, leading the way up the stairs, the building quiet despite me knowing it wasn't empty.

"What do you mean?"

She stopped and turned to face me. "Look at me." Then, after a moment, she grinned.

"Something funny?"

"You actually made eye contact. Once upon a time you'd have thought I was headless. Look at you now, acting all mature and shit."

"In all fairness, I am in a relationship." That, and her current outfit wasn't designed for maximum cleavage as her old wardrobe had been, not that I was about to say that out loud. What? I'm only human ... mostly anyway.

"Dare I ask how the meatwad being in your ex's body is affecting things?"

"Still figuring that shit out. Probably best to leave it at that for now."

She inclined her head. "Which I'm more than happy to do. But getting back to the point, the me who was dragged down into that cavern was a busy woman with a full schedule. The me who woke up covered in black demon jizz, not so much."

"Beelzebub bukkake, there's gotta be a market for that."

"I'm surprised you're not already a lifetime subscriber. But that wasn't my point."

"I know."

She let out a sigh, opting to ignore my stupidity. "Let's be realistic. I can't just walk back into the Pandora Foundation looking like this. Plastic surgery is good, but not *this* good." Ego, thy name is Sally. "It's way too early to make any decisions, but I can't help but think Sally Carlsbad is about to have an unfortunate accident ... one in which her body is never recovered."

"Carried off into the woods by Sasquatch maybe?"

"Here's a thought. How about I think this through without your help?" She turned and started up the stairs again. "Good thing I kept all those old IDs."

"Old IDs?"

She nodded from up ahead. "Yep. Contrary to the popular belief that Village Coven was above the law, a few of us – Star, me, and a couple others – made it a point to always have extra passports and social security cards handy ... just in case."

"In case of what?"

She let out a chuckle. "Despite what Night Razor would have had us believe, not every situation could be solved with a trail of bodies."

I couldn't help but smile. "Please tell me you have at least one with Sally Sunset on it because, if so, I have got to see that shit."

"Nice try, doofus, but no such luck. Most of it is under Sally Pemberton."

"Pemberton?"

"That was Jeff's last name."

"Wait," I said, slowing as we neared her floor. "So were you two...?"

"The only things that asshole was married to was cocaine and whatever unfortunate piece of tail he compelled to his bedroom at any given time. No. Think of it as a subtle fuck you, just in case I ever got a chance to make a run for it."

"No offense, but I think I prefer Sunset."

Her posture appeared to stiffen, likely from the unpleasant memories of her time serving beneath Douche Razor. "All things considered, me too."

CALM, COOL, AND DEBT COLLECTED

Though the front door of the building was pretty much a free for all, I'd taken the time in the ensuing weeks to at least fix the lock on Sally's apartment itself. Much as I'd needed a place for the new Village Coven – note to self, come up with a better name – it felt wrong giving them unfettered access to the building.

With the help of Christy's magic, we'd also taken care of the worst of the damage done by Sally's kidnappers, meaning her place was waiting for her to move right back in.

Thank goodness I'd remembered to grab her new keys on the way out, saving me the embarrassment of having to undo all my work by breaking down the door just to let us in.

"Didn't you say this place was infested with the undead?" she remarked as we stepped inside.

"I think that was actually your word, not mine. But anyway, the new recruits are probably asleep."

"No doubt, but I'm surprised at least one didn't wake up with all the noise we were making. How many are we talking about anyway?"

"About half a dozen."

"That's it?"

"Unfortunately, we've had to dust more than that."

"Can't say that's really too surprising." She looked around, then turned back to face me. "By the way, about how many vamps did your fucktard of a friend make with that shitty hand cream of his?"

I shrugged. "Probably best not to ask."

"Spill."

"I mean, it's not as bad as it could've been. Between the news, Christy's scrying, and the fact that martial law hasn't been declared, we're pretty sure a lot of the new vamps didn't survive their first sunrise."

"But I'm assuming that leaves plenty who were smart enough to stay indoors."

"Um ... yeah."

"So, exactly how fucked are we?"

"Not to sound pessimistic but I'd say in every hole, double penetration at the very least."

She let out a heavy sigh. "Sounds like one of Night Razor's old parties."

"Wait, what?"

"Make yourself comfortable," she replied, ignoring my outburst and heading for her bedroom. "I need to change."

"What for?"

"I love Christy, really I do, but please don't ever let her pick out clothes for me again. That goes triple for the new Icon."

"Remind me to tell you how he almost hung himself trying to put on a bra for the first time."

She slipped into the room and started to close the door behind her. "Remind me not to ask."

For someone who'd woken up from an extended magic induced coma to find their entire existence fundamentally changed, Sally seemed to be taking it all in stride.

I stayed with her for the rest of the morning and well into the afternoon. My plan was to be there when the others finally woke up, so I could drive home the point that Sally was not on the menu.

It had to be done, although I was holding out hope that it wouldn't be a life or death necessity. Reasoning with hungry vampires was like trying to explain to a drowning man that breathing was overrated. Sated vamps, however, were a different story, and I'd made it a point to keep my recruits stocked in overpriced pig blood.

Regardless, even a well-fed vamp could be unpredictable. I knew damned well that these people were no longer alone in their own heads. That by itself was an X-factor. A vampire could be chatting away one moment and covered in buckets of blood the next. I intended to make sure these guys knew full well that none of those buckets had better belong to any of my friends.

In the meantime, I kept Christy up to date via text message while Sally went about her business. In between us talking and me bringing her up to speed on things, she made several phone calls. I pretended not to eavesdrop but did anyway. Some were to the Pandora Foundation. Others were to banks or her portfolio manager.

I detected a definite undertone of her setting the stage to possibly move on. Yet, at the same time, she maintained a calm businesslike manner about her – almost as if she knew this day might come.

Before I could discuss it with her, though, she made one last call that was one hundred percent her old self.

"You're a life saver," she said into the receiver. "See you Wednesday. Yes, noon sharp. I won't be late."

When she finally hung up, I was sitting on the couch with a raised eyebrow. "I didn't mean to listen in..."

"But you did anyway because you're a prick."

"Pretty much," I said with a nod. "Anyway, I couldn't help but notice the name Alfonzo being mentioned."

"So?"

"As in our Alfonzo?"

"No," she replied. "As in *my* Alfonzo. As far as I remember, you wouldn't even let him give you a manicure. Your loss by the way."

I raised my hands in surrender. "I'm sure. Anyway, did I perchance hear correctly?"

"Yep. He's flying in from L.A., making a special trip."

"A special trip? Did you threaten to kill his family or something?"

She laughed. "It's called friendship, dumbass. Not to mention loyalty. I was one of his best customers back in the day."

"Um, you killed him so he could serve as your undead hair stylist for all eternity."

"True, but that was merely a compliment to his skills. Besides, afterward, as way of offering up my gratitude, I just so happened to help finance his new studio in California, where I might add he has a waiting list at least three months long."

"Unless your name happens to be Sally?"

"What good are favors if you can't call them in? And, much as I appreciate my divine makeover..." She fingered a strand of green hair. "I prefer to choose my own color combos. God, I hope he can strip this stuff out."

"Yes, because being stuck with punk rock hair is truly the worst problem imaginable."

"Don't be a little bitch, Bill."

"Speaking of which," I said, taking the opportunity to change the subject. "It's just the two of us now. Are you okay? No offense, but you seem really calm for someone who went through hell and back."

I thought she might dismiss me outright, tell me to grow a pair, but instead she sat next to me, put her hand on mine, and looked me in the eye. "No. I'm not even remotely okay."

"Oh."

"I'm terrified, confused, and angry beyond all belief." After a pause, in which my eyes might've opened a bit wider than normal, she added, "Relax, it's not at you."

"Who then?"

"Gan, Komak, mages in general, whatever did this to me ... Gan."

"You said Gan twice."

"I know. Killing her with my mind is cathartic. Gives me something to look forward to."

I didn't dare to disagree.

"As for being calm, this isn't my first time around the block. It's not like I'm a kid again, alone and scared in a big city while predators close in around me."

"Big city, as in...?"

She chuckled. "You know how I've never told you about how I became a vampire?"

Ooh, her origin story. "I may have noticed, once or twice."

"Well, get used to it because I'm not starting now." *Grrr!* "Anyway, what I meant is, I know trauma. It's been a part of my life for so long, I almost don't know what to do without it. It's partly why I've spent the last five years helping others cope with it. So this," she gestured at herself, "is just one more log to throw on that fire."

"That and," I replied with a grin, "looking like a stripper again might, just might, classify as a first world problem."

"Fuck you." But then she smiled, too. "Do you honestly think I don't know that? Trust me, beneath all of that fear, all of that survival instinct, is a small part of me that's screaming 'I'm back, motherfuckers.'"

I couldn't help but think the same. Before being kidnapped, Sally had pretty much sidelined herself with regards to the magical weirdness, and with good reason. She was done with it, out. Yeah, she might be there to play wise kung fu master and dispense the occasional bit of wisdom – or tell us we were being dipshits – but this was no longer her fight. And I was happy to accept that.

At the same time, though, as much as I'd grown to enjoy having Christy by my side, a part of me had been dreading the concept of change. Back in the day, Sally had been my partner in crime. As mismatched as we might be, somehow together we were more than the sum of our parts – like a fucked-up Voltron force.

It was jumping the gun to assume that would all change now that she was sporting her old looks again, but I couldn't lie and say a small part of me didn't hope to see her back in the saddle.

But that would have to be her choice and it would need to be made wisely. Before, she might've been five foot nothing in heels, but she had the power of the undead behind her. She'd been strong, fast, durable, and pretty much merciless as fuck. But now, hair and eyes aside, so far she seemed fairly normal, minus maybe that little incident back at Christy's – and there was no telling if that was just some random one-time quirk, hard to believe as that might be.

"Just do me a favor," I said. "Maybe hold off on diving into ... anything really, at least until Christy can do some research and we know you're okay."

Sally rolled her eyes, the look on her face suggesting she wanted to tell me where I could shove my advice, but I think we both knew she was too smart for that.

"Fine. I'll be careful. Baby steps, I promise."

"Awesome." I noted the shadows growing long outside her window and glanced down to check the time. "Care to go and meet the new troops?"

She actually let out a laugh. "No offense, Bill, but if your idea of *taking it slow* is meeting a pack of vampires, I can't wait to see what a busy day looks like."

KEEPING AN EYE ON THE KID

"...this is Jessica, and this is Stewart, and, last but not least, this is Leslie."

Sally glanced back at me. "I'm surprised you didn't give them superhero names, for old time's sake."

"Don't think it didn't cross my mind."

"Wait," Stewart replied. He was an older guy, mid-forties, about a hundred pounds heavier than me, and seemed to be perpetually covered in a thin sheen of perspiration. "We get superhero names?"

"Yeah," Sally said. "You're Captain Sweatstain. Congratulations."

I stepped in front of her before she could piss off more of the new recruits. Sure, they might not look like much at first glance, but they were all undead predators, in theory. Still, it was maybe best to not kick that hornet's nest too many times.

"Let me reemphasize, and I cannot stress this enough, Sally owns this building. She is off the menu. If you so much as touch a hair on her bright green head ... hey!"

"Let's cut the bullshit," she said, shoving her way past me. "There's only one unbreakable rule here. Touch me and I will fucking end you." Her voice was steel itself and I was suddenly transported back five years, watching her read the riot act to the other Village Coven vamps, some of whom were older and more powerful than her. "You may feel stronger than you've ever felt before and, believe me, I know how intoxicating that can be. But you know what? Those feelings lie. You aren't invincible, especially to someone who knows how to fucking take you down. That person is me. Remember that and you'll live a lot longer. Are we clear?"

Amazingly enough, there was nothing but nods from the new crew, which spoke volumes to the fact that a new day had indeed dawned for Village Coven ... or whatever I eventually decided to call it.

Jessica, a mousy girl with short brown hair, freckles, and thick glasses – thank goodness I wasn't the only one with shitty eyesight – stepped forward. She kind of had a Velma from Scooby Doo vibe, not helped by her raising her hand before speaking. "Crystal clear," she said. "And may I just add thank you. The last couple of weeks have been confusing, not to mention terrifying. I went to visit my grandmother, then the next thing I knew I woke up covered in blood and..."

Sally made a hurry up gesture, the look on her face suggesting she couldn't have cared less.

"Um, anyway, I just wanted to thank you for taking us in and giving us a safe, rent-free place to stay while we figure this out."

"We'll reexamine that rent-free part at some point in the near future," Sally replied, "but for now you're welcome."

"All right," I said, catching their attention again. "That's it. Make sure you drink up before heading out for the night. No biting anyone, no getting into fights, no trouble. Am I clear? Oh, and make sure you start heading back by around three AM. Even if you're over in New Jersey for whatever reason, that should give you plenty of time to get back before sunrise."

I dismissed them, then Sally and I turned to head back up to her apartment.

She raised an eyebrow at me as we hit the stairs. "You gave them a curfew?"

"Think of it more as a suggestion for their wellbeing."

"Guess I shouldn't be surprised you recruited nothing but nerds."

"I'm pretty sure they can all still hear us."

"Ask me if I care," she replied. "The first rule of establishing dominance is never let them see you sweat, something that one guy needs to work on."

I nodded. "Yeah, you'd think the undead would be less ... damp."

"Can't say that's a thought I really needed in my head."

I opened my mouth to reply, but then felt a buzz in my pocket. Retrieving my phone, I glanced down at the message on the screen. "Huh."

"What is it?"

"It's from Christy. She managed to make contact with that Falcon guy I was telling you about."

"The rich, good looking one?"

"No," I replied deadpan. "The other one."

"You don't wear jealousy well."

"I'm not jealous, simply cautious. I don't even know the guy."

"But she does." I glared at her until she finally grinned. "Relax, I'm just fucking with you. What's the rest say?"

"He's working tonight but is willing to meet with us on the job."

"A meet and greet with the NYPD? I'm sure that won't end badly."

"I think it's just with him." I glanced at the message again. "Yeah, I wouldn't doubt they have him working on stuff they don't want the normal cops to see."

"Or get eaten by."

"That too."

"Could end up being a self-correcting problem then."

"I won't lie and say that hadn't crossed my mind." We reached her door and my next question just sort of popped out of my mouth of its own accord. "Want to tag along?"

So much for me suggesting she take it slow.

She inclined her head. "Tempting, but I think it's best if I stay in for now ... unless, that is, you really need me."

A part of me desperately wanted to say yes, but the reality was I hadn't meant to ask her that. It just sort of blurted out. No, what I wanted was for her to ease back into her life, whatever that might be now, and not stupidly throw herself in harm's way. "We should be fine. I'm more worried about you being here alone."

"I'm not too concerned about the nerd herd."

"They're still vampires."

"Trust me, well aware. I'll lock my door and take precautions."

I didn't bother to ask what those precautions were, but it wouldn't have fazed me in the least had she confessed to having a few extra guns stashed away. At the very least, I was pretty sure the silverware in her kitchen was the real deal. Even so... "If anything happens..."

"Relax. I've got you on speed dial. Anything else, *Dad*?"

She probably had a point. Sally was close to twice my age, even if she no longer looked it. She'd survived stuff that would've broken me. I needed to trust her. But that didn't mean I had to be completely serious about it.

"Yes, be sure to eat your brussels sprouts, young lady, or so help me I'll take away your stripper pole for a whole month."

After double checking to make sure my new vamp recruits were set for the night, and then triple checking my phone to make sure Sally hadn't called in the meantime, I hopped in my car to head back to Christy's place. Since she'd told me we'd be meeting Falcon later but hadn't been specific where, I took it to mean her plan was for us to zap there together. Or at least I hoped it was. Magi teleportation kind of sucked, but it sure as shit beat driving all the way across the city again just to meet with this clown.

Ugh, Matthias, talk about a name that screamed pretentious douche. And then there was that bullshit from the TV, his "I prefer to be called Mentor" douche-baggery. Goddamn, how many sticks did someone need to have jammed up their ass to be that full of themselves?

I mean, yeah, in some ways it was no different than Dave wanting to be called doctor, or a lawyer signing their name with esquire. They technically earned the right through school and hard work. But, at the same time, there were plenty of other titles that were little more than pompous bullshit. Hell, in the space of five minutes I could go online and be proclaimed Reverend Bill Ryder. Shit, throw in a donation, and I could get that upgraded to Saint or Pope. Maybe that was a new coven tradition I should start. Down with coven masters, up with coven popes.

Pope Freewill Bill Ryder did have a ring to it ... assuming I wanted to listen to both Tom and Sally mercilessly rag on me about it.

I stewed over that idea for far longer than I should've on the ride back to Brooklyn, despite having much bigger things to worry about. But, with any luck, talking to Falcon would yield some clues for one of those bigger things – namely finding Ed – thus justifying going out of our way to meet with this smarmy English dick-biscuit.

Truth be told, I was still mentally ragging on the guy when I reached Christy's apartment, but it was time to put my game face on. The sun was down, the time for predators was nigh, which meant I should at least try to man up a bit.

Christy met me at the door. "How's Sally doing?"

"Settling in disturbingly well."

"Any..."

"So far all seems normal. No more random blasts of power," I replied, figuring that's what she was getting at. "Ready to go?"

"I can't, at least not yet." She stepped aside to let me in. "I don't have anyone to watch Tina."

"What happened to Tom?"

"He left. Said he had some business to take care of. Wouldn't tell me what, though."

Huh. That wasn't typically like Tom. Usually he was an unedited open book. Even so, he was an adult, albeit an unemployed one with too much free time on his hands. "Another training session with Vincent maybe?"

She shook her head. "Kelly said something the other day about him heading out of town. I think he's trying to mobilize some of his old Templar contacts."

"Getting the Bible-belt gang back together again? Wonderful."

That was probably unfair. Yeah, the Templar had been first class fuckheads back in the day, but some had chilled out over the years, especially with no supernatural evil left to fight. Vincent, for example, had ended up married to Kelly, Christy's coven sister. Now, instead of burning her at the wooden stake, he was staking her with his wood.

"It's not like we couldn't use the extra help," Christy said, dragging me from that somewhat disturbing reverie.

"True. I'm just hoping that the past doesn't repeat itself. I don't like getting automatically lumped in with all the things trying to kick my ass."

"Me neither."

"Oh, speaking of Vincent, and by that, I mean totally changing the subject to his wife..."

Christy shook her head. "Still no word. I don't know. Maybe she went with him."

That probably made sense. Sadly, it narrowed down our babysitting choices to roughly no one. After realizing Tina had enough magical potential to level the block, Christy had made the wise decision to preemptively cross most of the local teens off her list. We'd both seen *The Incredibles*. We knew how shit like that could turn out. And I wasn't about to suggest bringing Tina along.

It might be different if we were meeting this Falcon guy for coffee, but he'd *graciously* offered to slot us in while working a case. I didn't know what that entailed but had a feeling he wasn't staking out the local Chuck E Cheese's. Under other circumstances, I'd have suggested Sally, but now ... well, that seem perhaps an unwise choice, at least for the time being.

With her out of the running, that probably meant we were shit outta...

Hold on a second.

I was just about to suggest that I go alone when a thought hit me.

"Wait here," I said, turning around.

"What for?"

"I think I know the perfect sitter and, best of all, he'll work for kibble."

YOU SAY POTATO...

Christy opened the door for me again roughly twenty minutes later.

"Ready to head out?"

"I still need to get a... What is that?!"

Tina, however, was far more open minded when it came to the ... err lovable pet that lurched past me into her apartment. "DOGGIE!"

She ran across the living room with all the abandon of a child on Christmas morning and threw her arms around Glen's neck, hard enough to have probably given an actual dog whiplash.

"Bark," Glen replied, doing his best to lurch his tail back and forth, which only served to amplify how much he didn't even remotely resemble a normal healthy dog.

After a moment, Tina stepped back, her nose wrinkling. "Ewww. The doggie smells funny. Can I give him a bath?"

"Of course you can, sweetie," I said. "Right, Glen?"

"Sure," he replied. "I mean ... bark!"

Christy let out a pained sigh. "That is..."

"Perfect, isn't it?" I held up my hands. "Listen, I know what you're going to say, but we're short on options and Glen's an adult." Or at least I assumed he was. "Aren't you, Glen?"

He peered up at us with the two mismatched eyeballs currently bugging out of the dead dog he inhabited. "Well, in human terms, I crawled out of the primordial sludge of my home approximately two hundred and seventeen years ago. By my own people's gauge of maturity, however..."

"See? He's over two hundred. If you can't trust a double centenarian these days, who can you trust?"

Oddly enough, Christy didn't look impressed.

"Besides," I continued, "Glen has both of our numbers and will call if there's even the slightest bit of weirdness, right?"

"Of course, Freewill," he replied cheerfully. "See?" He opened his mouth wide and a tendril of protoplasmic goop came slurping out of it, holding an old Nokia phone. After a moment, he sucked it back in. "I'm all set to help in any way I can."

"Be sure to put that somewhere if she gives you a bath, okay?"

"You got it. And do not worry, Madam Witch. I will keep your spawn as safe as a sixteen-legged strix-roach gestating within its mother's digestive tract."

I blinked several times before turning to face Christy again. "And does it really get any safer than that?"

Despite her misgivings about leaving her child in the care of an eyeball blob wearing a dog corpse, even Christy had to admit it fell into the any port in a storm bucket. There was also no denying Glen had helped us out greatly down in the Source chamber, so we kind of owed him the benefit of the doubt.

I mean, shit, I probably would've sooner trusted Tina in his care than with her own father – not that I would've said that out loud in present company.

Rather than argue, Christy instead read him the riot act and then proceeded to go through her own personal babysitter checklist – full of emergency numbers, bed times, shows that Tina wasn't allowed to watch, and an incantation to recite which would activate the apartment's magic dampening wards in case she decided to throw a tantrum.

That last one might've been a recent addition.

Finally, giving me one last look that said I'd be up shit's creek without a paddle if Glen screwed this up, we stepped through the doorway ... and into Christy's bedroom, where she had a small sending circle inlaid into the floor.

"Be good for Glen," she called to Tina before closing the door. "We'll be back a little later."

"Okay, Mommy."

Then we were alone in her room facing each other inside a cramped circle.

"Kinda cozy in here," I joked.

"Not really in the mood."

"Sorry." I should have left it at that, but for some reason I decided to push my luck. "Speaking of which, have you talked to Tom yet?"

"About what?"

"About you and him ... and me, and how this is all going to work, or not work?" Amazing that I didn't have a career as a high priced motivational speaker, wasn't it?

"When have I had the time to?"

It was a fair answer. After all, she'd been as busy as me, even busier if we're being honest. In addition to helping me patrol for vamps, she'd been juggling a full time job with trying to contain her daughter's burgeoning magical potency, amongst everything else on her plate.

I was happy to leave it at that, for now, but apparently she wasn't finished.

"It's ... it's not that easy, Bill. Things are moving so fast now. I've barely had time to think of anything that hasn't had to do with magic, vampires, or what happened to Sally. I know it's not fair to you, but Tina is still getting to know her father and..."

"And you don't want to mess that up."

"I don't want to mess *any* of it up." She leaned in, put her arms around me, and our lips touched.

I *really* should have left it at that, but I had to press my luck like the dumbass I am. "But you are going to talk to him about it at some point, right?"

The moment instantly destroyed, she backed away and fixed me with a glare that would've sunk a battleship.

"And I'm shutting up now." Ugh. Why did I get the feeling that Glen might look like a canine, but I was the one getting put in the doghouse?

Taking a deep breath, she pulled out her phone and called up the browser.

"What are you doing?" I asked, trying my damnedest to adopt a businesslike tone.

"I know the cross street where Mentor Falcon wants to meet, but I need to visualize it, so I'm calling up Google Maps."

"Makes sense. Where are we heading?"

"To the Bronx," she replied curtly.

"Ah, such wonderful places you take ... oh shit!"

The upside of sending circles, for Magi anyway, was they acted as a focus, allowing them to move quickly without the need for incantations, powering up, or holding hands. The downside, for everyone else, was there was little to no warning before it happened.

One moment I was making a bad quip to try and break the ice, in the next intense light flashed in front of my eyes and I felt my very essence dematerialize. *Ugh!* It was like my body had been dropped into a giant blender set to atomize. For a split second, I was both nowhere and everywhere at once, a decisively unpleasant experience. And then it was over. I was reassembled at the speed of thought, finding myself standing in what appeared to be a playground that had seen better days.

My stomach lurched, reminding me how much I disliked traveling that way, but fortunately my vampire constitution was more than up to the task.

As the spots before my eyes cleared, I took note of a nearby chain link fence, beyond which lay a basketball court. "He invite us here to shoot some hoops?" Knowing my luck, this guy would be good at it, too.

"I doubt it. Keep your eyes peeled."

Yep, I said to myself, *that's me, just keeping a lookout for a smarmy British millionaire with an epic porno stache.* Considering the neighborhood, he probably wouldn't be too hard to spot. Unless he was glamoured up the ass, he'd likely stick out like a sore...

All at once, a shiver ran down my spine. It was that sort of feeling that screamed you were being watched. Forget searching for some Doctor Who reject, my instincts were demanding I get the fuck out of Dodge instead.

What the hell?

It was times like this I had to remind myself that I was a vampire, one of the lords of the night. Yeah, there was a predator roaming these streets tonight, and it was me.

Now to only hope I could make myself believe that.

Still, a part of me knew I was being silly. What out here could actually hope to threaten the two of us?

Almost as if in answer, a sound caught my ear – like the drip of water from a leaky faucet. No, not water. More like the pitter patter of little feet, a lot of them.

"You hear that?"

Christy turned to me. "Hear what?"

Of course she hadn't heard it. The sound had been low enough for my vampire senses to pick up, but that was it. Duh! For all I knew, I actually *was* hearing a dripping faucet.

"I am sensing some strange energy in the air, though."

Or maybe not. "Define strange energy. Are we talking bad cell phone coverage, short wave radio..."

"Old energy, not of this world."

"Um, the Martians have finally landed?"

The look she gave me was all the answer I needed. Too bad. I could've gone for an alien encounter. Would have broken up my week a bit. Not to mention, I really wanted to know who was closer when it came to faster than light travel: Star Trek, Battlestar Galactica, or if we should all start sucking down spice.

Alas, warp drive was probably the last thing I needed to worry about as there came a garbled scream from nearby.

"What was that?"

"Maybe someone having really good alleyway sex?" Christy narrowed her eyes at me, to which I sighed and forced myself to get serious. "Come on. That came from across the park, behind that building I think."

Though I could've left her in the dust with my vampire speed, I didn't relish leaving her by herself out here – nor charging in alone, for that matter. Whatever was going on up ahead, I didn't get a vamp vibe from it. No, the sounds I'd heard were unfamiliar, as if lots of little things were running around. Sure, it could've been midget vampires, but somehow I didn't think so.

Keeping pace beside me, Christy began to power up – a mix of colors suffusing her hands and body. Normally, Magi spells had this infuriating way of being color coded, letting you know in advance how fucked you were. I could only guess that she was maybe gathering noncommittal energy, waiting to see if we needed something defensive or face-meltingly hot.

Good call on her part, albeit unsubtle as all hell out there in the dark. Still, I'd take easily spotted over dead, so I kept that opinion to myself as we rounded the corner of the building.

Though my freshly regained vampire powers hadn't done shit to fix my near-sightedness, they offered the perk of military grade night vision. That wasn't always a good thing, though. Problem was, there was some shit you simply couldn't unsee.

Case in point. We were just in time to see some guy, probably homeless judging by the mismatched clothing he wore, being swarmed.

Unfortunately, we were too late, judging by the sounds that reached my ears – the rather unappetizing smack of multiple mouths greedily slurping down whatever they could tear off.

Whatever these things were, they were small – the largest being maybe a foot and a half tall. I could only see them from behind, but I got the sense of deformed humanoid bodies with short squat legs, arms long enough to drag on the ground, and hunch-backed bodies covered in crudely stitched clothing.

"Hey, you fuckle draggers! Over here."

"So much for the element of surprise," Christy said with a sigh.

Some people have no sense of style.

Most of the creatures ignored us, continuing to gorge themselves on the homeless guy ... and, um, pretty much everything else they could get their hands on. I saw cans, a bottle, and I'm pretty sure even a rock get stuffed into greedy mouths seemingly caught up in a feeding frenzy.

A couple of the little buggers, however, turned to face us, giving me instant insight that their backs were their good sides. Scraggly reddish sideburns covered pointed ears. What lay in between wasn't much better – a sloping forehead, bloodshot red eyes, a squat nose, and a mouth with exaggerated thick lips covering heavy yellowish teeth. Ewww.

"Any idea what these things are?"

"No," Christy replied, worry coloring her voice. That wasn't good. She was pretty much our resident expert in magic and the nasty shit it could produce. "If I had to guess, I'd say they're either new or very old."

Old or new. Neither was a particularly encouraging concept. On the flip side, ugly as these little troglodytes were, they were still pretty small. A lone homeless guy caught unawares was probably easy prey for them, but I was pretty certain a vampire and a witch would make this a whole other ballgame.

The few who spotted us immediately screeched something in a guttural language I couldn't even begin to understand. Then, before their fellows could be bothered to pull themselves away from their appetizing meal of dead guy and garbage, they launched themselves toward us at a loping run that would've been almost comical had I not already seen these things fuck up someone's shit.

"Stand back," Christy said.

"Ladies first."

She held up her hands and the indiscriminately colored power she'd been gathering flared up in a flash of purple. A half dome of energy formed about ten feet in front of her, blocking the creatures' advance...

... for about half a second before they stepped right through it.

The fuck?!

That was new.

The a'chiad dé danann are magical parasites. Such attacks will do no good.

I paused for a moment as I tried to process what my subconscious had just spat out. The what de' what were magical parasites? What the fuck did that even mean? And during what drunken stupor had I heard that shit?

Either way, it was pointless gobbledygook at a time when action was needed.

Fortunately for us, where defense failed, there was always a solid offense to fall back on.

"My turn!" I stepped past Christy – still staring wide-eyed at her failed spell – and punted the nearest of the little pricks.

It went flying headfirst into a nearby dumpster, hitting it with a solid *clong* and the crunch of bone. It slid to the ground in a smear of strangely colored blood and landed in an unmoving heap.

One of its friends was hot on its heels, leaping into the air far higher than I would've thought its stubby legs capable of. However, I was ready for it. I swung a left hook which caught it in the jaw, driving it into the side of the building we were still next to.

Caught between the rock of solid masonry and the hard place of my fist, the creature's skull popped like a zit, drenching my hand in brain goo.

"Anyone else want some?" I asked idly, letting the creature drop to the ground and giving my hand a shake to knock some of the nastiness off it.

"I think his friends are going to take you up on that."

I looked over and, sure enough, the rest had finished their meal – leaving so little of their victim behind that I was pretty sure the cops wouldn't need more than a couple of wet naps to clean the rest up. "Um, care to try again?"

"My pleasure," Christy said, her body already alit with angry red energy. That was more like it. This was the color you saw when the Magi meant business. It was perfect for turning motherfuckers into flash-fried motherfuckers and, since this Falcon asshole was nowhere to be seen, I guess it fell to us to finish this fight.

I quickly stepped aside, far enough out of Christy's crosshairs that I wouldn't lose my eyebrows from any ambient heat, and then she let loose with a blast of what could only be called pure hellfire.

The spell slammed into the group of ... whatever my subconscious had called them, like the fist of God, engulfing them all as they were still helpfully huddled together for our killing pleasure.

A wall of fire rose up, brilliant enough that we both backed away a few steps.

And that was all she wrote for...

"It can't be," Christy gasped, disbelief coloring her voice.

Couldn't really blame her on that one.

The flames before us receded as quickly as they'd risen, but they didn't disperse or disappear. No, they were ingested. A half dozen apparently still hungry mouths were pointed skyward as the power from the spell was quite literally eaten by them – sucked down like it was nothing more than strands of burning spaghetti.

It was crazy. This was the same spell Christy and other Magi had successfully used against the Jahabich, rock monsters from the center of the Earth. Yet you'd have thought she'd thrown these fuckers a plate of guacamole instead of a flame strike hot enough to fuse stone.

And the unpleasant surprises weren't done yet. The creature I'd punted into the dumpster was rising again. It grabbed its head, hanging at an unnatural angle, and snapped it back into place with a crunch of bone.

"Bill!"

She needn't have bothered. Sound and movement from much closer had already caught my attention, and I turned to find the one I'd smashed against the wall likewise rising. The damage I'd done to its skull was filling in, like attaching an air compressor to a deflated balloon.

It was like the regenerative capabilities I'd seen on much older vampires, except even more so, since a splattered skull was usually something even a vamp couldn't get back up from.

Not so with this guy. Within seconds, he looked good as new and plenty pissed off.

But I wasn't out of tricks yet. No sooner had the little troll closest us gotten up, when I extended my claws and slashed straight down, carving a gouge right down the center of his pug-ugly face.

Christy was likewise switching gears, going for the try try again philosophy when something absolutely refused to die. She screamed out an incantation in that unintelligible Enochian language of hers. A moment later, the dumpster across from us upended itself and landed atop the bulk of the nasties.

"That should buy us some time."

Except that I was pretty sure it wouldn't. As quickly as the metal bin settled over the creatures, trapping them inside, there came a horrific grinding sound from within as if something – or a lot of somethings – began scraping against the walls.

"Is it me or are they eating their way out?"

"Not you," Christy replied. "Look!"

Sure enough, the one whose face I'd just julienned was in the process of healing, its nose growing back between the two malevolent eyes that stared up at us.

"Fuck! Maybe we should think mean thoughts at them."

"What?!"

"Magic and claws aren't working, so I figured we should try something new."

"Not helping, Bill."

"Neither is anything else." I kicked the nearest one away, back toward where his friends were already chewing their way through the dumpster. We had maybe seconds at most before the world's nastiest ankle biters were free again. "I don't suppose you brought a gun."

"While I've always been partial to the classics," a smarmy accented voice said from behind us, "alas, that won't work, mate."

I turned, already knowing who I'd see. It was Falcon, mustache and all, making his grand entrance at last. He was decked out in that business casual action wear that only movie stars and wannabe male models could pull off – wearing a button-down shirt with the sleeves rolled up and a loosened tie around his neck.

It did nothing to improve my opinion of him.

He was carrying a couple of loaded down plastic bags for some reason. Guess he'd stopped off at the grocer before coming to watch us all get killed.

"You're late," Christy said.

"Couldn't be helped, luv. Some poor blokes over on Tremont were stuck on a fire escape while a few of these little blighters were busy gnawing their way up the ladder."

"Whatever the fuck," I replied. "I hope you brought some serious mojo with you, Matt, because otherwise you're just in time to be the next appetizer."

"I prefer Mentor Falcon, Freewill."

Huh. Guess my reputation preceded me.

He stepped to the opposite side of Christy, just as the metal skin of the overturned dumpster split, allowing the grime covered micro-demons to pour forth. *Shit!*

"Listen. I'll call you Mentor or even fucking Millennium Falcon if you want, so long as you brought something useful to the table."

"An apt choice of words." He threw something at one of the creatures. Whatever it was, it slammed home square into the beast's nose with a solid *thonk*. Rocks? That was his secret weapon? Oh, we were so royally...

That thought trailed off as the projectile seemingly melted into the creature's face, which collapsed in on itself where it had been struck.

It fell to the ground, where the rest of its body followed suit, until it looked as if it were merely a deflated balloon, instead of a nigh unkillable imp.

Both Christy and I turned toward him, wide-eyed.

"Here." He handed us each a grocery bag. "Just do us all a favor and aim well. This is all they had."

I took one without question – now was not the time to argue – then looked inside where I saw the words Idaho Russet staring back at me.

"Um, these are potatoes."

"You have a keen eye, Freewill," Falcon replied, throwing another at the creatures.

Christy glanced from him to me, then shrugged, pulled one out, and let fly, taking down one of our rapidly advancing enemies.

Oh shit! They were almost on us.

Suspending my disbelief for how freaking weird this was, I dug some spuds out of my bag and began chucking them at the monsters, feeling like a complete imbecile.

Too bad I couldn't aim for shit. Sorry to say, but growing up I was more likely to hide in my room with my Gameboy than play catch with my dad. However, being that our enemies were both numerous and disturbingly close, I hit more than I missed – each impact taking another of the stupid little gremlins out of the picture.

And stupid they were. As we whittled their numbers down with our combined assault, they didn't bat an eye. There was no sign of retreat or surrender, just a faceful of mashed potatoes followed by horrible death, until I eventually managed to peg the final one with a good sized spud right in the crotch – enjoying the confused look on its face as it collapsed from the dick on out.

When at last all movement before us had ceased, we dared a look around. Whatever these creatures were, they'd pretty much dissolved into little more than piles of wet mud once they were dead. Come tomorrow, this place wouldn't look anything else other than dirty ... minus maybe the overturned dumpster and murdered hobo.

But first things first.

"What were those things?" Christy asked. "I've never seen anything like them."

Once again, my subconscious offered an answer I'd neither asked for nor realized I knew. "They're called the a'chiad dé danann," I said idly, totally butchering the words I'd heard in my head. "Or at least I think they..."

I trailed off as I found both Christy and Falcon staring at me, looks of disbelief on both of their faces.

The latter stepped forward, getting so close that I could've licked his mustache had I wanted to ... which I really didn't.

All at once, his eyes flashed red.

"How the bloody hell did you know that?"

WIKI-FREAKS

"**W**hoa, back off, Mary Poppins. I'm not even sure exactly what I just said. It just sort of ... came out."

Falcon's eyes flashed again. "You'll forgive my reluctance to believe you, but that seems an oddly specific string of syllables for one to simply spit out."

I opened my mouth to reply but, much as I hated to admit it, he was right. "I don't know. Honestly. Maybe I heard it on Jeopardy or something."

"That name you just said," Christy replied, looking at me like I had two heads, "it sounds similar to ..."

"That's because it is," Falcon said, backing off a step, which was good because popping him in the face was starting to sound tempting. "The a'chiad dé danann are, in laymen's terms, what one might call a primitive forerunner of leprechauns."

"How does that even remotely sound like leprechaun?" I asked.

"The original pronunciation, obviously."

Yeah, obviously. "So, what? These guys were eating Lucky Charms back before they put those purple horseshoes in?"

Christy, perhaps sensing that I was veering into territory that would likely get me blasted, stepped in. "I'm familiar with the tuatha dé danann..."

"That makes one of us," I muttered.

"...but I've never heard of these."

"Not many have, luv," Falcon replied, giving her far less shade than he was affording me. Already, I could feel myself entertaining fantasies of his gruesome death. "There's not a lot written about them because they're rather ancient." He glanced at me. "Hence, why I'm curious to know how your *friend* here just so happened to have their name on the tip of his tongue."

"Well, if they're so old then how come *you* know what they are?" I shot back, rather lamely.

"I presume you've heard of the Falcon Archives," he stated, as if that were common knowledge. "But if not, I can assure you it is the single most comprehensive library of magic on the planet."

"Quite the humble brag."

He let out an irritatingly polite chuckle. "False humility has nothing to do with it. The fact of the matter is, we have texts which predate even the Fertile Crescent. Put simply, once I started tracking these creatures, I was able to cross reference what I learned and use that information to identify probable suspects."

"Suspects?"

"It was either the a'chiad dé danann or the xusia, an ancient race of pygmy demons from the Southern Andes. They're remarkably similar considering the vast geographic schism between..."

I held up a hand. "Yeah, that's real fucking interesting. So, you're telling us you followed a few footprints, then somehow had time to research a pile of dusty old scrolls and still get lucky? And yet you call me suspicious?"

"Hardly, mate." He reached into his pocket, causing me to tense up, but Christy stepped in and put a hand on my shoulder.

"Hear him out."

"My thanks, Ms. Fenton," Falcon replied, sounding annoyingly pleasant. "Or is it Mentor Fenton these days?"

Christy nodded then smiled at him, looking far too charmed by his bullshit for my liking.

"You were a student at the Academy, weren't you?"

"For one semester," she replied.

"It was a ways back, but I seem to recall us sitting together during a dreadfully dull lecture on the practical applications of phrenology."

Christy grinned even wider. "I'm surprised you remember that. I was barely able to stay awake."

"An inquisitive mind such as yours is hard to forget, especially when accompanied by such beauty."

"Yeah, this is all fascinating, I'm sure," I replied, stepping in again. "But we're on a timetable here. We need to get back so we can relieve the babysitter ... the one watching Christy's daughter."

Maybe a bit petty of me. But fuck it, I was bringing a knife to a nuclear missile fight. I needed every advantage I could get. This guy was tall, rich, good looking, rich, British, and rich. I'm not saying I felt inadequate next to him – I mean, I'm the fucking Freewill, for Christ's sake – but, if one of those proto-leprechauns decided to pick that moment to resurrect itself and rip this guy's face off, I wouldn't have complained much.

"A daughter?" Falcon replied to her, sounding not the least bit put out. "How utterly charming. And I dare say, if she's even half the witch you are then I foresee her making a fine mentor herself one day."

I made a hurry-up motion. "Hello? All that stuff I was busy accusing you of? Remember that?"

"Ah, yes." He glanced my way again, as if noticing I was there for the first time, then pulled his hand out of his pocket, revealing nothing more than a cell phone. "Tell me, Freewill, what do you think we've been doing these past five years?"

"Considering I didn't even know you existed? No idea."

"Fair point, friend, and not entirely surprising considering your former affiliation with the First Coven. No offense, but my organization preferred to do as little business with that lot as possible." Before I could comment on that, he continued. "To answer the question, as part of an effort to modernize, we've had a team of volunteers working nonstop to digitize the archive and make it available via... What is that word again?"

I stepped in and looked over his shoulder. "You put it on a wiki?"

"Do you mind?" he asked, quickly covering the screen.

"Not at all. Especially since you don't seem to mind putting the text of the freaking Necronomicon on the web."

"First off, that's not a real book. Secondly, unlike that messy ordeal up in Amherst some years back, I've been assured everything has been secured to the utmost degree."

"What messy...?"

"Excuse me," Christy said, interrupting. "Not to be disrespectful, but Bill's got a good point about the risks involved."

"I understand the sentiment." Once again, the tone Falcon took with her was far more cordial than the attitude he was throwing at me. "But the ability to cross reference texts in a fraction of the time it used to take is invaluable. In addition, there is one major plus in our favor. As adept at the arts as many of our kind are, it's rare to come across a Magi who isn't confounded by email, much less anything more elaborate. Not a lot of hackers amongst our number."

"Crackers," I corrected.

"Those either," he said dismissively. "And access is strictly limited. Regardless, it's a good thing that I was able to discern these blighters' weakness. Because believe me, they don't have many."

"Potatoes," I said, more to myself than anything. "No offense to these shitbags, but that's a really stupid weakness."

Falcon actually laughed, well, more a proper British titter anyway. "Indeed, Freewill. Dangerous as they are, there's a reason they haven't been seen since the dawn of civilization. Although the history books will have you believe that these beauties..." he held up a potato, "weren't introduced to Europe as a food crop until the sixteen-hundreds, what they fail to mention is that they were in high demand as weapons thousands of years earlier. It just wasn't until much later that some bloke dropped one into a pot of boiling oil, only to realize it tasted divine with a pinch of salt."

"Um ... thanks for the history lesson, Alton Brown."

He smirked as if amused by my lack of enthusiasm. "Never discount the mundane, friend. Not to flog a broken horse, but most history books love to blather on about how humanity moved from being hunter gatherers to farmers as one of the key steps of civilization. Bollocks. Early agriculture was as much about waging war as it was about keeping one's belly full. No offense, Freewill, but you should be glad this sort of knowledge is mostly forgotten."

"Why? Should I be worried that someone might try staking me with a carrot?"

"Carrots, no, but you'd probably be chuffed to know that scarcosinum is extinct. And before you ask, it was an herb indigenous to northern Africa that also happened to be excessively potent as a vampire repellant."

I backed up a step. "Hold on. There's such a thing as vampire repellent?"

"*Was* such a thing," Christy said. "It went extinct around the Dark Ages. From what I read, a group of Magi tried to recreate it about a hundred years ago but were unable to make it work."

"Don't think that was by accident," Falcon replied. "The vamps eventually got cagey to the fact that their enemies were cultivating it. That's right around the time they started pulling back into the shadows, convincing the simple folk that they didn't exist anymore. Within a couple generations, farmers began wondering why they were wasting field space on a junk plant that smelled bad and tasted even worse. It was killed off domestically, then the First Coven, clever nutters that they were, took care of the wild variant before making sure to burn every detailed reference, so that nobody could breed it back into existence. And they were damned thorough. There's nothing but vague references to it, even in the Falcon Archives."

This guy sure did love saying his family name, as well as yammering on about random shit that had nothing to do with the point at hand. I was about to say as much when Christy steered us back on track.

"We thank you for the insight as well as the assistance, Mentor Falcon."

"Please, call me Matthias."

Grrr!

"I appreciate that, Matthias," she continued. "But we should probably talk about the real reason Bill and I wanted to meet."

"Bill," he repeated, turning toward me. "I have to say, many of us found it refreshing to hear a Freewill going by such a mundane title, especially after a long run of tossers with names like Vara the Unconquerable, Abdalla the Merciless, or Vehron the Destroyer."

"I'm familiar with that last one, thanks. But Christy's right. Enough with the tangents."

Falcon nodded. "Fair enough. My assumption was that you wished to inform me you were active in this city."

"Partly," Christy said. "But also to let you know we're on the same side."

"The same side, eh?"

"Yeah," I replied. "We've been busting our butts trying to corral the recent vampire problem."

He raised an eyebrow. "Ah, so that's been your doing?"

Huh. I didn't realize he was already aware. Guess maybe we'd been doing a better job than I thought. "Pretty much. We've been trying to rein in those willing to listen to reason. And those who aren't..." I mimed sticking a stake through my heart. "Hold on. How did you even know someone was hunting vamps? It's not like we leave bodies behind."

"No, but there is psychic residue," Christy explained. "Easy to find, if someone knows what they're doing."

Falcon nodded. "Precisely. Or in some cases there's simply too much random dust to be anything else. I must admit, I'm impressed. Has it only been the two of you?"

I shook my head. "No. We have some friends who've been helping out. Another witch, and a former Templar." There was no point in mentioning Tom since, so far as I knew, he'd managed to kill nothing more than time. "And it's not that impressive. I mean, I think between all of us, we've managed to dust maybe ten or twelve rogue vamps."

"Ten or twelve?" he repeated. "That doesn't add up. I'm talking about scores over the last few weeks."

What? "Wait, how many?"

"Believe me, I'm not exaggerating. I've asked the local hospitals to keep me in the loop regarding any bite victims who come in. When I first got here, it looked like we might have the beginnings of an epidemic on hand, but the number has been dropping steadily. Far as I can tell, someone, possibly plural, has been dusting the undead with great aplomb. And word is apparently spreading. I'm hearing that those who haven't been hit have started lying low."

Christy and I shared a glance. Our small team had been pretty open about our numbers. We were all doing our part to keep New York from turning into open season on humans, so I couldn't think of any reason the others might decide to be humble about their success. It's not like we'd have given them shit for going over quota.

So then who or what was responsible for the numbers Falcon was claiming?

I remembered back to the other night. That woman I'd met, the one who called herself Char. She'd made short work of one of the vamps I'd been after. Still, impressive as she'd been, it seemed a stretch that she was responsible for racking up that high of a body count in such a short time. Unless that is, this Falcon guy was shitting us.

"You're sure it's that many?"

He reached into his pocket again, and once more I found myself tensing – as if expecting him to pull out the elder wand and go all avada kedavra on my ass. Instead, reality was far more mundane and infinitely more douchey. He pulled out a vape pen and proceeded to take a suck on it, blowing out a ring of smoke with a strawberry scent to it.

I swear, if I found out this guy moonlighted as the barista at an upscale coffee house...

"No doubt about it," he said after another puff. "I've been keeping detailed records."

"And you're certain it wasn't these proto-leprechauns?"

Falcon shook his head. "Positive. They'd have simply eaten them, dust and all."

That wasn't a particularly pleasant thought. I didn't relish the idea of ever being dusted. But being staked sounded preferable to ending up in some caveman's colon.

After a few more moments, he let out a sigh. "Bollocks. I was really hoping it was you lot. Would have saved me no small amount of headache."

"So you could arrest us and be done with it?" I asked, testing the waters. Though I knew it made sense to make contact with this guy, a part of me had wondered if I'd simply be signing my own arrest warrant in doing so. Better to get that out of the way now, so at least the option of knocking his block off was back on the table.

"Hardly," he replied with another puff. "The boys in blue won't take kindly to vigilantes in their city, don't get me wrong. That sort of nonsense only works in the comic books. But fortunately for you, I'm merely a consultant. My job is to assess and curtail these happenings, and if I so happen to require outside assistance, well, that's strictly at my discretion."

"Good to know."

He raised an eyebrow at me. "Funny you should even ask, though."

"Why?"

"Because you know full well that I'd be hard pressed to bring you in, even if I wanted to."

That caught my attention. "I do?"

"How so?" Christy asked.

"You're having a laugh, right?" Falcon replied, no doubt noticing the confusion on our faces. "The old treaties. The ones between the vamps and the authorities of this fine state."

"What about them?"

"They've all been reinstated."

What?!

CRAMPING MY STYLE

"What do you mean the old treaties are back?"

Falcon shrugged. "Well, not old, as in dawn of time, but the ones your kind seemed to have in place in nearly every metropolis of note. I imagine the ones in Europe and Asia are older. However, only a handful of those..."

"I don't need a history lesson." I glanced at Christy and then back to hipster Harry Potter. "You mean the treaties that kept the cops from forming an anti-drac task force back in the day?"

"One and the same, as I'm sure you're fully aware," Falcon replied. "The current Commissioner pulled me aside when I first got here, for a little locked door tête-à-tête on what I could and couldn't do. I was informed in no uncertain terms that vamps were off the table. Anything having to do with their kills I was to call in and that was it, no matter how distasteful I might find it."

"But you just said..."

He waved me off. "I know what I said. Vamps killing humans might be outside my charter, but I was never told I couldn't investigate whatever might be killing them instead."

I turned to Christy. "Did you know about this?"

She shook her head. "How would I? Back when there was a vampire nation, they didn't exactly keep the local Magi in the loop."

That was a good point. Stupid question on my part.

"I have to say, Freewill, you move fast." Falcon took another hit from the metal dong of his vape pen. "The eldritch energies have been flowing again for mere weeks, yet it sounds like you've wasted no time. Word on the street is that the Shanghai treaty was reinstated five days ago, and Los Angeles right after. You must have one hell of a little black book in your back pocket."

"Me? You think I did that?"

"Didn't you? Far as I've heard, you're one of the few vamps of note to survive the purge of five years ago."

Flattered as I was to hear it, nothing could be further from the truth. I mean, shit, I wouldn't even know who to talk to in my own city, much less in fucking Shanghai.

Wait a second. Shanghai... Goddamn it!

I could tell by Christy's face that she'd reached the same conclusion – Gan.

"Bill didn't reinstate those treaties, Matthias," she said, making me cringe at hearing his name on her lips.

"Yeah, I can barely ask my tenants for a year over year rent increase. I'm not quite up to negotiating wholesale murder on behalf of an entire species."

"But I think we know who did," she continued, "and it's part of why we wanted to meet, aside from letting you know we're here as allies."

Falcon actually laughed at her words. "Sorry, luv. Not trying to make fun of this. It's just that back before all this happened, mages and vamps occasionally worked together, but nobody fooled themselves into thinking we were allies. We find ourselves in interesting times, indeed."

I couldn't help but agree, although I kept my mouth shut. Spud save or not, I wasn't about to hand this Falcon guy more of my trust than was warranted.

"Please go on and pardon the interruption."

Christy thanked him, then continued. "I assume you're aware of the circumstances under which magic returned."

Falcon again grinned. His debonair demeanor was really starting to get under my skin. "While I may not have been present for the opening ceremonies, word has reached me that a certain charming sorceress within arm's reach had a hand in it."

"Okay, enough with the bullshit flirting," I snapped, losing my temper. "You know full well that Gansetseg was behind everything. She recruited a bunch of mages to fuck over the ones who were already busy trying to fuck over the world. The question being, did you have your dick in that first group's apple pie or the second's?"

Silence descended upon the alleyway as I realized I may have gone a tiny bit overboard. Both Christy and Falcon were staring at me – him wide eyed, her looking a wee bit angry.

Yeah, I almost certainly could've handled that more diplomatically.

"He's not..."

"Gansetseg?" Falcon asked, interrupting her. "You mean the former Prefect of the Gansu province in China? Adopted daughter of..."

"I know who she is. You don't have to recite her LinkedIn profile."

"You're suggesting she was behind all of this and you think I..."

"What Bill is *trying* to say," Christy cut in, putting a not so kind emphasis on my name. Oh boy. In the beer pong of relationships, I had a feeling I'd just sent the ball rolling beneath the couch. "...is that she and a handful of elder vampires survived the purge. In the last five years, she's managed to manipulate events to not only facilitate the Source's reopening, but at a scale none of us would have previously thought possible."

That about summed it up. Gotta hand it to Gan. She didn't think small.

"Others?"

"At the time," she replied. "None of them survived her plans. In fact, it would seem she used them as nothing more than sacrificial pawns."

"We're talking Emperor Palpatine level shit here," I added.

"What she was able to accomplish," Christy continued, making it a point to ignore me, "was far greater than anything my incantation was capable of, leading me to believe she somehow had access to resources far above and beyond what she should have."

"Excuse me for reading between the lines, but you think she may have gained access to the Falcon Archives? That's a serious accusation."

Christy nodded. "And one I don't come by lightly, Mentor Falcon."

I couldn't help but notice the use of his formal title again. It was all I could do to keep from screaming, "In your face!" at him. Petty of me, but a win was a win. Now to hope he broke down and confessed. If so, we could call it a night – after beating the shit out of him until he told us where Ed was being held.

Ah, if only life could be so easy.

If Falcon was either insulted or preparing to throw himself to his knees and beg for mercy, he didn't show it.

"It's fairly well known that the vampire nation kept their own extensive archives. Archives that, if the rumors are to be believed, rival my family's."

That much was true. I used to hear the vamps in charge gloat about it all the time. Colin, in particular, late unlamented douche that he was, seemed to take great pleasure that he had a library card, whereas I didn't rate one.

"So I've heard," Christy said. "The problem is, we don't know enough to even make a guess as to whether they'd have contained anything remotely like the level of arcane knowledge Gansetseg would've needed."

She glanced my way for a moment, as if checking whether I had anything better to offer, to which I simply shook my head.

"You're not incorrect," Falcon replied, sounding far less put out than I was hoping he'd be. "Those old vamps were as secretive as they were pragmatic."

Indeed they were, even amongst their own number.

Once again, my subconscious seemed to have an opinion on something, although this time I couldn't really argue. I mean, shit, when it came to secrets, the CIA and KGB could've both taken lessons from the First Coven.

"But that bit of speculation does bring us back to point one," Falcon continued, looking far more thoughtful than insulted. "We don't know what kind of information the vamps deemed of importance, but we know our own endeavors. If the knowledge to do such a thing exists anywhere in this world, it would almost certainly be within the Falcon Archives."

It truly was amazing that this guy was somehow able to speak without choking to death on his own smugness.

"Tell you what," he said, "it couldn't hurt to ask. I'm not aware of any dealings with this Gansetseg, but that doesn't mean it can be ruled out. Gaining access to the archives is considered a sacred honor among our people, one not handed out lightly. All the same, it must be acknowledged that the last five years have been ... difficult for our kind. But then to be approached with the proverbial golden goose – the restoration of magic? One can easily imagine even the most stalwart defenders of our ways being hard pressed to turn down such an opportunity. Truth be told, I'm not sure I wouldn't have considered it myself."

It was neither the confession I'd hoped for, nor did it bring us any closer to finding Ed, but, in the end, Falcon offered to do some digging for us. That seemed to satisfy Christy, although I'd be lying if I said it didn't leave a bad taste in my mouth. Call me paranoid, but I got the sense that Falcon was withholding information.

Had I been older, I'd have maybe been able to use my senses as a sort of lie detector. But if that were the case, I could've simply punted those proto-leprechauns all the way into the Hudson and not have to be saved by Mr. Potato Head's mustache attachment.

Either way, our business was concluded for now – outside of maybe some more pointless sniping on my part. As such, we took our leave of the illustrious Mentos Falcon or whatever he wanted to call himself.

Christy stepped close to me and, without saying a word, zapped us back to her bedroom – although I had a feeling no invitation for a sleepover was forthcoming, especially once she laid into me.

"You can't just accuse a wizard of his standing like you did."

I was tempted to argue that yes, I could and would if I felt the need to, even if it ended with me dodging fireballs. However, I could understand her being a bit upset. The guy had saved us, only for me to kind of lose my shit on him. Diplomacy thy name is not Bill Ryder.

"And flirting? *Really?*"

"What? He was obviously hitting on you."

"No, he wasn't. And even if he was," she snapped, "don't you think we have more important issues to deal with?" Sadly, it was a rhetorical question, as she kept on going. "Matthias was right about those creatures we fought. They're old. Even when we were fighting them, I could sense that."

I saw we were back to Matthias again, but in the interest of not being yelled at more than I already was, I kept my mouth shut on the subject. "Okay, and?"

"So why are they back now and, more importantly, why are they here?"

"Because nobody celebrates Saint Patrick's Day quite like New Yorkers?" Her eyes instantly flashed red, causing me to back up a step. "Sorry!"

"You need to stop that."

"Stop what?"

"What you're doing. You're falling back into the same habits from five years ago. You don't act, you react, and that includes the things you say. You're supposed to be an adult. This is serious business, not a joke."

I held up my hands in a placating manner. "I do take this seriously, believe me." Then, before I could do something smart, like try to make this better, I added, "But come on. We fought Neolithic leprechauns tonight. Even you've gotta admit that's pretty fucking ridiculous."

"We could have died."

"But we didn't." Hey, at least I didn't bring up the fact that I was technically already dead.

"You don't get it." She took a step forward, power crackling around her. Oh yeah, I'd gone and put my foot in my mouth. "We can't afford to..."

She was interrupted by the sound of the bedroom door being pushed open.

A moment later, a freaky-ass dog thing came clumsily lurching through it.

"Bark bark bark... Oh, it's you Freewill. You're back." Glen stared at us, the two mismatched eyes bugging out of his head doing nothing to improve my mood. "I thought it might be an intruder. I was coming in here to frighten them off."

"Yeah, I'm sure that would've terrified them."

"Thank you. I've been working on my ferocious growl. Want to hear it?"

"Maybe later, Glen."

"Is Tina okay?" Christy asked, thankfully distracted from laying into me more.

"She's perfectly fine. Fast asleep as a matter of fact. We had a really fun evening."

I raised an eyebrow as I realized his *fur* was damp in some spots, whereas newly bare patches of skin shone at various points along his rump and torso. Taking a quick whiff, my eyes began to water from the overpowering floral scent coming off him, mixed with an underlayer of death. "Is there a reason you smell like you stepped on a lavender scented land mine?"

Glen turned toward Christy. "My apologies, Madam Witch, but you are currently all out of body wash. Also, the hair trap in your tub might be a bit clogged."

"I'm assuming Cat gave you a bath," I said dryly.

"Six, as a matter of fact. It was great fun."

Christy let out a sigh and rubbed the bridge of her nose. "I'm going to go check on..."

"No worries. We'll let ourselves out."

On the short drive back home, I pointedly ignored Glen's repeated requests to roll down the window so he could hang his head out. Fucking method actors. The hell with that. His so-called disguise was even worse now, and I had no interest in horrifying the shit out of any late night pedestrians we passed on the way.

Besides, I had more important matters on my mind, and some of them didn't even have to do with the fact that Christy was obviously pissed at me.

The old treaties were back. That couldn't be good.

Don't get me wrong. I didn't care to end up arrested or in some government lab being dissected. But, at the same time, how long would it be before things got out of hand now that the cops' hands were tied?

In the past, the coven system had kept things in check. Now I was alone, the sole vamp trying to rein things in. Well, okay, maybe I wasn't as alone as I thought, especially not if Falcon was to be believed.

Someone else was out there hunting vamps. But who? And were they friend or enemy? I had a feeling it was only a matter of time before I found out. And knowing my luck, the answer wouldn't be in my favor.

We got back home, where I tossed my keys onto the end table and Glen sloughed off his dog suit like it was a pair of rotting shoes.

"That is never going to stop being disgusting."

"Maybe a new collar will help," he offered.

"I sincerely doubt it."

"Oh, and I heard there's a good dog groomer down on Sixth."

"Don't push your luck."

"Who's pushing what?"

I turned to see Tom stepping out of the bathroom, wearing a t-shirt and boxers – a not atypical thing for him to wear at night, although a part of me couldn't help but note he now wore it infinitely better than in the past.

Gah! Talk about needing brain bleach.

"Where'd you disappear to today?" I asked.

"I had shit to take care of. What are you guys up to?"

"I had the privilege of babysitting your daughter," Glen said.

"Cool. How'd that go?"

"She is a most wonderful child. And she gives such lovely baths."

Tom raised a quizzical eyebrow, then glanced once at the lifeless dog suit sitting on the floor and shrugged. "How about you, Bill? Anything good going on in Freewill World?"

"I was with Christy most of the night."

That got me an instant stink-eye. "When I said good, I meant..."

"Relax. We were working. Besides, I'm pretty sure she's mad at me."

That seemed to cheer him up, much to my displeasure. "Oh?"

"We met up with that Falcon guy, and I might have said some stuff about..."

"You talked back, didn't you?"

It was a bit more complicated than that, but still... "Yeah, I might've."

He shook his head, then paused to brush some hair out of his face. "I probably shouldn't tell you this, being that I'm totally working against you two as a couple, but I'm your friend and bros before hoes is a sacred covenant. Anyway, I learned this lesson the hard way, many *many* times, and now you need to learn it. When Christy gets in a mood, you don't talk back. Don't even apologize. Just avoid eye contact and nod."

"Avoid eye contact? She's not a mountain gorilla."

"No. She's a witch. A gorilla will only tear your arms off. A witch will fucking turn you inside out then set fire to whatever's still twitching. Don't get me wrong, I love Christy, but even with Icon powers I'm not stupid enough to get on her bad side."

"Women are strange."

"Yes, we are," he said with absolutely no sense of irony.

"Speaking of Icon powers, is that what you were off working on tonight?" I stepped past him into our kitchen nook, where I opened the fridge and pulled out both a beer and a pint of pig blood.

"Nah. I had other shit going on. Hey, grab me one, too," he said, holding his stomach. "And if you ask which, I'm gonna kick you in the nuts."

I grabbed an extra beer for him. "You okay?"

"I feel better than you look." When I stopped to glare at him, he added, "Relax, I'm fine. Think I just got a bad burrito. My guts feel like someone wrapped a vise grip around them."

The three of us walked – well, okay, Glen slithered – over to the couch. "Just for the record, I think I'll take food poisoning over Neanderthal leprechauns."

"You're shitting me," Tom said.

"Please tell me the witch was able to capture video of you dispatching them."

"Not this time, Glen," I replied. "Next one, I promise ... just so long as I remember to bring some potatoes with me."

"Potatoes?"

"Long story. And no, before you say anything, there was no pot of gold at the end of this rainbow, unless you count the color of their teeth. And trust me, I wasn't getting close enough to see if they were real."

"Oh shit," Tom said, standing up again. "Thanks for the reminder. I almost forgot."

"Forgot what?"

Rather than answer me, he walked back into his bedroom. Okay, whatever.

"Up for some TV, Glen?"

"Sure thing, Freewill. I think there's new episodes of Santa Clarita Diet on Netflix. I love that show."

I glanced at him. "You would."

"Here you go," Tom said, returning with a pocketbook in hand. I gave it a raised eyebrow to which he replied, "What? It's still a shit-ton cooler than a fanny pack."

"Can't disagree."

"Anyway, here's my share of the rent." He pulled out a stack of bills and placed them on the coffee table in front of me. "And next month's as well."

"You do realize I own the building, right? And, considering you were dead, I'm cool cutting you a break."

"I know, but dead ain't the same as being a deadbeat. Although, if you're waiting for five years back rent, you can go fuck yourself."

Screw it. I wasn't going to argue with free money. "Finally bit the bullet and asked Christy for..."

"Fuck no. Remember that thing I said I was working on? Well, it paid off big time."

"You discovered the power of prostitution?"

He flipped me the finger. "If I did, I can guarantee my price for you would forever be one dollar more than you're worth."

"I'd be remiss in pointing out..."

"That you've already sampled the wares? Trust me, dude. I'm well aware. It's why I make it a point to triple wash my vag every time I shower."

"Thanks for the visual."

"Just don't jack off to my memory."

"You've pretty much guaranteed that'll never happen. So, anyway, the money..."

"It's simplicity itself." He flashed me a smug grin. "I'm stuck in this body, so I figured I'd make it official."

"Make what official?"

"I managed to get copies of both my social security card and driver's license."

"Your driver's license, but...?"

"By mine, I mean Sheila's. And yesterday I hit fucking pay dirt." He reached into his pocketbook and pulled out an ATM card. "I finally got access to her checking account. Or should I say, *my* new checking account?"

IT'S ALL RELATIVE

"**I**sn't it brilliant?"

"No, it's not brilliant," I replied. "It's a fucking federal crime."

"How so?"

"You're not her."

"My DNA would say otherwise. Besides, at no point did anyone ask if I'd come back from the dead in possession of another person's body. So technically I didn't have to lie."

"Yeah, but what if she ... what if we find a way to bring her..."

It was a thought I'd toyed with but hadn't dared to give much credence to. We'd already pulled off the impossible, bringing one friend back from the beyond. I had a feeling fate owed us dick-all going forward with regards to doing it again.

"If we do, we do," Tom replied, as if he couldn't have cared less. "I'll cross that bridge when it happens. Easier to ask forgiveness than permission, I always say. Besides, better for me to have it than for it to sit around collecting interest for some fucking bank. You're with me right, Glen?"

Glen raised a portion of his gelatinous body in what I guessed was an indifferent shrug, before going back to ignoring us in favor of the TV. Smart blob.

Tom sort of did have a point, but in his own twisted way, which I understood far too well. "Just be careful, man. If you don't keep a low profile, someone is going to notice, like her family or..."

Tom's eyes opened wide but not with fear. He had that insane glee about him he seemed to only get when he was thinking of doing something cataclysmically stupid. "That's a great idea! I should call her mom. Maybe I can get birthday and Christmas gifts out of the deal."

"That's not what I..."

He interrupted me mid-admonishment to double over, holding his stomach. "Ugh!"

"That's karma."

"No, dude," he replied. "That's dinner not agreeing with me. Hey, you don't happen to know if Sheila was lactose intolerant or anything like that?"

"Not that I'm aware of."

"Oh well, then I shall suffer in silence until the god of epic shits calls upon me to make a sacrifice unto his porcelain altar." He turned and started back toward his room.

"Going to bed?"

"In a bit," he said. "First, I have some important work to do."

"Define important work."

"There's an eBay auction I've had my eye on, and I want to make sure no fuckers outbid me. Christmas is only a few months away and I know a little girl whose room could use some Thundercats."

Sleep was a long time coming and not just because being a vampire made me naturally nocturnal. All at once, it seemed the moving parts of my life were spiraling out of control. Just a few weeks ago, everything had been so normal. *I'd* been so normal. Now I had no heartbeat, my sorta maybe girlfriend was a witch, and I was fighting prehistoric leprechauns in my spare time.

Yet, amidst all of that mental baggage, I found my thoughts, oddly enough, turning toward Gan. Not in a fond way, mind you, and certainly not in a jacking off to way. No. She was still at the top of my shit list. Worst of all, she'd absconded with Ed for purposes that I would've bet my arms, legs, and even balls, were nefarious. With her the likely party behind these reestablished treaties – because who else would even know to do so – and with Ed the only neo-vamp capable of siring new ones, I could only guess her plans called for torturing him until he made her an army of minions.

Then there had been the disturbing thing she'd said about a great destiny awaiting me – that fate was not as finished with my ass as I hoped. Well, okay, almost everything she said was disturbing in some form but, with magic now back, that had been extra freaky. Yes, it was possible she'd been doing nothing more than affirming her insane love for me, but it worried me nevertheless – especially now that the weirdness seemed to be ratcheting up again.

I couldn't help but have a sense of foreboding for the future as I finally drifted off to a fitful sleep.

Come the morning, I was able to shake off some of that baggage and focus instead on a bit of work. The cash Sally had bequeathed me from Village Coven's old funds had been pretty sweet, more than enough to buy me some nice things and make a few solid investments. But it wasn't quite inheriting the Getty fortune. Doing some light consulting helped keep the coffers full. Also, it was nice to not be tied to a 9 to 5 workday.

Last time shit had hit the fan, I'd tried to juggle my commitments to my job with stopping the apocalypse – which had resulted in a global supernatural war, along with the added insult of being fired.

I was about two hours into updating a client's database architecture – not the most scintillating assignment I'd ever seen – when the downstairs bell buzzed. Almost immediately, I tensed up. Lately, unexpected company only served to remind me of the two neo-vamp goons who'd stormed into my place and beat the crap out of me – effectively kicking off everything that had followed.

Fortunately, those assholes were dead and most of the new assholes in my life didn't have my address, yet.

If anything, it was probably for Tom. I wouldn't doubt that the jackass had sprung for overnight shipping with his ill-gotten gains, likely for some useless piece of shit.

I got up and hit the intercom button, expecting to hear that I needed to sign for something. "Hello?"

"Bill?" a female voice replied.

"Yeah?"

"Let me in please. It's Kara."

Kara?! As in Ed's fiancée? *Oh shit!*

The cat was already out of the bag. She knew I was home. Why hadn't I ignored the doorbell in favor of focusing on my work? I mean, it's not like being paid wasn't a valid excuse.

I probably should have feigned illness or maybe answered back with, "no habla ingles," but instead I panicked and hit the buzzer to let her in, backing away from it in horror a moment later.

The truth was, Kara had been calling ... a lot. Most times I'd let it go to voicemail. The few times I'd answered, however, I'd been super vague – always lying about being on the way out so I couldn't talk, with Ed either perpetually busy or always in the can.

At first, I'd fed her some bullshit about him losing his phone. Then I'd told her he'd decided to stay out here a few weeks longer to help me with a contract. After that, it had been a string of minor bad luck – food poisoning and a late summer cold.

At first, she seemed to accept it all with few concerns. But fast forward a couple of weeks and the excuses were starting to wear thin. It was one thing for him to miss the occasional call from his fiancée, quite another for him to blow her off completely for three weeks running.

Truth be told, I'd been considering using the nuclear option of telling her that Ed had met someone else and they'd run off together. I mean, technically that wasn't entirely untrue. It was just leaving out that he hadn't been given much say in the running off part. Yeah, that would've been a total dick move, but it somehow seemed kinder than telling her that her husband to be was, in fact, no longer human.

And I had a feeling that was going to be an issue. Kara knew about vamps, had even been one for a short while in the days before the magic got turned off. The thing was, despite her being okay with her undeadness at the time, she'd since soured on those days – quite a bit as a matter of fact.

Had she been ignorant of the paranormal, this would've been a lot easier. But with her in the know, explaining Ed's predicament was going to require some dancing around on my part.

My foot brushed against something and I looked down, noticing the pile of matted fur on the floor. Shit! Forget mere dancing, I'd need Patrick Swayze level moves to get through this if the first thing she saw was Glen's dog suit.

Picking it up – eww, freshly washed or not, it was still gross – I carried it over to Glen's bedroom by my fingertips, opened the door, and tossed it in.

Okay, that was one hurdle crossed. Normal people typically didn't keep things like that lying around. Now to just make sure she didn't look in ... oh crap! The refrigerator.

I had at least three quarts of pig blood on the top shelf, and there was little chance of disguising it as nothing more than tomato juice.

My ears picked up the sound of footsteps walking up the stairs. Only another floor or two to go. Okay, I could do this. I raced to the kitchen nook and rearranged things in the fridge as best I could. Thank goodness Tom had picked up takeout last night, so I was able to stack his crap in front of mine.

That done, I took one last look around. It wasn't the neatest apartment on the planet but, unlike Christy's place, it didn't scream, "Hey, supernatural creatures on the premises!" I turned back toward the door, noting there was nothing in sight that might ... fuck!

Tom had left his freaking sword hanging on the coat hook. Jesus Christ! That thing was like seven hundred years old. You'd think he'd maybe know to not hang it up like some half-assed umbrella.

There came a knock at the door.

Okay. No time to hide it, but that was fine. It was just a sword. Almost every gamer had at least one or two these days. Hell, I had a copy of Frostmourne still hanging on my bedroom wall.

All right. *All's normal here*, I told myself. All I had to do was play stupid with regards to where Ed was. If she pressed the issue, I'd ... I had no idea.

Screw it. When in doubt, go with improv. I pulled the door open and plastered a fake-ass smile on my face. "Kara! What a surprise. What brings you back to the east coast?"

She was in her early twenties, just a bit shy of the age I'd been when I'd first gotten indoctrinated into the ranks of the undead. However, it would've been easy to mistake her for being older. She wore her light brown hair much shorter these days and had minimal makeup on. The look complemented the light blouse and long skirt she wore, giving her a bit of a teacher vibe. It was a long way from the wild child she'd been during our time together in Pandora Coven.

I'd considered her a hottie in my younger hornier days, and the truth was she still had it going on in the looks department, but now there was a much more reserved air about her. I guess being an ex-vamp had affected us all differently in the end. In her case, it had made her grow up a lot more quickly than she might've otherwise.

Still, she and Ed had found common ground in the months following the end of all magic in the world, and an unlikely romance had blossomed – one which had survived the past five years.

And, now, I realized, as she stepped in and gave me a curt hug, I was likely going to be at least partially responsible for destroying that fairy tale.

Yay me.

"Is he here?" she asked without preamble, her eyes hard. Obviously, she'd come prepared for this.

I was debating the merits of asking, "Is who here?" when the other bedroom door popped open.

Oh crap!

In all my panic, I'd overlooked one major detail. Yes, Kara was Ed's fiancée. But she was also Tom's little sister and, as far as she was concerned, he was still quite dead.

Tom, being somewhat less deceased than she assumed, stepped out of his room, wearing the same t-shirt and shorts combo from the night before.

"I feel like shit," he grumbled before noticing us both standing there. "Hey, Bill. Oh, hey, sis!"

And just like that, things became infinitely more complicated.

STAYFREE-WILL

"Sorry, can't talk ... about to blow."

Tom clenched his stomach and ran past us into the bathroom, slamming the door behind him.

Kara stood there for a moment, shock upon her face, before slapping me on the arm.

"Ow! What was that for?"

"Jerk! Does Christy know about this?"

Christy? "You mean about the fact that..."

"That you're back with your ex?"

What?! "Wait. You know about me and Christy?"

"Duh! We do talk, you know. I like to hear how my niece is doing." She stepped further in, continuing to glare daggers at me. "I wasn't sure what I'd find here, but this..."

"There isn't any *this*," I replied, holding up my fingers in quotes.

"So you're saying you're not back together? That you just so happen to be casually shacking up?"

"We're not shacking up. He, I mean she, needed a place to stay. That's all. We're done. There's nothing going on here."

"And I'm supposed to believe you?"

"You just saw her step out of that bedroom, not mine, correct?"

That was impeccable logic even for an angry woman, at least enough so that she stopped shouting at me for the moment. However, then, just as I thought reason might've taken hold, allowing us to discuss this in a rational way – one that might give me a chance to come up with a suitable lie for Ed's disappearance – her eyes opened wide.

"What? Do I have something in my teeth?"

She raised a hand to her mouth, as if unwilling to say what was on her mind, before finally asking, "Is *he* in there?"

"He?"

"Ed!"

"Huh? Why would Ed be in there?"

"Don't play games with me, Bill. I know they were close at one point. Hell, he even ran that damned company of hers for a while."

"Um, yeah. That's because we all thought she was dead at the time."

"So you're telling me that if I go in there, I won't find my ... my ... Eddie bear?"

Eddie bear? Oh God. Don't laugh. Do not laugh, Bill. Now is not the time.

Too late. I couldn't help the grin that broke out on my face.

"This isn't funny!"

"Um, actually, it kind of is." I quickly held up a hand. "But no. Ed's not in there. I swear. Seriously! You're free to look."

"Fine. Maybe I will."

She stepped to the door, hesitating for a moment as if waiting for me to admit I was bluffing, then flung it wide open – revealing nothing except for the fact that her brother, who she didn't know was her brother, was every bit the slob he'd always been.

"See? No Ed."

She turned back toward me. "Is he here?"

"No."

"Do you know where he is?"

"Um..." *Come on, convincing lie, where are you?!*

"Is he okay?"

"W-why wouldn't he be?"

"I'm not an idiot, Bill. Do you think I didn't notice that he came to visit you right around when things started getting weird again?"

"Oh, you noticed that?"

"I watch the news. People are saying the Strange Days are back."

"So I've heard. But you know reporters. They love their sensational headlines."

She stared hard at me, as if trying to discern if I was simply playing stupid, which I most certainly was. I swear, I really needed to invest in a poker face one of these days. Her glare intensified and I knew I was moments away from cracking. Goddamn, I was such a wuss. "Listen, maybe he ... stepped out for..."

"I swear to God," she said, "if you know something and you're not telling me..."

"Oh shit! What the fuck?!"

Saved by the bell.

We both turned toward the bathroom, where the cry had come from. What the hell was that idiot doing now?

"Fuck me! Get in here, Bill!"

What the?

"No! On second thought, stay out there. You don't want to see this."

"Is she okay?" Kara asked, concern overriding her anger at me for the moment.

"Okay is a very subjective concept."

A moment later, the bathroom door opened and Tom peered out, a towel wrapped around his waist. "I need you to do me a favor, man. No questions asked."

"Okay. What do you need?"

"Can you run to the store and buy me some tampons ... or maybe those pad things?"

"What?!"

He popped his head back in for a moment before peeking out again. "And maybe some detergent and cleaning supplies while you're at it. Trust me. This shit is not pretty."

Tampons? *Oh!* Just fucking great. It figures this would happen while Christy and I were having a spat.

"Is everything okay in there?" Kara asked.

Sadly, Tom was too far gone in his pity period party to answer rationally. "Fucking A, dude. Why the fuck did you have to bring me back in a woman's body?"

Son of a bitch. And there we were, back to complicated again.

Kara unzipped her purse and walked over to the bathroom door, pulling out a few wrapped objects of the feminine variety. "Here, I always carry a couple extra."

"Ugh, no fucking way," Tom cried.

"Why? What's wrong with them?"

Please don't say something stupid.

"I can't use your stuff. That would be like us ... sharing dildos."

So much for that.

Tom made as if to duck back in, then apparently thought better of it and grabbed Kara's offering anyway. "Fine. Give me those, but I swear if you tell Dad about this..."

He slammed the door shut, leaving Kara to turn toward me, looking kind of doe-eyed, not that I could blame her. "Did she hit her head or something?"

"Let's go with something."

"Goddamn it!" The bathroom door opened again. "I don't suppose any of you know how these things are supposed to work."

"You're on your own, man," I said, a moment before realizing my slip of the tongue. "I meant, woman ... since that's exactly what you are. Besides, aren't these things ... y'know ... instinctual?"

Kara turned and gave me a raised eyebrow that suggested she thought me an idiot, probably not far from the truth. Dear god, why couldn't some fucking Neanderthal hobbits pick that moment to attack? Even better if they managed to kill me.

"Fuck this noise." Tom reached out and grabbed Kara by the arm. "You're elected, but don't think this means we're going to start changing in front of each other at the gym or anything."

"You don't go to the gym," I replied, but he'd already dragged his confused looking sister into the bathroom and slammed the door shut again.

Kara stepped out a few minutes later with a curt, "No, I'm not doing it for you. Figure it out."

The moment she was clear, she fixed me with a glare that told me I really should've made a run for it – daylight or not – when I had the chance.

"That's not Sheila, is it?"

"Physically, yes. Mentally ... not quite."

She took a deep breath as tears gathered in her eyes. *Oh boy*. "My brother is dead."

"Yeah, about that..."

"We had a funeral."

"I know. I was there."

"My parents are still a mess about it. Hell, I'm still a..." She turned and glanced back at the bathroom door. "No. *Now* I'm even more of a mess."

"If it helps, we all thought he was dead, too ... until recently anyway."

"What do you mean, until recently?"

"Sit down. I have a feeling he's going to be a while."

Making it a point to stay out of punching range, I explained to her how Tom's ghost appeared not long after the magical pulses began – his soul having somehow been fused with a dormant extradimensional power source in the shape of an action figure.

From there, I switched gears, telling her how Sheila had sacrificed herself to save him, and in doing so made him the new Icon – skipping the part about how he sucked at the job so far.

"And you didn't think to tell any of us?" she cried once I was finished.

"Of course I did, but it's not really my story to tell. And even if it was, what was I going to say to your parents? Hey, you know how your son died five years ago? Well, turns out we were wrong. Oh, and now he's back in my ex's body."

That seemed to get through to her and she nodded as if to acknowledge I maybe had a point. After a moment, though, she replied, "But why didn't you tell me? I used to be a part of this. I would have understood."

I didn't have an easy answer, other than Ed – in the days prior to his kidnapping – had gone out of his way to explain how she was very much not cool with her short-lived tenure as a vampire. Fortunately, though, I didn't need to actually say that out loud because Tom picked that moment to emerge from the bathroom, lurching his way over to us in a duck walk of sorts.

"Sorry," he said, "I've been meaning to tell you I was alive, but I've been sorta busy."

"Why are you walking like that?"

"Because I've got three of those fucking things shoved up against my cooch. It's ... kinda uncomfortable."

"You do know you're only supposed to use one, right?" Kara asked, her eyes still wet with tears but the reality of the situation apparently starting to sink in.

"Yeah, but they looked kind of skimpy. So, I figured more is more." Kara opened her mouth to reply, but a sudden look of horror crossed Tom's face before she could say anything. "Oh shit!"

"What is it?" she asked.

He turned to me instead, though. "I just realized, this body, it works. *All* of it."

"Yeah, and...?"

"Dude. What if I get knocked up?"

"How? Unless you're telling me you've been hopping on random dicks in your spare time."

"Fuck no. I'm strictly a vag-man. But, like, what if I sit on the wrong toilet seat or something?"

The look on Kara's face said she was finally starting to come to terms with the fact that the dumbass words coming out of Sheila's face hole were, in fact, things her brother was more likely to say. "You do realize it doesn't work that way, right?"

But Tom was already on the move, heading toward our kitchen nook, where he proceeded to start opening up the drawers.

I stood and watched as he rummaged through the place. "What are you doing?"

"I'm throwing out our turkey baster, just to be on the safe side."

Before I could comment on that, Kara put a hand on my arm. "Okay, let's back up a second here. Magic is back and so is my brother, in a sense. I ... get that. So, is there anything else you're not telling me ... like about..."

"Fuck yeah," Tom replied conversationally, continuing to root through the cabinets. "A whole shit-ton of stuff has happened. Bill's a vampire again, our new roommate is an extra-dimensional eyeball blob named Glen, and Ed was kidnapped by Gan."

Son of a...

Kara narrowed her eyes at me. "Gan?"

"I think I mentioned her when we were both at Pandora. Gansetseg, former prefect of China, old as dirt and batshit crazy."

"What does she want with my Ed?"

"He's a vamp again, too," Tom rather unhelpfully added, still looking through drawers despite the fact that we didn't even own a turkey baster.

"How?! Was he...?"

"No," I said, realizing there was no longer any reason to play it coy. My phone buzzed in my pocket, drawing my attention for a moment, but I ignored it. This had waited long enough. "He wasn't bitten. Far as we can tell, he technically never stopped being one. He just sort of ... I dunno ... went into remission for the last five years." Realizing that likely wasn't helping, I quickly added, "At least that's our theory. But hopefully now you realize why we've been..."

"Lying to me?"

"I was going to say omitting certain details."

"That doesn't make it better," she snapped.

"I know, believe me. But the truth is we didn't want to freak you out or give you reason to get involved in this shit. Gan is not someone you want to mess with, trust me."

"So, where is she keeping him?"

"We don't know. But believe me, we're doing everything we can to find out. It's just ... it's a big world and Gan controls all the resources of the First Coven."

Kara wiped her eyes. "Do you think he's..."

"I have absolutely no doubt he's fine. This wasn't just some random drive by. Gan doesn't do anything without a reason, including taking people."

"Yeah," Tom said. "If she wanted him dead, she could've iced his ass no problem."

I turned and glared at him. "Not helping."

"Actually, he is," Kara replied, still sounding on the verge of abject misery. "I remember you telling me about her. She was dangerous, wasn't she?"

"Not was, *is*."

She nodded, looking like she was doing her best to hold it together. "Does this have anything to do with what Ed was

... is? You know what I mean. He was different from other vampires."

"We think so. That's why we're certain he's okay. He's one of a kind, unique." Hopefully that was good enough for her. I really didn't relish having to explain that Gan was likely keeping Ed around for the express purpose of making baby neo-vamps loyal to no one but her. There'd been enough surprises lain at her doorstep for one morning.

Or so I thought.

Because, of course, Glen picked that moment to plop out of his bedroom, causing Kara's eyes to open so wide they nearly fell out of her skull.

He stopped mid-slither and stared back, about half a dozen eyeballs of various sizes wearing a look of similar surprise. "Um ... bark?"

Before I could make proper introductions – or she could scream – my phone buzzed in my pocket again. Grateful for the reprieve, I pulled it out and glanced at the screen ... only to find that gratitude drying up in the space of an instant.

There was a voicemail from Sally waiting for me – the contents already transcribed into text.

You need to get over here ... now.

MODERN ART

"I have to go. It's Sally."

Kara immediately perked up at the mention of her name, no doubt because Sally had been her former coven master. "What's wrong?"

"I'm not entirely sure, but safe to say things have been getting weird again."

She looked me in the eye. "The news was right, wasn't it? The Strange Days are starting again."

A part of me wanted to tell her that they were long past getting started, but I realized that might do nothing except freak her out more, when she was already pretty well on the way there.

Still, until I received an engraved invitation to the end of the world, I chose to hold onto at least a bit of optimism.

"I don't know. We're still figuring shit out. But for now, sit tight." I hooked a thumb at Tom. "You two probably have some catching up to do anyway." I paused for a moment, a thought hitting me. "That is, unless you have another training session with Vincent this morning."

Tom shook his head. "Haven't heard from him in three days. Far as I'm aware, I'm free to be treated to a catch-up breakfast."

"Okay, go with that." Once again, it seemed nobody had any idea where Vincent and his witchy wife had gotten off to, but they were adults. They could handle themselves. Hell, for all I knew, she was celebrating getting her powers back by taking them on a second honeymoon to Valhalla, or wherever Magi jetted off to get their freak on.

"Why do you need training?" Kara asked.

Before Tom could answer, I pointed a finger at him. "No showing off your lack of sword skills in the apartment. I'm still mourning the loss of my favorite coffee mug."

"Pussy," he replied.

"Shall I accompany you, Freewill?" Glen asked. "It'll only take me a moment to put my disguise on."

I didn't really have time to slather on a ton of sunscreen, nor did I care to test my luck with city traffic when my friend needed me. That meant, with the sun up, the trip into Manhattan would have to be below ground. I could only imagine trying to explain to any nosy metro cops that Glen was my service dog. That, and I also didn't fancy traipsing into Sally's place with a rotting four-legged corpse lurching by my side. Undead I might be, but I still had standards.

"It's fine, Glen. I can get there faster on my own. Besides, it's probably nothing. For all I know, she's just pissy because one of her new residents redecorated without her say so."

"If you're sure."

I wasn't, but none of us really knew what had happened to her during her tenure as a human wall plaque. For now, it was probably safer to minimize the risk to others, even if I wasn't too keen on risking myself. "It's all good, man. Stay here, be a good host and, um, guard the place from any intruders."

I turned toward the door, glancing back at him. "And no biting the mailman."

As a paranoia measure five years ago, I'd had an emergency sewer exit built into the building's basement, fully expecting to never use it. Now I was glad as shit I'd forked over the cash. I had a feeling it was going to get a lot of use over the next ... well, eternity, as I currently didn't see any way of reversing things this time – not unless I planned to turn into an adventuring globetrotter, searching the world for the thirteen mini Sources Gan had created by destroying the original.

There are far worse fates than adventure.

Well, yeah, I guess there were and ... huh, my subconscious was doing it again, offering up unasked for opinions.

Sadly, I'd been down this road before. Much as I wanted to think these thoughts were coming from me, I had a feeling that wasn't the case.

"Not now, Dr. Death," I said, attempting to return Sally's call.

No answer, of course. So, I left a quick voicemail telling her I was on the way, before clambering down the ladder to the filthy muck below.

Fortunately, my murderous alter-ego didn't seem in the mood to argue. That was good because last time around I'd almost had to blow myself to bits to finally exert control over him, something I wasn't keen on reliving.

At least there was one upside to being a vampire. Disgusting as it might be in the New York City underground, and believe me I wasn't exaggerating, at least there was little chance of me contracting the plague. For a vampire, there was nothing down there that a good shower couldn't fix – hopefully anyway.

As I traversed the tunnels to the nearest subway station, I reminded myself that the rules had changed. Much as I wanted to believe that troglodyte leprechauns were the worst that I'd have to worry about – and, in all fairness, those fuckers had been pretty nasty – I had a feeling it was unwise to be complacent.

Needless to say, by the time I made it to the maintenance entrance of the 86th Street Station, I'd managed to spook myself pretty goddamned well. Go figure. Me, a creature of the night, the so-called legendary Freewill, was happy as a clam to finally step into the artificial light of the station and hop on a train bound for Manhattan.

Sadly, my underground adventures weren't quite over yet. Since I'd grabbed neither sunscreen nor a hoodie on the way out, I still needed to traverse the wonders of the Manhattan tunnels in order to make it to Sally's.

The only upside was that her place had originally been purchased as a safe house for our former coven, meaning it came standard with a subbasement sewer entrance, as all coven properties had back then.

Sewer to sewer service between Brooklyn and Midtown. What a world we lived in.

Thankfully, I made it there with no problems, save one or two economy sized rats giving me the side-eye along the way.

But that's about as far as my luck held.

I ascended to the back stairwell and had no sooner popped my head up, when a *whoosh* of air told me to get out of the way as fast as I fucking could.

CLANK!

I just barely managed to duck as a shovel blade cut through the air where my noggin had been only moments earlier.

My only thought as it slammed into the far wall was, oddly enough, *how did I manage to piss off Sally this time?*

"Oh shit! Sorry."

Alas, she wasn't the culprit. I looked up to find Jessica standing there, surrounded by most of the other members of Village Coven 2.0.

I was about to lay into her for almost making me a foot shorter, when I realized how pale they all looked – well, paler than usual. In fact, they were all huddled together like frightened puppies during a thunderstorm, the living kind, not whatever the fuck Glen was pretending to be.

I held up a hand to silence their incessant apologies – goddamn, we'd come a long way since the days of the original Village Coven. "Okay, what's going on. Is Sally okay?"

"S-Sally?" Jessica sputtered. "You mean that ... that witch you brought here?"

"She's not a witch. Or at least I'm pretty sure she isn't. Christy's the Magi. Remember her? I brought her over last week..."

"Who cares?" Leslie snapped, her brown eyes momentarily flashing black. "That ... thing killed Stewart!"

That was pretty much the end of the coherent information I was able to glean. What followed was a panicked babble of accusations and fear. Yessir, ladies and gentlemen, here was the latest generation of nocturnal predator.

That was a secondary concern, though, compared to Sally. Much as I considered these new vamps my responsibility, she came first. It probably wasn't fair to them, but oh well. Life wasn't fair. Why should anyone expect the afterlife to be?

I pushed through the mass of vampires huddled on the first floor, ignoring their pleas for my safety – crazy as that even sounded to me – and headed toward the stairs. Not a single one of them followed me up, though. Guess I was flying solo on this one, but that was okay. This was Sally we were talking about. She'd been my partner in crime through the worst of the worst. I wasn't about to puss out just because a few folks were accusing her of wanton murder – which, truth be told, wasn't exactly a new thing.

Still, so far as I was aware, the last time Sally had taken a life was five years ago – some unfinished business with a former coven mate. Sure, she'd recently put a bullet in Gan's head, but that didn't count since Gan survived – and had really deserved it.

The thing was, much as I wanted to believe Sally was okay after being flash fried by a godlike entity, I wasn't an idiot. There was no doubt we were sailing in uncharted waters here, and I had a feeling we were about to hit our first real rapids.

I made it to her floor where, at first, everything appeared normal. But then I started down the hall toward her door, noting there was some kind of stain or discoloration on the wall opposite her apartment.

As I got closer and my angle improved, however, I saw more details and the picture it painted was not a pleasant one.

It was a smear of ash and blood, still chunky in some places, in the vague shape of a human body – as if a vampire had somehow exploded and been dusted in the exact same moment. But that made no fucking sense.

Cut a vamp and they'll bleed, at least until they healed. But kill a vamp and no such dice. All you got for your trouble was a pile of ash. Sure, there were poisons that could retard the process but – call me crazy – I was pretty sure Sally didn't keep any on hand, not unless there was something in her kitchen cabinets she wasn't telling me about.

This, though, it was almost like whatever happened had been so fast or violent that even the vamp's death hadn't been enough to compensate, resulting in what could best be called a fucking mess.

So engrossed was I by the disgusting spectacle that I barely registered the sound of the door opening behind me, or the footsteps that followed.

"Something is definitely not right with me," Sally's said from over my shoulder.

"You don't say."

PTO

"**Y**ou up for some day drinking?"

"Yeah," I replied, forcing my eyes away from the gruesome display, "I could handle a bottle or two."

"Good. Come on in and join me."

Sally was already dressed for the day, looking considerably more fashionable than she had when last I'd seen her – wearing a lowcut blouse and miniskirt combo that probably wouldn't have passed muster at her foundation. Despite the horror show right outside her door, I allowed myself a brief smile.

"Let me guess," I said, as we stepped inside, "whatever happened out there necessitated a quick outfit change."

She shook her head. "Nope. Oddly enough, didn't get a drop on me."

"A rather ... nonchalant response, if you don't mind me saying so."

"Would you rather I be like those screaming pussies you recruited?"

"In all fairness, I can kinda see why they might be upset."

"Point taken," she replied, walking over to the wet bar. "And it still beats some of the crew we used to run with. I

155

swear, most of those assholes would've been out there rolling around in that mess."

"I don't doubt that. I'll take freaked out over freaking dickheads any day of the week." I stood where I was, watching her go about her business. "But enough of them for the moment. How are you?"

Sally spared an eyeroll my way, a very familiar gesture. "You can stop walking on eggshells, Bill. I'm still me. Although what me we're talking about is maybe up for debate."

"Not following."

She pulled two glasses out. "I should be upset, like *really* upset. I know that. And a part of me is..."

"But the rest?"

She let out a bitter laugh. "It's strange. I'm not sure if it's having this body back again or simply a result of what I went through down there, but all at once it's like the last five years never happened. All that time, relearning how to be a normal person, learning to let my guard down and let people in. And yet, despite all of that, those old defense mechanisms were still up here," she tapped her forehead, "waiting for the day when I needed them again. I'll say this much, Night Razor did a hell of a job acclimating me to this life."

"By being a murderous asshole."

"True enough." She filled the glasses with ice then turned my way. "What are you taking?"

"Tequila works for any day that ends in a Y."

"You are such white trash," she said with a chuckle before pulling out a bottle of Patrón and pouring it in both glasses, filling them to the brim. If she was trying to kill us via alcohol poisoning, at least it was with the good stuff.

She walked over and handed me a glass, raising hers in a mockery of a toast.

"Sure you can handle all of that?" I asked. "I mean, I'm a vamp, but you're..."

"Guess there's only one way to find out," she replied, downing a healthy slug of tequila.

Fuck it. I followed suit, then we both sat down, half-empty glasses in hand. "All right, spill. Tell me why the wall out there is going to need at least a dozen fresh coats of paint."

Sally took another sip then nodded. "It ... just happened, right before I called you..."

"Glad to hear it wasn't yesterday and you're just getting around to telling me now."

"Don't make me kick your ass."

Considering what had apparently gone down just a few feet away, it wasn't really my ass I should've been worried about. "Let's back up a bit. You say it just happened?" She nodded. "And shall I assume that's what's left of Stewart out there?"

"The sweaty guy? Then yeah, that's him."

"So what did he do? Threaten you? Try to break down the..."

"He knocked on the door and asked if I wanted to play Jenga with him and the others."

I glanced back toward the still open doorway, my keen vamp ears telling me none of the others had mustered up the courage to follow. "I'm gonna go out on a limb and assume that you *really* didn't want to play."

"Don't be a jackass, Bill. You think I wanted to do that?" I held up my hands in a placating manner and she continued. "He asked, I said no. He tried again. I said no again. He started to get mildly annoying, telling me they didn't want me to feel left out and all that bullshit. I wasn't in the mood, so I meant to tell him to go the fuck away ... and *that* happened instead."

I hooked a thumb back at the door. "All of that from mildly annoying? Seriously?"

She nodded, draining her glass. "Yeah. It wasn't anything more. I wasn't angry or pissed off. Heck, I didn't even know the guy from a hole in the head. All I wanted to do was go back to bed."

"So he woke you up?"

"Not exactly. I've been awake all night. I tried reading, watching a movie. I even popped a few Ambien."

"Okay, so you were tired and cranky?"

Sally narrowed her eyes at me, making me wonder if perhaps I should put in slightly more effort to not be mildly annoying. "Cranky yes, but not tired. I'm wide awake. I don't know. Maybe it's the fact that I just woke up from a three week dirt nap."

"Could be."

"Anyway, what I'm trying to say is I didn't mean to kill him. I don't like board games, but even at my worst, I never murdered anybody over one ... except maybe that one time with Dreamweaver, but that bitch was a cheater."

"Dreamweaver?"

"She was a bit before your time."

"I'll assume I don't want to know."

"Probably a good call. Anyway, what I mean is that I just wanted this guy to go away and leave me alone. But what happened instead..."

I wasn't entirely sure I wanted to hear this next part, but I kinda needed to. "Go on."

"Remember back at Christy's apartment, when I picked up Tina?"

"Kind of hard to forget."

"Well, it was like that, but more so ... and there was a focus to it that wasn't there before. It was like one moment I felt a tingle inside of me, but before I could even stop to think about it, he exploded. You saw..."

"Oh, believe me, I saw it."

She shook her head. "I'm telling you, I've seen vamps blown to bits before, but never like that."

"Do I want to ask?"

"Save it for another time."

"Noted. And then afterward you called me?"

"Your voicemail anyway."

I grinned guiltily. "I was busy dealing with Tom stuff."

"Oh. Let's assume I don't care then."

"Fine with that, but I tried calling you back. You didn't pick up."

She stood and walked over to the kitchen counter, where she gestured to a small pile of broken plastic and electronics. "That one's easy enough to answer."

"What the hell did you do to it?"

"I had just finished calling you when the others came looking for Stewart. They freaked the fuck out, which I was afraid was going to set me off again. So, I screamed at them all to go back downstairs and..."

"And what?"

Sally looked slightly embarrassed. "And I might have thrown it against the wall to drive home the point."

"Oh." I can't say that didn't make me feel slightly better, knowing she was trying to protect them, even if I doubted she'd admit it. "Better the phone than them."

"Tell me about it."

I got up and walked over to where she stood, looking down at the ruined mess of electronics.

She glanced up at me as I approached. "So, what do you think?"

"I think," I replied, meeting her eyes, "that you can borrow someone else's cell next time you need to make a call."

"Don't make me go all Jenga on you."

There was little doubt we were well outside my area of expertise with this one. Although, the fact that I'd been able to crack jokes around Sally and not be blown to bits was a promising sign. It told us that perhaps there might be more than base annoyance at play here. That was good because otherwise the simple act of going out to grab a bite to eat could end up being disastrous, much less anything more stressful.

Unfortunately, that was the limit of my insight. All I could do beyond that was be there for her.

This required knowledge above and beyond what I had to offer. I wasn't sure who might have that kind of know-how, but I had a good idea where to start.

Now to hope she wasn't still pissed at me.

I dialed Christy, hoping she wasn't planning on ignoring me because this really couldn't wait.

Fortunately, though, she picked up on the third ring.

"Hey."

"Um, good morning. How are you feeling today?"

"Okay, I guess," she replied cautiously, sounding as if perhaps she didn't want to start anything over the phone. Couldn't exactly blame her for that. "Listen, I just got to work..."

"Yeah, about that..."

I proceeded to fill Christy in on where I was and what had happened, with Sally adding color commentary from the background.

"How's she doing now?"

"She seems fine to me. Well, not fine, but okay, if that makes any sense. Um, what are you doing?"

"Me?"

"Sorry, not you," I said, glancing at Sally, who was calling up Skype on her laptop.

She waved me off then walked into her bedroom, presumably to complete her call in private. How rude. "Never mind. Just Sally being Sally."

"All right. Stay with her. I'm heading over."

"But I thought you had work."

"I do. Just give me an hour or so to hex the office so they don't realize I'm gone."

Huh. I'd almost forgotten how useful magic could be for day to day fuckery.

We said our goodbyes and I hung up. There wasn't any cutesy couple stuff about counting the minutes until we saw each other – which probably wasn't surprising considering the topic of discussion – but there also wasn't any curt iciness either, or at least none that I could sense. I kept my fingers crossed. The last thing I needed was the cold shoulder on top of what was already looking to be a stressful day.

Sally rejoined me about five minutes later, stepping back out of her bedroom.

"Let me guess. Time to renew your Pornhub subscription?"

"Does my name look like Bill Ryder?" she replied. "I made a quick call to the cleaning crew."

"Cleaning crew?"

"Yep. Same company that used to service Village Coven. I knew there was a reason I kept re-upping their contract." She paused to take note of my expression. "Don't look at me like that. They do good work. Do you know how rare it is to find a place that'll clean an apartment top to bottom, including windows?"

"Not really."

"And if any special *circumstances* arise," she said, adding air quotes, "they don't ask questions, provided one remembers to tip them well."

"That's ... disturbingly convenient."

"No. That's the beauty of the human race. There's always someone willing to step in and fill a niche."

"They must be a hit with the mob."

"How do you think we found them?"

For the sake of plausible deniability, I decided against asking further questions. Instead, I tried to steer the conversation back to the reason I was here – her. "So, getting back to what happened. You were telling me how you felt before..."

"Before I changed the subject with a generous splash of tequila?"

"Pretty much," I replied with a grin. "But seriously. How are you really doing with all of this?"

"I'm still trying to figure out what *all of this* is."

"No doubt, but I meant with what happened to Stewart. Because, no offense, you seem pretty chill."

"Do you really have to ask that?" At my raised eyebrow she let out a humorless chuckle. "Who am I kidding? Of course you do. And you're right. A small part of me is hoping it all comes crashing down, that it'll hit me all at once and the next second I'll be in tears lamenting the loss of inhuman life. But I'm pretty sure I know myself by now, and I don't think that's going to happen. Don't get me wrong, Bill, I'm not happy about it and I sure as shit wish I could take it back. The thing is, I guess there comes a point when you have so much blood on your hands that you barely notice a few extra splashes."

"Yeah, but that was the old you."

"Is it? Are you certain? Because I'm not. Remember what I said when you first got here, about the last five years feeling like they didn't happen? Did you ever wonder about that, that all this time we've been living in nothing more than a pleasant illusion?"

Taken aback by the question, I simply replied, "Can't say I've really ever thought about it."

"I'm starting to. For thirty years I was a killer, plain and simple. I didn't start out that way, but I grew into the part and, after a while, even learned to enjoy it. Don't look at me that way. Talk to me in another half century or so and see how you feel. I mean, yeah, there was something inside of me driving that urge, fanning those flames, but let's not pretend I was a hostage in my own head because I wasn't. When that ... part of me left, you'd think it would've been a relief. But over the course of all those years, the rest of me grew up, accepted who I was. And I've had time to think about it since then and the truth is, I can't lie and pretend every person I ever killed was because some devil made me do it. Does that make sense?"

I wanted to say no but couldn't. "Yeah. It kinda does."

"And does it scare you?"

"A month ago I might've said yes, but today ... not really. Old habits really do die hard."

"Interesting choice of words." She took my glass from me and headed back to the bar. "Top you off?"

I nodded and she poured us both another generous libation. Hmm. The beauty of being a vampire was it took a lot to knock me on my ass. So, it's not like I needed to be stingy with the liquid courage. But Sally was something else now, so I was curious to see how this went. Worst case was she'd sleep it off while Christy and me tried to figure out what was going on.

She returned, handed me my glass, and continued. "If it had all been because of that thing inside of me, I'm pretty sure I'd be having nightmares until the day I died. But you know what? I sleep like a baby at night, or at least I used to. How's that for fucked up?"

I shrugged. "We did what we had to do to survive."

"Don't fool yourself there, sport," she said with a grimace. "Hell, for a while there ... after it all ended anyway, I really did wonder if that meant I was an evil person."

"But..."

She held up a hand. "I know, I didn't say anything. This is the sort of stuff that only haunts you when you're alone and it's late at night. But if I was really bad then doing good wouldn't feel good. And I like doing good – back at Pandora Coven before it fell, then later at the Foundation. Then Tina came along and – don't tell Christy I said this, it'll ruin my rep – but I just love that little girl to the dickens."

"Did you just say dickens?"

"Bite my ass, fuckface. Better?"

"Much."

"Anyway, what I'm saying is..." She paused. "Actually, I'm not sure what I'm saying."

"You were talking about the last five years being an illusion."

She nodded and put down her glass. "Guess this stuff is going to my head. But yeah, it's exactly like that, as if we were allowed to live in a dream world for all that time. But then, the moment you told me about those magical pulses, I got the impression that it was finally time for us to wake up again. In a way, I think that was the moment that old mindset started waking up again, as if knowing I'd be dragged back in. That's probably why I seem so nonchalant about everything." She gestured back toward the door. "And apparently I was right. I mean, look at you, back to being the Freewill, and me back to ... well, looking good – amongst other things."

"It's the amongst other things part that kind of worries me."

She met my gaze, her strange emerald eyes staring at me hard.

"Me, too, Bill. Me, too."

BIRD WATCHING

Christy arrived at Sally's place a short while later. By then, the cleaning crew had shown up to take care of the Stewart shaped mess congealing in the hall.

Having seen my fair share of movies, I expected either some surly no-neck goons or a suave talking gentleman in an expensive suit. Instead, what we got was a quartet of meek Hispanic ladies who set to work immediately, as if this was nothing more than the turn down service at a hotel. However, rather than checking if we needed more toilet paper, they stripped the wall down to the studs, shoveled the mess into heavy-duty plastic bags, then carefully matched the paint and built it back up again.

All of it without asking a single question.

Holy shit. I had no idea what Sally was tipping these ladies, but I had a feeling it was way past the limit of my credit card.

When Christy finally got there, they simply stepped aside with polite nods and continued cleansing the murder scene of any trace of evidence. Gotta admire a strong work ethic.

Sally let her in then shut the door, as if nothing of interest were going on outside. It was no doubt to give us some privacy, because covering up blatant homicide was one thing, but talking magic in front of some randos might actually make it weird.

Either way, that train of thought derailed almost immediately once Christy stepped up and poked a finger into my chest. "I am seriously annoyed with you right now, mister."

Oh crap. She wanted to do this *now* in front of Sally? I could practically feel my balls shriveling up at the prospect. Go figure, back when he'd been in his own body, I'd taken great joy in giving Tom shit regarding his nuts being in Christy's purse. Wow. It really did suck for the shoe to be on the other foot.

With nowhere to run, I saw no other choice but to fall on the proverbial sword.

"Listen. I'm sorry about the way I acted. It's just that I can be ... a bit insecure at times and..."

"I'm not talking about that," she replied, adopting a wry grin. "I meant Tina. Ever since you and Glen left last night, she's been asking nonstop when we can get a dog."

"A dog?" Sally asked.

"I'll explain later," I replied, turning Christy's way again. "Are you still...?"

"We'll talk later," she said. "But I'm more tired than anything else right now."

"Shall I assume it's not because you spent the night crying your eyes out on my behalf?"

She pursed her lips and gave her head a shake. "Not quite. I was knee deep in research."

"Let me guess," Sally said. "About me?"

At that, Christy looked slightly embarrassed. "Actually no. I was busy trying to find more info about the a'chiad dé danann."

"Proto-leprechauns," I explained. "We fought a bunch last night." Sally glanced between us for a moment, to which I added, "It's been a robust twenty-four hours."

"Join the club."

"Sorry," Christy said. "I'm not trying to downplay what happened to you. It's just..." Her nostrils flared and she raised an eyebrow at me. "Have you been drinking?"

"A bit."

"It's not even noon yet."

"I know." Suddenly feeling like I was ten and Dad had caught me sneaking peeks at Skinemax again, I tried to explain. "But you really needed to see what happened before the merry maids out there cleaned up the worst of it."

"That bad?"

"On a scale of one to messed up ... batshit insane."

"For once, Bill does not exaggerate."

Christy shook her head, looking dismayed. "Now I wish I'd been a little more focused on this last night instead."

I shrugged. "It wasn't your fault. I'm the one who gave the all clear."

"You didn't give the all clear, dumbass," Sally replied. "I sent you home. This is on me."

"I'm pretty sure we can all share the blame," Christy said.

I gave half a nod. "In all fairness, it's not like we have a rulebook for any of this – other than not asking Sally to play Jenga."

"Bite me, asshole."

Christy raised an eyebrow. "Jenga?"

"Inside joke," I said, before clarifying, "not really all that funny actually. Let's grab a seat and we can explain." As Sally led us into the living room, I figured it wouldn't hurt to sate my curiosity while the topic was still fresh. "Learn anything new about those leprechauns, by the way? Maybe some other stupid thing they're allergic to?"

Christy shook her head. "Not really. I was more focused on trying to figure out why they've reappeared after all this time."

"Leprechauns in New York," Sally remarked. "Pretty sure I've seen that movie."

"You're thinking about..."

"It was a joke. I don't actually care," she interrupted before turning to Christy. "So, before we get to my shit show, any luck deciphering why the five boroughs have been invaded by little green men?"

Christy sat down and shrugged. "Nothing concrete, but I'm working on a theory."

"Please tell me it's a good theory."

"And you just guaranteed that it's not," Sally replied.

Christy inclined her head. "She's right. It's not. I was wondering about these creatures, not so much what they are, but the fact that I'd barely even heard of them. Not to toot my own horn, but I consider myself fairly learned in the dark arts."

"Something I don't think either of us would disagree with," I said.

She flashed me a quick grin, acknowledging the compliment. "I got to thinking, then I pulled out some of Harry's old history texts. They're mostly filled with ancient legends and prophecies from the early days of the Magi, but it was able to give me an idea of the state of the world back then, so I could try and compare it to now."

"I, for one, can attest that the internet is a wonderful thing."

"You would never have survived the seventies," Sally remarked.

Christy waited for us to finish, then said, "I'm pretty sure I've mentioned this before, but our world has been in a slow decline for millennia, at least in regard to creatures from beyond the veil." We both nodded, so she continued. "To give an example, as crazy as things got during the war between the vampire nation and Forest Folk, it was nothing compared to thousands of years ago."

I raised my hand. "Are we allowed to agree to disagree? Because things got pretty fucking crazy against the Feet."

"Sorry, I don't mean to downplay it. The thing is, outside of the Jahabich themselves, we didn't really encounter anything we shouldn't have."

"No offense, but I'm not sure if you remember that Jahabich prison at the center of the Earth and all the pants shitting horrors contained within. I mean, we're talking giant slime covered bat monsters and..."

"I'm well aware," she replied. "And true, a good deal of what was seen at the height of the war was not exactly common in this day and age. But we're also talking allies of both warring races ... creatures known to them, if not to you."

"Yeah, Bill," Sally said. "Not to be harsh, but the Draculas had an Olympic swimming pool of knowledge compared to the thimbleful of what they told you." Before I could say anything to that, she added, "Same with me. I saw snippets at best during my time, but it was enough to tell me I'd have needed another thousand years to barely scratch the surface."

I leaned back, not quite following any of this. "Okay, so there's a lot more out there than I'm aware of. The point of all this?"

"The point is," Christy continued, "that the creatures we saw, while fantastic, are just the tip of the iceberg compared to what used to roam the land. The ancient myths make mention of myriad creatures, some we're familiar with today, but also others that have no equivalent to anything we know of. Take dryads, for instance. They aren't exactly common, but the Magi have known about them since before the Peloponnesian Age."

"Aren't those like, Greek Treebeard things?"

"Thus proving my point," Sally stated.

"Not exactly," Christy said. "But the bottom line is, while a layman might not know what they are, we do. But those things we fought last night. They're different. They're so old, that even the Magi consider them nothing more than a myth."

"So ... where have they been all this time?"

"Who can say?" she replied. "All we really know is that the world has changed over time. For whatever reasons, some creatures were exterminated, others left this world, and still more were cast out never to be seen again. What we saw last night was the equivalent of finding a living dinosaur."

"Jurassic Park: The Bronx. Why has nobody written that yet?" Both ladies glared at me, so I quickly tried to cover my ass. "Sorry, but it kind of fits. I mean, some old guy finding their DNA in amber makes as much sense as anything else."

"It's always fascinating watching your mind do the exact opposite of work."

Christy wisely chose to ignore both of us. "What I'm trying to say is that over time the natural order created a sort of balance if you will, even with regards to unnatural beings. Some creatures were driven out, while others asserted dominance. Over time, things changed until it became the world we knew. Chaotic as it was, there was still a balance of power, one that had come to be over thousands of years.

Except, by doing what we did, destroying the Source, we inadvertently upended that balance."

"Why does that not sound particularly good?"

"Because it's not," she replied to me. "It means that the rules have not only changed, they've been thrown out the window. There's no telling what could show up in our world now that the old gatekeepers are gone. Today it might be the proverbial devil we know, but tomorrow we could be facing something that hasn't been seen since the dawn of time."

"I'm guessing that means we should start stocking up on potatoes."

"Potatoes?" Sally asked.

"Apparently, they are the holy hand grenade of tubers."

"If you say so," she remarked dubiously. "Either way, sounds like we screwed the pooch big time by opening things up again. What a surprise."

"Not us," I said. "Gan."

Christy nodded, then gestured toward Sally. "Which brings us full circle back to you. Gansetseg never named whatever entity she'd forged a deal with. I think that was purposeful. Almost all known pantheons have rituals associated with them for summoning, appeasement, even banishment. If we knew what she had made contact with, it would be the first step in knowing how to deal with it."

"Except it's not about her," Sally said. "At least not anymore. Whatever that thing was, it zapped me instead. So what does that mean? Do I need to worry about being banished to some netherworld, or maybe ritualistically cleansed by fire?"

"Don't be silly..."

Christy shrugged uncomfortably. "I won't lie to you. If it comes down to it, yes."

"Wait, what?"

Oddly enough, though, Sally smiled. "I appreciate the honesty and, don't worry, no offense taken."

"But it could be worse than that," Christy said, because of course it could be. "What if Gansetseg took things a step further?"

"How does one take a deal with the devil a step further?" I asked, really wishing I hadn't.

"By making a deal with a devil that nobody remembers," Sally surmised.

Christy nodded. "Exactly. The old texts don't just make passing mention of day to day threats the world has long since forgotten. There's ... *more*."

I reached up to rub my eyes. "I'm going to regret asking what more means, aren't I?"

The look on Christy's face told me all I needed to know. "I'm working with limited resources here, and there's a lot that's open to interpretation, but I still found a few scattered references that seem to hint at unnamed gods and demons – entities whose names haven't been uttered since mankind first discovered fire, and for good reason."

All at once I was wishing I had another glass or three of tequila. "That's ... not even remotely reassuring."

"It's not," Christy agreed. "But there is one major plus in our favor here."

"Sally's new hair color? Because it is kinda funky."

"No. And before I continue, let me just say this is nothing more than mere speculation on my part, but it seems sound to me. Whatever happened to Sally was intended for Gan – some kind of deal or reward maybe, even beyond getting her immortality back. So whatever it is, it stands to reason it was something she wanted. That's perhaps our one advantage. Sally got it instead."

"Too bad it didn't come with an instruction manual," she replied with a heavy sigh.

"Hold on," I said. "Let's back up a bit here. How would one even know how to reach out to a god...?"

"Entity."

"Excuse me?"

"We have no idea what she actually made contact with."

"Fine. Entity. How would Gan even figure out how to reach an entity that nobody remembers? The whole nobody remembering them part kind of covers that."

Christy opened her mouth to answer, probably either to confirm what I was hinting at – that Gan likely had help from a smarmy stool pigeon masquerading as a bird of prey – or to yell at me for bringing it up again.

However, Sally beat her to the punch. "The First Coven would've known how."

Christy's eyes met mine and there was little doubt what she was thinking. Guess I should've prodded Sally a bit harder to join us at the meetup last night.

"Maybe not directly," she continued. "But I have no doubt shit like that and worse was in their old archives. If Gan was maybe able to gain access to them..."

"No maybe about it," I interrupted.

"What do you mean?"

I smiled sheepishly, knowing she wasn't going to like what I had to say. "You might've missed a few things while you were busy being held captive at the Earth's core." I quickly filled her in on the fact that Gan had laid claim to the First Coven's lair, their fortune, and presumably everything else they owned – including the vast records they'd maintained.

When I was done, Sally let out a deep sigh. "Remember earlier when I asked how fucked we were? You probably should've led with that."

"Sorry. Was distracted by the dead guy outside."

Christy, fortunately, was there to keep us on track. "You're sure that kind of information would've been in there?"

"No, of course I'm not sure," Sally replied. "Outside of a couple fact finding missions for James over the years, I didn't rate access. But Colin did."

Alas, it was a function he was phenomenally adept at. What the? I tried to ignore my subconscious and its apparent newfound admiration for the oily douchebag. "So ... he told you about...?"

"No way. That asshole wouldn't have told me the time of day if he'd been tied up outside at high noon. But, he never turned down an opportunity to gloat. Hell, he even bragged this one time about how they offered him a position as an archivist at the home base in Switzerland, but he turned it down because he felt his true destiny was to lead." She let out a laugh. "Hah! We all know how that one turned out."

"Too true," I replied with a grin.

"That still leaves us back at square one," Christy said, bringing us out of the pleasant reverie of Colin's final fate.

"Wish I could offer more." Sally leaned forward and tented her fingers. "But the betting girl in me says this is an easy call. The Dracs were pretty OCD when it came to data. If someone somewhere had access to forbidden knowledge, you can be certain they wanted it, too. And they were good at collecting it. *Really* good. We're talking about a repository of fucking evil that is unmatched in all the world."

I shared a quick glance with Christy, to which she replied, "Perhaps not entirely unmatched."

"So, you're telling me there's a secret wizard library that's potentially equally as terrifying as the First Coven's?" Sally asked after we'd brought her up to speed for the second time in an hour. "Why doesn't that make me feel any better?"

"It's under strict lock and key," Christy said. "Though I don't know the specifics, the acolytes of the Falcon Archives are supposedly placed under several strict geas to ensure they're unable to divulge what they know, even if they want to."

Left unsaid was that wouldn't have meant shit during magic's five year hiatus.

Sally turned to me after a moment. "What, no gay ass joke? Look at you being all adult and shit."

"You're just lucky Tom isn't here right now."

"Tell me about it. I should play the lottery."

"Can we focus here?" Christy chided.

"Sorry," Sally said, smirking. "You were talking about Magi compulsion, right?"

Christy grimaced uncomfortably. "It's ... a necessity. Otherwise, we would never..."

"Relax. I lived in a glass house for thirty years. I'm in no position to throw stones."

"The problem with all of this," I said, "is as much as we know, there's too much we don't. We have two vast storehouses of ancient knowledge, one or both of which has the answers we need to help Sally. But it's not as if we can just walk up to either like they're a branch of our local library."

Silence descended upon the apartment for several seconds, broken only by the sounds of the cleanup crew as they finished up outside.

"So how do we fix that?" Sally asked at last. "I mean, let's stop focusing on the problem and figure out some solutions, even if they're half-assed."

"We need answers, plain and simple," I said. "The thing is, we don't even know where Gan is. And even if we did..."

"She'd be unlikely to help *the whore*," she replied, using air quotes and a healthy dollop of bitterness. "At least without there being something in it for her."

"Probably meaning me. A sacrifice which I..."

"That leaves the Falcon Archives," Christy stated, cutting me off.

"Yeah, but..."

"No buts. We can't afford to wait on this. We need to gain access, even if it means swallowing our pride and apologizing profusely." She fixed me with a stare, causing me to shrink down in my chair.

"Sorry."

Sally smirked. "Looks like someone is eating crow for dinner tonight."

"Bottom line is we have no other choice," Christy continued, ignoring her. "Matthias is the only person with the knowledge and pull to help us. Now we just have to hope he's willing to."

LIBRARY CARD

"Are we really sure this is a good idea?"

"Considering our lack of other options, yes," Christy replied, sitting next to me on the PATH train.

Sally sat across from us in the otherwise empty car. After reaching out to Falcon and getting him to agree to another audience with us, we'd headed out – taking the sewer exit, thanks to my extreme sunlight allergy.

That itself had been ... interesting, watching the vamps of Village Coven 2.0 scatter as we approached, or more like as Sally approached.

Sadly, there really hadn't been time to offer up any reassurances to them outside of, "Everything is under control," which had sounded as fake to me as it probably had to them. Oh well, chalk it up to yet another on the growing list of fires that were in need of putting out.

Once we reached the nearest station, Christy had helpfully broken out the magic to ensure we got a car to ourselves and could thus talk freely on the short trip downtown. Ironically enough, Falcon had instructed us to head to the docks on West Tenth, the neighborhood where Village Coven once had a safe house. We'd be stepping onto the same turf where Night Razor had met his end. I swear, the more things changed the more fucking weird they got.

Talking to Falcon was potentially a double-edged sword. On the one hand, if his archives had knowledge of what had done this, it would certainly cast light that the accusation I'd thrown at his feet yesterday, the same one he was supposedly looking into, was possible. But if he had no clue as to what had zapped Sally, well, then we'd be stuck in the same spot we were now, knowing jack shit.

Then there was the issue of taking Sally to meet him, something I wasn't particularly comfortable with. He was here to catalogue, investigate, and put an end to any paranormal weirdness he found, and she now potentially fell into that category.

Still, the alternative was to leave her home alone with a bunch of freaked out vamps while I tried my best not to stick my foot in my mouth again. Probably not a great strategy all in all.

I suppose I could've given her the keys to my apartment but ... well, let's be realistic here. I fully remembered the damage that had been done there in prior years. Did I really want to send Sally to a place that she freely admitted to thinking was a shithole?

Yeah, so instead I'd brought her out into the public domain, where she could potentially endanger untold lives if she gave in to the general stress that is New York City.

So nice to see I hadn't gotten any better at thinking this shit through in the intervening years. Oh well, at least if Sally lost her cool and went all supernova, I'd probably be caught in the blast and thus no longer burdened by whatever horrors my lack of foresight had wrought. That's me, a glass is half full kinda guy.

"Are we sure there's no other Magi we could've called for a second opinion?" I asked, dragging myself back to the here and now.

"None I trust," Christy replied.

"Kelly's still AWOL?"

"She isn't AWOL. Fine, okay, maybe she is. But I'm sure she and her husband have just as much to deal with at the moment as the rest of us."

"Liz, maybe?" She narrowed her eyes at me to which I quickly held up my hands in supplication. "Relax, it's only a suggestion."

Guess that was to be expected. Liz had orchestrated an attack on Christy's home not too long ago that had put her child and friend in danger, not to mention left one of her neighbors dead. Still, beggars couldn't really be choosers.

"Remember what I said about what I'd do if I ever saw her again? It still stands."

"I knew there was a reason I always liked you," Sally commented.

Christy grinned at her then turned back toward me. "As for the other local covens, or former covens anyway, I'm not sure what help they'd be. Far as I've heard, it's been mostly a nonstop party in the vast majority of the Magi community. I spoke last week to a few of the witches from my support group. If anything, they're drunker now than they were when they didn't have magic."

"Not sure I can blame them," Sally replied. "But even so, there's gotta be other wet blankets out there. I mean, back in the day we ran into plenty of humorless shitheads from the magic world, no offense."

Christy waved off the concern. "Trust me, I know. Harry had contacts with most of the Mentors on the east coast, as well as a few High Mentors. Problem is, a lot of them died down below when we stormed the White Mother's lair. And those that didn't ... well, five years is a long time. The old gatherings have mostly been abandoned, the lines of communication gone stale. I even reached out as far as New England. A few of the covens up there were known to have fairly extensive collections, but no dice. Some of the former Mentors are missing, a few didn't return my calls, and at least one died of lung cancer in the ensuing years."

I winced. "Let me guess. Lack of magical health insurance."

"Pretty much."

"So that leaves us this guy we're going to see," Sally surmised. "And we don't exactly trust him, do we?"

"Nope."

"Yes, we do."

Sally glanced at us both then raised one eyebrow. "At least he's local."

We reached our stop to find a bit of luck thrown our way, and by that I mean my way. A weather system had moved into the area. It had been partly cloudy earlier, but now a light drizzle had begun, meaning I could traverse the final few blocks without having to don a Unabomber motif.

The place had been cleaned up quite a bit in the days since Night Razor's reign had ended. Back then, it had been a haven for derelicts in need of a place to piss, puke, or pass out – in short, the perfect spot for vampires to pluck victims off the street without anyone caring.

Now, however, the vast majority of the old warehouses had been replaced with buildings full of closet-sized *luxury* apartments, no doubt priced for one-percenters with more money than sense. Progress? Yes. Positive progress? Debatable.

But we weren't there to scope out new rental units. Christy led us past them to where a few of the old warehouses still stood, walled off with a rusty chain link fence that looked to be in good enough condition to stop basically nobody from crossing its threshold.

We made our way to a gate, chained but not locked, telling us this particular entryway was more ceremonial than anything. As far as security went, the owners of this place obviously had few, if any, shits to give.

"There's ... something here," Sally said as we approached it.

Or maybe not.

"A glamour," Christy confirmed. "How did you know?"

"I'm not sure. I just did."

"Bill?"

I took a sniff of the air. From past dealings with older vamps, I knew that it was possible to smell the magic in the air. And once upon a time – when I'd developed control over the mindless brute inside of me – I probably could've done so. However, the clock had been reset on my vampire tenure so, while all the scents were greatly multiplied, all I could sense was garbage, decay, and the not too clean water of the Hudson. "Nope. It just looks like a fence to me."

Christy held out a hand for a moment, no doubt the Magi equivalent of a check for traps roll, then she led the way through the gate.

I wasn't sure what to expect as we crossed into the derelict parking lot. After all, I'd seen glamours before and knew they were capable of showing a reality completely different than what was actually happening. However, as I stepped in, noting the air shimmer around me, I saw nothing different than what I'd seen on the outside.

"Okay, am I crazy or was that the world's shittiest illusion?"

Christy shook her head. "It actually makes a lot of sense, showing what things look like under normal circumstances. It just so happens nothing out of the ordinary is going on right now that would need to be masked."

"I guess that makes sense."

"There's more here," Sally said, her head cocked to the side. She was wearing sunglasses to mask her freaky eyes, but I could still see her glancing every which way.

"You're not wrong." Christy made another gesture and immediately began to glow with yellowish energy. "Behold."

The air before us once again shimmered, and suddenly the empty lot lit up in all directions for about fifty feet around us.

Countless sigils, glyphs, and wards appeared, all glowing bright yellow. Some were painted on the cracked pavement. Others were on the sides of dumpsters, trash cans, and light poles. Still more hung in midair, like magical spider webs waiting for unsuspecting *flies* to walk into them.

"Holy shit!"

"Am I wrong?" Sally asked, "Or is this pretty much a Magi minefield?"

Christy lowered her hand and the sigils disappeared from sight, not really making me feel any better, as I hadn't exactly memorized their locations. "More or less. It's an impressive amount of work to do in such a short time for such a large space. And I think those were only the tip of the iceberg."

She continued onward, but I caught her arm. "Are you crazy? You just said..."

"They're all inert at the moment," she explained with a grin, obviously at my discomfort. "Otherwise we wouldn't have made it even this far."

"And if they hadn't been?" I asked, not even remotely comfortable walking through the magical demilitarized zone around ghetto Isengard.

"The wards around the gate are relatively low level," she said, calmly and collected, as if we weren't surrounded by enough magic to blow us to several hells at once. "It's meant to daze, confuse, and redirect people. It gets more serious, however, the further in we go."

"As in the direction we're currently headed?"

"Bravery thy name is Bill," Sally remarked. "What's the matter? You want to live forever or something?"

"Forever, no? Past the next five minutes? Preferably."

Christy turned to me, amusement etched onto her face. "Relax. Like I said, they're inert."

"And how much effort would it take to make them not inert?"

"The wave of a hand, chum," a voice called to us from further in, Falcon's.

I glanced that way to find him standing in the doorway of a derelict warehouse down near the waterline.

He was leaning against the door frame, shirtless. *Motherfucker!* Night vision aside, my eyesight wasn't exactly supernaturally charged, but even from this distance I could tell the asshole was ripped.

"You know, luv," he called out with a laugh, turning his attention to Christy, "it's rude to show off another wizard's party tricks."

Oh, how I was beginning to hate this guy.

I made it a point to be last in the door – partly because I didn't trust this asshole as far as I could throw the fucking Titanic – but also for somewhat pettier reasons.

Sure enough, I detected Christy's gaze making a quick crawl over Falcon's annoyingly perfect washboard abs. Then came a far more blatant stare by Sally, over the rim of her sunglasses.

Et tu, Bitchy?

"Excuse my dress," he said, acknowledging both with a nod. "Just finished a long shift down in the sewers. Was finishing up my third shower when you texted, luv. Didn't expect you lot to get here so quickly. Sending?"

"Subway," Sally replied.

He smiled back at her. "I take it you're the reason for this visit. Mentor Matthias Falcon at your service. Sally Carlsbad, I presume?"

However, before I could opine whether he'd been snooping magically on us, he added, "Relax, everyone. I simply cross-referenced what Mentor Fenton told me with what we already had on file about the Freewill. No extraordinary cleverness required." He then turned his focus squarely back to Sally. "Although, judging from your most recent media photos, Miss Carlsbad, I'm going to assume your American cameras tend to add a few years."

"Sally is fine," she replied. "My last name is still up for debate, at least going forward."

"Very well, Miss Sally. Please make yourself at home and kindly forgive the mess."

I was planning on very much not forgiving any mess as I stepped past him, but then found myself scooping my jaw off the floor.

Holy shit!

I'd expected ... well, a warehouse. We'd had one back in the Village Coven days and it looked exactly like you'd expect a warehouse to look, just a wee bit more ominous. I'd expected old shipping crates with a cot off to the side, along with maybe a chemical toilet and a sink – all of which would have at least served to make me feel marginally superior in a petty way.

Instead, it was like stepping foot into a palatial estate as imagined by the folks who'd built Hogwarts.

It was as if someone had designed a studio mansion – all the comforts of luxury, but in an open floor layout with an extra dose of freaky thrown in. There was a massive leather couch close by with a large screen TV floating in midair in front of it. An indoor waterfall, of all things, emptied into a crystal clear pool off on one end. And that was just the start. All around us, the trappings of wealth and magic combined into sheer spectacle. There wasn't even the customary girders and rafters above to break up the illusion. Instead, a bright blue sky complete with blazing sun shone down upon us ... obviously fake as I didn't immediately turn to dust, but of course not before I flinched in a very unmanly way.

Goddamnit!

That alone made it tempting to grab this asshole's douchetastic mustache and give it as much of a yank as my vampiric strength would allow.

Before I could let that fantasy play itself out, though, the entire place began to pulse with a greenish yellow glow.

"Any reason for the disco lights?" I asked, tearing my eyes away from splendor which made Alexander the Great's old quarters back in Switzerland seem practically humble by comparison.

"Those are my personal wards," Falcon replied, sounding far more guarded than he had a moment earlier.

"No offense, dude," I said, totally meaning to cause offense, "but if you knew we were coming, why didn't you shut them off like the outside ones?"

"I did."

Oh. "Just for the record, if I'm about to get vaporized, I totally blame y ... OOF!"

Before I could finish my pithy accusation, a bolt of blue energy slammed into me, lighting up my nerve endings and dropping me to the floor like a sack of wet shit. My only solace as I hit the rich mahogany flooring – who the fuck installs hardwood in a warehouse – was seeing that same energy envelope Falcon and knock him ass over teakettle to land in a crumbled heap.

But who...?

That was answered a moment later, as I managed to turn my head enough to see Christy – still awash with bluish power – throw herself to the floor, her hands laced behind her head as if being arrested ... or ducking for cover.

What the fuck?

Sadly, the answer to my unspoken question came in the form of pure devastation, as if God himself had taken affront to Falcon's abode and decided to smite it with both middle fingers.

An invisible wave of intense pressure flattened me against the floor, letting up a moment later, only to be replaced by the sound of seemingly everything in this entire fucking place being blown to pieces.

It was only after it passed that I realized, pride notwithstanding, I was mostly unhurt. I pushed myself to a sitting position to find that only Sally remained standing, a look of shock and confusion etched onto her face.

All around us, the opulent dockside palace was in shambles. Where there had been rich magical excess mere moments earlier, now there was just a rich magical mess. The TV was busted, the couch was in tatters, and the waterfall now looked more like a cesspool. In fact, the only thing that appeared untouched was the illusion of a clear blue sky far above us. Glass half full and all that shit.

"Oh crap," Sally said. "I did it again, didn't I?"

"Is everyone okay?" Christy asked, pulling herself to her feet, looking a bit windblown but otherwise unhurt.

Last to recover – *hah* – was Falcon, but he had to be all flashy to make up for it.

"What the bloody hell?!" he cried, standing up, an angry green glow surrounding him – battle magic if I had my colors right.

Not a great look for him, or us for that matter, if he decided that all of our asses had to die. On the upside, at least it would give me an excuse to pop the guy in his perfect chin.

His ire, however, appeared directed entirely at Christy, since she seemed to be the culprit behind zapping our asses, for whatever reason. Can't say I minded having anger pointed elsewhere for a change, but if he thought I was going to just stand there while he went all avada kedavra on her, he had another...

"I'm sorry about that," Christy said, raising her hands, "but it was better than the alternative. Believe me." She indicated the destruction around us which, in all truth, was pretty extreme. It was as if someone had rolled a giant wrecking ball through the place.

"Explain," Falcon ordered, his tone not at all to my liking, "and make it good. I will warn you, those weren't my only wards."

Looking around the place, I highly doubted that. Everything the guy owned seemed to have been reduced to a pile of junk more suited to how this place looked on the outside.

"You knew I was going to blow, didn't you?" Sally asked.

Oh shit.

I remembered what she'd done to Stewart, and that had been over nothing more than a freaking board game. Yet here was Falcon, lit up like Times Square, flashing colors of a variety that was probably a bit more stressful than asking if we wanted to play Parcheesi.

Though a small part of me wouldn't have minded seeing him reduced to a gallon of Magi paint, Christy was right. He was our best bet for figuring out what was going on, for now anyway.

Fortunately, Sally's attention seemed entirely focused on Christy for the moment.

"Mostly," Christy replied to her. "Not a hundred percent, but I figured worst case was apologizing for a stun spell."

"What do you mean by that?" Falcon asked.

"Um, yeah, what he said," I added unhelpfully.

Though I enjoyed being tazed about as much as a swift kick to the balls, Christy's spell couldn't have come at a better time. What Sally had done here had utterly dwarfed the comparatively minor blowback of the prior day.

"Back at my apartment you had a similar ... episode."

"Is that what we're calling it now?"

Christy shrugged then continued. "I've been thinking it over, wondering what caused it, and the only thing I keep coming back to is Tina."

"Kids are stressful? You don't say."

Sally turned toward me and narrowed her eyes. "Here's an idea. Maybe let the non-idiots talk for a bit. Go on."

"Tina radiates far more ambient magic than a typical witch. She's like an entire battle-charged coven in one tiny body."

"Not following," I said.

Much to my consternation, though, Falcon jumped right in with, "Bloody brilliant! My wards..."

"Exactly. The second I saw them going off, I realized what was happening."

"Care to explain for those of us who prefer fighter classes?" I asked, annoyed at the fact that I was playing catch-up again.

"The wards," Christy replied. "Deactivated or not, they and this place in general represent a lot of ambient magic in the air."

"Then how come the ones outside didn't do anything?"

"It's the concentration, mate," Falcon replied, "helped by four walls and a ceiling. A man's home is his castle after all."

Ah, I was beginning to catch on. "So, what you're saying is that Sally is an open flame and magic is kind of like gas fumes to her."

"Crude, but effectively correct," Falcon confirmed, although I couldn't help but bristle at the dig. "Pull out a lighter in the general vicinity of a propane grill, for example, and not much will happen. Open all the ports on an oven in a sealed room, however, and it's a different story."

"Guess that means I should avoid the local Magi conventions," Sally replied.

"No doubt. But that isn't all there is to it, is it?" Falcon asked.

Sally shook her head then gave him a rundown on what had happened back at her place, leaving out a few minor details, such as the obviously shady cleanup crew.

"Hmm, so there appears to be a conscious element to it as well," he concluded after a moment, "or a semiconscious one anyway."

"Activated when she's annoyed, it would seem," I added, "which, just for the record, is pretty much how she usually is."

Sally turned my way, her eyes narrowed behind the sunglasses that inexplicably still remained on her face. "Which you're not helping much at the moment."

"Don't make me disinvite you to game night."

"Oh no. Whatever shall I do?"

Falcon stepped in and put a hand on my chest, easing me back. "If annoyance is indeed the key to this power, then I might suggest it best to not antagonize her."

"Bill's not antagonizing me," she said in response. "This is barely a slow Tuesday for us."

"The bottom line is we simply don't know enough," Christy told Falcon, effectively steering us back on track from the tangents we seemed insistent on taking. "We have only the barest clue what triggers it, and that's all. We don't know what else she can do, if anything, the limits of her power, whether it's dangerous to her, any of it. All we know is that something granted her these powers, powers that were meant for someone else."

I nodded. "And which I'm thinking we're all now really glad that certain someone else didn't get."

"Am I perhaps reaching in assuming this unnamed someone is the same Gansetseg you accused me of being in league with last night?"

"Accused is such a strong word."

"The same," Christy admitted, shooting me a look. "But what we talked about last night got me thinking. What if the thing she struck a deal with is ancient, like those a'chiad dé danann – something long since forgotten by man and Magi alike? If so, there'd be no mention of it even in our historical tomes, except perhaps the really old ones."

"Kinda like how Cthulhu shows up in the original Deities and Demigods, but was cut from later editions?"

All eyes turned toward me for a moment. Geez, everyone is a critic when the gamer in the room speaks.

Falcon resumed talking to Christy, utterly ignoring me like the dick-biscuit he was. "And if this theoretical being was willing to make a deal with a mortal, to reignite the Source, it must have a vested interest in our world. Thus, if we can figure out what it is, we could possibly protect ourselves against whatever that vested interest might be."

"And help our friend here."

"Of course," he replied, stroking his mustache. "Assuming such a thing is possible."

"Excuse me?"

Ignoring me once again, he turned to Sally, his expression grim ... or as grim as it could be with that ridiculous dead otter on his face. "I'm sorry to have to say this, but it's best if you understand upfront. Some power simply cannot be controlled, merely contained. And once a person is touched by it..."

"They're fucked?" Sally replied, sounding strangely nonplussed by his premonition of doom and gloom. "Story of my life. What else is new?"

"Not going to happen," I said. "We'll find a way to fix this."

She smirked. "And if you can't, I guess I can just take over the world."

Falcon didn't seem to appreciate her sense of humor, but I was happy to feed into it. "Have you seen Washington lately? Doubt you could do worse."

"Exactly."

"The point is," Christy said, once again steering this rudderless ship back onto the straight and narrow, "we still don't know where Gansetseg is, so we need an alternate source of knowledge to combat whatever she did. We need access to the Falcon Archives."

All eyes turned to Falcon, a few of them aimed at spots other than his face. *Grrr!* He, in turn, fell silent, an unreadable expression upon his mustachioed mug. He stepped away, toward one of the piles of debris left in the wake of Sally's little outburst. Digging through it for a moment, he pulled out a t-shirt, dusted it off, and then put it on. Of course it was skintight, doing nothing to make the situation better. Fucking A! Where was this guy's uptight prim and proper British attitude when you needed it?

"Kindly take off your glasses and sit over there," he finally said to Sally.

After a moment, she did as asked, picking up an overturned stool and taking a seat upon it.

Falcon bent down slightly and began to circle her position, studying her as if there was going to be a quiz later.

"Take a picture, it lasts longer."

Apparently, he seemed to agree with my advice, pulling his cell phone out of his pocket and tapping the screen as he continued to circle her.

"What are you...?"

But Christy silenced me with a quick, "Let him work."

Not one to take good advice when it was given to me, I stepped in nevertheless and took a peek over Falcon's shoulder.

"What'cha doing?"

In response, he quickly lowered the phone again, turning off the screen in the process. "Do you mind?"

I held up my hands and backed away a step. "Just making sure you're not taking any upskirts to jerk off to later."

"Like you've never tried," Sally said with a scoffing laugh.

I spun back toward Christy to find her eyes narrowed. *Oh crap.* "She's just joking. I mean I never..." That might've been a bit of a lie, but now seemed a poor time for the whole honesty is the best policy schtick.

After a few more minutes of Falcon circling Sally like some sort of smarmy mustachioed shark, he turned to the rest of us. "I think I have what I need here. I'll be in touch if I discover anything useful."

Christy shared a quick glance with me, for the moment looking just as confused as I was. "I'm not sure I follow. We came here to ask for..."

"Access to the Falcon Archives, I know," he replied. "But you must understand the archive is considered one of the most valued treasures of the Magi community, as well as one of its most highly guarded. There are tomes contained within that absolutely must not fall into the hands of the average lay person, much less some of the maniacs out there."

Oh yeah, this guy wasn't full of himself at all. Listening to him talk, I was reminded of the Templar, the group of holier than thou assholes Vincent used to belong to, convinced that they and they alone were the guardians of God's scripture.

"Except I'm neither an average lay person nor a maniac," Christy said, her voice tight in the way it used to get when she was preparing to chew Tom a new asshole. "I'm a Mentor in my own right."

"I didn't mean to imply you weren't," Falcon replied smoothly.

"If this is about what was said last night..."

"Not at all. I'm speaking of established protocol, nothing more. The simple fact of the matter is that few of our number are granted access to the archives at any given time, and that is only after a lengthy application, review, and background check. There's a rigorous vetting process, not to mention the need for positive testimonials from noted Mentors and High Mentors alike."

"Huh, and I thought the vampire nation loved their bureaucracy," Sally remarked, putting her sunglasses back on.

"Fine," Christy said after a moment. "Tell me what you need. I counseled a lot of our people during the years we were powerless. I'm sure they'd be happy to vouch for my credentials."

"Alas, that's an issue unto itself. Any Magi who fell upon hard times during the quiet years would automatically be considered suspect and thus unreliable in their testimony. As for those who weren't..."

There came an uncomfortable pause during which Sally gave me a warning look, although I had a feeling it wasn't directed at me.

"Who weren't *what?*" Christy asked.

"Christine, you ... how do I put this gently? You developed a bit of a reputation back before the Source fell. I believe one of our very own High Mentors accused you of treason. Then there was that kerfuffle with your former Mentor, Mr. Decker." He held up his hands in a placating manner, as if realizing he was venturing into dangerous territory. "I understand your motives, believe me. I lost my family to that nasty business, something that wouldn't have happened had they the foresight to question the White Mother's return as you did. Yet, the vetting protocol remains."

"So, you're saying I'm not qualified?" The temperature in the room seemed to drop about thirty degrees.

Heh. Guess being rich, good looking, and British didn't automatically preclude one from shoving their expensive loafers down their own throat. Good to know.

"I'm saying it would likely take some time to grant you clearance, time, I dare say, that we simply do not have. Your friend here, if I am not mistaken, has been chosen, whether willingly or not, to be the Earthly avatar of a being lost to time. Now, I don't pretend to understand the whims of the myriad forces beyond the veil, but very few myths are known for expounding on the patience of the entities they're based upon. Thus, I am offering to lend my time in helping research the issue for you, so we can all come to a satisfactory conclusion before things get further out of hand."

Though he tried to keep his words diplomatic, there was a take it or leave it quality to his voice that Christy no doubt picked up on. The look on her face said it all: she wanted nothing better than to give this fucker a piece of her mind, but he had us over a barrel.

So, instead of blasting him – verbally or otherwise – she simply nodded after a moment and said, "Thank you, Mentor Falcon. We appreciate any and all help you can provide. All I ask is that you keep us in the loop."

"Of course. I'll make every effort to. However, I do have a request of my own to make."

"Please speak it."

I couldn't help but notice that Christy had fallen back into the formal speech her people seemed to favor during their ceremonies – probably to keep from losing her shit.

"One moment please."

Falcon stepped to another pile of debris, the remains of a desk from the look of things. He rooted through it for a few moments before returning with something in his grasp.

He handed it over to Sally, giving us a chance to get a good look at it.

Oh crap. We're all gonna die.

"I'm afraid I must insist you wear this."

"Is that...?"

Sally's tone instantly turned every bit as icy as Christy's, maybe even a few degrees frostier, but Falcon cut her off. "Yes. It's similar to the bracelets required by those under house arrest, magically reinforced – albeit hopefully not enough to set off your ... condition. Rest assured, you are not actually under arrest. But I will need a way to find you if the situation warrants it."

"Why not just use a fucking cell phone like everyone else?"

"Because I'm afraid this goes beyond that. Mobiles can be forgotten or turned off. That, alas, is unacceptable, at least until such time as I can narrow down the identity of the entity who has enchanted you."

"You can take your fashion accessory and shove it up your..."

"Perhaps I didn't make myself clear. As a Mentor of my people and, more importantly, a duly deputized official representing the New York Police Department, I must *insist*."

As Sally's previous episode seemed to have been triggered by annoyance, I had no idea how she managed to show the restraint necessary to let us walk away from this situation alive.

Nevertheless we did, with her wearing the tracking bracelet and looking none too pleased about it.

At the same time, the implied threat had been hard to dismiss. I'm pretty sure neither of us gave a single solitary shit as to what the Magi wanted, our close friends aside. However, making an enemy of the NYPD was not in our best interest. Yes, according to Falcon, the old treaty between New York and the vampire nation had been reinstated, but that no longer applied to Sally as she now clearly fell into the "other" category – the kind he'd been brought in to assess and, if necessary, deal with.

It was exactly as I'd feared when Christy had contacted him about this issue. He was waving around his weight as a duly appointed representative of the city, here on assignment to stamp out potentially dangerous *things*. The message was loud and clear. The only person keeping Sally from being listed as one of those things was Falcon, and if we wanted to keep it that way, we'd need to play ball.

So it was that we walked away from the docks with seemingly little to show for our efforts, save giving a stranger the ability to track my friend like a chipped dog. Yet I couldn't help but feel a sense of smug satisfaction.

Despite the fact that Falcon had us over the proverbial barrel, I'd gotten everything I'd hoped for from this meeting.

Now to see if I could make use of it.

* * *

A SLIGHT DETOUR

"**W**ill you stop staring at me. I told you, I have it under control."

"And yet Falcon's warehouse says otherwise, not that I had a problem with you trashing the shit out of it."

"I kind of got that impression." Sally held up her arm, the one with the rather unfashionable accessory attached to it. "Listen. I know why I'm inclined to dislike that guy, but what's your beef with him?"

"I just don't like his attitude."

"Uh huh. Let me guess. You're worried that Christy is going to consider all the things you don't bring to the table, then she's going to look at him with his rock hard abs, money, and magical mastery, and realize she could easily upgrade to first class seating?"

Motherfucker! "No."

"I thought so. Small dick syndrome at its finest."

"I do not have a small dick!"

All in all, I probably could have picked a better time to shout that than while still in the relatively crowded 86th Street subway station.

Hurrying up to the drizzly streets above, I said, "Getting back to the point at hand, how can you be sure you have it under control?"

"First off, we just took mass transit without killing every single annoying asshole on our train, but mostly because I've been thinking about what happened with what's his face."

"Stewart?"

"Yeah, him."

"And?"

"And, I'm beginning to think it was a bit more than base annoyance. I mean, otherwise, I'd have leveled the entirety of the Metro system on the way there and back."

"All things considered, probably a reasonable conclusion."

We'd split up shortly after leaving Falcon's formerly pristine abode. Christy was still in a snit over his refusal to grant her access to the archives, even though she claimed she wasn't. Color me skeptical, especially since she'd answered my inquiry about how she was doing with, "fine," – in that tone females used when they're actually at DEFCON 1.

Thankfully it didn't appear aimed at me this time.

Before going our separate ways, we'd taken a moment to gather our thoughts and discuss things. Neither of us wanted to leave Sally alone, both for the safety of others as well as her own now that Falcon had her in his personal Find My Friends app. A quick examination by Christy was enough to conclude that the perp bracelet he'd given her was warded in ways designed to *discourage* its removal.

Taking it off might've hurt Sally or it might've discharged enough magic to cause her to go all Mount St. Helens again, which probably would've been a bad thing in a crowded city.

Truth of the matter was Christy was probably best suited to keep Sally company, being that she had half a clue. Problem was, she also had Tina, or would in a few short hours. Christy's place was warded up the ass, yet none of us was willing to bet that it would be sufficient to keep Tina from exuding enough residual magic to set Sally off.

I had a feeling we might've gotten lucky that first time. Maybe Sally's body had still been waking up from its extended power nap. The damage inflicted to Falcon's warehouse, though, had been a magnitude beyond that. If it occurred again, who knew what could happen?

That meant I was once again elected for babysitting duty, not that I minded in the least.

Sally minded, though, especially once I suggested we head back to my place in Brooklyn. Thing was, her home was currently still full of vampires who were now absolutely terrified of her. That would need to be remedied and soon, but for the moment I suggested a time out might be beneficial for both parties.

Sally, proving that – despite her assertions otherwise – she hadn't fully regressed back to her old *kill them all and let God sort it out* ways, agreed ... for now anyway.

"Shit!"

"What is it?" Sally asked, as I stopped on the sidewalk.

"Tom's home."

"So?"

I'd been so busy thinking of the lack of ambient magic at my place that I hadn't considered the other part of the equation. "So ... I know you said you think it was more than mild annoyance which set you off, but at the same time he's been known to..."

"Piss me off by sheer virtue of his stupid existence?"

"More or less."

"Now augmented by Icon abilities, which I'm sure he's using in a less than intelligent manner."

"I'll ... plead the fifth."

"Color me not surprised, but I should still be okay. Like I said, I think I'm beginning to understand what happened."

"Care to enlighten me?"

"Gladly." She indicated we keep moving, which was probably better than standing there being rained on. "That Stewart guy triggered me, but I don't think it was really him. More like he just happened to be sweating in the wrong place at the wrong time."

"Go on."

"I was ... not in a good frame of mind this morning. I'd been up all night, pacing back and forth, wondering what that little bitch had done to me."

"Gan?"

"You know any other little bitches?"

I kept my mouth shut on that one and simply shook my head.

"I'm not going to lie, Bill. I'm scared. I mean look at me... Not like that, jackass! Think about it for a change. It's like I was granted everything I wanted. But there's a catch to that wish."

"I one hundred percent understand. This one time in Dave's game I wished for my bard to be the hottest act in the land, and ended up being burnt at the stake instead, after

I..." I paused as I realized she was staring at me with one eyebrow raised, and not in a kindly way. "I meant, please continue."

"Fucking nerd." She rolled her eyes and let out a pained sigh. "Anyway, back when I was a vampire, I knew what those catches were – bloodlust, compulsion, Colin." She chuckled at that last one. "Now, though, I don't even have the benefit of knowing. I have to figure this shit out from scratch."

I stepped in and put a comforting arm around her, which she allowed ... for about three seconds.

"Okay, that's enough. No free feels."

I quickly moved out of her reach. "Let me guess. Planning on notifying your former clientele to keep their wallets handy?"

"See? This is what I mean by having a handle on things. You'll notice you're still in one piece."

Oh yeah. I'd forgotten about things for a moment – shooting off my mouth while completely ignoring the fact that it was potentially throwing a lit match into a pool of rocket fuel. "Good point."

"That's what I mean. Same with the meathead. You might both annoy the shit out of me, but you're known quantities."

"And Stewart wasn't?"

"As I said, wrong place wrong time. I realize now he caught me at a low point. It wasn't even about some stupid board game. It was..."

"The straw that broke the camel's back?"

"More or less, although call me a camel again and I'll reconsider my stance on you two."

"Point taken."

"The thing is, I know he was just trying to be friendly, but he caught me at a moment when all I wanted to do was lash out. And the thing is, I'm sure a part of me knew that. It's like, even as I was telling him to go away, I was silently screaming at the heavens – in a sense killing him with my mind, just because I needed to do it to someone. It just so happened that it wasn't only in my head."

"That's ... kind of terrifying."

"You're telling me."

"But understanding it..."

"Is the first step to controlling it, I know. I just hope I'm right."

"Even if you're not," I replied, "I'm sure you're close. You have this nasty tendency to be right more than you're wrong."

"I do, don't I?" she said with a grin. "I still need to know for sure, though - find some way to test it without hurting anyone. And then there's that ambient magic thing. No offense to the tyke, but I may have to miss her next birthday party."

"Send her a card with a lot of money in it. I find that works like a charm when it comes to kids."

"I guess some part of her has to take after her father," Sally remarked before turning back to the subject at hand. "The other problem is whether this new body of mine has any more surprises awaiting me."

I nodded. "If we can figure out what did this to you, we might have a better chance of answering that."

"Yep, but right now it seems our new wizard friend holds all the cards in that game. Can't say I'm all too comfortable putting my faith in a stranger."

This time it was my turn to grin. "He might not have *all* the cards."

"Sounded that way to me."

"Let's just say I might have an ace up my sleeve."

"Oh? Do tell."

"Not yet. I need to see if it pans out first. Just give me a few hours to test whether I'm on to something or just spinning my wheels."

We arrived back at my place to find no sign of Tom, Kara, or our resident blob for that matter. I can't say that bothered me much. It potentially gave me the time I needed to work on my little research project, without having to worry about being asked to go on a tampon run.

"I see all's quiet on the stupid front."

"Yeah, I guess they went out."

"They?"

I explained to her how Kara had paid us a visit.

"Oh. How'd she take the news that her brother was alive and her boyfriend is Gan's new plaything?"

"A bit better on the first front than on the second."

"Not surprising."

"Yeah. I'm hoping Tom's able to keep her distracted for now. The last thing we need is her panicking and filing a missing persons report."

"Where do you think they went?"

"No idea," I replied, stepping into my bedroom to retrieve my laptop. "Maybe she took him out for his first mani-pedi."

She let out a laugh. "I would've liked to have gotten video of that."

"Future blackmail?"

"You know it."

The thing I've always loved about programming is getting into the "zone" – that perfect mental harmony where the problems of the world seem to fade away and all that remains is the logic of the code. I mean sure, there was the madness of debugging and trying to find a missing semicolon in a ten-thousand line rat maze of nested subroutines, but that simply added to the challenge.

Mind you, the project I was working on was less about coding something new and more about hitting a particular problem from multiple angles. But the same rules applied. Either way, a few hours passed – me working, while Sally busied herself with watching TV and complaining about how much my apartment sucked.

In fact, the entire day might've passed without incident had not the door to Glen's room finally opened and he came slithering out, blinking about half a dozen eyeballs our way.

Fortunately, I'd brought Sally up to speed on my newest roommate, which resulted in her barely raising an eyebrow as he undulated toward us.

"Freewill," he bubbled, before turning several eyeballs her way. "A pleasure to make your acquaintance again, Mistress Carlsbad. May I say, you look considerably less crusty than last I saw you."

The side of Sally's mouth raised in a half grin as she leaned forward. "I don't think we were properly introduced down in that hellhole. Sally is fine."

"A pleasure then, Mistress Sally," Glen said, quivering as he blinked multiple times. "And might I say, you have the most captivating eyes."

"Um, thanks."

"I guess you'd know," I replied, closing my laptop for now. "Anyway, didn't realize you were here."

Glen sloshed over. "I must have dozed off after the Icon left with his sibling." All at once, his eyes opened wide – quite the freaky thing as he had at least twenty of them floating around in his gelatinous body. "The Icon! I almost forgot."

"What about him?"

"He said to tell you they were going to Pennsylvania."

"What's in Pennsylvania?" Sally asked.

"Far as I know, Hershey Park, construction, and all the fireworks money will buy," I replied before turning to Glen. "Did they say where they were going?"

"To see the Progenitor's father. The Icon's sister seemed somewhat agitated about him."

All at once the mirth drained from my tone. "Wait, Ed's stepdad?"

"I believe so. I overheard them talking, and it seems the Progenitor was only one of the reasons for her visit. His father was the other."

"Why didn't she say something?" Then I realized how stupid of a question that was. Kara had barely stepped through the door before getting beaten over the head with the fact that her brother was alive. I could see how that might be a bit distracting. "Is something wrong with Ed's dad?"

Glen raised two ... um ... flagellum in an "I don't know" sort of gesture. "I don't believe so, but she said something about weird things happening at his home."

"Weird things," Sally echoed. "That's kind of vague."

"She didn't seem to know, only that she was worried about him."

"That doesn't sound right." I turned to Sally to explain. "Ed's pop is a bit of a prepper. Lives in a big ass cabin in the woods. Was the guy who kept us in shotguns back in the day, no questions asked. We were a little nervous about him living where he was, back when the Feet were busy turning everyone into fucking trees, but we never heard a peep from him about it. I mean, seriously, the guy's pretty unshakeable."

She nodded, taking it all in, before turning to Glen. "And yet Kara thought something was wrong?"

"Yes, Mistress Sally." Glen locked all his eyes on her again. "Enough so that the Icon volunteered to accompany her. Hopefully he remembers to take video. I would so love footage of his glorious battles for my scrapbook."

"Hold on, who said anything about glorious battles?" I asked, a sinking feeling beginning to form in the pit of my stomach.

"The Icon. He said he was going to kick ass and take names."

"Of course he did." I pulled out my cell phone and dialed him. *Fucking idiot.* What did he get himself into now?

A moment later, *I Threw it on the Ground* by The Lonely Island began to play from the counter of our kitchen nook ... where the dumbass had left his phone.

Sally stood up. "Let me guess. We're taking a ride to Pennsylvania to save the meathead and his sister?"

"It's probably nothing," I replied, not sounding even remotely convincing. Less than a month ago, this would've been easy to dismiss, but not now. Call me paranoid, but I'd seen firsthand some of the things that were beginning to crawl out of the woodwork now that magic was back.

There was also the fact that Sheila had been formidable – possessing powers and skills that made her nigh untouchable. Tom's mastery of both, however, was questionable at best.

Not to mention, I liked Ed's stepdad. Sure, I'd always gotten the vibe that he thought we were all a bunch of pussies, but there was no denying he'd been cool to us in years past. If he was in trouble and Tom was his only backup...

That pretty much sealed the deal.

"You should stay here."

"In this shithole?" Sally asked. "Not happening. You leave me alone in this place and I'm liable to do the sensible thing – burn it the fuck down. And that has nothing to do with stress."

"But..."

"Besides, it's time I accepted the fact that, like it or not, I'm back in the game."

"It's been all of two days."

"I know that, but I can't let my partner run off and get his stupid ass killed now, can I?"

INTO THE WOODS

"**B**ark bark bark!"

"All right, that's it!" Sally reached over to the control panel and began to close the back window. Glen's *head*, which had been busy lolling in the wind, got caught in it for a moment, but then he gave it a yank and pulled it back in, sending fur flying.

"Sorry, Mistress Sally. Just trying to act the part," he bubbled from the backseat, still inside his creepy ass dog suit.

"Yeah, well your acting is going to get us thrown in jail for animal cruelty. And stop calling me mistress." She took her eyes off the road for a moment to glare at me.

I pretended not to notice, continuing to stare at my laptop screen.

Glen had insisted on coming along, and arguing only served to slow us down, so I'd relented fairly quickly. However, being that it was at least a three hour drive to Pop's place, I'd requested Sally take the wheel so I could continue working on my project.

"Don't ignore me. I'm not your fucking chauffeur."

"I'm not ignoring you," I lied. "I'm working."

"You still haven't told me on what."

"I don't want to get anyone's hopes up until I'm sure it'll work."

After a moment, she let out a sigh. "I must have rocks in my head, but okay. This had better be good, though."

"It will be," I said idly, hitting a few more buttons before finally pressing enter. A moment later, I watched as my screen reloaded, filling with data, and telling me I'd succeeded. *Bingo!* I called up my email client, added all the information that was needed, and hit send before disconnecting the cellular modem and closing the lid.

"Giving up already?"

"Have some faith," Glen said, his dog face leaning forward so it was between us. "The Freewill is strong, ferocious, and smart."

"Damned straight," I replied, patting his head. "Good boy."

"Bark!"

Sally rolled her eyes from behind the wheel. "You two were made for each other."

"Is this guy an axe murderer or what?"

"Just keep going. He's way back ... oof! And watch the potholes."

"The entire road is potholes," Sally complained. "Assuming you can even call it a road."

"Pop Vesser likes his privacy."

"This isn't privacy. This is the sort of place a vampire coven would own to make sure nobody could hear all the screaming."

I couldn't really deny that. Even with my vamp-enhanced night vision, the dirt road felt cramped with the trees seemingly just inches away. Not helping was the fact that my car, a late model Toyota Camry, was most definitely not built for off-roading. With the gloom of the rapidly darkening skies bearing down upon us, it was easy to forget that we weren't the soon-to-be victims in a horror movie.

"There," I said, pointing ahead, despite it being obvious. The lights shining at the end of the dark wooded path were pretty hard to miss.

Equally hard to miss, as the trail widened onto a large front lawn encircled by a gravel driveway, was the massive log cabin which stood out like a lit beacon against the dark forest around it. In truth, it was far less Little House on the Prairie and more Lex Luthor, looking more like one of those luxury manors they showed to rich yuppies looking to spend a million dollars *roughing it*. I didn't doubt Pop could have gotten that amount or more had he ever decided to sell, but he'd built all of this himself – his personal pet project over the years, something to do in his spare time after Ed's mother had passed away.

The effort and craftsmanship showed, as well as contrasting to what useless bags of skin Ed, Tom, and me were comparatively. So much so that Tom and I were actually forbidden from helping out whenever he was looking to add a new room or renovate something. Ed, being his stepson, wasn't so easy to banish, but he usually got relegated to bullshit tasks like running to the local hardware store for more nails.

On the flip side, I doubted Pop Vesser could've pulled off the voodoo I'd just done with my laptop.

Sure, he could build a livable shelter with his own two hands but, once the machine apocalypse finally hit, we'd see who was more useful when it came to keeping the Terminators away from Sarah Connor.

Motion-activated floodlights lit up the immediate space as Sally pulled in behind a rental car, Kara's probably, and cut the engine before tossing me the keys.

"Um, Bill?"

"Yes?" I replied, turning toward her.

"Just for curiosity's sake, does Ed's dad know about *him*." She hooked a thumb over her shoulder, almost poking our pseudo-canine companion in the eye ... one of them anyway.

"Glen?"

"Not specifically, but all of it. You know, vampires, witches, monsters?"

I opened my mouth, then quickly shut it as I realized my potential strategic blunder in bringing Glen along for the ride. "Um, not really."

"So all this time, you and your idiot roommates kept coming over here, asking for guns, and he'd just give them to you, no questions asked? What kind of nut is this guy?"

"He's not a nut. He was just concerned about his darling stepson, and said son's upstanding friends, living in the crime-ridden hellhole that is Brooklyn."

"Or, let me guess, it was a crime-ridden hellhole *after* you fuckheads got done explaining it."

I grinned sheepishly. "We may not have exactly dissuaded him of that notion."

She threw a glance back Glen's way before facing me again. "This ought to be worth the price of admission."

"It'll be fine. Hey, Glen, any chance you can ... I dunno, sound more like a real dog? Oh, and maybe pull your eyeballs back in a bit so they don't look like they're about to shoot across the room."

Glen tilted his head to the side, looking almost doglike in the process – a good start – then he sucked the two bugged out eyes back in a bit. The end result looked somewhat more natural, if with a bit of an uncanny valley vibe to it.

"I can't really see all that well like this," he said.

"That's fine. There isn't much to see, or at least I hope there isn't. Oh, and no talking."

"You got it, Freewill. I mean ... bark!"

"Close enough." I turned to Sally. "Put your sunglasses on. And if Pop says anything about Glen, just tell him he attacked some drug dealer and ate his stash before we could stop him."

Kara met us at the door.

"What are you doing here?" Then she looked down, saw Glen, and lowered her voice to a whisper. "And why did you bring that thing with you?"

"Why didn't you tell me that Pop was in trouble."

"I tried to, but I got distracted by ... oh, I don't know ... learning my brother was alive and on his period."

"Tom has his period?" Sally asked, a grin spreading across her face.

"Sally?" Kara leaned in, her eyes opening wide at the sight of her former coven master. "Is that you?"

"In the flesh. I know, I look great. Don't ask. It's a long story."

Kara turned my way. "Is there anything else you want to tell me?"

I shrugged. "It's kind of a running narrative. So is Pop okay?"

She stepped aside to let us into a large foyer that opened up into an expansive living room with high ceilings, picture windows, and a heavy wooden beam that ran the length of the room at the second story level.

"Swank," Sally remarked.

"I wouldn't mind keeping a summer bucket here," Glen said before I glared down at him. "I mean, bark!"

Oh yeah. No way this wasn't becoming a complete cluster fuck.

"I don't know," Kara said, ignoring Glen. "He seemed all flustered over the phone, but you know Jacob. Now that we're here, he's acting like it's no big deal. Says it's probably just some stoned hippies."

I turned to Sally. "Pop's not his actual..."

"I get the picture," she interrupted, an eyeroll visible behind her glasses.

"Tom ... I mean, *Sheila*, asked him to show her around. I think he, she, wanted to do a perimeter sweep."

"A perimeter sweep? That's ... actually pretty thoughtful of him to..."

Before I could finish, though, a familiar grizzled voice cried out from further in the house. "Kara! Come and tell your fool friend here that there's no reason to be tinkering around in my storage shed." A moment later, Jacob "Pop" Vesser stepped into the living room, headed our way.

He was in stark contrast to his stepson. Whereas Ed was thin and wiry, Pop had arms that bespoke of a life of hard work, with multiple tattoos peeking out from beneath his short sleeves. He was about my height, had graying mid-length hair, a full beard, and a bit of a gut, albeit one that served to make him appear more formidable than fat. Truth of the matter was he looked more like a reject from Orange County Choppers than a carpenter. Appearances notwithstanding, though, he'd always been close with Ed and his sister, treating them like they were his own.

The older man stopped when he saw us, his eyes instantly turning my way. "Billy boy! I didn't know you were heading up this way."

"Billy boy?" Sally asked.

"Don't start," I hissed at her before turning my full attention Pop's way. "Hey! Good to see you. I was ... in the area."

"Let me guess, you smelled the ham I got slow roasting in the oven and decided to pop on by."

"Um..."

"Just messing with you, boy," he said with a chuckle before turning serious. "You're welcome to stay for dinner, but I'm glad you're here, nevertheless. That girlfriend of yours is out back acting like she owns the place."

Girlfriend? Oh yeah. Sheila and I had still been together last time I'd spoken to him – not to mention her body hadn't been possessed by another soul. "Um, she's not really my girlfriend anymore."

"No? Then what are you doing all the way out here?" Before I could answer, he looked past me to where a certain four-legged friend stood. "And what in hell is wrong with your dog?"

Shit! I glanced down, prepared to give Pop a sob story about how Glen was a rescue with some incurable disease, but the words died in my throat as my gaze fell upon him.

The eyes in Glen's head were still retracted, looking almost normal – if one squinted hard enough. The problem was more his mouth ... and the eyeball-filled tendril of slime currently protruding from it.

Fuck me sideways with a rusty garden hoe.

"That is super gross," Kara remarked, not helping matters in the slightest.

I turned my back on Pop and lowered my voice as much as I could. "What the hell are you doing?"

"Sorry," Glen bubbled back. "But I couldn't see anything." Then, after a moment, he added, "I mean bark!"

Jesus fucking Christ!

TOY STORY

All of us turned slowly back toward Pop. I wasn't sure whether to expect shock, surprise, fear, or for him to run for one of the myriad gun cabinets scattered throughout the place.

Instead he folded his arms across his wide chest and let out a small sigh.

"I see the newspapers were right. The Strange Days are back, aren't they?" He stepped over to the dry bar on the far side of the living room, grabbed himself a bottle, and began to fill a glass with it. "I take it that's why I haven't heard from Edward lately. Scotch anyone?"

He was taking this far more calmly than he had any reason to.

After a moment, Sally stepped forward, taking her sunglasses off and revealing her freaky eyes – because why not at this point. "Single malt?"

Pop raised one eyebrow by the barest amount but simply replied, "Of course. We're not savages here."

"Then count me in."

Finally, I found my voice again. "Am I missing something or are you taking this way too well?"

Pop handed Sally her Scotch then turned to face me. "Do I strike you as stupid, son?"

"Um, no, sir."

"Good, because I ain't. I might not have a fancy degree, but I've been around a while and seen my fair share of weird. Or did you really think I bought those bullshit stories about gang violence and drug dealers gone wild?"

"You didn't?"

"First off, Eddie couldn't act his way out of a paper bag. Second, this ain't the nineteen-seventies anymore and you don't exactly live in Fort Apache, the Bronx. Oh, and him asking if I knew where to buy silver bullets wasn't all too subtle either. No offense, but you boys were either elbow deep in that mess or on so many pills you thought you were."

"Oh."

"And now with him up and disappearing, yet Kara telling me everyone's been acting like it's no big deal, well, excuse me for putting two and two together."

"When you put it that way..."

"All I want to know is whether my boy is okay."

I wasn't sure how to answer that, but fortunately Sally was there to step in while I had my foot buried in my mouth.

"We don't know where he is, but we have every reason to believe he's fine. The person who took him... Ed has unique abilities, which they kind of need."

"And you're sure of this?"

"As certain as we can be," I replied, trying to sound confident.

"Okay then. That'll have to be good enough for the moment. Just tell me you're doing everything you can to bring him home. I promised his Mom that I'd look after him and Maggie. Not sure how possible that is nowadays, things being all frigged up again, but least I can do is get your word on the matter."

"You have it, sir. We're doing everything we can to find him and bring him home safe."

"Good enough, I suppose. Now, about your girlfriend..."

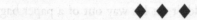

"You're serious?" he asked, leading the way outside to the storage shed – shed being a bit of a misnomer as the structure was the size of a two car garage, built every bit as well as the house. "You're telling me that ain't your girlfriend, but that other friend of yours, the dead one, stuck inside her body?"

It was just the two of us – Kara, Sally and Glen having stayed inside at Pop's insistence.

"As serious as I can be when it comes to Tom."

"Does Kara know?"

"She does now."

"That's good. Must be a load off her conscience. What about that girl Tommy was seeing?"

"Oh, trust me. She's aware."

He stopped in the gloom and fixed his flashlight on my face. "Exactly how deep into this are you boys? And don't lie to me. I was minding my tongue back there in front of the ladies, but I have a nose for smelling bullshit."

It was tempting to tell him that there was no need to mind his tongue in front of Sally, as being a mass murderer had desensitized her to potty language, but I figured that could wait for now. Instead, I decided to lay out all my marbles. He'd already figured out the bulk of things anyway. And besides, it wasn't like the vampire nation was still around to bitch me out for these things.

"This deep," I replied, extending my fangs and causing my eyes to turn black.

"Vampire, eh?"

"Yes, sir."

"You drink blood?"

"Yep."

"Turn into a bat?"

"Nope."

"Got a weasely fella back home named Renfield who eats cockroaches?"

"I guess you could say that was Tom's job. He used to work in finance after all."

"How many people you killed?"

Oh crap. "Um, directly or indirectly?"

Pop gave a grunt then started walking again. "Maybe some questions are best left unanswered."

"Might be for the best."

"That thing back there in the house. That ain't no dog, is it?"

"Glen? No. Definitely not."

"Good," he replied. "I've had to put down dogs that looked a lot healthier than he does. Didn't fancy having to take him out behind the shed with my shotgun."

"I appreciate that. Speaking of the shed, you sure Tom's still in there?"

"Tom, Tammy, or whatever the hell he calls himself. But yeah. Couldn't get him out of there. That's why I came back to the house looking for Kara."

"And exactly what's in there that's got his attention, if I might be so bold to ask?"

We stepped through the door of the *shed*. The lights were on, but Tom was nowhere to be seen – not exactly a major deal as the place seemed to house several rooms. However, I could definitely hear something – or someone – moving around further inside.

Pop had explained to me that the 'shed' had originally been built as a guest cabin. After Ed's mom passed away, though, he repurposed it, setting aside space in it for stuff that used to belong to Ed and his sister from when they were kids.

It didn't take me much longer than a nanosecond to guess what might've caught Tom's attention.

Following my ears, I turned a corner and found my roommate happily rooting through boxes that didn't belong to him. I paused for a moment, the image before me still strange. It was Sheila's body, but the insane gleam in her eye firmly belonged to my best friend.

I cleared my throat, so as to get his attention.

Surprise shone on his face at seeing me, for a moment anyway, before he got caught up in his own personal mania again. "Oh, hey, Bill. You gotta check this shit out." He turned and held out an action figure. "Ed used to play with fucking Captain Planet. Can you believe that? How much you want to bet his favorite was that Ma-Ti fucker?"

"What exactly are you doing?"

"I was kinda wondering the same thing myself, *Tommy boy*?" Pop said, stepping up beside me.

"Hey, Mr. V," Tom replied, seemingly unconcerned to hear his secret was out. "I guess Bill filled you in."

"That he did and..."

"Holy shit! He has the original Ninja Turtles." He glanced our way, then quickly added, "Not that they're worth anything. In fact, everything here is just taking up space. How about I take it all off your hands for, say, twenty bucks?"

"This isn't fucking eBay, dickhead."

"Shhh," he replied. "Adults are negotiating here."

"No, we ain't," Pop said. "All of that stuff belongs to Eddie."

"I'm well aware but, being one of his dear friends, I also know deep in his heart he'd want me to give them a good home."

I stepped forward. "I thought you were supposed to be sweeping the perimeter."

"I did. There's a lot of trees. They didn't look threatening."

"But this place did?"

Tom stopped rummaging through the boxes and turned to me, a pseudo-serious look on his face that said I was about to be fed a double-decker bullshit sandwich. "Am I the only one here who's seen *Child's Play*? I'm simply ruling out one possible cause."

"Cause? Of what?" I turned Pop's way. "Sorry, didn't mean to get caught up in his stupidity, but what's going on? I kind of only heard half the story."

Pop glanced away, looking embarrassed. "It's nothing more than me being a foolish old man, is all. I even told Kara as much."

"Yeah, but it worried her enough to come out here."

"I was ... exaggerating, that's all. Must've been in a mood. Been seeing all that stuff on the news and spooked myself, that's all. Believe it or not, even an old codger like me can get the heebie-jeebies when he's all alone. Probably nothing more than a bunch of hippy freaks too stupid to know when they're trespassing."

One didn't need vampire hearing to realize his tone had changed. Where before he'd been gruff and direct, now I could sense discomfort and ... maybe even a little fear in his voice.

"See, Bill? All's well," Tom said, continuing to violate Ed's childhood.

Okay, maybe one *did* need vampire hearing to notice those things, or at least basic human empathy.

"Let's back up a bit," I replied to Pop. "You said hippy freaks. What exactly do you mean by that?"

"Like I said, boy, it's probably nothing."

"Humor me ... please. It's just us. We don't have to tell the others."

He let out a sound of disgust after a moment or two. "Fine. But only if you promise me you'll do everything to find my Eddie."

"I already told you I would. I meant it, too."

"I know, but sometimes an old bastard needs to hear it said twice."

He stepped away, back toward the entrance, looking out one of the windows to the dark woods beyond. Maybe it helped him to think, or maybe it was just easier for him to open up when there was no eye-contact. Either way, I waited for him.

"It started maybe a week and a half back." He paused, then added, "No, I guess it goes back a bit further. Maybe three weeks in total, right around the time the news folk were yammering about weirdness over in the city. Bunch of cock suckers, if you ask me. Stuff happens in the sticks, they could give a shit less. But anything happens over in Philly, and they can't jam their noses up its ass fast enough. Anyway, that's neither here nor there. What matters is what I heard."

"What you heard?"

"Yep. Might be unrelated to the stuff that came after, but I'll mention it all the same. I was sitting out back enjoying a smoke when it was like all hell broke loose. We're talking animals hollering like crazy, snarls, growls, all of it. Went on til way past midnight. Never saw anything, mind you, but it was like every beast out there in the woods went crazy."

Three weeks. That coincided with what happened down below in the Source chamber. Was it possible that the animals sensed things changing? "Huh. And after that?"

"Nothing," he replied. "Was quiet for a while after that. Figured maybe it was a fluke, or something had gotten into the water."

"But you heard it again?"

"Nope. Like I said, I'm just mentioning that first bit, but what happened after was nothing like it."

I turned toward where Tom was fiddling with an old *Bop It!* toy. "Are you listening to this?"

"Not really."

Goddamn, as far as Icons went, he was useless. I turned my attention back toward Pop. "Go on."

"I was out grabbing some oregano from my garden." He glanced back at me, a wry grin on his face. "I know, a fella like me with a spice garden, but there ain't no seasoning as good as that which you grow yourself. But that's beside the fact. I was out there when the forest suddenly got real quiet, you know like when a predator is near. Thought it might be a bobcat. We get them from time to time. Then I heard a few branches break, like something was walking around. I shined my lamp out into the trees. Didn't see nothing, but I swear I could feel myself being watched. Not ashamed to say I slept with a loaded rifle in arm's reach that night."

A chill began to creep up from the base of my spine. I knew all too well the feeling of being watched in the woods. What came afterward, though, was usually much worse, especially since it often came attached to fists the size of bowling balls.

Turd is dead and the Feet are gone, I told myself, suddenly wishing I'd stayed in Brooklyn.

"Whatever was out there, it came back the next night ... and it brought friends. I could hear them out there circling the place, a bit closer, but not close enough for me to catch a glimpse of. I ain't no scaredy cat, but after that I started making it a habit to finish my chores before the sun went down. And if I did feel the need to sit out on my porch, believe me when I say I had a box of .30-06 cartridges next to me the entire time."

Smart, although I personally would've opted for bazooka shells myself. Rather than say that, though, I replied, "Is that all?"

Pop actually laughed at that. "If that were all, boy, we wouldn't be having this conversation. Not the first time I been spooked out here. Catch even the bravest man in the right mood and he'll jump at his own shadow. No. That's not all. Could've been my ears playing tricks on me, but every night it seemed they got a little bit closer, yet I never saw a thing. Would've chalked it all up to my imagination, as a matter of fact, had they not started speaking to me."

Oh fuck. I could feel my knees beginning to involuntarily shake. "Speaking to you?"

"Oh yeah. Plain as day, even if I never could see the mouths making the words."

"And ... um ... one of those words didn't happen to be T'lunta by chance?"

He turned back toward me, a look of confusion on his face. "Say what?"

"Never mind. What did they say to you?"

"They said they knew who I was. But that wasn't the thing that turned my nuts to jelly, pardon my saying such. No. It was what they kept saying after that. Whispers from the woods, coming from a dozen places all at once, all saying the same thing."

"And that was?"

"Bring us the progenitor."

The Progenitor ... oh shit!

"Whatever the hell that means."

I stepped up behind him, mindful of the darkness beyond the window and the things that could be lurking in the trees beyond.

"The good news is you're not crazy."

"Oh?" he replied.

"Yep. But the bad news is I think we really need to get our asses back to the house and figure out just how many guns you own."

THE NAKED FOREST

Thankfully, Tom's control over his aura was shitty enough that I was able to grab him and drag him out without even singeing my fingers. Sadly, the downside was that didn't bode well for us in case whatever was out there decided to get nasty.

"Please tell me you brought your sword," I said as we headed back to the main house. My eyes easily cut through the darkness, but that didn't mean much considering we were surrounded by trees and vegetation on all sides. There could've been a whole army of Feet or god knows what else standing out there, and I wouldn't have seen shit.

"No. Why would I have?"

"Oh, I don't know. It's not like you came out here at the bequest of someone who was freaked out about things in the woods ... oh, wait. You did!"

"You don't have to be a dick about it."

Pop glanced back as he led the way. "Mind telling me what's scary enough to spook a vampire? And don't go pretending you're not worried. You're about as good an actor as my Eddie."

So much for that semester I spent with the NJIT drama society. "Believe me, there are lots of things that can scare a vampire ... really bad things."

"I was afraid of that. Care to be more specific?"

"Wish I could be. All I know is that something out there asking for the Progenitor is not a good thing."

"Why's that?"

I stopped as we reached the expansive back porch of his home. "Because they're talking about Ed."

"Wait. You're telling me Eddie is this progenitor person they're..."

"Yes. It's a long story, way too long to get into now, but there's some people out there who refer to him that way. And if whatever is out there is asking you about him, that means they know who you are and what your relation to him is. And, no, I have no idea what that means other than there is absolutely no way it can be a good thing."

That was probably an understatement. As of the last time I'd seen them, Ed and Gan were the only two neo-vamps left, with Ed being the only one who could procreate, or at least pass it on to others. That said, I had every reason to believe Gan was gleefully forcing him to make more for her. After all, that seemed the sort of batshit thing she'd do. But then who was out here looking for him? Had some of her newbie neos escaped and then fled to the backwoods of Pennsylvania for no other reason than to pester Ed's stepdad?

That seemed a stretch even for the weird shit I normally dealt with. So that likely meant something else was out here. That's what made it terrifying, dealing with an unknown – mostly because it seemed every unknown I came across was worse than the last. Not helping was that the woods were traditionally a bad place for vamps to be. Though there was no indication the Feet had returned, they'd had allies aplenty back in the day, some of whom might have a vested interest in making sure that Ed didn't live long enough to sire a new race of enemies for them.

True, Ed wasn't with us now. But it seemed a fool's errand to hope they'd simply take no for an answer, not when their schedules were free enough to allow for nightly harassment of an old man minding his own business.

Yeah. No way was this good news.

We stepped into the house, thankfully finding the three companions we'd left behind doing little more than milling about.

"Remember that time I threw Bill out my office window and he almost hit you on the way down?" Sally asked with a laugh as we entered the room.

"I would have liked to have seen that," Glen replied from his dog suit.

"Not the Freewill's finest hour, right Bill?" She turned toward us, no doubt noticing we weren't in a laughing mood. "What happened?"

"Nothing yet," I replied. "But that doesn't mean it's not going to."

I'd like to say I brought all three stragglers up to speed, but Sally was the only one among them who really counted, at least in a situation like this. Kara was too far removed from the situation these days and Glen – well, it was hard to take him seriously looking like a zombie Irish Setter. Sally, on the other hand, had experience dealing with crises, far more than me as a matter of fact.

That done, I put it up for a vote. "So what do you guys think? We hop in the cars and get the hell out of here or what?"

"You want me to abandon my home?" Pop asked, sounding like this was a battle he was more than willing to take up.

"Think of it more like an extended vacation."

"Think of it more like you being a pussy," Tom replied.

I shot him a glare, but then Sally said, "Much as I'm loathe to agree with you on anything, no matter what body you're wearing, you're right."

Tom grinned at me. "Told you you're a pussy."

"Not that, idiot. But the truth is we don't know what's out there. For all we know, it might be nothing more than a couple of drugged up jackasses like Jacob said." I opened my mouth, but she quickly talked over me. "I don't think it is, not with what they're saying, but we won't be any better off if we leave here without knowing. If we don't put a face to these voices, they could find him again and he'd never know it."

"So, you want us to take a stand ... out here in the woods?"

"I know what you're thinking, Bill, and if it turns out you're right, believe me I'll be the first behind the wheel pulling out of here, whether or not any of you are with me. But I think we need to, at the very least, consider this a fact-finding mission first."

"If he's right about what?" Pop asked.

Tom, subtle as always, was happy to spill those beans. "I don't suppose you've had any Bigfoot sightings lately?"

"Better than the Jahabich," Kara commented.

"Don't even joke about them," I told her.

"Bigfoot?"

"Enough!" Sally snapped. "Let's stow the speculation for now." She inclined her head toward Pop. "How long do we have? I mean, before the voices usually start in with their shit."

Pop glanced over at the large grandfather clock on the side of the room. "Hard to say. Can't exactly set my watch by them, but if I had to guess, maybe an hour or less."

"We can work with that. The plan is simple enough." She gestured toward him and Kara. "You two stay inside. The rest of us will fan out, try to get a bead on whatever's out there. If it's nothing, we'll scare them off ... maybe break a few bones to teach them a lesson." I opened my eyes wide at that. "Just being realistic. If it's more than nothing, then we can regroup and consider our options."

"I'm not sitting in here, missy, while you go out there and risk your neck," Pop protested. "This is my home."

"Chivalry is not dead," Sally replied with a grin.

Much as I wanted her out there on the front lines, I realized Pop had a point, although perhaps not for the same reasons. "He's right. We don't know the extent of ... well, anything you can do."

"Do?" Pop asked.

"Yeah, those eyes and green hair aren't merely a fashion statement."

"Oh. Figured that was just the look these days. Didn't take you for ... anything else."

Sally smiled. "You have no idea."

"Yeah, but I do," I replied, cutting in. "I'm serious. We don't know anything about your durability or healing or much else for that matter, other than you occasionally explode."

"Is that code for something or do you mean..."

I turned to Pop. "Believe me when I say that once you get indoctrinated to the strange, it only gets weirder."

"So it would seem. Regardless, I'm not hiding in here like some scared rabbit. This is my land, my home. And before any of you ask, yes I'm willing to die defending it. But I'm hoping it doesn't come to that. So far, these voices in the woods, they've been frightening yes, but they haven't actually done anything threatening. I'm hoping maybe between us all we can scare them off without any bloodshed."

Ah, the ignorance of those who were new to the program. Sadly, for all involved, the orientation could be a real killer.

Pop might not have known much about the supernatural, but he sure as shit knew guns. More importantly, he was an avid believer in home protection. Going through his wares was like taking a shopping spree right before invading a third world nation. Though I myself wasn't really a gun fan, or much of a shot for that matter, I wasn't about to argue right then and there.

It was semi-automatic shotguns for both me and Kara. High capacity and easy enough to use. They pretty much destroyed anything in front of them, which I could dig, especially if whatever was in front of me was eight feet tall and covered in shit-stained fur.

Pop himself took a high-powered hunting rifle. As for Sally, her eyes lit up when she saw Pop's collection of handguns, deciding on an oversized revolver that looked like it was designed for random elephant encounters.

"That's a Taurus Raging Bull," Pop said, upon seeing her heft it. "That there will take down a water buffalo but, I'm warning you, it kicks like a mule. No offense, little lady, but are you sure you don't want something a bit more ... manageable?"

"Offense taken," Sally replied, opening up a box of cartridges that looked big enough to sink a battleship. "Don't worry about me. Believe me when I say bad things can come in small packages."

And if that didn't sum her up, I didn't know what did.

Tom was the only one we didn't arm, at least the only humanoid, being that none of us trusted him to not shoot himself or one of us by mistake. But that was fine. He wasn't stationed on the so-called front lines anyway.

The plan we eventually agreed upon called for him and Kara to hang back inside. In theory, he was to protect her if anything went wrong but, being that his powers worked like shit and she had the gun, the unspoken thought was that it was kind of the other way around.

I wanted Glen to stay behind, too, but he insisted on helping out. I wasn't sure what he could do, but it's not like his dog body could get messed up much worse. Besides, if there was anyone who would make a good lookout, I guess it was a little blob filled with eyeballs.

That said, I wanted to play this smart. Sally and I were ostensibly the heavy hitters of the group, so I insisted we take the back of the house facing the woods – where the majority of the *sightings* seemed to occur. Though he wasn't happy about it, Pop agreed to take watch out front with Glen.

A pair of high-powered walkie talkies from his shed ensured we could keep in touch as we stepped outside and began our watch.

"Anything going on back there? Over."

"All's quiet on our end," Sally replied. "Nothing out here but..."

I interrupted her with a squeal of panic as a beetle big enough to land on an aircraft carrier parked itself on my arm."

"*What was that?*"

"Our resident vampire losing his shit over a bug. Over."

"Thanks for that," I groused, checking to make sure there were no more on me.

"Anytime."

"How does anyone live out here with these freaking insects? I swear, city roaches look downright adorable next to these fucking things."

"You are such a wuss," she said, clipping the walkie to her waist.

"I don't understand why they're bothering me and not you. You're the one with the freaky glowing eyes."

"Don't be jealous."

We'd been standing out back in the darkness for maybe forty minutes. Though Pop had floodlights surrounding his property, enough to light up the immediate area like it was the middle of the day, we'd turned them off soon after coming outside.

As it turned out, Sally's strange eyes weren't just for show. Though she said it was different from her vampire days, she'd apparently gained some sort of night vision in the deal. Different was one word for it. I'd nearly jumped out of my skin upon stepping out into the darkness and seeing her eyes light up like a glow in the dark kid's toy.

Freaky as it was, though, it allowed us to both keep watch without any flashlights or other aids that were probably of limited use out here with all the fucking trees.

I'd love to say the ability to see in the dark meant I was calm, cool, and collected as we maintained our vigil, but fuck that noise. I swear, it was like every bug, bird, and animal in the vicinity was walking around, eating, screwing ... or dive bombing me from above. I kept spinning toward sounds in the woods – weapon raised – certain something was coming for us, only to realize it was nothing more than a deer taking a shit or something equally benign.

"Relax, Bill," Sally said, apparently growing tired of my twitchiness. "You're wound up so tight you're liable to shoot yourself, or shoot me, which will make you wish you actually shot yourself."

"Hard to relax in this place."

"I understand. Believe me, I do. Listen, I know this might be counterintuitive to a pussy like you, but all of those sounds are a good thing. So long as everything out there is going about its business, it means nothing strange is going on."

"Did you hear that on Animal Planet?"

"No. I heard about it by not being a fucking dumbass."

"Touché." I glanced at the dark woods, seeing a whole lot of nothing. Rather than complain about the bugs some more, though, I decided to circle back to the whole reason Sally was here to begin with and not relaxing at home. "So, how are you holding up?"

"Better than you, obviously."

I pointed a finger at her forehead. "I meant, how are you feeling up here?"

"A lot better than your nuts are going to be feeling if you don't get that finger out of my face." Needless to say, I did. "Thank you. No offense, but I don't know where you've been."

"Actually..."

"And I don't want to know. Although, speaking of which, have you heard anything from Christy lately?"

"Way to change the subject."

"I'm good that way. Not to mention, I think you've psychoanalyzed me enough for one day. I appreciate it, don't get me wrong. But enough."

I held up my free hand in supplication. "Okay, fine. You win."

"As it should be. So, you hear anything from her, or is she back to giving you the cold shoulder?"

"Hold on." I pulled my phone out and checked it, momentarily blinding myself with the glow from the screen. "Nope. All's quiet."

"You did tell her we were coming out here, right?"

"Um ... well, I did email her earlier."

"Nothing says romance like an email."

"It's not that," I replied. "It's just, I'm trying not to smother her. A lot has changed in the last few weeks. She's got her powers again. Same with Tina, except tenfold."

"Tom's back," she added.

"Yes, he is. And just in time for me to once again be lacking in the pulse department."

"Do you really think that matters to her?"

I let the question hang between us for a moment. "I'm not sure it doesn't matter to *me*."

"Oh, so you're only into immortal chicks now?"

"It's not that. It's more... I'm not sure I'm..."

"Good enough for her?" Sally opined, finishing the sentence for me. "Especially now that she has a choice between you two chucklefucks and hot Harry Potter?"

"You really do suck at pep talks, you know."

"So I hear," she replied with a grin, somehow made a wee bit sinister by her glowing eyes. "But the truth of the matter is, you're right. You're not good enough for her."

"You know, you really missed your calling as a therapist."

"Just being realistic here. Christy's a hell of a catch. She's smart and sexy..."

"Let me guess. She reminds you of yourself?"

"I didn't say she was *that* smart and sexy. But she's also a magical prodigy, one who's survived things that would break a normal person. You don't find someone like that standing on every street corner."

"You would know all about street corners."

Rather than point her hand cannon at me, Sally actually laughed. "There's the Bill I remember. Seems so long ago, doesn't it?"

"Yeah, but at the same time it's like it was yesterday."

"True. But back to what I was saying. Christy *is* too good for you. But, she was also too good for Tom – way too good if we're being honest here. Almost infinitely too good, actually. I swear, that moron must have a whole platoon of guardian angels watching his back, or maybe guardian pimps."

"Is there a point to all of this?"

"What? Oh yeah. The reality is Christy's a hell of a catch for anyone. She's almost a force of nature. That said, she's also an adult, one who can make her own decisions. And apparently those decisions include dating far below her weight class."

"Not following."

"What I'm saying, dumbass, is stop beating yourself up. Christy is with you because of who you are, in fact, despite who you are. Just the same way she almost married the meathead in there, even though he has his act together about as well as a meth addict standing atop a mountain of free drugs. Give the girl some credit. She knows who you are, what you are, and yet she still hasn't run away screaming. Offhand, I'd say that bodes well for you."

"But everything..."

"Yes, everything is fucked up now. Not going to argue with you there. And I won't lie and say it won't be enough to possibly screw things up for you guys. In fact, it probably will. But what I am saying is that, whatever happens, it won't necessarily be because you don't measure up."

Huh. In a roundabout way that was actually really nice of her to say – in a sense. Thing is, though, it's not like she was saying anything my own subconscious hadn't been screaming at me. If anything, her conclusions were far kinder than whatever the person in the mirror was saying back to me every morning. In fact, her words were almost enough to make me consider that...

There came the sound of a branch cracking from somewhere out in the woods, nothing I hadn't heard a dozen times in the last hour. However, it was soon followed by another and then several more.

"So, what do you think about what I just said?" Sally asked.

"What I think," I replied, as all the sounds of the forest suddenly seemed to grow quiet at once, "is we should get our asses ready, because company's about to arrive."

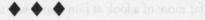

"Put your sunglasses on," I whispered.

Sally wasn't stupid. She put them on, covering the freaky ass glow, then she unclipped the walkie and lifted it to her lips.

"We have possible contact. Stay alert. We're not alone out here. Over."

She once again secured the radio, freeing up both hands for the massive revolver she was packing. Small girl, big gun. Why hadn't anyone made that into a movie yet, or maybe a porno?

I was armed, too, but opted to keep my gun at my side, for now.

Whoever had been visiting Pop in days past probably was more than aware he was packing, but that hadn't scared them off. Nevertheless, I didn't want to appear overly aggressive until I was given reason to.

Scanning the surrounding tree line, I began to see shapes moving around in the gloom of the woods – accompanied by the sound of leaves crunching underfoot.

That alone, oddly enough, made me feel a bit better. One main advantage the Feet had over us – besides being big as trucks – had been their unearthly stealth. You'd be all alone one second, then your head would be crushed the next and you'd never see it coming. Comparatively speaking, whoever was out there now, though, was moving with all the grace of a herd of hippos.

"Oh, yeah, this isn't fucked up at all," Sally said from my side.

I turned my head, wondering what she was talking about, and saw that at least one of the nighttime intruders had gotten bold enough to step almost to the tree line, giving me far more of a look at him than I wanted.

It was a guy, just a regular looking guy – a bit below average height, thinning hair, slightly overweight. In fact, the only thing that stuck out about him was that he was bare-assed naked.

The fuck?

"That stoned hippies theory is starting to sound more and more likely."

"Tell me about it," I replied, as I caught sight of someone else, and then another – all similarly clothing impaired.

I wasn't sure what had changed. Perhaps it was the fact that Sally and I were the ones standing out here and not the person they normally harassed, but either way it seemed these naked weirdos were picking tonight to be bold.

And no, it wasn't to our benefit. The fantasy of nude beaches was a haven of beautiful flesh and perky boobs. Too bad most people weren't swimsuit models. If anything, the ones I could make out were far closer to me than Sally on the hotness scale.

On the upside, at least I didn't have to worry about any accidental boners making these negotiations weird.

"Nice night for a walk," I called out, hoping maybe a bit of pop culture could break the ice.

"You're neither Jacob nor the Progenitor," the first of the nudists said. Huh. Guess he wasn't a Schwarzenegger fan. His loss.

"Sorry about that. The Progenitor couldn't make it. He sends his apologies, asked if we could come in his stead to see what this shit was about. Listen, no offense, but I've seen some pretty big mosquitos flying around out here tonight. I don't know about you, but I sure as hell wouldn't want to be walking around with my dick flapping in the wind."

"Good job, Bill. That ought to do it," Sally remarked from beside me, before raising her voice. "What do you want with the Progenitor?"

"He's the herald of the new race," another voice replied, this one a scrawny middle-aged lady.

"Yeah, and?" I prodded.

"And we want him, asshole!" a third person, another male, replied from somewhere behind the tree line. At least this guy was direct.

"What for? So he can bite you all in the ass?"

"No, fuck face," the same voice replied. The owner stepped forward, revealing himself to be a big old bear of a man, thick with muscle and fat – the kind who wouldn't have looked out of place eating at a truck stop, assuming he was wearing pants. "We want to end him."

Oh crap.

"We're finally free now. Ain't we?" he cried out, eliciting a chorus of "Hell yeah!" and other affirmations from all around us – at least a dozen voices, maybe more.

This was becoming less and less promising by the moment.

"And we plan to stay that way, don't we?"

Another round of agreement followed.

"We'll never go back to the way it was!"

I glanced sidelong at Sally, not wanting to take my full attention off the crazed nudist mob. "Any idea what the fuck they're talking about?"

She shook her head. "My vote's still on them being stoned outta their gourds."

"Good point. Think maybe they got their hands on some bad shrooms?"

"No idea, but they're about to get their hands on some hot lead." She took a step forward, gun raised.

So much for me playing good cop. It was time for the bad cop to flash her badge.

"Listen up, assholes," she cried. "I don't know what you dickheads want and I don't care. The only thing I give a shit about is that you're trespassing and pissing me off. So I suggest you go back to whatever bar you stumbled out of, put on a pair of sweatpants, and stay the fuck away from here." She pulled back the hammer on the massive gun. "Or else I can guarantee something bad is going to happen."

Sadly, something bad *did* happen, but not in the way any of us were expecting.

As Sally finished up her not-so-idle threat, her body began to glow – bluish white light suffusing her entire form. At first, I was afraid she was about to blow again, something that wouldn't have boded well for either the folks in the woods or the house behind us. However, she hadn't lit up at all during her previous episodes, especially not anything like this. More important was the fact that she was staring down at herself, as if equally surprised at what she was seeing.

The bracelet on her wrist let out a single beep.

In that same second, the glow around her intensified, like she was standing in the middle of a spotlight, and then it simply winked out – revealing nothing but emptiness where she'd stood. There was no trace of Sally left, as if her presence here all along had been nothing more than a figment of my imagination.

The fuck?!

Silence descended in the backyard of Jacob Vesser's home. I expected triumph or perhaps manic glee to show on the faces of the naked weirdos surrounding me, but instead their expressions mirrored the shock on my own.

No. That couldn't be right. I was simply projecting. These bare-assed fuckheads were obviously to blame. I didn't know how, but they'd somehow lashed out at Sally in retaliation. Lashed out and killed her...

She's not dead. Stop for a moment and think about it.

The voice inside my head gave me pause, even as I'd begun to raise my weapon.

It forced me to take stock of the situation, push back the outrage that was demanding I open fire on these fuckers for what they'd done.

Fine. There'd been a flash of light and then she was gone – not dissimilar to how a vamp might die and turn to ... except that it wasn't the same at all. Sally wasn't a vampire, at least not anymore. We didn't know what she was. But even if she had been, there'd been no heat, no combustion. And there certainly wasn't any pile of dust where she'd been standing. Hell, there wasn't anything there at all. It was like she'd simply ... vanished.

Son of a...

And that's when it hit me. This wasn't a disintegration. I'd seen this exact same thing happen many times. It was like Magi teleportation, or sending as Christy insisted on calling it. Of course, Sally wasn't a Magi either, but who was to say what her new powers might or might not include?

Where she'd gone was a whole other story, though. No idea on that one. She could've zapped across the yard or to the freaking moon for all I knew. However, I wasn't exactly in a position to figure that out right then, being that suddenly I was all alone against a small horde of naked maniacs.

"What the fuck was that?" the mouthy nudist cried.

And it seemed the momentary ceasefire was over. "Um ... you tell me," I cried out.

"What the hell is going on back there?"

"Bark!"

I glanced over my shoulder to find both Pop and Glen making their way around the side of the house. So much for waiting for our signal – not that I could've given one if I wanted to, as Sally still had the freaking walkie.

Pop flashed the beam of his Maglite past me and toward the trees, alighting upon the truck driver looking guy who so far seemed to be the leader of this group.

"Is that you, Hobart?"

"Vesser," the man replied in greeting, not looking happy to have his identity revealed.

"Where the hell are your pants, man?"

A reasonable question, under far more reasonable circumstances.

"I'm sorry you had to see my face, Jacob."

"Stay back," I warned Pop as the people in the tree line began to step forward, their aggressive stance suggesting they weren't stopping by for a neighborhood barbecue.

"Where's Mistress..."

"No time for that, Glen, watch him. As for you fuckers..." It was time for the ace up my sleeve. A little something to show these inbred hillbillies I wasn't playing. As I turned back toward them, I darkened my eyes and extended my fangs. "Back the fuck off. Last warning!"

The beam of Pop's flashlight fell upon my face in the same second. Couldn't have timed it better had we planned it.

If the crazed nudists had been surprised by Sally's vanishing act, that was nothing compared to the look on their faces upon seeing me.

Eyes opened wide as they stopped dead in their tracks. Oh yeah, this was more like it.

"It ain't possible," Naked Truck-driver said. "There ain't none of you left."

I felt safe in assuming he wasn't talking about a guy wearing glasses. So, these dipshits were up on who the Progenitor was, but hadn't gotten the memo about regular vamps being back, too. Guess word traveled slow out here in the boonies.

Still, the fact that they knew about vampires at all was a bit worrying.

Truth of the matter was, young vamps like me were tough but we weren't invincible, and there were more than enough of these yahoos to make my night even worse than it already was.

Fortunately, I remembered the lessons of my early days with Village Coven. Back then, Sally had told me that attitude was half of every battle, sometimes more so. I hadn't believed her until I'd actually tried it myself – adopting the persona of Dr. Death and doing my best to act the part.

The results had likely saved my life, all thanks to her.

Time to see if this was one piece of bullshit that hadn't lost its fragrance. "You have no idea how wrong you are, Bubba. If you know about vampires then maybe you've heard of the Freewill. And if you haven't, then please allow me to introduce myself." I extended the claws on my free hand to add a bit of extra zing to the threat.

Oh yeah, still got it.

Those I could see all turned their attention toward Large Marge there, the one Pop had identified as Hobart. Fitting. He looked like a Hobart.

Hobart, for his part, started to back away. *Yes!*

However, rather than run off like a whipped dog, he said, "You and your top coven ain't never gonna lord over us again. I swear it!"

What the?

Before I could say anything to that, he turned, cupped his hands over his mouth, and cried out, "Myra! Get over here!"

Myra?

I figured I'd give him the benefit of the doubt and assume Myra was a Doberman Pinscher or maybe a German Shepherd. At least that would be reasonable. The alternative was that he'd called for some chick to come out here and face me instead. I mean, don't get me wrong, I didn't consider myself a sexist, but that seemed to be a serious pussy move on his part.

Or at least it did until I saw the glow emanating from the forest.

"What in hell?" Pop said.

"You can do it, Freewill," Glen cried out. "I mean ... bark!"

Oh, for fuck's sake.

The stupidity behind me, however, was not my concern as the glow intensified, almost as if ... it were heading this way.

Sure enough, a few moments later the bushes a couple of yards away parted to reveal a woman. So much for Hobart showing some dignity here. I mean, yeah, this was definitely better than some slobbering Grendel's mother-like monster named Myra, but still.

Unlike her beer-gut afflicted brethren, she was in good shape, not naked, and was obviously glowing. She had long red hair and wore a flowing white robe – similar to ones I'd seen before. Needless to say, if her being lit up like a Christmas tree wasn't a dead giveaway, her attire was.

"Stay back," I told my companions. "She's a Magi." Duh! That probably wasn't particularly useful for Pop. "Um, they're dangerous."

I hadn't been expecting an appearance by Ginny Weasley, but it wasn't like I hadn't tangled with witches before. If I could close the distance between us without getting blasted, I could take her out no problem – hopefully.

The witch locked eyes with me as she stepped to the edge of the tree line. I could read arrogance in her gaze as well as recognition. Even if she didn't know my face, she'd likely heard of the Freewill. She pursed her lips, then opened her mouth, no doubt to say something obnoxiously arrogant about how I was a filthy beast, beneath her attention, blah blah blah.

"Fuck him up good, boys!"

Okay. That was unexpected. Instead of austere formality, like I'd come to expect from the Magi, I'd gotten their lot lizard cousin instead. Ah, rural Pennsylvania, never a dull place to be.

I tensed up as her crew, still standing among the trees, began to whoop and holler. I guess in the valley of the naked, the person with one clean set of britches was queen.

Myra Sixpack, no doubt spurred on by their cheers, began to glow brighter as I readied myself to move – fully expecting a bolt of either red or green death to come flying my way any second.

Instead, though, the glow of magic abruptly changed to purple as a dome of energy formed around her. So much for clubbing this witch like a ginger baby seal and being done with it. Still, it wasn't like I'd never seen this trick...

Before I could finish that thought, Myra raised her hands and a bolt of yellowish power erupted from the top of the dome. It flew up into the space above us to a height of about fifty feet.

The fuck? What next? Was she going to try selling me fireworks out of the back of her pickup?

I was about to tell her I wasn't impressed by the light show, when the energy above us coalesced into a glowing sphere, taking on shape and form until it resembled...

Huh. That kinda looks like a full moon.

Okay, this was one stupid-ass mage. Seriously? An illusion of the moon was even more useless than conjuring a fake sun. I let out a laugh at the dumbassery on display.

However, the sound of my voice was almost immediately drowned out by an angry snarl which rose up from nearby.

Another joined it, and then more. Moments later, the air was filled with them.

I turned and caught sight of Hobart, busy foaming at the mouth. He still looked like an out of shape redneck, but was now an out of shape redneck with red eyes, jagged sharp teeth, and a coat of black fur that was rapidly expanding to cover his naked ass.

He threw back his head and howled at the illusion of the moon, an act echoed by all those around him as they changed from man to beast.

Oh, you have got to be fucking kidding me.

WEREWOLF 359

I desperately hoped that Sally was alive and well, wherever she was ... because I had every intention of kicking her ass when next I saw her.

One of the first things she'd told me upon my awakening as a vampire was that werewolves didn't exist. They were a myth, nothing more. Bigfoot was real, witches were real. Hell, even shapeshifting rock monsters were real. But werewolves? Nope, just a myth created by cavemen after smoking too much peyote.

Tell that to these guys, though. Apparently, these fuckers hadn't gotten the memo that they were nothing more than the product of drugs and Hollywood special effects.

"Freewill?"

"Stow it, Glen," I said, wide eyed. "Still processing this myself."

I remembered seeing *The Howling* years back and being impressed – and not just because of that scene where two people turn into monsters while fucking each other's brains out, although, in all fairness that part may have spurred a few wank fantasies over the years. The thing that stood out most for me had been the cool transformation of man to wolf beast.

Interestingly enough, Hollywood hadn't gotten it entirely wrong. The spectacle playing out before me looked painful and sounded disgusting as fuck, as a chorus of crackling bones and rippling flesh filled the air.

Sadly, the end result wasn't Tinsel Town's more recent concept of werewolves, in which shirtless hunks turned into oversized dogs. I could've dealt with that a bit better than the bipedal monstrosities taking shape all around us.

Take Hobart for instance. He'd already started off large, a good six foot two if not taller. But I watched as his body expanded, Incredible Hulk style, to at least seven feet. He still had a beer gut – this wasn't some instant CrossFit workout – but his arms, legs, and shoulders had enlarged to even things out. As for his face, it was getting uglier by the second. Matted black fur now covered it, not doing nearly enough to hide the exaggerated muzzle forming at the front of his face or the mouthful of rottweiler teeth contained within. And then there was the...

Fucking nasty! Was he actually taking a shit mid-transformation?

Oh wait, no. He was just growing a tail, and what a ratty tail it was, more like something that belonged on an oversized possum.

So engrossed was I, that for a moment I forgot he wasn't the only one there. All around me, people were completing their transformations into monsters – still naked by the way, as, unlike the movies, the fur covering their crotches wasn't nearly heavy enough to obscure their junk. *Ugh*! I wasn't sure what was worse, the teeth or the red rockets a few of them were proudly exhibiting.

The females weren't much better off, some of them now sporting four sets of floppy tits down their torsos. Eww. I could understand why movie makers had made the changes they had.

Sadly, none of this served to downgrade the threat these things represented. Some of them dropped to all fours, their forelimbs now long enough to support it, while others remained bipedal. All of them, however, started to growl and not in a friendly "wanna play catch" way.

"Okay, done processing," I cried. "Take Pop and get inside, now!"

"Like hell. This is my house, and I'll... What the hell are you doing?"

"Sorry, sir, but the Freewill knows what he's talking about. Hey, watch the fingers."

I didn't bother to turn to see what was going on between them, trusting Glen to figure out some way to ooze them inside. I had bigger problems to deal with, from creatures that somehow managed to make even worse dogs than my new roommate.

It was only then that I remembered I was armed. Thank goodness! Never before had I been so glad for the Second Amendment.

Lifting the shotgun, I called out, "I don't want any trouble, but I'm more than happy to give you fuckers the Old Yeller treatment."

If my threat intimidated them, they didn't show it – all of them now snarling and foaming at the mouth as if they were nothing more than rabid animals.

"I'm warning you," I said, taking aim at the nearest.

"You think that's gonna save you?" Myra called out to me from behind her purple force dome. "You don't know nothing, you dumb fuck!"

I can't say I held particularly high opinions of most Magi I'd met, and she wasn't doing much to change that. Just what the world needed, a trailer trash Morgana.

She was the least of my concerns right then, though, which probably said exactly how fucked in the ass I currently was.

And then the impasse was over as my ears picked up the sound of feet pounding upon the soft Earth.

Not today, Fido.

I spun, noting one of the werewolves closing the distance between us with disturbing speed. Too bad he wasn't quite as fast as my trigger finger.

BOOM!!

The weapon was loaded with buckshot, meaning all I needed to do was aim in the beast's general direction, which suited me just fine. It had been five years since my last shooting lesson, and I'd pretty much forgotten it all by now. As far as gunfighters went, I was less Wyatt Earp and more Wyatt Twerp.

But that was okay. The werewolf was large, a moving wall of flesh and fur, and my ears had told me right where it would be. Even Tom would've been hard pressed to miss ... maybe.

A sizable chunk of the wolf's muzzle disappeared in a spray of blood and gristle. It let out a choked yelp as it fell to the ground grabbing at its ruined face.

"Bad dog," I said with a triumphant smirk. "Now who's next ... OOF!"

Apparently *I* was, as one of the creatures slammed into my side, hard enough to make me wonder who'd brought a truck to a monster fight. I skidded to a halt on the grass, a massive mutt atop me, and just barely managed to bring the gun up between us before it could chomp down onto my face.

Instead, its jaws clamped shut onto a mouthful of American made steel, strong enough to ... to actually do jack shit. The housing of the shotgun immediately began to deform as the creature bore down on it, treating it as if it were nothing more than a dollar store chew toy.

Well, isn't that just fucking wonderful.

Snarls and growls filled the air from every direction, telling me I was perhaps seconds away from being literally dogpiled. That might've been a cute place to be if this was a litter of golden retrievers, much less so with Cujo's uglier cousins.

Fortunately, I wasn't exactly helpless. That, and I'd seen all of the Underworld movies. Not sure how useful that was, as I wasn't wearing skintight leather, but you used what you had – and what I had was a whole arsenal of vampire powers.

Extending my claws, I let go of the now useless weapon and raked a furrow across the beast's arm and chest, feeling its hot blood spill out and ruin my favorite *Metal Gear Solid* shirt. The wolf monster didn't like that, not one bit. It pulled back and yipped in pain, giving me enough leverage to shove it off and roll back to my feet.

Out of the corner of my eye, I saw the werewolf I'd blasted also getting back up, its ruined face apparently not enough to keep it down for the count. Well, wasn't that just fucking grand. I swear, once, just once, I'd like to fight a monster that had a below average constitution score.

However, that was a gripe for later. I quickly dove to the left to avoid another of the charging beasts, then leapt over a third before it could make me its bitch.

Dodging and weaving was keeping me alive, but it wasn't doing shit to win this fight. With their superior numbers, it was only a matter of time before I zigged when I should've zagged. The only thing in my favor at the moment seemed to be that these assholes were fighting as individuals as opposed to trying to pen me in. There was also the issue of...

Hold on a second.

While the immediate area contained enough of these things to ruin my evening, there seemed to be far fewer dogging me than I was expecting. What, had some of them run off to chase rabbits?

The sound of snarls from closer to the tree line caught my ear, and I allowed myself a moment to check it out. Myra was surrounded by no less than three of the monsters. They were circling her, growling. Then, one of them leapt at her flank, bouncing harmlessly off her magical shield, only to push itself back to its feet and try again.

The fuck? Had her less than eloquent oration skills offended the wolves' sensitive ears, or did they maybe know an asshole when they smelled one?

All at once, the force dome made sense. She hadn't raised it because of me. It had been to protect her from these things. If anything, she seemed to be as much in control of these beasts as I was, which was to say not at all. Sadly, unlike her, I didn't have a handy dandy forcefield to save my ass, having to rely on being a moving target.

Although not for long apparently. A couple of the wolves had managed to close in while I was busy gawking at Princess Everclear. Fucking A! I really needed to stop worrying about everyone else in situations like these, especially the asshole who'd sicced the fucking monsters on me to begin with.

The only advantage going for me was that, unlike the Feet, these things weren't exactly the stealthiest fuckers on the planet. As I kept an eye on the one in front of me, a growl from behind telegraphed that an attack was incoming.

I turned, just in time to sidestep and plant a fist in the side of the backbiter's face. Hopefully no one from PETA was around to see this because teeth cracked as its head whipped to the side,

Sadly, so did something in my hand.

Ow!

It was like punching a rock, which really shouldn't have been surprising. Growing up, one of my cousins had owned a Newfoundland. Thing was the size of a small bear and built like a tank. However, it was little more than a puppy compared to these things. Though they weren't quite Sasquatch sized, I'd have easily placed most of them around the four hundred pound mark or more, making them easily big enough to fuck up my day.

The one I'd decked hit the ground stunned, just as another growl from my flank caught my ear, causing me to dive out of the way as something massive and hairy just barely missed me.

Fuck! This must've been how caribou felt being surrounded by a wolf pack. Yeah, well, the hell with that. It was time to teach these guys that I wasn't just some deer in their headlights. This was one bag of dogfood that bit back.

Or something like that.

Recovering as quickly as my vampire reflexes would allow, which was pretty darned fast, I spun and leapt at the one that had just tried to attack me, catching it before it could fully turn around.

I landed on its back then, before I could realize how potentially stupid my plan was, I grabbed hold of its head with both hands and twisted with everything I had.

Come on. Don't have a fucking adamantium skeleton.

CRACK!

The werewolf yipped in pain as I shattered its vertebrae, then crumbled to the ground. I had no way of knowing if this thing was down for good, but at the very least it seemed to be out of the fight. That was good enough for me.

Sadly, it seemed to be enough for them, too, as silence suddenly descended upon the yard. I stood and found at least half a dozen sets of red eyes all glaring at me. Even the ones who'd been circling Myra, the wicked witch of white trash, were now focused my way.

"You gone and done it now," she said, safe behind her force bubble.

"Eat a bag of first cousin dicks, as if you haven't already."

Despite my witty retort, it looked like I was the one who was about to be thoroughly boned, as the werewolves began to spread out, encircling me.

So, of course, I did the sensible thing and made it worse for myself. "Aw, what's the matter? Did I send one of the puppies to the pound?"

However, if this served to piss them off even more, they didn't show it. Hell, I wasn't even certain they could understand me. Seemed to be a bit of a communication gap between vamp and dog.

One thing soon became crystal clear, though. As the pack continued to surround me, one of them stepped forward. Though it wasn't exactly wearing a nametag, the big old beer belly protruding from its gut told me who it likely was.

Hobart rose to his full height, towering over me as he slowly approached. As for the rest, they seemed to be doing little more than watching and perhaps making sure I didn't turn tail and run.

I wasn't sure if wolves did this in the wild, having made it a point to miss most National Geographic specials these days, but in human terms it seemed fairly obvious what was happening.

Hobart was the big dog in this pack of rawhide rangers. I'd hurt one of them badly. Now it was up to him to teach me that I wasn't worthy of pissing in the tall grass with him and his bros.

Too bad for this fucker I'd done this dance before, with monsters bigger and badder than him.

True, I'd either lost most of those fights or had to rely on Dr. Death, but that was then. This was now. I was older, more mature, more confident in my ... whoa!

Apparently, I hadn't learned a goddamned thing when it came to not getting caught up in my own internal dialogue. Hobart stepped in, his stride allowing him to easily cover the distance between us, and took a swipe at me – the fingernails of his hands having lengthened and thickened into, well, dog nails, except much sharper looking.

I barely jumped back in time to keep my guts inside my body. Two could play at this game, though. I raced in behind his swing and slashed at him with my own claws, drawing four rivulets of blood down his arm.

Unfortunately, the minor damage I'd caused was for naught as it put me in prime position for him to simply reverse his swing – catching me with a backhand that knocked me on my ass a good ten feet away.

Ugh. These things definitely weren't lightweights in the strength department. Neither were they when it came to speed. I'd no sooner landed when my view above became obscured by a wall of black fur.

I barely rolled out of the way in time to avoid being squashed like a bug, but at least that allowed me to get to my feet before Hobart could right himself again. Using my vampire speed to my advantage, I stepped in, looking to knock a few of this thing's teeth out. If I could put Hobart down, maybe the others would ... um, tear me to pieces more respectfully.

Oh well, I'd cross that bridge when I...

Or not.

Hobart-wolf spun, far faster than I expected, and caught my fist – closing his hand over mine like a vise grip.

Uh oh.

Guess he finally remembered that whole opposable thumb thing.

The bones in my left hand screamed in protest as he put on the pressure, but then a whole other type of pressure exploded in my right eye as he slammed a fist into the side of my head, dislodging my glasses so they dropped to the ground at my feet – albeit that was probably the least of my worries.

The world greyed out around me and my knees buckled, but Hobart wouldn't let me fall. Holding me aloft, as his hand began to turn mine into pulp, he punched me in the face again, causing me to spit out teeth and a generous mouthful of blood.

"Kick his ass real good, Hobart!"

I'd never been one to advocate violence against women, but right then I wanted nothing more than to deck that fucking witch.

However, first I had to get past this asshole – easier said than done as blood was now freely dribbling out both sides of my mouth, as well as the shattered remains of my hand.

He hit me again, swelling my right eye shut and making me feel all woozy.

A few more of these and I'd be done for. With no other vamps around to bite and Sally vanished to god-knows-where, I was on my own with not a lot to fall back on, except...

"C-come on, Dr. Def," I slurred, my swollen tongue making speech difficult.

By now, I couldn't even feel my left hand, save for a dull ache, letting me know it was nothing more than a sack of rent meat and broken bones.

"ARGH!"

Hobart struck again, this time with his claws, digging four deep furrows across my chest – tearing my shirt to shreds, along with most of the rest of me.

"Any ... y-year ... now," I sputtered, rapidly losing cohesion.

He's most vulnerable where he's at his most dangerous.

That voice in my subconscious, the one who'd somehow known what proto-leprechauns were, spoke up again – not that its advice made much sense.

Last time I was in a situation like this, I'd gotten lucky with a cheap shot to the nuts. However, Hobart in his werewolf form was considerably larger than Night Razor had been, not to mention he was holding me in a position that made a solid dick punch difficult to pull off.

And now the voice in my head was telling me it was too dangerous anyway. What? Did he have a toxic taint or something?

Another blow to the side of my head knocked loose that bit of internal dialogue, along with another molar, scattering my thoughts to the wind.

Sensing victory, mostly because I was losing badly, Hobart threw back his head and actually began to chuckle. It was a throaty unpleasant noise, made worse by the drippy ass tongue lolling out the side of his mouth.

Wait ... his tongue.

Most vulnerable where he's most dangerous. Well, what was more dangerous than a monster wolf's teeth?

Dr. Death hadn't been talking about Hobart's dick after all. What a novel concept.

Of course, that still left open the *how* part of this equation. Sadly, Hobart didn't leave his tongue hanging out long enough for me to grab hold of it. He finished his little inside joke, then lowered his head to face me again, opening his jaws wide as if preparing to...

Fuck it. I'd done worse.

Before he could chomp down on my favorite face, I lashed out with my free hand, reaching inside his mouth and burying my claws into the flat of his tongue.

Disgusting as it was, the look on his face – his red eyes opening wide as saucers – more than made up for it.

Sadly, less encouraging was when he clamped his teeth shut.

JESUS MOTHERFUCKING CHRIST!

A moment later, I fell to the ground. My left hand looked like a crumpled paper bag while my right was missing three fingers, but I was free. As for Hobart, he backed up pawing at his mouth, opening it just enough for me to make out my severed digits inside, the claws still embedded in his tongue.

"How'd you like the taste of that, asshole?" I spat.

Too bad it was a momentary reprieve at best. The upside of killing vampires was that you didn't have to worry about disposing the bodies. Same with dismemberment. Outside of some poisons that could retard the process, cutting off a piece of a vamp resulted in that piece quickly turning to ash. Any second now, the three spikes stuck in Hobart's tongue were going to dissolve like the world's worst tasting cotton candy, leaving him free to fuck me up some more and angry enough to give him reason to.

I barely had enough working digits left to dial a phone, much less put up a fight. My healing was good, but not good enough to make a difference in the next couple of seconds. I needed to...

Shots rang out from behind me, coming from inside the house. They were followed by a woman's scream, causing all the wolves around me to turn in that direction. *Shit!* I'd noticed earlier that there didn't seem to be as many werewolves out here as I'd expected. Had some of them gotten inside?

If so, that couldn't be good.

On the upside, it was a momentary distraction, one I'd be remiss to ignore.

Taking advantage of the confused dog faces around me, I hooked my glasses up from the ground then turned and bolted, leaping over the werewolves forming the rear vanguard and crashing through one of Pop's plate glass windows to land in his kitchen.

I needed to make sure my friends were all right, but with any luck this change of venue would also bring with it a change in the current fortunes of this battle.

HERO IN A HALF ASS

I swung my arm, catching everything that was on the counter next to me and knocking it all to the floor. Glass shattered, knives scattered, and the entire place was covered in a greasy mix of flour and vegetable oil. With any luck, the resulting mess would slow down my pursuers for a second or two.

As the icing on the cake, I yanked open the oven door, instantly filling the room with the succulent odor of cooked ham. If that didn't keep these slobbering mongrels busy for a few minutes, I didn't know what would.

That done, I turned my attention toward the direction of the living room, where an entire symphony of destruction seemed to be playing out – another gunshot, the sound of furniture shattering, and voices crying out.

"Ow! Goddamnit! Come on, work already!"

"Get out of the way, girl!"

"I'm not a girl, dumbass!"

"Bark!"

Mixed in with it all were a chorus of snarls, telling me my earlier fears had been correct.

There was neither time to be subtle about things, nor much opportunity – considering my current lack of working digits.

I was tempted to charge straight ahead, through the wall and into the living area, but then I took note of the wall itself. This place wasn't made of drywall and a few scattered studs like most dwellings. Everything was solid wood, solid being the operative term. But maybe that was a good thing.

Taking the time to step through the kitchen doorway instead, I turned and upended a nearby china cabinet with my shoulder, seeding the floor with debris and more broken glass – just as there came another crash from up ahead. There was no more time to waste on covering my tracks.

I stepped into the living room to find a scene of chaos. Pop and Kara stood off to one end, the couch flipped to afford them a modicum of protection. Both were armed and Pop had apparently wasted no time in gathering the rest of his guns, as a small arsenal lay stacked between them.

A few feet away, Glen was engaged with one of the werewolves ... sorta. They were circling each other: the beast growling, Glen lamely attempting to growl back. This was the sort of weird shit you didn't see in most nature documentaries.

However, of far more pressing concern, and where both Pop and Kara were both trying to get a clear shot, was another wolf that had fallen upon Tom.

Crap!

My friend was on the floor, clearly overpowered. The wolf was slashing and biting at him, just barely kept at bay as Tom's aura would flare to life at the last second, deflecting each killing blow, only to then fizzle out again.

"Come on! Work, you piece of shit!" he cried, sounding more annoyed than terrified, which wasn't entirely surprising.

I might not be the poster child for the ideal vampire, but there was little doubt he was the shittiest Icon in history –

something I might've found amusing under better circumstances. Sadly, all it did for us now was fuck us up the ass.

Screw it. Time to take matters into my own hands, or lack thereof.

I bolted forward, head down, hoping Pop didn't pick that moment to decide he had an open shot.

"Freewill!" Glen cried out, but I ignored him, shoulder-checking the werewolf and sending it tumbling away from my friend.

"Now!" I shouted. "Empty the clip and don't hold back."

"This ain't got a clip, you ignorant fool," Pop snapped.

"Who gives a fuck?! Just shoot it and keep shooting."

That spurred them to action and, a moment later, the room erupted in a barrage of gunfire.

The downed wolf was peppered with bullets. As for the one facing off against Glen, it recoiled from the sound then – perhaps sensing it was outnumbered – turned and fled into the night, out the broken remains of the front door.

Too bad I had a feeling it would return soon enough, and with reinforcements.

Pop and Kara ceased firing long enough to toss away their newly emptied firearms and pick up others from the pile, but the wolf they'd blasted appeared to be down for the count.

As for Tom, I stepped back allowing him room to get up. "I'd offer you a hand," I said, holding up my mutilated appendages, "but, I don't have any to spare."

"Thanks, man," he replied, climbing to his feet, a bit bruised but otherwise no worse for the wear. He couldn't control his aura for shit, but thankfully it still seemed to work instinctually. "What the fuck happened to you?"

"I gave these assholes the finger ... then another, and another."

He actually grinned. "Werewolves. How cool is that?"

"I'll hold off judgement until I can count on my hands all the ways this is most definitely not cool."

Speaking of which, Pop stepped around the couch to where we stood. "Hot damn, son. You need a hospital."

"Don't worry. They grow back."

"They do?"

"Hopefully. Everyone here okay?"

"I think I might be missing a piece of my tail," Glen replied.

"I'll take that as a yes."

"Where's Sally?" Kara asked, a look of panic in her eyes.

"Gone. I don't know where, but don't worry. What matters is those things didn't get her. I'll explain later..." There came a crash and several snarls from the direction of the kitchen. *Oh shit!* Guess one ham could only do so much. "Make that much later, after we're miles away from these fucking things." I turned to Pop. "Listen, I know what you said about defending your home..."

"Fuck that. I can always build a new one."

"A more than reasonable answer," I said, turning toward the remains of the front door.

"Offhand, I'd say we're more royally fucked than the Queen of Denmark's strap-on."

Can't say my friend was wrong, at least on that first point.

My plan had been simplicity itself: grab one of the cars out front – mine or Kara's rental, didn't really matter which – and drive the fuck away. We could always figure out a plan of action later, when we weren't stuck in the middle of a bad horror flick.

Sadly, it seemed the werewolves had already seen that movie. Both cars were trashed – tires shredded, windows smashed, hoods and roofs both caved in, with it all topped off by a big pile of dog shit in the front seat of my Camry ... because why not.

There was a chaotic element to it, though. This didn't feel planned or thought out. Both vehicles looked like they'd been attacked simply for being there. And here I thought most dogs liked car rides. I dunno, maybe they thought our plan was to take them all to the vet.

Either way, the end result was us being thoroughly screwed.

"Come on," Pop said, heading off into the darkness, as howls filled the night air. "Garage is this way. My truck's inside."

Or maybe not. "Think it's okay?"

"Hopefully," he replied, sounding as if he had his shit together far better than the rest of us. I could see where Ed had gotten his blasé attitude toward danger. "I keep it locked up tight. Don't trust the local teenagers."

"I'm sure that goes double for teenaged werewolves."

"You ain't wrong, boy." He led the way toward another large structure off to the side of the house, as seemingly all around us the night air was rent with the sound of monsters. "Let's hurry. Gonna take a few minutes to prep. Was replacing the water pump earlier when Kara pulled in."

"A few minutes, eh?" Tom asked, bringing up the rear.

"Yep. Was gonna change the oil, too, but I figure that can wait."

No argument there on my part. We reached the garage. Unlike the house and storage shed, this structure was made of sheet metal, probably a prefab. Ultimately, though, I didn't give a shit about the construction, so long as it was sturdy enough to hold until Pop could get us out of there.

He unlocked the door, then stepped in and turned on the lights, illuminating the workspace. Unlike the shed, this was one big open area – large enough for Pop's truck, a full-sized Ford F-150, as well as some work benches, a canoe, and more tools.

Once I was in, I turned around. "Lock the door behind ... um, Tom?"

I stepped back to the doorway and poked my head out. There was no sign of him. What the fuck?

"Where is he?" Kara asked, stepping to my side.

"I don't know."

"Do you think one of those things..."

I held up a hand. "No. We'd have heard it and seen it, too. That aura of his would've lit up like a magnesium flare ... probably."

"Then where is he?"

I would've heard one of those werewolves approaching us. Of that I was sure. Subtle, these things were not. But, in all the chaos, listening to these things howl up a storm, I might've missed a much smaller set of feet heading away from us. After all, why would I have bothered to keep an ear out for something so cataclysmically stupid?

But, again, this was Tom we were talking about. I swear, I needed to put a leash on that idiot some days.

"We have to find him."

"No," I said, turning to Kara. "*I* have to find him. And trust me, I can. You get in there and lock the door, let Pop finish his work. If we're not back in ten minutes, leave without us." I considered all the monsters likely still in the area. "Fifteen tops."

"But..."

"It'll be okay," Glen said from behind her, his voice full of exuberance. "He's the Freewill and she's the Icon. It'll take more than a pack of ravenous bloodthirsty monsters to stop them."

"Thanks for the vote of confidence, pal," I said, turning away.

Now to only hope his faith in me wasn't as misplaced as I feared.

I had a sneaking suspicion where the moron had run off to, but to be safe I let my nose guide me. Back before Tom had taken up residence in her body, I'd been intimately familiar with Sheila's scent – maybe a bit too familiar now that I thought about it. Even in my early days as a vamp, I'd been able to pick out her scent from the crowd, her unique odor unmistakable to me.

Yeah, definitely a bit of creep factor there. Goddamn. I'm surprised she hadn't taken out a restraining order against my stalker ass.

The thing was, Tom didn't use any of the same beauty supplies she did. His morning routine mostly consisted of generic soap, or at least I hoped it did. That said, beneath it all, he was still in her body and thus carried her scent. As much as I knew he'd give me endless shit if I ever admitted this out loud, I was certain I could still track him if need be.

Heading in the direction I was sure he'd fled, I took a deep breath through my nostrils, letting the scents of the night air fill my sinuses. What a surprise. It mostly smelled like a fucking kennel.

Don't get me wrong, it could've been worse. In the past, I'd made the mistake of taking a sniff while in the vicinity of Sasquatches, all of whom smelled like rancid maggot-covered ass. Smelling those fuckers had been like an olfactory kick to the balls. This, while not exactly pleasant, at least didn't make me want to shove wooden dowels up my nostrils in the hopes of never smelling anything ever again.

The wind carried far more than the odor of dog, though. There were the underlying scents of the forest — trees, dirt, animals, and more. Oh, and in case you're wondering, yes, bears do shit in the woods. I caught a whiff of cheap perfume, pretty much the opposite of what Sally used to wear. However, that wasn't Tom. I had a feeling the Eau de Kmart belonged to Myra. Seemed more her style.

There!

With so many other competing scents, it was almost easy to miss, but I finally caught Sheila's — err Tom's that is — scent floating on the breeze. It brought back memories of a different time, a different us, but that was all in the past. Pleasant as she might've smelled, she was Tom now, which meant there was no way in hell I wanted to make this into a habit going forward.

Sure enough, I was right in my assumptions. The idiot had headed straight for the storage shed. It should've been pure suicide to go that way but, amazingly, the backyard was mostly clear now. Myra was gone, too — probably headed back to the nearest state fair so she could be crowned Miss Corndog or something.

I didn't allow myself to be fooled, though. The werewolves were definitely still in the area. I could hear them crashing around in the house, snarling and probably trashing the place. Others had apparently moved off into the woods, probably to terrorize the local rabbit population.

Nevertheless, I stuck to the deep shadows as I tried to make my way across the yard unseen.

So far there'd been no sign of Tom, or his corpse, proving that once again fate smiled upon the mindbogglingly stupid.

However, as I caught sight of the storage shed, I realized his luck likely only stretched so far. The door was open with the light on inside. That itself wasn't the damning part so much as the fact that I was certain I wasn't alone in noticing it.

Yes, he might've been an idiot, but he was also my best friend. Tempting as it was to leave the doofus to his fate, I had to make sure he was okay.

I raced forward, stepping inside the door just as he rounded a corner heading my way, a box held unsteadily in his hands.

"Oh, hey Bill. Truck ready to go?" he asked, as if he'd been doing nothing more than packing for a road trip.

"Seriously, dude? What the fuck is wrong with you?"

"Before you judge me, let me just say I'm doing this out of the spirit of altruism."

"Are you now?"

"Hell yeah. I mean, we're gonna find Ed, right? Well, when we do, I guarantee it'll warm his heart to know that I saved his childhood memories from a bunch of asshole furries."

"The same childhood memories he's left here for years and never once mentioned?"

"Not my fault he doesn't appreciate the value of collector's items. And if he doesn't want them, I know a little girl who will. Now are you going to stand there like a douche or help me out here? This isn't easy with my gimp arm, you know?"

"I think I'll choose the douche option. Drop that shit and let's go."

"No way."

"I'm serious."

"Or what? You'll drag me out?" he replied with an asshole grin, eying my ruined hands.

"I still have teeth."

"Save the sick kinks for any desperate prostitutes we come across."

Tempting as it was to simply club the shit out of him, I turned and said, "Fine. But keep up and don't be surprised when I stand back and let Pop kick your ass."

"Whatever you say, Captain Hook."

I stepped back into the night air, before stopping dead in my tracks at the realization that we'd been a hair too slow. Tom nearly ran into me a moment later, the box partially obscuring his view.

"The fuck, dude?"

There was no need for me to answer, though. The reason became blindingly obvious a moment later as snarls filled the air around us.

Just as I'd feared, our luck hadn't held out. Two werewolves were waiting outside, flanking us as they crept out from around either side of the shed.

"Drop the box and run," I hissed. "I'll cover you."

"Fuck that noise. We can take these assholes."

Cool as the idea sounded in theory, I'd already tangled with these things enough for one day. "I'm serious. There's no time to fuck around with..."

There was no time to finish my sentence either. The wolf to our immediate left charged toward us. I turned to face it, but my ears told me the other was on the move, too. Sadly, there wasn't much I could do about it, not barely functional as I was.

I stepped forward, hoping Tom's aura was usable enough to at least keep the other monster at bay.

The werewolf came at me high, its full height dwarfing mine. That was fine. I'd played this game of chicken before. I charged forward, ducking low at the last minute and hoping I didn't end up with a face full of wolf dick.

The werewolf's momentum didn't allow it to stop before I hoisted myself up, catching its body in the upswing and catapulting it over me – pretty much the only move I had that didn't require working hands. Thank you, years spent watching WWE matches.

I turned to see it land on its back about fifteen feet away, just as the other one plowed into Tom like a living freight train, sending toys flying and him tumbling to the ground.

Thankfully, his aura had partially activated at the last moment, sparing him from the multitude of broken bones he would've likely suffered otherwise. Unfortunately, the collision with his shield of faith didn't appear to have fazed the werewolf in the slightest. No surprise there. I'd seen Sheila at full power and Tom wasn't anywhere near that. His current aura was a nightlight compared to her nuclear bomb.

"Run!" I shouted, stepping over Tom and intercepting the beast before it could launch itself at him again. I planted my feet and braced myself against the werewolf's massive body, doing what I could to hold it back. Using the broken stubs that had been my hands to keep the beast at bay hurt like a motherfucker, not to mention I had to bend my head low to keep the fucking thing from treating my face like a giant McNugget, but somehow I managed to keep it from advancing.

"Go!" I repeated.

"Hold on. Just one more second."

You have got to be fucking kidding me... "OOF!"

Strong as I was, it wasn't enough, especially against a creature that made me look Sally-sized in comparison. It managed to free one arm, tossing me away like I was nothing more than a squirrel it had grown tired of chewing on.

I landed hard, rolled, and came to a skidding halt on my side.

Back near the shed, the wolf I'd tossed over my shoulder was clambering to its feet, but that was almost a secondary concern compared to the one that had thrown me – now in prime position to gut my best friend, who was still scrambling in the dirt trying to pick up a bunch of freaking toys.

"Look out!"

He glanced up just as the beast swung a massive paw at him. Instinctively, because I knew the greedy moron wouldn't have ever done so purposely, he held up his hands to ward it off, along with the pair of Teenage Mutant Ninja Turtles in them.

Somehow, Tom managed to flinch back at the last moment, keeping his head but resulting in one of the toys being shattered to pieces. It flew out of his hand, a tiny shower of plastic body parts hitting the ground a moment later, with Leonardo's head landing in the grass about a foot away from me.

Sadly, a cheap action figure wouldn't be the only casualty this night if I didn't do something quick.

Come on, Dr. Death. Now is not the time to play... HOLY SHIT!

A blinding flash of brilliant white light erupted from the spot where my friend knelt, like someone had set off a briefcase nuke beneath him, causing me to quickly cover my eyes before they melted out of my head.

"You fucking piece of dog shit!" Tom screamed, displaying an outrage one might more expect from someone who'd just witnessed their favorite pet run over.

I blinked back tears as pure white faith magic radiated out of him – powerful enough to drive the werewolf back several steps and for my eyebrows to start smoldering.

Tom pushed himself to his feet, glowing with fury and holding the remaining figure out before him – Rafael from the look of it.

"Do you ... have any idea ... how much..."

All at once, his aura seemed to concentrate around Rafael's plastic form.

"THAT FUCKING THING WAS WORTH?!"

With that, a burst of dazzling white energy shot forth from his outstretched hand, slamming into the werewolf like a speeding bus. The creature burst aflame as it was flung backward, shattering a big ass oak tree that was in the way.

What in the ever-living fuck?

Bark, wood, and burning fur rained down from above, somehow missing us both. Good thing too, because I was kinda busy trying not to shit my pants at what had happened. From what I could tell, the werewolf had been utterly obliterated in the blast. Nothing but a twitching mound of steaming organs remained. As for its buddy, it might've been nothing more than a dumb animal, but even animals had survival instincts. It stood up tall, its red eyes open wide, then let loose with a stream of piss between its legs and took off running.

"How'd you like that?" Tom cried at it, before turning toward me still aglow. "Oh yeah! Final flash, bitch!"

He wasn't whistling Dixie either. "What the hell was that?"

"I ... actually don't know. Didn't realize I could do that."

"I-I'm not sure you're supposed to be able to," I sputtered, at a complete loss for words.

"It was pretty fucking rad, though, wasn't it?"

There were a lot of things I could've said right then, but disagreeing with him wasn't among them.

There was no way the werewolves in the house, much less those still prowling around outside, hadn't heard what was going on. I mean, shit, that blast had sounded like World War Three.

I had no idea what that had even been. Based on what I knew about Icons, and what I'd seen with my own two eyes, their powers were defensive based – their true threat coming from their ability to wade into combat with their faith auras up, allowing them to incinerate most supernatural foes on contact. Nothing I'd ever heard of suggested they could fire it out like a freaking Kamehameha wave. If Sheila had been saving something like that as a last resort, she'd never once mentioned it.

Either way, I doubted that was the case. If so, I wouldn't have come close to killing her in our battle five years ago, crippling her arm in the process. Had she been capable of such an attack, she'd have surely used it. If not against me, then against Calibra or Alexander.

Something didn't add up here.

Then again, I sincerely doubted there'd ever been an Icon like Tom.

Either way, playing Blue's Clues with this mystery wasn't in our best interest right then. We still needed to get the fuck out of there. So, in the spirit of friendship and not wanting to get blasted myself, I offered Tom a compromise of sorts.

"Three. That's it. No more. Grab them and then let's go!" I put as much *Dr. Death* as I could into my voice, hoping it worked.

Thankfully, my best friend was a lot of things, but an alpha male wasn't one of them.

"Fine," he groused, picking up two additional pieces, a Street Shark and a red Power Ranger to go with the turtle still in his hand. That done, he turned toward me expectantly. "Well, what are you waiting for, a fucking invitation?"

If it weren't for the fact that I was currently lacking in the hand department, I'd have smacked him upside the head.

Instead, we raced back the way we'd come, heading toward the garage. I fumbled with my pockets trying to hook my phone, desperately hoping we hadn't taken longer than I'd told Kara to wait, only to pull out a crushed hunk of plastic and glass. Fuck me! I really needed to start buying insurance for these things.

"Come on, before they leave without us."

"You don't need to tell me, dude," Tom replied, his body still aglow, albeit thankfully not enough to burn me as we ran side by side.

"You might want to douse the light show."

"You might want to tell me how. This body didn't come with instructions."

"Then how the hell did you do that back there?"

"Was hoping you had some ideas."

Our banter was drowned out as a chorus of howls rose up in the night, spurring us on faster ... or Tom anyway. I could've left him in the dust, but you don't do that with buds, even dumbass ones.

Finally, we reached the side door of the garage. I was tempted to barrel through it, but then remembered the people inside were armed and likely to shoot first and ask questions later.

Instead, I stopped and knocked with my elbow, yelling out, "Open up. It's us!"

A moment later, Kara let us in. Sure enough, Pop was standing behind her, his weapon raised, with Glen alongside him.

"How are we doing on time?"

"Best not to ask," she replied before turning to her brother and punching him in the arm, his faith aura doing nothing to stop her human fist. "And you, jerk! What the hell was that?"

"Ow! I was saving my good friend's cherished childhood." Tom looked down at the remaining toys from his ill-timed side quest. "A few of them anyway."

Pop stepped forward. "You blasted idiot. You could have gotten us..."

"Trust me, that option is still on the table," I interrupted. "Let's save it for later. For now, let's get the fuck out of here."

"Good plan."

Tom's aura had diminished to little more than a slight glow around him, but it was still more than I cared to sit next to in a cramped truck cab. And that wasn't even counting if anything set him off again. Likewise, I wasn't the only one his powers might affect.

"Glen, you're with me in the back." I turned to Pop. "Don't worry about us. We'll be fine. Just gun it."

"If you say so, son," he replied, climbing into the front seat of the massive pickup. Tom took shotgun, giving us a bit of buffer from him, while Kara got in the backseat.

Pop started the engine then activated the automatic garage door.

"Hold on tight," I told Glen as we settled into the pickup's bed. "This could get bumpy."

"You got it, Freewill," he replied, sounding like he was having the time of his life. "Bark!" A moment later, a tendril of slime reached out of his mouth and wrapped itself around one of the tiedowns in the back. Whatever worked. I grabbed hold of one as well, best I could anyway with my few working fingers.

Pop revved the engine as the garage doors opened up, the headlights revealing – *oh, fuck me* – a front yard full of werewolves. So much for a clean getaway. Standing among their number, about twenty yards away, was a big beer-bellied bastard – Hobart.

"There's too many to drive around," Pop yelled, rolling down the window.

"Then drive through them," I called back. "These aren't some poor doggies crossing the road. Run these fuckers down, I say."

Left unsaid was the fear that it wouldn't work. The truck was big with a lot of horsepower, but we were dealing with supernatural predators here – ones easily strong enough to give as well as they received. If they managed to stop us, we'd be fucked as certainly as the guests of honor at a Japanese gangbang.

"We'll take out as many as we can," Pop called back, gunning the engine one more time. Through the back window I saw his hand move to the gear shift, preparing to give it his all.

Before he could hit the gas, though, there came a pained yowl from somewhere out front.

A splatter of blood splashed the ground right outside the garage, followed by the body of a werewolf which went flying past us to land unmoving in the dirt.

What the hell?

Another wolf bounded across the front of the garage, likely looking to investigate, but it was stopped as a large hairy fist appeared from the other side, slamming into the first beast's jaw and sending it to the ground.

The fist had an owner, another werewolf – a big sucker with slightly lighter fur than the others, dark brown and a bit less ratty looking. It stepped in front of us, glanced our way, and then actually held up a palm as if indicating we should wait a moment.

Then it picked up the wolf it had just decked, spun, and flung it across the yard ... where it slammed right into Hobart, knocking him ass over tea kettle. Huh. Nice shot.

Probably stupid of me, but I slapped the top of the cab to get Pop's attention. "Hold on."

"What?" he shouted back.

"Let's give this a second."

"Are you sure?"

"Not really."

Hey, at least nobody could accuse me of bullshitting them.

The brown werewolf made eye contact with me and actually gave a single nod of its head, before turning and racing into the front yard. The other beasts, seemingly unhappy that this newcomer had just embarrassed the fuck out of their leader, swarmed it from all sides. But, where they were charging wantonly at him, like a bunch of rabid trash pandas, it was obvious this newcomer was fighting strategically.

It sidestepped one, then grabbed it before it was out of reach and flung it face first into another group, using their numbers against them.

Another wolf leapt upon its back, and the fucking thing tossed it off with a goddamned judo throw.

"Kung fu werewolf for the win!" Tom shouted from the front, echoing my thoughts.

I had no idea who this new wolf was or why it had picked now to appear but, after a few moments, it became obvious what it was doing. It wasn't fighting these things to put them down for good, but instead tossing them back and forth, stunning some and scattering the rest as it seemingly cleared a path for us.

No fucking way.

Almost as if reading my mind, it turned toward us and waved one massive arm in a "come on" gesture.

Fuck it. That was good enough for me.

"Go!" I shouted. "And try not to hit that one."

"I ain't stupid, boy. Now sit down and grab hold of something."

I did as told. "Hold on tight, Glen."

"Oh, this is so exciting."

I stared at the little weirdo as the truck started to move. "We really need to have a talk about your definition of exciting."

And then Pop began to speed up, making me close my mouth lest I end up ingesting any of those giant tree beetles still buzzing about.

The brown wolf stepped to the side and actually gave us a thumbs up as we passed. I followed it up with a wave of thanks, as if he were simply another motorist who'd stopped to let us pull out. Lame, but it was all I had.

As Pop accelerated toward the dirt lane that would hopefully take us out of this horror show, the brown wolf hightailed it into the trees – just as the others were starting to regain their feet.

Whoever that wolf was, they'd just saved our asses.

Sadly, I realized as we drove away from Pop's house, we were leaving with a whole lot more questions than we'd arrived with.

As if my week couldn't get any weirder.

FROM THE FRYING PAN...

Despite being certain that something would leap out from the trees at any moment, leading to a desperate battle in the bed of Pop's truck, we somehow managed to make it back to paved roads and what passed for civilization in rural Pennsylvania without further incident.

I was just starting to think we were home free when the inside of the cab lit up from within, like someone had turned on a million-watt lightbulb. Recognizing the pure brilliance of faith magic, I scrambled as far back to the end of the cab as I could, just as the truck screeched to a halt on the side of the road.

"Jesus, Tom!"

"What the hell are you doing, you idiot?!"

Okay, that sounded somewhat less panicked than I'd assumed it would.

"Everything all right up there?" I called back, as the light dimmed and went out.

"Not unless you call being blinded all right!" Pop shouted.

"Sorry," Tom said.

"What do you mean sorry?" Kara scolded. "You could have killed us."

"I was just testing to see if I could make it work again."

"Seriously?!" I cried. "And you thought now would be a good time to do that?"

He rolled down his window and stuck his head out, the glow completely doused. "Don't be such a pussy. When inspiration hits, you go with it."

"Is that so?" Pop replied. "Well, don't go with it when I'm driving, not unless you want to walk your ass back to..." He turned around in his seat toward me. "Where are we going anyway?"

How the fuck did I end up as leader of this lifeboat? Oh wait. I was one of the three supernatural monsters onboard, and the only one who wasn't either an obvious dumbass or wearing a disgusting dog corpse. Yay for being elected by default.

Sadly, I didn't have anything that even remotely resembled an answer for him, so I did the smart thing ... I stalled.

"Take us back to the city. We'll figure it out on the way."

It wasn't a great plan, but it was likely better than sitting there with our thumbs up our asses. We were out of the woods, literally, but still in an area that it would've been generous to call sparsely populated. I had no idea whether those werewolves were in a mindset to follow us but, if they were, I highly doubted we were anywhere close to being safe. Best to keep moving and find a major highway as soon as possible.

Pop pulled into a gas station just before we hit 80 East toward New York. As I filled the tank, he ran into the convenience store, returning with a t-shirt to replace the blood-stained mess I was still wearing – "I Survived Pennsylvania" emblazoned boldly on its front. Glad to see at least someone had a sense of humor about what had happened.

Being that Tom had seemingly found his off switch, Glen and I climbed into the cab with Kara – making sure to remind the new Icon that he'd best not fuck around with me sitting right behind him. It gave us a better chance to talk on the way back, not to mention made it about a thousand percent less likely that we'd get pulled over by the cops.

Sadly, there wasn't much to talk about. We had tons of questions about what had happened and who had saved us, but were seriously short on answers, other than what we'd seen with our own two eyes ... or two dozen in Glen's case.

There was also still the question of what the fuck had happened to Sally.

Fortunately, I realized we needn't be alone when it came to figuring this shit out.

"Glen, do you have your phone? Mine got trashed in the fight."

"Sorry, Freewill. I left it back at the apartment."

Go figure, same place Tom's was. Glad to know they were two peas in a pod. I turned toward Kara with the same question.

"I left mine in the car." She let out a sigh. "Can't wait to explain this one to the rental company tomorrow. Guess I should've sprung for the extra insurance after all."

She wasn't alone there. My car had been trashed, too, and it was no rental. *Shit!* I had a sinking feeling there was going to be a lot of mass transit in my future. Just what I needed to make my week any...

Double shit! I remembered that I'd also left my laptop on the passenger seat, as if my fucking luck could be any worse.

At least my game saves were backed up to the cloud. Glass half full, I guess ... half full of werewolf shit anyway.

All right, that was enough of that. Everyone here was alive, that was the important thing. Besides, in the grand scheme of things, Pop had lost a lot more than any of us. Speaking of which...

"I hate to ask, Pop, but can I borrow your...."

"No can do, Billy boy. Don't own one. Damned things give you brain cancer."

Somehow, I wasn't surprised to hear him say that.

The rest of the long drive was spent decompressing. Pop put on the radio – country, of course – causing me to tune out and mostly just stare out the window. Truth be told, I was both tired and hungry. I'd grabbed some pig's blood before leaving with Sally, but big battles had a way of taking it out of one, even a vampire, and that wasn't even counting the energy it was likely taking for my hands to heal.

Looking out the window allowed me to do my best to ignore the fact that both Pop and Kara were starting to smell pretty tasty.

So instead I focused on Sally. On the grand scale of things, she was way higher on my priority list than dinner. I closed my eyes and tried to remember exactly what had happened. Sally had been threatening those yahoos then *zap*. There'd been no warning, no indication, no...

Except there was. Go over it once more, slowly this time.

Fucking know it all subconscious. Dr. Death was definitely getting too big for his britches. Even so, it's not like I had much else to do, so I followed his advice and focused on that moment ... playing it again and again in my head until... Holy shit! The asshole was right. There was something I'd missed – that damned bracelet had beeped right before she vanished. But had that been the cause or simply a result of something setting it off?

I had no way of knowing and, with no working phones in reach, that left me with few options for finding out. Fortunately, one of those options was knowing the little birdie who almost certainly had a clue as to what had happened to her. And I was going to get answers from that fucker no matter what.

By the time we reached the city, the crushed pulp that had been my left hand had mostly sorted itself out, leaving it pretty close to functional. As for the other, my index finger had partially grown back, with the other two not far behind. Thank goodness for vampire healing!

I instructed Pop to drop us off in Midtown, then told him he was more than welcome to crash at my place in Brooklyn.

"I appreciate that, I really do," he replied, "but I'm good. Got me a time share down in Cape May that I know for a fact is empty right now. Gonna head down there and hole up for a bit. Figure out what to do once it's daylight and I got a few hours of shuteye behind me. Maybe all of this shit will even sound sane by then."

"Doubt it."

He glanced at the rest of us. "It's a big place with plenty of room. You're all more than welcome to join me."

No go for me, as I had too many things to do. Likewise, I had a feeling I might need Tom's help for them. As for Glen, no way did I want him a hundred miles away, walking around in a creepy dead dog with nobody to supervise him. However, that left at least one good candidate for keeping Pop company.

"You should go with him," I said to Kara. She opened her mouth, probably to protest, but I was ready for that. "Listen, it's really not much safer in the city right now. No werewolves, but we have other crap to deal with. And I have a feeling it's going to be a bit of a late night for us." I looked at the clock on Pop's dashboard. "Later night anyway. I promise, I will keep you both in the loop about Ed. There's no reason for me to hide this stuff anymore. It's about as out in the open as this shit can get."

I could see she was warring with the decision. On the one hand, my words hadn't exactly been comforting, speaking of dangers still to come. On the other, I knew she didn't want to be a part of this world anymore. Yeah, she was now firmly in this mess again, by virtue of both her brother and fiancé, and I didn't know of any good way to fix that, but I was at least giving her a temporary out.

In the end, former vampire or not, she'd been through enough for one evening, so she finally agreed to go ... after throwing several threats my way that I'd better keep my word or else.

Pop pulled over and we said our goodbyes. Kara gave Tom a big hug, telling him to keep safe, and likewise promising to be in touch so they could discuss how to break his miraculous resurrection to their parents. Then she climbed back in, taking shotgun this time.

Pop waved to me, but then he turned to Tom. "No offense ... um, son, but those toys you got there. You do realize those belong to my..."

288

"Trust me, we know," I said, interrupting. "But also trust me that it's best if he holds onto them. Believe me, you're not going to find any safer hands right now."

That was bullshit. I mean, Tom would almost certainly *try* to protect them, likely with his life – greedy nutjob that he was – but the reality was their future was probably a wee bit less certain in his hands. Still, my answer seemed to mollify Pop for the moment.

"All right. I suppose it don't hurt none. You bring my boy back safe, you hear?"

I nodded. "You have my word, sir."

"Good enough. I'll hold you to it."

They promised to give us a call once they were settled in, then he and Kara pulled away – disappearing from sight down the next block as they turned and headed toward the Holland Tunnel.

At least they were safe for now. As for us...

"So where to, Freewill?" Glen asked, looking up at me with his freaky bugged out eyes.

"The docks. I have a stool pigeon I need to have a word with."

"Will you knock it off? People are staring. It's bad enough they can already see Glen."

"Bark!"

I looked down at him. "Not helping."

"Chill, asshole," Tom replied. "I'm just testing shit out. Jeez, when did you become my grandma?"

"Fine, but test your powers where people can't see you. They're not exactly subtle, you know."

"Fuck it. Let them take a picture and post it to Instagram. See if I give a shit. Besides, this is the first time I've gotten this faith crap to work right, so I want to make sure it's not going to fizzle again."

Working right might've been taking it a stretch too far. I'd never seen Sheila do what he'd done back there in the woods. Fortunately, Tom at least had enough sense to not try that here. Blowing a hole in the side of a building was definitely not going to go unnoticed. As it was, though, him constantly flaring up as we walked wasn't really helping either.

"Seriously, dude, I think I'm starting to get the hang of this. It was all about having something to focus on."

"Makes sense," I replied. "Except that Sheila's focus was on ... oh, I dunno ... helping people."

"Yeah, but most people are assholes."

"Takes one to know one."

If Tom was insulted by my quip, he didn't show it, continuing to look down at the ill-gotten gains in his hands. "I get it now. It's kinda like when I found Optimus Prime at that flea market. You remember that?"

"Hard to forget."

"It was like ... I had a connection with him."

"It," I countered.

"Huh?"

"It was a freaking toy, not a person."

"Eat a dick, grammar Nazi," he replied with no real rancor. "When I had him with me, it was like there was this tingle in my fingertips. Kind of like how your hand gets when you've been jacking it too long."

"That's a metaphor I could do without, thanks."

"I believe it was actually a simile, Freewill," Glen bubbled from next to me.

"Who's the grammar Nazi now?"

"Except now it's different," Tom continued, ignoring our banter. "Same focus, but that tingle is like all over my body. And back there with those werewolves, it was like me grabbing hold of that tingle and shoving it right up their asses."

"So you're equating the power of faith to a dildo now? Nice."

"I think I understand, Icon," Glen replied. "Those items in your hand function in the same way the former Icon's sword did."

Tom nodded. "Yeah, I guess so. Except I can't use her sword for shit, especially not with this gimped arm. But that's okay, I like this stuff better anyway. Fuck that ren faire bullshit." He turned to me. "Speaking of which, how much do you think we could get for..."

"We are not selling the sword," I snapped. "It belonged to fucking Joan of Arc."

"Yeah, but I don't need it now. And think of what some rich history nerd will pay for that shit? We could ... oh fuck. Not now." He stopped and put his hands over his stomach.

"What's wrong?"

"Pit stop time. Can't talk, need to find a place to..."

There was a Wendy's across the street. Without further preamble, Tom raced over and inside, headed toward the restroom.

Ah fuck it. It's not like I couldn't use a piss break, too.

I debated whether to tell the staff that Glen was my emotional support dog, then decided to just leave him on the sidewalk and go. Who the fuck was going to try stealing him?

Sure enough, he was there when I got back – after picking up an order of fries. If anything, people were giving him a wide berth as he stood there wagging his tail in a haltingly disturbing way. Can't say I really blamed them.

Feeling much better with an empty bladder, I waited for Tom to join us.

"Women," I said to Glen. "Always gotta take forever in the can."

"In all fairness, Freewill, both of your sexes utilize an inefficient process when it comes to waste management."

"Oh?" I replied, vaguely aware that I was having a public conversation with a talking dog.

"Yes. I merely allow my excretions to collect on my surface layer so it can evaporate. Much easier that way."

I made a mental note to never touch him again. "I'll have to try that some time."

Tom finally rejoined us. He stepped out, smiled, then held his arms out to the side. "Ta da! How do I look?"

"Exactly as you did three minutes ago."

"I know. Isn't it great? No leaks or anything."

"Not following."

"Kara showed me how to change a pad, and I think I finally figured it out."

I couldn't help but grimace. "I didn't want to say anything in front of your sister, but shouldn't you already know this shit?"

"Why the fuck would I?"

"Oh, I don't know. Maybe because you're an adult, who used to be in an adult relationship, and who somehow managed to father a freaking child for Christ's sake."

"First off, there's no used to be. Secondly, rather than being a jack-off of all trades, like you, I chose to specialize in what I'm good at – sliding it in and letting the magic happen."

I turned away shuddering. "I so did not need to know that."

"The truth hurts ... but it hurts so good."

"Someone should hurt you so good."

"Hey, be nice to me. It isn't easy being a chick. On the way out, some fucker offered me his chicken nuggets for a blowjob. Cheap asshole could have at least thrown his Frosty in, too."

"At least it's good to know you have a backup job in case this Icon thing doesn't pan out."

"Fuck you."

"No thanks. I have intelligence standards and you no longer qualify."

It didn't take long for us to reach the pier Falcon was currently calling home. There was a strange stillness in the air as we approached. It was quiet, almost too quiet. Of course, that could've been nothing but my paranoia, having just walked away from a fucking werewolf battle. Such things tended to leave one a bit on edge.

More than likely, it was simply a case of it being late and a work night. I glanced past the metal fencing standing before us, noting the boring normalcy of it all, and remembered the glamour Falcon had in place. For all I knew, it was designed to mute noise, too, prissy British twat that he was. Dude was probably used to some proper country estate rather than a filthy pier in the middle of Manhattan.

I told my two companions about the glamour, especially Tom, since it would effectively mask him if he wanted to flare up once inside, maybe. Icon powers tended to futz with magic, so there was no way to tell for certain. But I guess we'd cross that bridge ... in about three seconds.

Popping open the unlocked gate, we walked inside. So far so good. A few more steps and I noticed the air shimmering as it had before, and then we were through.

"Okay, we should be inside the glamour," I said. "Um, want to power up and see if anyone calls the cops?"

My logic was piss poor at best, but Tom wasn't one to question such things. He simply stepped forward a few feet, moving far enough away so as to not instantly kill me, held up the toys he'd purloined, with his good arm anyway ... and then hesitated.

"Waiting for an invitation?" I asked.

Tom smiled back at me with the look he got when a plan was forming in his mind – almost never a good thing where he was concerned. "Hold on. I want to try something."

"Please tell me you're not going to see if you can hit New Jersey from here."

"Nothing that cool," he replied. "Although that's not a bad idea."

"I'm going to look around, Freewill," Glen said, wandering away. "See if I can sniff out anything with my eyes."

"Wait, your eyes can...?"

"Check it out," Tom said, catching my attention again. He stared at the pair of toys in his hand, squinting at them.

"Check what out?"

"I'm concentrating."

"You look like you're trying to take a shit."

"Same general idea." The white aura of faith began to form around him, sputtering at first, but then growing stronger and steadier.

"Okay, and? Are you trying to see if your powers will wipe your ass, too?"

"While I don't dismiss that a faith bidet would be awesome," he countered, "not quite. Gah! How did she get it to work?"

"Get what to work?"

"Oh wait. I have an idea." He stared down at his bad arm. "By the power of Grayskull, I command you to heal!"

Heal?

Unsurprisingly, nothing happened for several long moments. Then he looked at the stuff he was holding and rolled his eyes. "Duh. Wrong catchphrase. Let's try that again." He touched the red Power Ranger to his bad arm and cried out, "Form Megazord, motherfucker!"

I was about to comment on how that was the absolute stupidest fucking thing I'd seen in quite some time, when the glow around his body coalesced into the hand holding the action figure ... and then down into his bad arm, causing it to be momentarily enveloped in brilliant white light.

When the glow cleared a second or two later, gone were the scars that had crisscrossed his upper arm, scars which I'd caused five years earlier.

Tom flexed his fist a few times, then spun his formerly bad arm around in a circle, seemingly with no pain. "Fuck yeah! Good as fucking new, bitches. No idea why she didn't do this herself. Goddamn, that is so much better."

I had no doubt it was. At the same time, a part of me was sort of insulted on Sheila's behalf. "You do realize she kept those scars for a reason, right? To remind her of her humanity and those she fought for."

Tom shrugged, the concept apparently going right over his empty head. "Yeah, well, when a new tenant moves in, you can't blame them for making a few improvements."

I was a bit split on that myself. At the same time, though, it was hard to forget the various new threats which seemed to be popping out of the woodwork. Honoring a memory was one thing, but I had a feeling we were going to need us all in tiptop shape in the days ahead.

Hell, for all I knew, we might need that in the next few minutes.

Still, it was kind of a slap in the face to her memory, and probably something we needed to talk about. That said, even I couldn't argue it might be best to table that discussion for a better time.

"Fine," I groused. "If this Icon gig doesn't work out, at least you can make a living jerking off two dicks at once."

Tom laughed. "You're just jealous that one of them won't be yours."

"Believe me, I'm not." I turned and looked around. "Hey, Glen!"

"Over here, Freewill," he called back from further in. His mouth was open and a tendril of goo containing an eyeball was extended out from it, looking at something on the ground.

"Be careful, man," I said. "This place is warded. You don't want to set one..."

There came a bright flash of blue light from where he stood, followed by a high whine of power, as if an electric transformer had just blown out.

"...off."

Before I could comprehend what had just happened, a smoking mound of fur flew past us to land in an unmoving heap upon the cracked asphalt.

Oh shit! "Glen!"

I HEAR YOU KNOCKING

"Douse the light show," I told Tom, as we both raced to where Glen lay.

"Sorry, man," he replied, dialing it back – a bit anyway. "Still figuring this shit out."

I wasn't really listening, though, being far more concerned with our other roommate at the moment. Poor little guy. He'd been enthusiastic, yeah, to a really fucking annoying degree if we're being honest, but he'd meant well. And instead of warning him to be careful while he'd wandered into a supernatural minefield, like I should have, instead I'd just stood there with my thumb up my ass watching Tom play with action figures.

Some friend I'd turned out to be.

"Glen," I cried again, reaching where he lay. "Speak to me, man!"

Arcs of blue energy continued to lance through the now smoldering dog corpse. As awful as it had looked before, it was a complete mess now. Part of its back leg had been blown off, the fur was missing in even more spots, and one side of its head had been charbroiled.

It twitched a few times, giving me hope, but then I realized it was likely just the residual power of the ward still coursing through the lifeless pile of meat before me.

"Oh no, man." I dropped to my knees next to him.

"Shit," Tom said from behind me. "Poor dude. Um, should we give him mouth to mouth or something?"

I rounded on him. "And what the fuck is that going to do? He doesn't have a mouth!"

"Wait, I know! I could try healing him."

Shaking my head, I turned back to where Glen lay. "We don't know what that would do to him. Your powers, the good parts anyway, mostly work on humans. The rest, it's meant to kill guys like me and him. I don't think..."

"Ugh ... Freewill?" a weak burbling voice asked from inside the dead dog.

"Glen?"

"I ... I think..."

"Yeah, buddy?" I asked, leaning down toward him.

"I think ... I found one of those Magi wards."

The crumpled corpse of the dog began to shudder in front of me, its legs straightening out as a pair of eyes bulged out from the semi-charred skull of the dead Irish Setter. The body continued to contort and jerk, until finally it lurched unsteadily to its feet – three of them anyway.

I backed up to give him room. "You're okay?"

"Dude," Tom said. "That was hardcore."

"Thank you, Icon," Glen replied, if possible looking even more disgusting now than he had. "Although, I fear I may need to consider a new disguise."

No shit. "Don't worry about that." I knelt down in front of him. "The important thing is you're okay. You are okay, aren't you?"

There came the sound of bubbling from inside the dog's body, pretty fucking gross if we're being honest here. At last, though, he replied, "Nothing appears broken, although I must admit that was most unpleasant. If it's all the same to you, I'd rather not experience being blown up again."

"No complaints here. Don't scare us like that, okay?"

He stared up at me from the now nightmarish dog corpse, as if someone had decided the world needed a fan film mashup of *Old Yeller* meets *The Living Dead*. He'd been borderline gross before. But now there was no way he was walking around in that thing without attracting a whole shit ton of unwanted attention.

"I suppose I should air this out a bit for now." A few moments later, the dog opened its mouth and the entirety of Glen came puking out of it. The dog body deflated and fell to the ground, leaving a pulsing mass of gooey eyeballs looking up at us.

A few of his eyes appeared to be blackened and, in some spots, his normal unhealthy mustard color was now a bit darker, but he otherwise seemed to be in reasonable shape for an amorphous pile of snot.

"Much better," he bubbled. "Although if it's all the same to you, perhaps I'll stand guard out here while you lead the charge forward."

That seemed a reasonable decision. I had a feeling we'd gotten lucky and he'd hit a stun ward, although it was a hell of a stun ward if you asked me. Nevertheless, I didn't care to press our luck again – at least with him.

Speaking of pressing our luck, though, I stood and turned around. Both the city street behind us as well as the warehouse at the far end of the dock appeared quiet.

Guess the glamour was still holding. That was good. As for Falcon himself, I don't know. Maybe he was sleeping, or locked in his bathroom jerking off to thoughts of Christy...

Okay, I really didn't need to go much farther than that.

This fucker had fitted Sally with that goddamned bracelet. That had been bad enough. But if he was in there, posh British cock in hand, muttering about how utterly marvelous it would be to plow my girlfriend at teatime, there was going to be hell to pay.

But first we had to get there.

"All right," I said, preparing myself for the hurt to come. "Glen, you stay and keep watch. Tom..." Was I really going to say this? Yeah, I was. "You're with me. Here's the plan."

Okay, it really wasn't much of a plan, but that was fine. In programming it was well known that sticking to the KISS method – in which one kept it simple, stupid – was often the way to go. Leave the in-depth planning to the Navy SEALs, I say. For this, we only needed to wipe out as many of Falcon's wards as possible – as it was painfully obvious the welcome mat was no longer rolled out – and make it to his door before he could make an appearance and go all Lord Voldemort on us from afar.

As far as ranged combat went, Magi definitely had the advantage over vampires. But I had an ace up my sleeve in the form of the Icon – the being who'd singlehandedly wiped out their race, until Gan came along anyway. Before now, I probably wouldn't have considered Tom a plus in any plan, but with him having discovered a trigger mechanism for his power – a trigger which I now realized shouldn't have surprised me in the slightest – we had a chance.

"Now!" I shouted, taking off at a full run on the left, while Tom screamed out "Thundercats Ho!" over on the right flank, causing his aura to light up around him.

Whatever worked.

Years ago, Sheila and I had carried out a similar plan against a group of witches holed up in the Bunker Hill Monument outside of Boston. It was simplicity itself. I attempted to set off the wards nearest me, but at vampire speed, so that I was hopefully already out of range when they went off.

Over on his end of things, Tom adopted a far more casual pace, moving through what we'd guessed to be the center of the magical minefield, his powers causing the wards in range to sputter and fail.

The smart thing would've been to let him take the lead and follow at a safe distance, but I wasn't dick enough to let him face all the danger alone. Not to mention, I considered it a piss poor strategy for us to group up, just in case Falcon made an appearance. True, his powers likely wouldn't work against Tom but, as any gamer worth their salt knew, staying too close together was practically begging to be hit with every area of effect spell in the Player's Handbook.

When in doubt, always go for the flank bonus.

I glanced over, happy to see things working on his end. With every step he took, something would light up – whether on the ground or in the air itself – then pulse and fizzle out.

Even outside of any doomsday prophecies, I could understand why the Magi might not be particularly fond of Icons.

Sadly, on my end, things were a bit different. Last time I'd done this, it had been in a magical forest, offering me tons of cover as shit blew up around me.

Here, I was out in the open, exposed as chunks of asphalt exploded from quite literally beneath my feet, my vampire reflexes being the only thing keeping me from being turned into a pile of something that resembled Glen's disguise.

The upside was that the wards at the periphery of Falcon's defenses seemed designed more to stun or scare than outright maim and kill. Christy had mentioned as much, and I'd also gotten that sense after seeing how Glen had fared. Though I had no idea how much punishment a pile of sentient eyeball goo could take, I felt fairly confident in assuming we'd still be squeegeeing him up had killing magic been involved.

That said, a small part of me felt shitty sending Tom in to deal with the hardcore stuff. However, his powers were best suited to it.

Of course, hardcore was a relative concept, especially as I set off one ward, leaping into the air a moment before the asphalt beneath me erupted in blue lightning, only to accidentally slam into one of the invisible midair sigils.

A gust of tornado velocity air blasted into my chest from seemingly nowhere, slamming me into the ground hard enough to make me wish my parents had used birth control. *Ouch.*

"Go, Freewill! You've got this!"

Not wishing to disappoint my cheering section, I flashed Glen a shaky thumbs up, then pulled myself unsteadily to my feet.

The only plus was that the momentary *nap* had given me a chance to rethink my strategy.

Based on both past experience and discussions I'd had with Christy, I got the impression Magi wards could get disturbingly specific if so desired. However, doing so required more work on the casting mage's part. Access to a hoity-toity archive of forbidden magic aside, Falcon had only recently come to New York. Yet the pier before us was practically drenched in defensive magic.

I didn't consider myself a betting man, but I was willing to wager that so many wards placed in such little time meant that he'd taken a wholesale approach to them. These weren't magical smart bombs so much as a shitload of eldritch landmines, happy to blow up for anyone or anything that set them off.

The thing with landmines, though, was those crazy enough to employ them probably didn't want them going off every time a mouse took a shit on one. A certain amount of pressure was needed. Seemed a logical guess that these were the same, otherwise Falcon would be out here with a mop every time a fucking pigeon flew past.

Now to test that theory.

I grabbed a few chunks of asphalt from the surrounding area, there being no shortage to be had. My best baseball days were well behind me, in that I'd never had any good days to begin with, but skill wasn't necessary here. All I needed were heavy enough pieces thrown with sufficient force.

I let fly with the first chunk, jumping in surprise when a purplish dome of energy – some kind of magical cage – sprang up around it.

Yes!

Glancing toward the warehouse, I saw no sign of a response from our host. Fuck it. The plan had been to make our way to his doorstep as quickly as possible, but maybe there was a bit of time to really rain on his parade.

I glanced down at the rocks in my hands. I'd found the combination to this asshole's safe. Now it was time to make off with the spoils.

303

"It's about time you got here."

"Fuck you."

Tom had the easy job, just moseying along like his shit didn't stink. I guess Falcon hadn't anticipated a Shining One waltzing in and utterly decimating his hard work. If he had, maybe he'd have laid a few actual landmines.

Things had been a bit more hit and run on my end, but eventually I'd made it to the warehouse entrance – breathing hard but with minimal damage to my person.

I waved over to where Glen still waited. "All clear if you want to head over."

"I'm good, thanks!" he called back.

To each their own.

I turned back toward the door leading inside. "Ladies first."

He casually flipped me the finger. "Age before beauty, fucker."

"Immortality before assholes you mean." I grinned then stepped up to the door.

Subtlety had already been damned so, rather than knock, I kicked the door open with a loud bang.

"Yoo-hoo! Anyone home?"

"You are such a dick, dude," Tom said with a chuckle.

"If you'd seen the way this guy was shamelessly flirting with Christy, you'd be up for some property damage, too."

"Fuck that noise. It's bad enough I got you putting the moves on my girl – unsuccessfully I might add. No way is this wrong-side of the street driving, scone-sucking dickhead getting away with that shit."

"I know this is probably a bad time to have that talk, but you do realize you no longer have the ... um ... equipment she prefers, right?"

Tom looked at me as if his opinion of my intelligence had dropped several notches. "Seriously? That's why they make strap-ons."

"And suddenly I'm sorry I brought it up."

I stepped inside, noting the place was still pretty trashed from my last visit. Guess that explained how I was able to kick in the door and yet still continue breathing.

"Whoa. What a fucking shithole," Tom said from behind me. "What the fuck happened here?"

"Sally happened."

"No way. Did she do that *thing* again?"

"Yeah. She did that thing ... times about a hundred."

"That's some kaioken level shit right there."

"Damned straight."

"So where is this Frieza fucking asshole anyway?"

"No idea."

I stepped in further and looked around, reaching out with my senses. Someone's scent still lingered in the air – probably Falcon's – but it was just that, lingering, not fresh. I was still catching up on the nuances of having vampire powers again, but if I had to guess I'd say it had probably been a few hours since he'd been here.

Fuck!

Although, truthfully, that shouldn't have come as a surprise. The reality was, if Falcon had been here, he'd have likely made his presence known the second Glen tripped his first ward.

But I realized that was okay. It might be petty, but a part of me was glad we'd trashed his defenses. The asshole had been dismissive to both me and Christy, treating her like a second-rate criminal even. Then there'd been that fucking house arrest bracelet he'd slapped on Sally – the one which had shunted her off to god knows where. For all I knew, she was even now being tortured in some Magi dungeon, all because Captain Mustache had deemed her a probable threat.

What a dick head. Where had he been when the rest of us had risked life and limb – and in Tom's case more – to save the world? Where had he been when a bunch of mages had gone rogue, allying themselves with Gan so as to unleash some godforsaken monstrosity on the world? Nowhere that mattered apparently. Instead, he'd waltzed into our city like he owned the place, tossed around a few potatoes, and pretty much declared himself Duke of New York.

Fuck that noise.

I spun and kicked over a bookshelf, already teetering on edge against the wall.

"So we're fucking this place up even more?" Tom asked.

"Debating it."

"Let me know, man, because I could use the practice."

I was about to tell him to have fun when a thought hit me. "Hey. How come when I get superpowers, you're all gung-ho to set me on fire, but when you get them, it's fun stuff like blowing shit up? Care to explain that?"

"Twenty bucks."

"What?"

"Yep. Back when you first became a bloodsucker, Ed bet me twenty bucks that you wouldn't be stupid enough to let us do all that shit to you. He was wrong and I got paid. That is what we in finance call a perfect day."

"You assholes made a bet about whether or not I'd let you kill me?"

"I may be the one with the vag these days, Bill, but you, sir, are eternally the bigger pussy. I mean, fuck all that. You heal like a motherfucker. You don't even have any scars to show for it, unlike me, I might add."

"What scars?"

"The ones I had ... before I figured out how to get rid of them."

I sighed and put my face in my hands, partial hands anyway. "I'm sorry I asked."

"So, are we going to trash this place or what?"

"Or what. He's not here, so there isn't much point."

"Okay, so what now?"

"No idea. I'm kind of hitting a dead end." I looked around, unsure of our next move, but then spotted something on the floor that had somehow been spared Sally's wrath. "But maybe not everyone is."

I bent to retrieve the cordless phone handset sticking out from beneath a pile of debris. It was a longshot, but maybe the base was still plugged in.

I hit the talk button and, amazingly enough, heard a dial tone. *Yes!* Finally, a bit of luck that wasn't entirely bad. I held it up to show Tom but noticed him wandering further into the once regal warehouse.

"Where are you going?"

"To this asshole's bedroom."

"Why?"

"I'm gonna leave a used tampon in his pillowcase."

"I thought you borrowed a pad from Kara."

"Dude, they're all tampons as far as I'm concerned. So, you in?"

I shrugged. "It's both gross and childish."

"I know."

I considered this for a moment. "Have fun!" Then I dialed Christy's number.

She picked up on the second ring. "Hello?"

"Thank goodness," I replied. "It's me."

"Bill? Where the hell have you been?"

"It's a long story, trust me on that. Listen, don't worry about me. I'm fine. It's Sally I'm worried about. She's..."

"She's right here beside me."

"Wait. She is?"

THE BLIND LEADING THE BLIND

Christy gave me the Cliff's Notes version of things. Long story short, she along with Falcon – of course – were both at Sally's place, where Sally had materialized some hours earlier.

They'd apparently been trying to get a hold of Tom and me ever since – not helped by us being phoneless, on the move, and with Tom's now functional powers futzing up their attempts to scry us.

Mindful of who was there with her, I decided to keep it vague. "My phone died and I totally forgot about Tom's powers. Sorry."

"It's fine. The important thing is you're both okay. What about..."

"Kara's good, too. She's with Pop. They're heading to Cape May."

"Why?"

"Um, just a little vacation. Y'know, to get away from it all. I'll explain when I get there."

"Where are you now?"

I glanced around the trashed, now wardless warehouse. "We're ... not too far away. I ... borrowed someone's cell to call you." I pulled away from the headset a bit. "Oh? What's that. You need it back? Listen, Christy. I've got to go. We're heading over now. Be there in a bit. Bye."

I ended the call, then tossed the handset away, hearing it clatter as it landed in a pile of something that looked like it was once a love seat. I mean, it's not like I was really messing up the place worse than it already was.

Tom rejoined me a moment later.

"Let's head out, man. Everyone is at Sally's place. You good?"

He grinned at me. "The package has been delivered."

I allowed myself a petty chuckle and then we stepped out into the night air to collect our friend.

Glen was back in his gross dog suit, waiting outside the chain link fence for our return.

"All good out here, buddy?" Somehow, I managed to resist the urge to pat his mangled head.

"Bark!"

"Shall I take that as a yes?"

"Indeed, Freewill. I spotted a few shifty characters lurking in the shadows but made sure to let them know I was standing here in faithful vigil."

"Good job, Lassie," Tom said, to which Glen wagged what was left of his tail.

"I bet those are fuckers who won't forget to spay or neuter their pets anytime soon," I replied, leading us away.

The subway would've been faster, but I didn't consider that a wonderful place to take a disgusting zombie dog. Not to mention, I didn't really consider it wise to be trapped inside a metal tube with people at the moment. My stomach had been rumbling since before our return to the city, and my game of magical ward tag hadn't served to make it better.

Truth of the matter was, my plan was to head over to Sally's, make sure she was okay, bitch Falcon out a bit, and bring everyone up to speed on the fact that werewolves were amongst our new problems. Once that was done, I figured I'd go downstairs and steal some of the coven's blood, then safely spend the rest of the night watching my fingers grow back. And that was it.

This fucking day needed to be over.

"So, we're all on the same page, right? Pop dropped us off uptown and we've been walking ever since. At no point did we head over to Falcon's personal birdcage and we definitely did not fuck it up even worse than it was."

"Nor did we stick a tampon in his..."

I turned to Tom. "Probably best to forget that altogether."

"Ooh. We could say we took a detour through a dog park," Glen offered.

I nodded. "Okay, that could work. You tried to play with some rottweilers, and they decided to use you as a chew toy instead."

"But I won in the end, right?" he asked hopefully.

"Sure you did, buddy."

"All dogs go to heaven," Tom replied, "but especially those who fuck with Glen."

He held up his hand and we high fived.

Maybe this new dynamic of ours wasn't so bad after all. Soon as we figured out a way to rescue Ed, we could...

Tap. Tap.

A low but persistent sound caught my ears as we turned onto Sally's block. The streets weren't exactly empty – they never really were in Midtown – which really wasn't helping my situation. I'd been making it a point to keep my head down as much as I could, so as to not tempt myself any more than I already was ... and I was pretty goddamned tempted. As it was, every person we passed smelled tastier than the last. Soon enough, it was going to drive me fucking crazy.

However, among the edible rabble hurrying this way and that, I spotted a lone woman walking slower and more carefully than the rest.

A moment later I realized why. She was tapping a long white cane out in front of her. Just as I noticed this, a group of barely twenty-something girls – all of them giggling, laughing, and probably high as balls, walked past, bumping into the blind woman and causing her to stumble.

They barely turned long enough to laugh out a false apology before continuing on their stoned merry way.

New Yorkers were famous for coming together during a tragedy, but that didn't mean there weren't tons of assholes in the bunch. Case in point.

I glanced toward Tom. Technically this was supposed to be his thing, last defender of humanity and all, but he seemed blissfully clueless. Typical.

Though I knew it wasn't smart, hungry as I was, it was still the right thing to do. And it's not like I hadn't been forced to curb my appetite before. I could behave for a while longer if need be.

"Hold on, guys. I'll be back in a second."

I stepped away, crossing over to the other side of the street, where the blind woman appeared to be regaining her bearings. As I approached, I saw she wasn't much older than the group who'd tripped her up – probably around my age when I'd first gotten dragged into this shit. She had short black hair, a Hispanic complexion, and was wearing a light jacket and dark glasses, despite it being night – which obviously wouldn't mean shit to her anyway.

"Hey," I called out, not looking to startle her. "Are you okay? I saw those assholes bump into you."

She turned her head my way and smiled, revealing straight white teeth. "I'm good, thanks. Happens all the time. Everyone here is always in a rush, even this time of night. You get used to it."

"Okay. Just wanted to make sure. That wasn't cool what they did."

"I appreciate it. Nice to see not everyone in this city is a pendejo."

"All right then." I turned, then hesitated, not really sure what the protocol was in situations like this. "Um ... before I go, is there anything I can help you with?"

"Is this your way of asking me out?"

"Um ... no. I just meant, um..."

She smiled again, obviously aware that I was trying to extract my foot from my mouth. "How about this? Help me across the street and we'll call it a day. Damned long blocks. Takes forever to reach the cross walk."

"I know what you mean, but sure. Um, here." I held out my arm to her. After a moment, she took it and we stepped to the curb.

Somewhere close by a car screeched on its brakes, not atypical for the city.

The scent of burning rubber filled my nose, distinct yet distant ... probably too distant for a normal nose to pick up. It was one of the benefits and curses of being a vampire. A single breath through my nostrils revealed layers upon layers of scents: the scalded tires, the general dirt of the street around us, Tom and Glen up ahead – a strange combination of Sheila's scent mixed with the rotting meat suit Glen was wearing. Beneath them all were many more layers, but none that I cared to spend much time on. Leave that shit to the bloodhounds, I say.

A few moments later, we stepped back onto the sidewalk where both Tom and Glen were waiting.

"A truly noble gesture, Freewill," Glen called out, before adding, "Bark!"

Out of the corner of my eye, I saw the blind woman raise an eyebrow behind her glasses.

"Um, I'm with two of my friends. I mean a friend and my dog."

She shrugged then let go of my arm. "Well, I appreciate the help, Mr. ... Freewill. Thank you."

"My pleasure."

She started to turn, heading in the opposite direction to where we were going, then stopped and cocked her head. "You may want to take your dog to the vet."

"I do?" I replied, eyes opening wide.

"Yeah," she said, once more turning away. "I can hear him limping ... among other things."

I managed to stifle a chuckle as she walked off. If only she could've seen Glen, she'd have instantly known he was long past the point where a veterinarian would do anything other than run away screaming.

"That chick was totally faking," Tom said, drawing me from my reverie as we finally neared Sally's building.

"Huh?" I'd been stuck in thought the last minute or so, something nagging me in the back of my mind that I couldn't quite put my finger on. Then again, a lot had happened in the past several hours. So it likely wasn't surprising that something about this fuckery of a day was bothering me.

"I said she was probably faking. You should have checked."

"How the fuck was I supposed to check?" I asked. "Wave my hand in front of her face like an asshole?"

"No way. Everyone knows that trick. What you've gotta do is pull out your dick. Nobody expects that. If they give a reaction, they're a fucking faker."

I was tempted to ask how he'd come to this revelation, then realized I didn't actually want to know. "Pass. The cops might have instructions to turn their heads the other way at vampires running wild, but I'd prefer not to push my luck."

"Pussy."

"I have quite the opposite, unlike you, and I'd prefer to not have it flapping in the breeze in Soho. Now remember what we talked about."

We made our way up to Sally's floor without seeing any other souls, living or otherwise.

That reminded me, I really needed to check on my aspiring coveners, but first things first. Making sure Sally was okay took priority.

Her door was already open for us. I stepped aside to let Glen and Tom in ahead of me, pausing for one brief moment to glance at the wall opposite her apartment, which was now good as new – maybe even better. You'd have never guessed someone had been utterly pulped there less than a day ago.

Needless to say, I knew who I was calling the next time my apartment got trashed.

"Miss O'Connell," Falcon's voice greeted from inside. "I've heard a great deal about you. It's a pleasure to make your acquaintance, Shining... What the bloody hell is that?!"

Oh yeah. I probably should've remembered that Glen looked like a walking nightmare before letting him saunter into a place where a wizard cop was waiting.

"It's okay, Matthias. That's Glen and he's just ... wearing a..."

Christy's voice caught my ear, especially the fact that we were back to Matthias again, so I quickly stepped inside. "It's a disguise," I finished for her, before lamely adding, "Still a work in progress."

"A work in progress?" Falcon asked, standing between Sally and Christy, and looking far too smug for my personal edification.

"Bark!"

"We, um, ran into some trouble with some stray dogs," I replied, sounding not even remotely convincing.

"Oh my god," Christy cried. "What happened to your hand?"

I held it up. "They were mighty big dogs."

"Ah, that explains it then," Falcon said, looking disturbingly dapper despite the late hour. If there was one thing I hated more than a fucker, it was a kempt fucker. "For a moment there I thought you might be trying to reintroduce zombies into the current state of affairs – nasty business that it might be."

I remembered the way Boston had once used them, as clerical help of all things. Can't say I would have minded an undead maid to keep my apartment tidy. "Wish I knew how."

"No," Falcon said, approaching me. "You really don't. Trust me on this, chap."

Well, that was far more ominous than expected. But fuck it. I wasn't here for this turd in a teacup. Instead I stepped past him toward Sally. "Thank goodness you're..."

"Save it," she replied, holding up a hand. "I'm fine. Just caught me by surprise. How about you? Did you manage to scare off those weirdos?"

"You aren't going to believe what those..."

Grrr! Realizing that Tom was about to blow his load in front of Falcon, despite our talk on the way over, I quickly jumped in. "Stoned hippies ... just like Pop thought. It was all a big misunderstanding. You know how those tree huggers can be." Realizing my acting was getting worse the more I spoke, I tried to change the subject. "Forget about them. False alarm, nothing more. What the hell happened to you and how did you get back here?"

"I was explaining that to your lovely companions when you called," Falcon replied. "It's a failsafe built into the bracelet. Think of it like an extra clever GPS, friend. It tracks where you are. If you get too far away from where you're supposed to be for too long, it activates and sends you right back to where you should be."

I glared at him, feeling my eyes blacken in the process. "And you didn't think to tell us that?"

"I was just apologizing to Miss Carlsbad about that oversight on my part. I didn't think it was a consideration, as I'd set it to its maximum range. That's more than enough to encompass the city and the surrounding boroughs. No offense, but I didn't expect you lot to go traipsing out to the wilderness the moment I sent you on your way."

"We're spontaneous like that."

"So I'm beginning to see. Anyway, we had ourselves a good sit down, cleared the air a bit. Next time you decide to go off on an adventure, just give me a call and it'll all be aces."

I turned toward Sally. "And you're okay with this? Asking for permission that is?"

"It's not permission," Falcon said. "Think of it more like ... like letting your bank know before you go off on holiday. Therefore, all your cards work right when you get where you're going. You know, don't leave home without it?"

"I know what that is." However, there was only one person whose opinion on that mattered and it wasn't his. I turned back toward Sally to see how much murder was showing on her face but was surprised to find it wasn't much.

She let out a sigh. "I'm not happy about it, but Matt makes a convincing argument. It's to keep people safe. So, for now, I can deal."

Matt?

Goddamn it! I so hated the British with their ... charm and sophistication!

The only upside was that we'd apparently caught Falcon's smarmy ass on the way out. Guess he wasn't too big on sticking around once a real man made the scene.

And no, I didn't really buy that either, but I needed something to make me feel better, especially with both ladies in the room making goo goo eyes at the guy.

"Now, if you'll kindly pardon me," he said. "I have a lot to do before morning – a mess to still clean up, not to mention some surveillance reports to go through. This doesn't leave this room, but those vampire killings we talked about..." He glanced over at Tom, who was standing there chewing on his fingernails, then apparently dismissed him as anything other than a moron. "It seems I may have ruffled a few feathers in my investigation. The local constabulary has received more than a handful of death threats, all with my name attached to them."

"That ... sucks."

"Quite the contrary. Means the guilty party is nervous and I'm getting close. That's a good thing in this business, chap."

"Hah," Tom replied. "With us, that usually just means Bill's about to get his ass kicked."

I shot him a dirty look, but Falcon was apparently too classy to acknowledge the dig at me.

Or too preoccupied with a certain witch.

"Christine, do be sure not to hold that particular incantation for long. The strain can sneak up on you."

"Incantation?"

"It's nothing important, Bill. Don't worry about it," she replied, before showing Falcon out.

"Ladies," he said as way of announcing his farewell. "Freewill, Shining One, um ... Glen."

"Later, dude," Tom replied, sounding nonplussed. At least there was one female – sorta anyway – immune to *Matthias's* insufferable charm.

Christy closed the door, but I waited before saying anything – listening as Falcon's footsteps reached the stairwell and started down.

With him finally gone, I walked over to where Sally stood.

"Listen, Bill," she said. "It's obvious you don't like the guy, but even you have to admit he's only trying to..."

"That's nice," I interrupted. "But I have a better question. Like, when were you going to tell me that werewolves fucking exist?"

DEAD CALM BEFORE
THE STORM

"Hold on, what?"

"Exactly what I said. Back when I was first turned, you specifically told me werewolves were just make believe."

"You did," Tom confirmed. "Bill told us all about it. Seriously bummed me out."

Sally raised an eyebrow at us both. "Did you morons huff from the same exhaust pipe again?"

"They do in a sense," Christy said, taking a seat on the couch. "Werewolves, not the exhaust pipe thing. I mean, we all know shapeshifters exist. The Jahabich were proof of that. And there are both nature spirits and some forms of fae that can assume animal forms."

"What about rednecks?" I asked her.

"Excuse me?"

"I'm talking naked, dueling banjos motherfuckers who turn into giant hairy monsters when some hillbilly witch shoots a magical moon into the sky."

Christy and Sally both stared blankly at me for several seconds, then Christy leaned back and closed both eyes as if deep in thought.

Couldn't blame her. This was a lot to take in.

"Sorry, dude," Tom replied, "but I was there, and you still lost me in that pile of word vomit."

"Yeah, back up a bit," Sally said. "What happened to the stoned..."

I took a deep breath and sat down as well. "They were neither stoned nor hippies. I just didn't want to say anything in front of Bird Boy." I held up my mangled hand again. "Bottom line is, I wasn't lying, but the dogs that chewed me up happened to weigh four hundred pounds and could stand on their hind legs."

I explained to them how things had rapidly gone downhill after Sally poofed away. Tom and Glen jumped in here and there to fill in the blanks or – in Glen's case anyway – to explain how awesome it was to see the Freewill in action against the vile hounds of hell.

"Damn. Can't believe I missed all of that," Sally said at last. "And you're sure a Magi caused it?"

"I don't know if she did *any* of it, but one was there and she poofed up a full moon for these assholes."

"The moon?"

"A glamour of it anyway, or so I assume."

"So she created an illusion of the moon and that caused them all to change? That doesn't make any fucking sense. That's like showing you a picture of the sun and hoping you burst into flames."

"Maybe not," Christy said, opening her eyes again.

"How so?"

She turned to me. "I can't believe I'm asking this, but what color did she glow right before casting?"

"Hah! I knew you guys color-coordinated."

"Don't be a dick to my woman," Tom chided. "Just answer the damned question."

I glanced sidelong at him but decided not to take the bait. "Give me a second here. It was a little chaotic. I know she cast one of those force dome thingies around the same time, but that was to keep the wolves from attacking her."

"They attacked her?" Christy asked, eyes wide.

"Yeah. It's like she triggered them but didn't actually control them. They were more like wild animals than people, except infinitely scarier and ... hold on. Yellow. Her hands glowed yellow and then she shot a blast of magic into the sky."

Christy nodded, although her expression seemed troubled. "I was afraid of that. It's possible she cast a glamour but one with a secondary mind magic element to it."

"And you've lost me."

She tented her fingers and closed her eyes again. Guess she was tired. I know I sure as hell was. "Again, this is mere speculation on my part. As far as I'm aware, nothing like what you're describing actually exists." I opened my mouth, but she wasn't finished yet. "I'm not saying you're wrong. What I mean is that simply seeing the moon shouldn't be enough. Such a profound physical metamorphosis would likely require a lot more than mere visual stimuli. It's like Sally said. Otherwise, you'd have people turning into monsters merely by watching the wrong TV show."

"So, you're saying she hypnotized these fuckers?" Tom asked.

"In a sense. Theoretically speaking, there would likely be a lot of factors at play for something like this to work. No, I'm not talking to you, honey."

I raised an eyebrow. "Excuse me?"

She held up a hand and continued. "What I'm trying to say is, there's likely other factors at play – the tides, slight changes in gravitational pull, or maybe alterations in brain chemistry. If I had to make an educated guess, this spell didn't simply make the moon appear. It caused those affected by it to actually believe – mentally and physically – that it was real."

"So ... hypnotized," Tom repeated.

"More or less."

I turned to Sally. "And you're certain you weren't shitting me about this stuff?"

"Not with all the fiber in the world. But seriously, Bill, I asked the same questions back when I was first dragged into the fold ... perhaps not as pathetically, but I still asked. And not just to Jeff, because it was obvious from the start that dumbass didn't know much about anything that couldn't be snorted. Besides, you were there when shit went south, both in Canada and down in Calibra's lair. We both saw a lot of weird crap, stuff I'd love to pretend didn't exist, but at no point did I see any dog men running around barking at the moon."

She had a point there. Although, speaking of dogs, I turned next to our resident blob. "How about you, Glen? You've been around a while. Any of this ring a bell?"

He'd thankfully shed his dog disguise at some point and was now merely a gross pile of eyeball snot. Definitely an improvement. His body quivered in response, his version of a shrug. "Nothing of the sort comes to mind, Freewill. Although, I once witnessed a pair of sea otters devouring one of the Forest Folk after it wandered too close to their..."

"That's fascinating. You'll have to tell me about it sometime," I interrupted, trying to keep us on point. "What about the Jahabich? Could they have survived and somehow evolved ... again?"

It seemed a valid assumption to me, but even Tom was able to shoot that one down.

"Okay, but what were they doing in Buttfuck PA?"

"That ... is a good question."

"A good question for a stupid theory," Sally said. "Don't forget, the Jahabich only took on the forms of the creatures they killed. So, for this to work, either they'd have had to kill a werewolf themselves or..."

"Or they killed a dog and a person together at the same time and somehow it all got frigged up in the mix." That seemed a stretch, even for us. "Which brings us back to square one, having no fucking idea where these things came from. Or how they're connected to vampires."

"Wait," Christy replied, popping her eyes open again. "What do you mean connected to vampires?"

"Something one of them said to me. Some jackass named Hobart. I mean, seriously, who names their kid that?"

"The point, Bill?" Sally prompted.

"Oh, yeah. Anyway, he told me that his people were free now and then he babbled on about top covens and being lorded over."

"Top covens? You mean the First Coven?"

"Hard to say. The guy was a bit of an idiot. But yeah, I guess."

Sally narrowed her strange eyes at me and took a deep breath. "And you didn't think to lead with this tidbit?"

"Sorry, but I figured the part about almost getting my arms chewed off by imaginary monsters was headline enough."

"That changes things," Christy said, looking none too pleased. "If they knew about the First Coven, then it stands to reason the First Coven knew about them, too. But in what capacity?"

"Maybe not." Sally picked up her glass from the coffee table and took a sip from it. "I'm not going to pretend James told me everything. But never once did he ever even hint at something like this. Not even in that smooth 'I'm obviously hiding something' way he had about him."

It was quite smooth, my subconscious suddenly offered. I hadn't guessed Dr. Death to be a fan of anything, much less James, but whatever. "Maybe they were, I dunno, a secret weapon."

"I suppose it's possible," Christy said, although she sounded doubtful.

Sally, however, seemed even less convinced. "If that were the case, then why didn't we see them in the final days of the war, when the Feet attacked Boston? Or when Alex's troops stormed the Source chamber. You can't tell me a platoon of werewolves wouldn't have been useful down there."

Christy nodded. "Sally's right. That doesn't make sense."

"Maybe they kept them as pets," Tom offered, as unhelpful as always. "Can you imagine that – some redneck on a leash taking a dump on Alex's rug? That would've been awesome."

I couldn't really disagree. However, during my brief time in the vampire headquarters, I hadn't seen any sign of giant doggie beds or oversized piddle pads. I mean, shit, they'd introduced me to a fucking death god, so why bother hiding a bunch of hicks who put the doggy in doggy style?

"This doesn't make any sense."

"No, it doesn't," Christy replied, sliding over and putting a hand on my arm. "But we'll figure it out. We always do."

Tom, never one to let an opportunity for cock-blocking slip, immediately moved to her other side, putting an arm around her. "We'll figure it out and kick their asses. *Together*."

"Yes, together," she confirmed with a smile, which quickly dropped off as she got back to the topic at hand. "But it still bothers me. I mean, I can understand them keeping it from you, Bill, and you too, Sally. You were part of the system and a good deal of that system involved secrets. But the Magi have existed side by side with the vampires since the beginning, and not always in harmony. What I'm saying is that each side kept tabs on the other. I can't see the vampire nation having a hidden army without us having gotten even a slight hint of it."

I opened my mouth to agree, but then a thought hit me. Hell, it was the same thought which had been bothering us all – except for Tom maybe – for a couple of days now: old things. "Wait, you said from the beginning. And we know that's true since Calibra was both the White Mother and the first vampire. But is it maybe safe to assume that those early days were kind of chaotic? I mean, we have email now. But back then, someone probably had to send a messenger pterodactyl and hope it didn't get eaten on the way."

She inclined her head and gave it a half nod. "I suppose that's not an entirely incorrect assumption."

"Well, what if this is another thing like those proto-leprechauns? Something old that's only coming back now because all the rules have gone out the window."

"Possible..." Christy opined.

"If so, then books and scrolls wouldn't bother mentioning them because there's been nothing to make mention of, until now."

"Yeah," Sally replied, "but did any of those naked mouth breathers out there strike you as being thousands of years old?"

And there was my theory hitting a brick wall. "That's ... a really good point. Remember some of the older vamps we used to deal with? You could tell right away they didn't really belong – talking like they'd just stepped out of a fucking time machine. But these guys, I wouldn't have batted an eye if their dicks hadn't been swinging in the wind."

"Superman had kryptonite," Tom replied. "Bill has cock."

I absentmindedly flipped him the finger, while Christy shook her head before once more closing her eyelids.

"Are you okay?"

"I'm fine. Stop changing the subject. The problem is, regardless of whether these things are brand new or so old that even Magi history makes no mention of them, we're stuck at square one. We have no way of researching what they are or how to fight them."

"Assuming there's even reason to," Tom offered.

"How so?"

"Well, we're in the city and their asses are back in the woods. Do we have any reason to think they'll try following us here?"

"Ed," I reminded him. "They were looking for him for whatever reason, and knew Pop was his dad. Now they know our faces, too."

"Fuck! I forgot about that."

"I'm not exactly expecting to go home and find these guys humping the neighbors' legs down in the foyer, but I'm not so trusting these days that I don't want to be ready for it."

Christy nodded, before opening her eyes to look at us all. A thin sheen of sweat had appeared on her forehead at some point. What the? "I hate to ask him for more than we already have, but we're going to need to bring Matthias into the loop on this. If these creatures were known to the First Coven, maybe there's mention of them in their archives..."

"Which are now that crazy hosebeast bitch's archives," Sally said.

"True, but the Falcon Archives go back just as far. While Matthias is looking for clues about the entity Gan conjured, maybe he can also check to see..."

As this exchange went on, I kept looking expectantly at Christy, waiting for her to drop the bombshell I'd sent her but, infuriatingly enough, it didn't seem to be forthcoming. Guess it was up to me to get this party started.

"Okay, hold on. We don't need *Matthiasshole's* help for any of this, not anymore."

"I know you don't trust him, Bill, but I really do think he's the only shot we have at..."

"No, he's not." Then, after a moment, when it became blindingly obvious she had no idea what I was talking about, I added, "Seriously? Did you not check your email today?"

"What are you talking about?" Sally replied.

"My secret project, of course," I said with a smile.

"You mean that wasn't just some stupid scheme to get free porn for life?"

Tom immediately perked up. "Wait, free porn for life? And was nobody going to tell me?"

"There's no porn," I replied before turning back toward Christy. "You didn't check your email, did you?"

"I checked it a few hours ago. Why?"

"Okay, and did you get what I sent you?"

"You're sending my woman porn?"

I shot Tom a glare. "No! There's no porn, free or otherwise. Well, there is, but that's not the point here."

Christy looked confused for a moment, but finally recognition dawned on her face. "Wait. You mean that message from earlier?"

"Yes!"

"The one with the random numbers and instructions that made no sense? I thought that was maybe a ... butt dial."

"You can't butt dial email." Okay, this was going nowhere fast. I needed to remember I'd sent technical instructions to someone not in the IT field. It was like asking my mother to check her DNS settings. "All right, let's back up a bit here. Do you have your phone on you?" She nodded. "Can I see it?"

Christy pulled it out of her purse and handed it over – a mid-spec Android model a couple of years old. I doubted it would be long before she was forced to upgrade, considering how our lifestyles had gone from normal to batshit, but for now it would do just fine.

I opened up her email, found my message, then got to work, all while – yep, you guessed it – she leaned back and shut her eyes again. Christ, it was like she'd developed narcolepsy in the few hours I'd been gone.

Okay, enough of that. I could ask if she was getting enough sleep once this was over. Hell, maybe we could even settle down for a nap together. For now, though...

"Those weren't random numbers," I explained as I typed. "It was an IP address. And those instructions were for an anonymous VPN I occasionally use when I ... um, don't want to be tracked by ... my enemies."

"Hey," Tom replied, "is that the same one we use to download hentai ISOs?"

"No, it is not. In fact, I have no idea what you're talking about." Was it getting warm in here, or was it me? Doing my best to ignore the eyeballs now turned my way, I continued to work.

"Is this one of those games you told me you used to build?" Glen asked hopefully.

"No such luck."

329

"Too bad."

He wasn't wrong, I considered as I set things up on Christy's phone. Some days I missed my old gig at HopSkotchGames.com. Making games had been a hell of a lot more interesting than debugging databases, even if I was now my own boss.

There was also the fact that I was a vampire again, meaning the chances of me working for another company and it not going tits up due to supernatural assassins or extradimensional incursions were...

My thoughts trailed off as my stomach grumbled, making me more than aware that at least a few of the people around me were edible. Hell, one of them was even menstruating, the scent so intoxicating that...

OH GOD! NO FUCKING WAY! I pushed that thought away, desperately wishing that brain bleach was a real thing. Gah!

"I ... I don't suppose one of you wants to run downstairs and maybe see if our resident coven has any blood to spare."

"It shall be my pleasure, Freewill," Glen replied, oozing back into his nightmare dog suit.

Yeah, that was probably not going to go over well. "Um, anyone else want to go with him?"

"I'll go," Tom said. "Standing here watching you dick around with a phone is about as exciting as it sounds."

"Thanks."

He and Glen stepped out, their footsteps echoing in my ears as they walked away.

"Sending a zombie mutt and the Icon to talk to a bunch of already skittish vamps?" Sally remarked. "I'm almost tempted to see how that works out."

"Maybe you can go all Dark Phoenix on them while you're at it, because that can only make things better."

"I'm going to pretend that actually meant something."

"Whatever floats your boat because..." I hit the last sequence of keys then checked to make sure it all loaded correctly. "I'm finished. Woo!" I leaned over to Christy and held out the phone for her. "Wakey wakey, eggs and bakey."

"I wasn't asleep." She opened her eyes, took the phone, and looked down at the screen, raising an eyebrow.

"Pretty freaking awesome, isn't it?"

Rather than offer up the gushing accolades I was waiting for, she simply looked confused. "It's a ... web page?"

"Not just any web page. Do a search for werewolves or maybe leprechauns and see what comes up."

"Why?"

I guess I was going to have to explain it to her. Ah, true genius is never appreciated. "The Falcon Archives."

"What about them?"

"You're looking at it."

"What?!"

"Hold on a second," Sally said, a trace of admiration in her voice. "You actually hacked the wizard Pentagon?"

"Hack is really too strong of a word. The protection on it is almost non-existent. No biometrics or two factor authentication, and the way they installed the SSL cert is a joke. Hell, they didn't even change the name of the admin account. I figured there'd be something more there ... maybe a magical firewall or two. But nope. All I had to do was run a few brute force password crackers and I was in like Flynn."

Sally actually smiled. "Look at you being all black hat and shit."

I grinned back, almost feeling like a supervillain monologuing his diabolical plan. "I got the idea the first time we met Falcon. He was busy sounding self-important, explaining how there weren't a lot of techs in the Magi world. Well, he's probably right. But he failed to take into account there's at least one competent IT guy on the vampire side."

"B-but, how did you even find this?" Christy asked. "There's millions of web pages out there and..."

"That bit of brilliance required no technical skill whatsoever, just a bit of social engineering." Seeing her blank look, I explained. "Remember when I got all up in his personal space when he was examining Sally? Well, I wasn't merely trying to be annoying. I mean, I kinda was, but I was also scoping out the web address. The rest was all about getting in and making sure it couldn't be traced back to us ... although, considering the security on display, I'm pretty confident about that one."

"Not bad, Bill," Sally replied. "Maybe you should hire yourself out."

I chuckled. "Bill Ryder: dragging ancient knowledge into the twenty-first century. Gotta admit, that'd make for a hell of a business card. Right, Christy?" I turned to find her staring at her screen, probably too engrossed with all the secrets she was learning to notice what I'd said. "Christy?"

She finally met my gaze, the expression on her face somewhat less than the adoring admiration I was hoping for. "This is wrong."

"What? Did I typo the password? Pretty sure it let me in just a moment ago..."

"No. What you did is wrong. You broke into the deepest secrets of Magi society."

'I know. Isn't it Cool?"

Red power flashed behind her eyes, instantly erasing all traces of glib on my tongue. "No. It is not cool. It's a violation of trust of the highest order." Then she added, "It's okay, I'm not mad at you."

"Oh. That's good..."

"Yes, I am mad at you, Bill."

Huh?

Sally looked between us for a moment, then got up. "Think I'm gonna go top off my drink ... and maybe make some popcorn while I'm at it."

Oh yeah, that was helpful.

"Okay, fine," I said. "Maybe it's a violation of Falcon's trust. I'll give you that. But don't forget this is the guy who shot you down when..."

"That's not the point," she snapped. "Yes, I was hoping he'd give me access, was angry when he didn't, but I respected his decision. And since then I've been thinking about it and realized he made the right choice. The archives have been kept under the strictest lock and key for millennia, and for good reason. The secrets contained within cannot be allowed to get out, even among our own community. Just because things have changed in the last few years, doesn't mean those values should change. The information within is still dangerous, perhaps now more than ever. And Matthias was right. My reputation in the Magi community isn't all that spectacular. What kind of precedent would he be setting by handing over the keys to a...?"

"Miscreant?" Sally offered. "Undesirable maybe?"

"Thank you," Christy replied dryly.

"Anytime."

"So ... you're not happy?"

"No, Bill. I am not." She put a hand on my shoulder, fortunately one that wasn't glowing with killing magic. "Listen, I know you meant well, and I appreciate the sentiment. But this isn't the vampire nation, or you pulling one over on the First Coven. These are the Magi, *my* people.

Technically speaking, they could see this as an act of war if they found out about it."

"*If* they found out," I repeated. "Did I mention the VPN you're using makes a couple dozen double hops? There's no way they'll..." I trailed off as I saw the look on her face. "That's not making it better is it?"

"Not really. Like I said, I appreciate the sentiment. It's sweet ... in a way. But this is something you need to stay away from." She took both my hands in hers, again with no death magic thankfully. "I know we need to find Ed and help Sally. And these new ... creatures simply add more complications to our already full plates, but we'll figure it out in our own way. Trust me on this, please."

"I do trust you."

"Then promise me you won't do this again."

Shit! I glanced Sally's way out of the corner of my eye and caught her smirking. Bitch. But she at least knew it wasn't always as simple as that. The truth was, this world of supernatural horrors, the one we all seemed to once again be getting sucked into, was not a nice place. Sometimes it required not nice solutions.

In order to win. Hell, in order to *survive*, we occasionally needed to do what had to be done. Taking the high road was all well and good in concept, but sometimes there was no way around the fact that you had to gut a motherfucker in order to stop them.

At the same time, pissing Christy off wasn't high on my list, especially since I was already walking on eggshells around her. Besides, this was kind of a specific scenario anyway. I could take one for the team – for her.

"Fine. No more hacking Magi archives."

"No more mucking about in Magi affairs period, not unless you run it past me first. This is for your protection, too. Most of my people aren't as understanding about these things as I am."

Damn it. She was going to hold me over a barrel with this, wasn't she? "Okay. I promise. Mind you, that doesn't count if they shoot at me first. Deal?"

"Deal," she said before leaning in to give me a hug, albeit kind of a curt one.

Regardless, I took the opportunity to stick my tongue out at Sally. Immature of me, yes, but you use what you have.

"And whatever you do," Christy added as she pulled away, "don't let Matthias know. He won't ... understand."

That was probably an understatement.

I sat back and chuckled. "Yeah. Safe to say he's probably already going to be ticked off."

"Why? What did you do?"

I grinned sheepishly. "We might have stopped by his place first. I mean, think about it. We had no working cell phone, were running from werewolves, and Sally disappeared right after her stupid bracelet beeped. There wasn't much I could do about those first two, but I had no intention of letting that third one pass."

"I'm flattered to know I made your top three for the evening," Sally replied from the wet bar.

"Don't let it go to your head."

"What did you do, Bill?" Christy repeated.

"It wasn't just me."

Speaking of the devils, my sensitive vampire ears picked up the sound of footsteps walking up the stairs. Seemed our two wayward companions were returning, hopefully without freaking out the already skittish vamps downstairs.

"I don't care who was there. Just tell me what you did."

"Fine. We may have set off some of his wards getting to his front door."

"Some...?"

"More like all."

"Do you realize how insane that is? You could've been killed!"

"This isn't my first rodeo, you know. Not to mention, Tom finally figured out how to use his powers, sorta anyway."

"Sorta?"

"Good enough to fizzle out everything he touched."

To be on the safe side, I took a quick sniff of the air – my paranoia already on its highest setting from this day's happenings. Sure enough, one of the scents headed this way was Tom. The other smelled like dead...

He has a distinct scent.

No idea why my subconscious was pointing that out, but whatever. Maybe Dr. Death was hoping for a new nickname: Captain Obvious.

But that woman did not.

Wait, what? I ignored Christy as she continued bitching me out, probably at my own risk, as I considered what I was hearing in my head.

What woman? The only other person I'd run into tonight, other than Kara, had been that blind chick who...

I thought back to that moment. It was simply meant to be a nice gesture on my part – helping her across the street – nothing more. But something about it had bothered me afterwards and I didn't know why.

At the time, I'd dismissed it as nothing more than me already being on edge. But now, the annoying voice in my head that suddenly seemed to be full of all sorts of useless information was finally chiming in.

More importantly, Dr. Death was right.

I remembered taking a breath as we crossed the street, idly analyzing all the scents which had filled my nose, and not realizing she hadn't given off any.

My eyes opened wide as I heard her voice in my memory.

"Is this your way of asking me out?"

That wasn't the first time someone had said that to me this week, and I'm not talking about Christy either.

Shit!

"...Yes, I admit perhaps he went a little overboard on his protections," Christy continued, seemingly mid-rant, "but you have to understand his position here. The media has already outed him and he's a known figure among the Magi. Whoever's been hunting down those vampires could very well have him in their sights. Taking down his wards might seem a bit of childish revenge, but there could be real world consequences..."

"I agree," I interrupted. "In fact, I think we should get over there *now*."

"I'm glad you realize what you did was wrong. But it's getting late and..."

"Char," I said.

"What?"

"Isn't that the name of that boogeyman you were telling us about?" Sally asked. "The one who kicked your..."

"Boogeywoman," I corrected. "And no, she didn't kick my ass ... entirely. But she did dust the shit out of a big ugly motherfucker of a vamp like it was nothing."

"What about her?" Christy asked.

"You're not going to like this, but I think she was hanging around outside earlier."

"No dice, man," Tom said, stepping through the doorway with Glen hot on his heels.

"Sorry, Freewill," Glen added. "But it would seem nobody was home."

"What do you mean, nobody was home? Where the fuck did they go?"

Tom shrugged. "Do I look like vampire friend-finder to you?"

"Who cares about that," Christy cried, dragging me back to the real issue at hand. "This person? You saw her outside and didn't say anything?"

"I didn't realize it was her. It's just now that it hit me. Her scent, or lack thereof, and something she said about a date."

"You asked another chick out?" Tom asked accusingly. "Not cool, dude."

"No. It was just something she said."

"Who?"

"That blind woman we met. I think she's Char. You know, the vampire slayer I told you about."

Tom slapped a hand down onto one of Sally's end tables. "I knew that bitch was faking."

"Shit!" I cried as yet another piece of the puzzle fell into place. "And she knew about this building, too."

"She knew about my home? How?"

"Not your home," I told Sally, "at least not at the time. You were still a hunk of rock. But I tried to recruit her for the coven. Told her she could come here if she needed a place to stay – that we wouldn't judge her."

Tom sighed. "Good job on the Amnesty International speech, dude."

"Not helping!"

"So, who was she here for, Matthias or the coven?" Christy asked, looking both none too pleased and also sweating profusely for some reason. What was up with her?

"I don't know. I mean, she knew what we were doing. That we were trying to recruit vamps who didn't want to be monsters."

"Vamps who are apparently no longer in the building, I might add," Sally said. "Do you think she got in and...?"

"I don't know," I replied, turning to Tom. "Any sign of forced entry or piles of dust?"

He shrugged. "None that I noticed. But we just knocked on a few doors. That's it. I didn't realize I needed to play CSI with this shit."

"Fuck!"

"All right then, who do we go after?" Sally asked, trying to be the voice of practicality amidst the chaos. "And before you say anything dumb, Bill, yes I mean we. Wait here." She walked into her bedroom, returning a moment later with the hand cannon she'd been wielding back at Pop's. "I hope Ed's father doesn't mind that I kept this, because I'm not giving it back."

"Probably the least of his worries," Tom remarked.

"True."

"The best idea is to split up," Christy said, turning toward me. "You track the..."

"No," I interrupted. "Tracking the vamps is a snipe hunt. We don't know whether they walked out the front door or the sewers. If they went down, it's going to be nearly impossible to find them on short notice. And if they went the other way, I don't think we'll be able to find them before she does. But we know where Falcon's going. If he's her target, then maybe we can get there in time to make a difference."

"Are you sure?"

I actually wasn't, not even remotely. Shit, the fact that she was calling him Matthias again almost made me want to buy ringside seats to watch the smarmy fucker get disemboweled. No! That was the monster inside of me talking. Hungry or not, I needed to be a man about this.

"I'm certain," I replied. "I screwed things up for the guy, I admit that. So now it's time for me to try and make it right again."

Hopefully without having to add, "or die trying," to any of that, because I felt bad, but maybe not *that* bad.

PLAYING IN TRAFFIC

Annoyingly, mobilizing for action meant a good deal of bickering about how exactly to mobilize.

On the upside, it was at least kind of comforting to know that some things were probably never going to change for us.

First thing we did was have Christy try to call Falcon – getting no answer, of course, because why would things ever be that easy?

That done, the quickest and likely smartest route was for us to let Christy apparate us to the docks or at least the surrounding neighborhood. Reappearing inside Falcon's glamour could be tricky, especially if we missed any of his wards. I didn't think we had but wasn't willing to bet my life on it.

The problem with that idea – as it tended to be – was Tom. Friggy powers or not, he was still the Icon, and Icons tended to play havoc with magical teleportation.

Christy suggested scouting ahead, but I ixnayed that. Bottom line was Char was dangerous, more dangerous than a freshly turned vamp should be. Christy herself was scary as fuck when she wanted to be, but it wasn't wise to pop in blind against an opponent who ... err ... pretended to be blind. Well, either way, I didn't like it, not when Falcon's place was relatively close by as it was.

"Fine," Christy said at last, looking strangely winded. "But I'll still have to meet you there. And no, I'm not asking."

"What do you mean? And seriously what's up with you tonight? One moment you go all power nap, the next you look like you just ran the Boston marathon."

Christy, however, ignored me in favor of Glen. "I hate to ask this, but can you babysit again for a bit tonight?"

"After we confront this wicked charred vampire?" Glen bubbled hopefully.

"No. Right now."

Suddenly a thought hit me and I stepped between them. "Wait a second. Who's watching Tina?"

"I am," Christy replied, "but I can't keep doing that and help out at the same time."

"Whoa, back up a second. What does that even mean?"

Seeing that I wasn't backing off easily, she apparently decided that explaining was the quickest way we were getting anything done.

"When Sally called, I wasn't about to leave her high and dry, but it's not like I have a lot of sitter options for Tina these days ... and, no offense, but I couldn't risk bringing her with me."

"Trust me," Sally replied, "None taken. The last thing I want is to put her in danger ... or level the building."

I raised an eyebrow. "Wait. That's what Falcon was talking about earlier, right, when he was blathering about incantations?"

"Yes. To a non-Magi it probably looks like I'm resting my eyes, but someone trained in the art wouldn't be fooled for a second."

"Fooled by what?" Tom asked.

"That I was splitting my consciousness between here and home."

"Holy shit! You can do that?"

She nodded, sweating even more copiously now. "Yes, but not easily and not for long. There's a ... glamour of me back home, mimicking my moves and voice here. Guess I got too loud at some point and woke her up. Either way, I'm not exactly winning any mother of the year awards right now."

"Are you kidding?" Tom replied. "That's fucking wild!"

She shrugged, but then offered him a tired grin. "Maybe, but it's also exhausting. So, please let me do what I need to do, so I can join you all at the pier."

"Hold on," I said. "No offense, but you look beat. Why don't you sit this one out? I mean, usually I'm happy to take whatever help I can get, but we're talking about one vampire here. I think we've got enough firepower between the rest of us to stop her and save Bird Brain's butt."

She shook her head. "If it was anyone else, I might agree. But I think it's best if I ... remain our liaison to Matthias. No offense, Bill, but..."

"You suck at this shit," Tom finished for her.

Sadly, she didn't disagree.

Christy zapped out of there with Glen a few moments later, the plan being for her to drop him off at her apartment then meet us outside the docks.

Glen wasn't too pleased being relegated to the position of guard dog but, in all honesty, there didn't seem to be a lot he could bring to the table for this mission – other than looking gross.

With any luck, we could talk this Char person down. When I'd first met her, I didn't get the impression she was a total psycho. Maybe a bit, mind you, but not in a spirit of vengeance sort of way. I mean, sometimes all you needed to do was convince someone to switch to decaf.

If not, well, we were going in hot. I don't care how quiet she was or how little scent she gave off, she was still nothing more than a lone vampire. As for us, we had the Freewill, the Icon, a witch, and whatever the fuck Sally was. And that wasn't even counting Falcon. Not saying this was going to be easy, but the truth of the matter was we were bringing multiple tanks to a knife fight.

Good thing, too, because this Freewill was just about out of gas.

The walk back to Falcon's pier was near maddening. Even so, it was better than taking the train. Ignoring that it was out regardless, on account of Sally sporting a gun big enough to kill the moon, being stuck in an underground tin can with walking bags of sweet, sweet blood was too much of a risk for me in my current state.

The people we passed on the street were tempting enough as it was. Pretty sure I was copiously drooling by the time we got close to Falcon's place.

Forget saving this wizard. He'd be lucky if I didn't fucking eat him.

"So what's the plan?" Tom asked, distracting me from thoughts of noshing on some smarmy British cuisine.

"Um, we stop this Char chick."

"Good job, Rommel," Sally opined. "If that isn't a hell of a strategy, I don't know what is."

"Do you have anything fucking better?"

I didn't really mean to snap at her. If anything, I was hoping she actually did have a better plan. Back during our Village Coven days, original not neo, Sally had always been the resourceful one, thinking several steps ahead. I was more the make shit up on the fly guy, something that didn't always serve me well.

At least both my hands were mostly functional by now. That was something. Too bad the extra energy required to heal hadn't done the rest of me any good.

"Sorry. I don't mean to be a total dick, but it's been a long night. What I meant is, do you have any insight I might've missed, so we can make this an easy in and out job?"

"Easy in and out job. Sounds like your sex life."

"Yeah," Tom agreed triumphantly. "But with someone else, not Christy."

I turned to glare at him, feeling my fangs descend. "Who do you think I was with before her?"

A look of revulsion crossed his face. "Fuck me, Dude. Now I need another shower."

"Douche for a douchebag," Sally replied.

He turned toward her. "Speaking of which, I don't suppose you know how to use...?"

She stopped and glared at him. "Let me point out that you might be bulletproof, but that won't stop me from emptying this revolver into your face if you even think of finishing that question." She then turned my way. "And to answer you, no. I don't have anything better."

"Seriously?"

"Seriously, Bill," she said as we started walking again. "I hate to admit it, but I'm rusty as all hell with this crap. I mean, for the last five years I've been hiring counselors, running fundraisers, and managing budgets. You know how many people I've had to kill in that time? Zero. Up until I woke up looking like this, I figured that was going to be my body count until the day I died."

"Hey, at least you've still got all your good parts," Tom replied. "I miss my dick."

"That probably makes you the only person on Earth with that particular issue."

"Although having tits is kinda fun."

"Dear God, we are so fucked if the world needs you to save it again."

Despite the tiredness in my bones and the gnawing hunger growing inside me, I managed to smile.

Maybe we didn't have a plan, but we had each other. And truth of the matter was, if I had to choose one over the other, I knew which one that would be.

"Um, Bill?" Sally asked after another moment, as we neared our destination.

"What?"

"You notice anything weird here?"

Weird was such a subjective term these days. Nevertheless, I took a quick look around. The street around us was quiet, true. But it was pretty late and, New York's reputation as the city that never sleeps aside, a lot of the residents here likely had to get up and go to work in the morning. I turned my attention to the block ahead, the darkness no issue for my vampire vision, and saw the chain link fence leading to Falcon's pier.

All looked normal to me.

"Who turned out the lights?" Tom asked after a moment.

I turned to glance at him and caught the glow coming from Sally's eyes. That caused me to take a closer look at my surroundings. The buildings around us were dark, again not exactly a shocker at this time of night. But so were the streetlights. I simply hadn't picked up on it, being way too distracted by both the mission and my hunger to pay attention.

"It's gotta be a coincidence," I said.

"Do we really ever get that lucky?"

I turned toward Sally, her eyes green orbs of luminescence staring back at me. "There's a first time for everything."

Yeah, I didn't buy that either. I spun back the way we'd come. Interestingly enough, the streetlights a block further up were all on. Likewise, I could see lit doorways of the buildings on either side of the road.

It was only here, close to both the Hudson and our destination, that the power was out. It might've still been a coincidence but, if so, it was an oddly specific one.

"Reach out with your senses, Bill," she told me.

"Why? I can already tell the power's out."

"Yes, Sherlock, but if other shit is afoot – like, oh, I dunno, dead bodies everywhere – that might give us a bit of a clue, don't you think?"

"You know, you could have just said that without the editorial."

"Well aware."

I knew it was no longer pc to call her a bitch, but at least I was safe in my mind to think it. However, right as she was to be cautious, I still hesitated. What if I did smell blood ... delicious wonderful blood? It was only a few weeks ago that I'd been out with Ed, only to watch as he went absolutely apeshit on some homeless guy, all because he was hungry.

Sure, whatever was in him had been starving for five years, so maybe that was an extreme example, but even so. Who was to say I might not lose my mind, only to end up licking the sidewalk clean next to a dead body? I mean, gross as that imagery should've been, it was kinda tempting, too.

"I can activate my Icon senses if you want."

Sally looked at Tom sidelong, the expression on her face not a kind one. "Do you even have Icon senses?"

"Um ... maybe."

"I sincerely doubt that, since you can't even smell your own bullshit."

I guess it was up to me. Bracing myself internally so that I didn't go running off like some hungry dog after a steak, I took a deep breath.

As usual, the first thing to hit me were the overarching scents of the city – most of which weren't particularly pleasant. I swear, it seemed I never had a reason to do this when we were next to something good like a bakery.

Dirt, asphalt, the Hudson, blah blah blah. All of that was meaningless as my olfactory nerves worked to dig deeper.

I readied myself. Blood, even faint traces of it, tended to hit my nose hard. Go figure. In some ways, vampires were like land sharks. Don't get me wrong, I doubted the fallout from a week-old nosebleed was going to set me off like a starving hyena. However, if there were fresh corpses about – the more the merrier – that was going to be like ringing the dinner bell.

Much to my relief, though, I didn't pick up anything. Well, okay, there was Tom and his ... um, time of the month. Thankfully, that was a horrific enough thought to scare even the creature inside of me back to silence. I think even Dr. Death had enough self-respect to choose starvation over sucking on one of Tom's used maxi pads.

That sobering thought aside, I realized there was definitely something on the wind – multiple somethings as a matter of fact. It wasn't blood, but some of it was familiar nevertheless. "Vampires."

"This Char person?" Sally asked.

"Doubt it. She knows how to mask her scent."

"Your nerd herd?"

"Not sure. I recruited them, but to be honest I didn't spend a lot of time sniffing them."

"Can't say I blame you on that one. Any idea how many we're talking about?"

I raised an eyebrow at her. "You're just trolling me now, aren't you?"

"Only partially. You really should know this stuff."

"What was that you said about being rusty?"

"Touché."

"Over there!" Tom cried.

I turned to find him pulling out one of Ed's action figures. In that same moment, his aura ignited.

Pity the idiot did so while I was less than five feet away.

I didn't think, I just dove toward the middle of the street. Thank goodness it was late enough for traffic to be nonexistent, otherwise I'd have been flattened for my troubles.

Rolling to my feet, safely out of range of Tom's faith aura, my eyes opened wide at the sight before me – although it wasn't at whatever Tom was pointing at.

His aura had ignited normally. If anything, it looked the same as I'd seen Sheila do countless times before, although she was usually holding a sword and not a Teenage Mutant Ninja Turtle. Fashion accessories aside, it was more Sally's presence that made me want to consider shitting a brick.

Rather than immolating her or even knocking her back, it was as if Tom's faith aura had hit a wall instead, visibly stopping a couple of feet short of touching her. Weirder still, where the aura touched whatever invisible barrier was around Sally, the energy flickered a dark green ... not unlike her hair.

What was powerful enough to stop faith magic?

Neither of them seemed to notice this phenomenon, their attention directed elsewhere. I was about to say something when suddenly Tom's aura went out, as surely as if he'd turned off a light switch.

Was it because of...?

"My bad," he said, all caution gone from his voice. "It's just Christy."

Sure enough, with the blinding glow from his power now gone, I could see past him to where Christy was stepping out from between two buildings and heading our way.

"Thanks," I said, dusting myself off. "I appreciate you almost blasting me over a false alarm."

"Sorry. I saw a flash of light and freaked out."

I guess I couldn't entirely blame him. Tom's idiocy aside, he likely had some instincts going on inside of him that reacted to Magi as well as vamps. After all, historically speaking, Icons were pretty much the bane of both our species.

Ah, how the mighty had fallen.

Tempting as it was to discuss what had just happened, I was more concerned with Christy. She looked absolutely exhausted. I could only hope she was no longer dividing her attention between here and Brooklyn.

"Sorry it took me so long," she said, breathing hard. "I wanted to work up a glamour to make Glen look a bit less ... disturbing, in case Tina woke up."

"Should have left him like he was," I joked. "She'd never ever bug you about wanting a pet again."

Christy smiled then said, "I hope I didn't keep you all waiting."

Sally shook her head. "We just got here ourselves."

"Yeah," Tom replied. "As far as rescue parties go, we kinda suck."

Sadly, no one among us could really dispute that.

"Any luck reaching Falcon?"

"I kept trying. No answer."

That didn't bode well. I had a feeling we'd dallied long enough. "So how about it, vampire hunters, shall we go hunt some vampires?"

"Vampires?" Christy asked, "as in plural?"

"Bill smelled some in the area," Sally explained.

"Ours?"

"Same question I asked."

"And same answer," I added. "I'm not sure, so why don't we keep our fingers crossed and find out?"

That was as good of a pep talk as I had inclination to give. But it was enough to get us all moving again toward the chain link fence separating our reality from the magical mystical wonderland of casa de Falcon.

"All looks quiet," Tom remarked as we reached the gate.

"Glamour, remember?"

"Oh, yeah. But seriously, how good could an illusion really be? I mean, if all hell was breaking loose inside, there's no way we wouldn't notice."

"Good enough," I replied as the air shimmered around us to indicate we were passing through, "that nobody called the cops on our asses last time we were..."

My voice trailed off as reality took over from the fantasy presented to the rest of the world.

But that was okay. I doubted anyone would've heard me anyway over the sounds of chaos and destruction going on just ahead of us.

Tom was wrong.

All hell was breaking loose, and we'd just stepped right into the middle of it.

HITTING ON THE DOCK OF THE BAY

I just had to be full of myself, didn't I?

It's just one vampire, I repeated in my head. *We were bringing a tank to a knife fight.*

I should've known fate would reward my lack of screaming paranoia with a good solid kick to the balls.

I'd latched onto the smell of vamps just minutes earlier, mostly because I could identify them, when what I should have focused on were the smells I couldn't put a face to.

Oh shit.

Falcon's warehouse was under assault. A purplish force dome had been conjured around it, flaring up with every hit it took. For the moment it was holding, but I had to imagine the strain was immense. The place was huge and the ... *things* attacking it all looked intent on the task at hand. Considering Falcon's resources, I had a feeling he wasn't powering this thing entirely by himself. No way was that possible. Some Magi were strong, but their reserves weren't limitless by any stretch.

But even with help, I doubted the force field would hold for long.

The vampires were the easiest to pick out, mostly because they looked human. They didn't move like humans, though, jumping and slashing at the barrier, while others tore up the asphalt as I'd done earlier and used it as projectiles.

On the upside, I didn't see my coven among their number, thank goodness, but I did notice one strange thing. All of the vamps in sight wore black armbands – just like those assholes I'd fought a few nights back.

"What the fuck?" Tom blurted out.

He wasn't wrong either. Oddly enough, the swarm of vampires was the most normal thing about this. Mixed in with them, running around like a pack of psychotic red-headed stepchildren, were a bunch of those proto-leprechauns.

Not good, as those things had been small but tough as fuck.

They weren't the only weirdos in the bunch, though. Standing out among them, like proverbial sore thumbs, were what appeared to be scaly bioluminescent fish men – like a Hollywood effects team was asked to update *The Creature from the Black Lagoon* but decided to drop acid first.

Needless to say, nobody was going to confuse these things with the little mermaid anytime soon.

Sadly, if my subconscious had any clue what they were, it kept that information to itself.

"This isn't good," Christy said, stating the blindingly obvious.

"You don't say," Sally replied.

"No. You don't understand. Look at them."

"I am. Kinda wishing I'd brought more bullets."

"Me, too," I replied.

"I mean really look at them." Christy turned to me. "Remember the other night when we ran into the a'chiad dé danann?"

"Kinda hard to forget."

"They were feral, chaotic."

"That's one word for it."

"Look at them now. Do they look like they're randomly destroying everything in their path?"

Recognition dawned as she spoke. Oh shit. "No. They all look like they're ... working together?"

"Exactly. Them, the vampires, and those ... other things."

Our resident expert on the paranormal was referring to a group of monsters as *things*. That was pretty much the opposite of reassuring.

Either way, she was right. Gone was the chaotic element that had seemingly driven the leprechauns the other night. Back then, they'd seemed more interested in eating absolutely everything they could stuff into their creepy troglodyte mouths.

Rather than snacking on the vamps they were fighting alongside, though, they actually seemed to be coordinating with them.

Same with the glowing gill-men. Disney movies aside, I had no idea how creatures with gaping fang filled mouths that looked more suited to catching trout than talking could even communicate. I mean, what? Did they glow brighter, once for yes twice for no?

Alas, that was unimportant. How these guys shot the shit wasn't the issue, so much as the fact that they'd all be shitting Falcon feathers soon if we didn't save a certain wizard's ass.

The warehouse shield flared again, as if to drive this point home. Whatever was powering it was apparently an industrial model compared to Christy's spell, as it seemed to be holding even the leprechauns at bay ... for now. But we were fooling ourselves if we thought it would hold indefinitely.

Too bad I had no idea how to...

"What's the plan, Bill?"

And just like that, my idiot roommate had elected me as the one to figure it out. I swear, if I didn't think I'd burst into flames, I'd punch his fucking lights out.

Great, now they were all looking at me. Wonderful. I had to think quick and come up with something that wouldn't get my friends insta-killed and leave Tina an orphan. Oh yeah, no pressure there.

Vampires are a known quantity. As for the a'chiad dé danann, some legends claim they abhor water.

"Thanks, subconscious," I replied for some reason. "What about those fish fuckers?"

"Who the hell are you talking to?" Sally asked.

"Um, just thinking out loud." Sadly, Dr. Death was once more silent on the subject of gill-men. Guess he wasn't a fish and chips kind of guy. Still, he'd given me something to work with. Now to hope it wasn't bullshit meant to fuck me up the ass.

Sadly, I had a choice to either trust his advice or make shit up on my own, something that didn't seem altogether wise.

"Okay, here's the plan. We know about vampires, how they fight and how they can be killed." I gestured to Sally. "Take Tom and do what you can to thin the herd." I turned to Christy next. "You need to keep those leprechauns busy. Try to..."

She shook her head. "We both saw what they did with my magic the other night. They..."

"Hit them indirectly then, shockwaves, explosions, that sort of stuff. Force them back if you can. They don't like the water. Filthy little fuckers were probably born before baths were invented."

Christy narrowed her eyes at me. "How do you know that?"

"I ... honestly, I'm not sure. But I'll explain later and maybe we can figure it out."

She nodded, albeit reluctantly, but it was obvious we didn't have time to hash this shit out now. Still, there was one additional thing I could offer. "Don't go crazy. Call your shots wisely. Don't let them wear you down."

"I'm fine."

"No. You're not."

Christy glared at me for a moment, but then her expression softened as she hopefully realized I was just worried about her. After a moment, she nodded again.

"What about you?" Sally asked.

I was about to tell her of my plans for a *fishing* expedition, when something else caught my attention — movement in my periphery. Glancing that way, I saw a lone figure heading toward the battle from the far edge of the dock. It was hard to tell, even with my night vision, but I would've bet there was something covering the top half of their face.

"I'll join you guys as soon as I can. I think I just found the ringleader of this asshole circus."

Our assignments doled out, I took off at vampire speed, hoping to flank Char before she saw me coming. She seemed focused on the siege going on ahead of her, so I might've made it had Sally waited a few more seconds to see if her marksman skills were still up to snuff.

The massive handgun went off with a boom of thunder from behind me, almost causing me to jump out of my skin

RICK GUALTIERI

despite knowing it was coming. I definitely needed to shake off the rust and get my head back in this psychotic game of death.

Sadly, one didn't need to be a vampire to hear the blast. However, Char, being one, likely heard it extra loud.

She slowed down, actually covering her ears with her hands before inclining her head in my direction.

Too bad it was a moment late and a dollar short.

She tried to sidestep me, and almost succeeded – nimble little psychopath. Even Gan might've been impressed. Pity that almost wasn't enough.

It was a glancing blow at best, catching her with the edge of my shoulder, but I was larger and had momentum on my side, so it was more than enough to send her tumbling across the asphalt, knocking the crowbar she was once again wielding out of her grasp and sending it clattering away.

Sadly, she wasn't in the mood to stay down and admit she was outclassed. In the time it took me to change course and advance upon her, she'd managed to scramble back to her feet.

"We've got to stop meeting like this," I said, throwing a punch at her uncovered jaw. Not overly gentlemanly of me, but it wasn't like she wouldn't heal fast.

It wasn't like she wouldn't block me either. She raised an arm, countering my attack easily and sending me stumbling past her off balance.

Strike one.

She wasn't the only one able to play vampire here, though. My ears registered movement behind me and I spun with a backhand. Again it was blocked, but the blow hit her arms hard enough to push her to the side, ruining her own attack.

358

"Aw, and here I thought you were beginning to like me," she replied, actually grinning.

"How's this? I like you just enough to take you out..." *Oh fuck!*

And just like that, I got caught playing the banter game when I should've been paying more attention to fighting. She caught my fist, spun, and launched me over her shoulder like I was a sack of moldy shit.

I landed hard enough to bounce once before ending up in a crumpled heap.

Ouch.

"Guess it was a good date, since you got laid ... out flat."

The only thing worse than losing a fight was losing a fight I should've been winning. And, truth be told, the only thing worse than that was losing to someone who was happy to talk shit.

"Now stay on your back like a good puta, Bill Freewill, and maybe you won't wake up as dust tomorrow. I'm willing to give you the benefit of the doubt since you helped me out once, but push your luck and I will end you."

"My name isn't Bill Free..."

Boom!

Sally was firing again, hopefully with more luck than I was having. It was deafeningly loud to my vampire ears, but nothing I hadn't experienced before. However, Char acted as if someone had just placed air horns on either side of her head and pulled the trigger.

She covered both her ears and screamed as the gunshot echoed across the pier.

Fucking newbs.

Hoping it wasn't a ruse, I scrambled to my feet and closed the distance between us, fist raised.

A part of me expected for her to grin at the last second and once again send me flying, but she actually seemed confused – looking around as if unsure of which direction I was coming from.

Being the sporting fellow I am, I decided to give her a hand – All Might style.

"TEXAS SMASH!"

Much to even my surprise, I caught her with a right to the kisser that sent her flying, busted nose and all.

That was more like it, not to mention considerably less embarrassing. Hopefully my friends, especially Tom, were too preoccupied to have seen the fight up until now. I'd eaten enough shit for one day. I didn't care for another mouthful.

Char landed a good ten feet away, appearing stunned from the blow.

And why not? I'd grown far too used to facing opponents for whom my best wasn't even in the ballpark. To actually fight someone where I had the physical advantage ... well, I wasn't a bully or anything, but fuck it. I could get used to this shit.

But first I had to end this, and that wasn't going to happen if I stood around acting like a self-satisfied douche every time I got a lucky hit.

That said, Char had been right earlier. I'd earned an out in her book and the truth was, she'd earned one in mine. And, despite everything, I wasn't entirely convinced she was evil. I mean, yeah, she was definitely a vengeful as fuck vampire slayer, but with most vamps being first class pricks I wasn't sure that counted against her.

One chance. After that, she was dust in the wind.

I leapt upon her prone form, pinning her down – hopefully.

Or at least I tried to. Dazed or not, it was like trying to wrestle an angry bobcat ... at least until Sally fired off two more shots in succession.

Char screamed in pain as she tried to break free from my grapple, but it was pure desperation, a far cry from the controlled moves she'd been kicking my ass with up until now.

"What the fuck is up with you?"

"I ... I can't...," she gasped. "It ... hurts."

"That's what she said."

Both the fight and the snark seemed to have gone out of her, though, as she lay beneath me wincing – and not from anything I was doing to her.

Taking advantage of the momentary lull in having my ass handed to me, I let go of one of her arms and ripped the mask off her face. Yep, no doubt about it. She was the one who'd been pretending to be blind earlier.

Hold on a second...

Her eyes were unfocused, darting every which way but my direction, and the irises were clouded over, like she had heavy cataracts or something.

"Holy Daredevil, Batman."

"T-take a picture, asshole," she snarled. "It lasts longer."

"I've got a better idea, blind fury. Call off your lackeys. Much as I hate to say this, Falcon is off limits." Left unsaid was, *for now anyway*.

"What?"

"Those monsters over there going apeshit against the warehouse. Call them off."

"How?"

"Um ... however you would do such a thing."

She stopped struggling and stared up at me, albeit not actually at me. "Are you seriously telling me, Bill Freewill, that you're stupid enough to think I'm controlling those fucking things?"

"Okay, first off, the name is Bill Ryder and I'm the vampire Freewill."

"Is that supposed to mean something?"

"Kinda ... I guess not. Wait a second. You mean you're not behind this attack?"

"No. I'm trying to stop it, moron."

HIND-BLINDSIGHT

I dared a glance back toward the warehouse. Sure enough, my friends were still occupied. Among the crazed monstrosities, the majority of which were still focused on turning Falcon's warehouse into an outhouse, I could easily make out Tom's white faith aura as he waded into the fray. Elsewhere, the angry red glow of battle magic told me Christy was busy doing her part, although hopefully being judicious about it.

They all seemed to be okay for the moment as well as not paying attention to me, which was good because suddenly I was feeling somewhat less than smart.

"Explain," I ordered.

Char made a dismissive sound. "I don't need to explain nothing to you, Freebill, or whatever the fuck you call yourself."

"Fine, then I'll explain." It was either that or play a game of "No, you go first" until such time as this entire place was reduced to rubble. "We came here to stop you and found an army of monsters instead."

"So you're not with them?"

"Would I be having a conversation with you if I was?"

As a show of good faith – fully expecting it to backfire in my face, thus proving the universe hated nice guys – I let go of Char and backed away, allowing her to get to her feet.

An unsporting asshole would've used that moment to double-cross me and, truth be told, it wasn't exactly like I didn't deserve it for being a trusting fool. However, Char merely picked herself off the ground and dusted herself off.

"No, I suppose not."

"So then same question to you," I said. "You're not with them?"

"With those assholes? No way."

"Then why..."

"I've been tracking those black armband fucks for like two weeks now. You already had the displeasure of meeting a few of their recruits."

"Hard to forget."

"Yeah, well, they're some crazy Aryan Nation offshoot or something like that. They've been on a rampage hunting down folks, both normal and like us."

"You mean vampires?"

"God, it feels so fucking weird to use that word, but yeah, I suppose."

"I can kind of guess why they're going after people, but why other vamps?"

"Best I can tell, they're looking to be the only game in town. You're either one of them or you're dust. But don't think for a second these pendejos aren't enjoying this shit."

And all at once it made sense. The dusted vamps Falcon had told us about. I'd been wondering how likely it was that one person could've been responsible, even someone with Char's fighting skills. But if I was hearing correctly, then maybe these assholes had the numbers to account for the extra killings. If so, then all the more reason to stop them. "And that's why you're after them?"

"Let's just say they made the mistake of targeting someone I cared about." Her fangs descended at what was obviously a painful memory, but a moment later she retracted them. "But even if they hadn't, I don't know about you, jefe, but the last thing the world needs right now is a bunch of super skinheads running amok."

"Not going to argue. But that still doesn't tell me what any of you are doing here right now."

"You ain't my babysitter, so I don't have to..." There came the sound of more destruction near the warehouse, telling us that perhaps now wasn't the time for an overdrawn heart to heart. "Okay, fine, long story short. That bird guy's been all over the news. Word on the street was that the armbands were planning to hit him before he could get to them."

"Wait, Falcon? So, that's why you were skulking around outside Sally's place when I ran into you earlier?"

"Don't know any Sally. I was just keeping an eye on bird guy, since I had a feeling he was being tailed. Interesting coincidence that he just so happened to be hanging out at the same address you gave me."

"Not really. I'm trying to make sure my people aren't on his radar. But hold on. If you were going to all that trouble to stop these guys, why didn't you just tell him?"

"Because he's a fucking cop and I don't need that shit. Now are you going to shut up and let me finish or what?"

I glanced nervously over toward where the assault continued. "Sorry."

"Apology accepted. Anyway, I was tracking him when things got weird."

"Weird?"

"Weirder. Out of nowhere, these goons just mobilized, but not in a normal sort of way. It was like all of a sudden these apes discovered how to shut their mouths and get shit done."

"Go on."

"I was scoping them out, debating when to make my move, when these other freaks showed up and they all started working together, like they had a playbook or something. Makes no sense, man, because before tonight, these jackasses barely tolerated each other. And now they're working with whatever those things are."

"Believe me, I get it. I tangled with those proto-leprechauns a few days ago..." I held up a hand. "Yes, that's what they are. And believe me, they didn't seem like the type for team-ups either."

"So what's going on?"

"Honestly? No idea. I thought you were calling the shots."

"Me? I mean, I'm flattered and all, but why would you think that?"

"Oh, I don't know. You show up wearing a mask, kick ass, and then you disappear just as quickly."

'And that makes me the bad guy?"

"Well, you have to admit, calling yourself Char is just a wee bit sinister."

She put her hands on her hips. "It's short for Charisma ... my name, dumbass."

"Oh. Well, what about having no scent or being so quiet? And don't tell me you just found some manticore venom lying on the street."

"Manticore what? That a brand of scent remover or something?"

"Scent remover?"

"Yeah. You can buy that shit on Amazon. My uncle's a hunter, told me all about it. As for being quiet, well, when you're like me..." She waved a hand in front of her eyes. "You learn the value of noise, as well as when not to make any."

I had a lot more I wanted to ask her, like how the hell she was blind to begin with. The only blind vamps I'd ever met had been crazed zealots, forced to jam hot pokers into their eye sockets every hour, since otherwise they regenerated like crazy.

Sadly, I had a feeling the rest of my Q&A would have to wait. I'd wasted enough time, time that should've been spent helping my friends.

Apparently, Char was of the same mindset.

"You got any more questions for me, Freebill? Or can we go stop the world from burning now?"

A temporary truce in place, or so I hoped, Char retrieved her weapon and then we both raced into the fray.

"This way!" I directed.

"No shit, dickless," Char shouted back.

Sightless she might be, but I needed to remember my Daredevil analogy from earlier. Almost everything about vampires was enhanced compared to when we were human. Well, okay, maybe not dick size, but that was already good enough ... not that I would've complained about having more.

Anyway, strength, speed, healing, check check and check. Equally important was the massive boost to our senses. Night vision was my personal favorite, but there was no denying both smell and hearing were amped up to crazy levels as well.

I could only imagine the experience was even more intense for someone who'd come to rely on those other senses.

Sure enough, she ran straight and true, seeming to have no problem homing in on her prey.

"I got the armbands," she said. "You go help with those other freaks."

"Right on. Soon as I top off the old tank."

"What?"

"Never mind. Hey, you remember that woman I was with earlier?"

"The one with the freaky dog?"

"Yep. Do yourself a favor and stay away from her."

"Why?"

I was about to tell her about Tom's white aura of faith before realizing that likely didn't mean shit to her. "She's dangerous to vamps. Get close enough and she'll melt you into goo."

"You keep some crazy friends, Freebill."

"You have no idea."

That was enough banter for now. We'd be upon the battle in moments at our current speed.

However, we were already close enough to notice that things were ... strange. And I mean stranger than vamps, garbage disposal dwarves, and Chernobyl brand fish sticks all working together.

It was more how they were working together that struck me as odd.

I'd run into fuckers like these armband vamps before. Though they could certainly be unpredictable, they tended to have one thing in common: most were fucking loudmouths. Go figure, white supremacists weren't exactly a subtle bunch. Now, though, they were all quiet, seemingly focused on the task at hand – the warehouse. And this was despite both Tom and Sally having waded into the battle.

Likewise with those freaky leprechauns. Those things had practically oozed buckets of chaotic crazy last time I'd seen them. Now, they, too, seemed way too focused and organized.

I spied Christy hitting a group from their flank, blowing up the asphalt beneath them and driving them toward the water as I'd instructed. However, rather than turn and swarm her, the creatures simply picked themselves back up and headed toward the purple force dome again – a dome which, if we're being honest, didn't look like it was going to hold for much longer.

It was the same with them all.

So focused were they on the task ahead, that none of them – fish, leprechaun, or vamp – seemed to notice me and Char coming up from behind them.

Once I was within range, I took a flying leap, landing upon the back of one of the vamps – a skinny fellow wearing a beaten-up biker vest, like he was some low-rent extra from Sons of Anarchy.

Focused – or compelled – as he was, he was still cognizant enough to put up some fight, but not enough to keep me from sinking my teeth into his neck.

Oh, fuck me that's good!

In terms of nutrition, vampire blood wasn't a replacement for the blood of the living. It was like trying to survive on nothing but caffeine and empty calories.

That said, in the short term it was like eating a Snickers when you were starving, satisfying as fuck.

Best of all, it hit my stomach like rocket fuel, adding this vamp's somewhat less than impressive strength to my own.

Yeah, that was the downside of the here and now. With the exception of Gan, pretty much every vampire on the planet was all of three weeks old. That meant the boost I got was modest at best. Still, doubling my power wasn't something to sneeze at. And fortunately, the effects were cumulative.

Either way, I drank more than was warranted, mostly because I was fucking starving, before snapping the biker's neck and dropping him like a bad habit.

"Holy shit," Char said from nearby. "What the hell did you do to him?"

"Nothing I suggest you try and copy."

My supernatural public service announcement over, I pressed on, taking down two more vamps in the line and adding their strength to my own.

A part of me almost felt bad hitting these guys in their blindside while they were busy zombie walking toward Falcon's warehouse, but it was a really small part.

Fuck it. This was how all battles should go: vamps lined up like a salad bar, waiting for me to top off the tank before moving on to the next.

Sadly, however, it seemed three freebies was all I was going to get.

I wasn't sure if it was me, or if I'd simply been the straw that broke the camel's back, thanks to the damage my friends were inflicting, but all at once the horde seemed to notice us.

Almost as one, a large portion of the vampires, fish men, and freaky ass leprechauns turned toward us, as if we were mosquitos who'd finally managed to annoy them enough.

Thankfully, by then I had enough of a boost to make me a legitimate threat.

I decked one vamp who charged at me, sending him barreling into a threesome of his buddies, enough to give me some breathing room.

Just then, my flank lit up with bright white. I turned in time to see two more vamps consumed by white flame as Tom headed toward where I was fighting.

"About fucking time you decided to join us."

"Sorry. Got a bit sidetracked. Thanks for leaving some for me."

"Anytime, bro." He spun, directing his toy-born fury at a pair of gill-men. "Um, Bill?"

"Yeah, man?" I asked, kicking another vamp in the nuts hard enough to Marty McFly his future grandkids.

"I don't mean to criticize your methods, but weren't you supposed to, y'know, ixnay the blind chick?"

"The blind chick has a name, chica," Char spat from where she was busy ninja throwing a vampire into a couple of his buddies.

"Change of plans," I said. "Turns out she's on our side."

Tom glanced my way as the fish men turned into a fish fry – proving his aura was lethal to them, too, thank goodness. "Really?"

"Yeah."

"Called that one like a pro, didn't you?"

"Bite me. And it's not like you were any righter. She actually is blind."

"So, a blind vampire is now on our side. That makes me feel so much better about our odds."

In response, I merely pointed toward where Char had waded into a pack of armbands. Despite being outnumbered, she dodged and weaved among them like a whirlwind – dusting assholes with her crowbar left and right – seeming to have eyes in the back of her head whenever one would try to flank her.

It didn't hurt that these guys weren't really fighting all that smart. If anything, they were attacking us with all the skill they'd used on Falcon's force field. However, they very much had numbers on their side, which was apparently what whoever was directing them was counting on.

Hold on, *directing them*.

Goddamn, some things never changed. Five years later and I was still a fucking idiot.

By myself, I was on equal footing with most of these vamps, save perhaps in terms of experience. However, amped as I was, I had one big advantage over them – and I wasn't talking about my effervescent personality.

Compulsion.

I mean, hell, I'd almost forgotten about it. Back during my first foray as a vamp, you couldn't take a shit without someone throwing out a compulsion. It was a way of vampire life, practically engrained into the day to day dealings of covens. That was then, though. Nowadays, there wasn't nearly as much reason for it.

And, truth be told, I was okay with that. Compulsion was, for the most part, evil as fuck: the act of asserting one's will upon others, like an asshole pimp version of Charles Xavier.

Hell, Sally, brilliant as she was, had been relegated to little more than a sex slave under Night Razor, and one could argue she'd gotten off easy.

All of that said, I didn't really have a problem using an asshole power against actual assholes. Yeah, I'd probably snag Char, too, but oh well. Sometimes the old omelet and eggs analogy worked best.

Time to see if I still had the touch.

"KNOCK IT THE FUCK O... Oh shit!!"

One moment I was standing there next to Tom, giving these dickweeds an order. The next, the world greyed out in a haze of pain so intense I was certain Sally had emptied her gun into the back of my head.

It was hard to explain. I'd had compulsions used against me before. They couldn't actually control me – that whole Freewill thing being more than a stupid name – but a powerful vamp could make a compulsion feel like a boot to the face. One of them, a shit-stain by the name of François, had even postulated that a strong enough one could probably turn my brain to mush. And the truth was, I'd been hit by enough doozies to believe it.

But that was receiving. Sending out a compulsion was usually painless ... at least until today.

It was like in the same instant I sent out the order, it was somehow fed back into my brain, except amplified a thousand-fold. It was as if my own voice had been weaponized, exploding in my skull like a sonic hand grenade.

And it kept repeating itself, over and over again, until all I could do was curl up inside my own consciousness and pray that it would finally kill me, bringing the torture to an end.

CHUMBALAYA

"Kamehameha! Shining Finger! Um, fire photon torpedoes? Why won't this shit work?!"

Three weeks on and it was still weird to hear Tom's words spoken in Sheila's voice. I had a feeling it would never stop being strange.

The bigger question was why the fuck was he bitching loud enough to wake me up?

I swear, some assholes just couldn't let others sleep in...

Except I hadn't been sleeping. Hell, I wasn't even lying down. Nearest I could tell, I was on my hands and knees, and what was beneath me was neither bed nor floor.

I shook my head to clear the haze. Bad move. Not only did everything feel disturbingly wet, but it was like a boot to the face. Goddamned hangovers were the fucking worst I tell you. Especially while the party was still going on, as evidenced by all the fucking noise around me.

Not a party. Now wake up!

The voice in my head functioned kind of like a cup of coffee, except far less pleasant. In the space of a second, I remembered who I was, where I was, and what I'd been doing.

Shit!

But not what had happened.

Last thing I remembered was compelling these vamps to stand down and then ... and then something exploded in my head, like I'd been sucking on a live hand grenade.

"You alive over there?"

If Tom's voice didn't serve to jolt me fully awake, the sizzle on my skin did. In his worry, he'd gotten a wee bit too close with that death aura of his. I let out a yipe to let his dumb ass know.

"Sorry."

I tried to nod my head, unsure if I was actually doing so, then opened my eyes ... to see nothing but red.

Except it wasn't the red I normally associated with Dr. Death. That was more like a haze of anger clouding my vision. This was actually red ... and drippy, too.

A moment later I realized why. I was staring at the inside of my glasses and the lenses were covered in blood.

That was the least of my worries, though. I pulled them off to see the ground beneath me likewise covered in a spreading puddle of my second favorite bodily fluid.

Reaching up to my face, I realized I was bleeding from almost everywhere: my mouth, my nose, my ears, and ... eww ... even my eyes.

Whatever had just happened, it was like half the blood vessels in my brain all picked the same moment to explode.

Truth of the matter was, I was probably lucky it hadn't blown my entire fucking head off.

Thankfully, the trickle was beginning to slake, no doubt my vampire healing starting to compensate for the metaphysical whisk trying to scramble my brain. Call me crazy, but I had a feeling the only reason I was still alive was because I was currently sporting the power of multiple vamps. Without that, I'd likely be *enjoying* the feel of my brain turning to dust inside my head, followed by the rest of me.

Taking a moment I likely didn't have, I sat up and wiped my glasses as clean as they were going to get.

"Dude, what the fuck happened to you?"

I spit out a mouthful of blood and gasped, "N-no fucking idea."

That was the god's honest truth. A vampiric compulsion was usually a one-way thing. It wasn't a boomerang that looped around, picked up a stick of dynamite, and then flew back in your face. Yet this one had seemingly done exactly that.

Had something changed? Was it possible that in reinventing vampires via his fucking hand cream, Dave had somehow mucked up the mix? I mean, if anyone could fuck things up in an epic way, it would be him.

That didn't feel right, though. Call it instinct or whatever you want, but I didn't think that to be the case. But if not, then what had just happened?

A ward that we'd missed perhaps? Or maybe some kind of protection that our foes somehow shared?

Either way, it didn't seem as if answers were forthcoming. All I knew for certain was that I wouldn't be trying that again.

Sadly, it had all been for naught anyway, as both Tom and Char continued to battle our seemingly undaunted foes, of which there were plenty left – the only upside being that they were still attacking us with all the skill of mindless zombies.

"T-this might be," I sputtered Tom's way, "a g-good time to make with the wave motion cannon again."

He narrowed his eyes at me, his aura burning around him but no death ray apparently forthcoming. "What the fuck do you think I've been trying to do? Goddamned thing won't work."

Of course it wouldn't. Why would anything be easy? "For fuck's s-sake."

Another booming gunshot was fired from nearby, catching my attention. However, it was accompanied a few moments later by a cry of, "Shit!"

I turned toward the warehouse and the sound of Sally's voice. She was further into the fray, having turned her gun against the fish freaks. Or she had anyway. Now she was holding it like a club, probably out of ammo, as a group of gill-men shuffled toward her.

"You guys ... hold the line or something, I need to help Sally."

"Is that the Sally who owns the building or are we talking about someone else?" Char asked, but I was already on the move.

My gait was a bit unsteady for the first few steps, but I managed to find my sea legs, heading toward where Sally was busy trying to fend off a trio of glowing fish men.

"Tagging in," I cried.

"Gladly." She stepped back, doing a double take my way. "Holy shit! What the hell happened to you?"

"Spontaneous brain hemorrhage," I replied nonchalantly, stepping up to the first creature and delivering a haymaker to the side of his stupid fish face.

FUCK!

The blow snapped the monsters head to the side, dropping it to the ground twitching. However, my hand had been left a bloody mess in the process. The hell?

There was no time to wonder why, though, as another stepped in, swinging a clawed ... um, flipper I guess.

Fortunately, these guys didn't seem all that fast on land, giving me plenty of time to raise my arm to counter. Another upside was these things didn't appear to possess much in the way of super strength. What a fucking relief to finally fight something I could overpower.

Sadly, that relief was cut short as pain lanced down my forearm and blood began to drip from it. No wonder, as there was now a deep gash in my flesh where I'd blocked the monster.

I reached out and shoved it away, sending it tumbling to the ground, but earning a bloody palm for my troubles.

Fuck me!

I took a closer look as the third tried to circle us, my glasses still a bit smudged. These things might not be the bodybuilders of the supernatural world, but I realized too late the translucent scales covering them from head to toe were apparently razor sharp. It was like their skin was a natural weapon, one I'd just scraped the shit out of myself against. Figures that nothing could be easy. You find a bunch of wussy monsters and it turns out they're covered in broken glass.

I turned back toward Sally, finding her thankfully blood free. "I don't suppose you brought any extra ammo."

"Oh, I brought tons. I was just standing here like a dumbass out of a sense of good sportsmanship."

"A simple no would've sufficed."

"What fun would that be?" she replied, stepping up alongside me. The third gill man lunged forward, but she bashed it upside the head, using the handgun as a club.

"Be careful," I told her.

"Careful and this job really don't go hand in hand."

"I'm beginning to remember that." I glanced down at my arms, glad to see my healing was starting to take care of the cuts I'd suffered beating these things up. All that remained of the damage were a few scratches and some bluish goo I'd managed to scrape off these...

Wait, I don't think that's goo!

My subconscious screamed out the warning a moment before a wave of nausea hit me, doubling me over. Almost at the same time, both of my arms went numb.

"S-sally," I sputtered, trying to keep from puking my guts out. "Be c-careful. I t-think, they're poisonous."

Just my luck. These things were like two-legged, razor sharp jellyfish. Well, kinky as it sounded, no way was I inviting Sally to piss on my arms.

That's okay. Life was already shitting on me enough.

Another of the creatures stepped in and slashed me across the face. It wasn't a hard blow, but it sliced open my cheek, spilling even more of my blood onto the ground.

Not good. I could feel the boost I'd gotten from those vamps starting to wane, and that wasn't all. The hunger I'd temporarily sated was starting to come back in force. Whatever I'd lost in the last few minutes was rapidly catching up on what I'd taken in, if it hadn't overtaken it already.

The side of my face went numb to match my arms, at least sparing me the pain of my face being fileted.

I wasn't out of it yet, though. Useless lumps of flesh they might be, but I still had my arms and their vampire strength. I swung my body, smacking the fish creature upside the head with a sloppy uncontrolled slap, sending it stumbling back into a pair of its fellows.

I tried to shout out a warning for Sally to fall back. We needed to regroup and find Christy. With any luck, she could make short work of these assholes. Unfortunately, with my face now feeling like it was pumped full of Novocain, what came out was more an incomprehensible slur of syllables.

"What?" she asked, trying to fend off more of the things.

Sadly, she made the mistake of turning her head at the wrong time, the sight of me likely not helping matters. "Holy shit, Bill, are you all ... ARGH!"

She let out a cry as one of the fishmen slashed her in the side. Then another stepped in and got her arm, sending the gun clattering uselessly away.

I tried to stumble toward her, but two more of the creatures turned my way, their attacks not particularly skilled but a hell of a lot more effective than my numb-ass flailing.

Bad as this was for me, it was going to be much worse for her. Within seconds, she was surrounded as the creatures closed in.

Realizing I wasn't going to get the job done with the useless meat clubs that were my arms, I kicked out at the creature nearest me, hoping my shoes were enough protection to keep my legs from turning to taffy. These fish things didn't appear to have balls to aim for, but their spindly legs turned out to be conveniently brittle.

I struck the ugly fucker's kneecap and it shattered with a sharp *crack*, dropping the beast to the ground to flop around like ... well, a goldfish out of water.

Unfortunately, this new offensive of mine was too little too late.

Sally screamed in pain as the creatures slashed at her from all sides, ripping her blouse and the flesh beneath it to ribbons.

Oh God. I'd just gotten her back from what I'd been sure was certain death. She'd been changed by the experience, but inside still seemed to be the same Sally. There was no way I was watching her die again.

No.

Fucking.

Way.

Come on! I screamed inside my head, hoping to finally coax the beast inside of me awake. *I need you, Dr. Death. Sally needs us!*

For a moment there was nothing, save me flailing about desperately with arms that felt like they were made of Silly Putty.

Then from inside my mind came an answer I didn't expect.

I'm sorry, but I can't.

The fuck?!

I wouldn't have blanched at being told to go fuck myself. But an apology?

Was Dr. Death having the disembodied spirit equivalent of erectile disfunction or what?

The hell with this!

Once again, it was up to me to save the day. With waning strength, a growing hunger, and arms more suited to flapping in the breeze than anything else, I still refused to give up. I would not lose Sally again ... not ... ever ... again.

Except, I realized in the next moment, it wasn't up to me.

I caught a glimpse of Sally's face as the fish men continued to swarm her, biting and slashing. Her eyes met mine and they flashed a brilliant green, as if powered from within, right as her expression changed from anguish to something far less forgiving.

What the...?

Call it instinct, Freewill's intuition, or just being freaked the fuck out, but in that moment I became certain that the person staring back at me wasn't Sally. I had no idea how or why, just that it wasn't her.

Whoever they were, though, one thing was obvious: they were pissed.

There was no way of knowing whether this was all in my semi-woozy head or not, but I dropped to the ground nevertheless – hitting the dirt as surely as if Christy had been there to zap me with a stun spell.

Lucky guess or not, it was the right move.

A split-second later, I was covered in guts, offal, and roly-poly fish heads as the creatures dogpiling Sally were, quite literally, blown to pieces.

Every single fish monster within ten feet of her was ripped apart as another of those shockwaves exploded forth from her. Those within twenty weren't much better off, as arms, legs, and skulls were all turned to pulp. Further back, even more were knocked to the ground – and it wasn't just them. My view suddenly unobstructed, I saw vampires and proto-leprechauns alike all knocked flat.

"The fuck was that for?!"

Apparently, the same could be said for at least one of my friends, too, as I spied Tom scrambling back to his feet, aura or not, and looking none too happy about it. On the upside, a few of the fish creatures nearest him were now burning like tiki torches.

Regardless of that, I couldn't help the chill creeping down my spine. I'd thought myself mistaken the other day, back at Christy's apartment, but it hadn't been Tom's shitty control after all. Sally's power had actually cut through his faith aura like butter. What the fuck could do something like that?

Sadly, that was probably the least of our worries. Whatever the fuck Sally had just done had blown right through Falcon's warehouse shield, too, canceling it out like an unwanted magazine subscription. Gone was the purplish force dome, as if it had never been there. The structure itself was undamaged, but I had a sinking feeling that wouldn't be the case for much longer.

As for Sally, she was somehow still on her feet – the air around her shimmering, as if it were a cold day and she was standing atop a hot grill.

The fish creatures had pretty much shredded her blouse, leaving her upper half clad only in an overpriced bra. However, though her skin was still stained with blood, there was no trace of the wounds she'd sustained. She was once again whole.

"FOUL DENIZENS OF THE DEPTHS," she cried in a voice that echoed across the dock. "YOU WOULD DARE LAY YOUR UNCLEAN HANDS UPON THE HERALD OF THE GREAT BEAST?!"

And if that wasn't ominous as all hell, I didn't know what was.

BEAST WARS

I wasn't exactly a newb when it came to weird shit. Same for my friends. If anything, my life had somehow turned into one of those CW superhero shows in which, over the course of a few seasons, somehow everyone I knew had joined my former one-man crusade to fight crime.

Problem was, the last couple of weeks had proven to be my personal Flashpoint, with the rules having abruptly changed.

For example, when someone talked smack to a bunch of monsters, usually one of two things happened: either they served up a plate of ass-kicking or got their butts handed to them. All in all, it was a pretty simple equation.

These days, however, our opponents seemed fond of checking off D – none of the above – when it came to situations we should've been able to call with our eyes closed.

The unlikely alliance of freaky ass monsters slowly clambered back to their feet, those nearest me as covered in the guts of their buddies as I was. Meantime, Sally's eyes continued to glow a sickly green as the air around her shimmered – despite giving off no heat that I could discern.

I expected the standoff to end with either us or a lot of fish monsters dead. Instead, though, the creatures all bowed their heads ... as if in subservience.

Okay, this is getting really fucking weird now.

They weren't alone either. The other two factions: vampires and proto-leprechauns alike, stopped what they were doing to turn Sally's way and lower their gaze.

Thankfully, Tom was on the ball where I wasn't – and he wasn't above doling out a whole basket of cheap shots.

"Eat all the cocks, motherfuckers!"

His aura reignited as he held one of Ed's toys aloft, and then he plowed into a trio of vamps, instantly dusting them.

Elsewhere, a section of pavement exploded in red fire, sending leprechauns flying.

I pulled my attention away from Sally long enough to see Christy. She was standing about fifteen yards away, atop an old dumpster that was lying on its side. She looked almost as exhausted as I felt, albeit considerably less bloody, but she was still somehow in the fight.

I waved at her, to which she pointed and shouted, "The warehouse! They're going to get in!"

"On it," I cried back, before adding, in a much softer voice, "In a second anyway."

Almost as if being reminded of their goal, the remaining beasts all turned back toward Falcon's abode, once again ignoring us.

Or most of us anyway.

I couldn't help but notice those in the immediate vicinity were now giving Sally a wide berth as they marched past.

"Um, Sally?" I tentatively asked. "You in there?"

It was slow going getting back up. My arms were tingling, the feeling beginning to return to them as my healing compensated for the poison in my system, but they were still close to useless. Likewise, my head was all fuzzy, although I had a feeling that was more hunger related. Either way, I was in shit shape.

Sally slowly turned toward me, her eyes still aglow, and a look on her face that appeared bereft of anything resembling humanity.

Oh crap.

And then she blinked and, in the space of a second, everything changed.

The air stopped shimmering around her, the glow left her eyes, and a look of confusion replaced the inhuman contempt that had been plastered across her face.

She looked down at herself, bloody and half-dressed, then met my eyes. "What the fuck just happened?"

"I was kind of hoping you could tell me."

She shook her head. "One minute, a whole school of those ugly bastards were in my face. Now..." she gestured around us, the creatures continuing to avoid going anywhere near where she stood.

I didn't have long to dally but fuck it. At the end of the day, Sally rated higher in my book than Falcon – even if most of this was my fault.

"Do you remember the great beast?"

"What the hell is a great beast? And, no, don't tell me that's what you call your dick."

"Well..." Okay, that wasn't helping, especially as I could now hear the sound of leprechaun teeth gnawing through the metal siding of the warehouse.

"Bill! Hurry! I don't have much left."

"On it," I call backed to Christy.

Sally made a small whipping motion but then grinned. "Shall we crash this party, partner?"

"No," I replied, not believing I was saying this. "Sorry, but the party's over for you. You need to stand down." She narrowed her eyes, no doubt readying to blast me with some snark. "I mean it. You just went all Zuul on these things. I don't know what the fuck that was, but until we figure it out, you're benched."

"But..."

"Go. Cover Christy's back but stay out of combat."

"You can't be..."

"I'm serious," I growled back at her, putting as much adult into my voice as I could.

I didn't wait for a response, whether it be in the form of insult or hurt feelings. Instead I took off, my arms still flopping about like I was trying to take flight rather than run. But whatever. In the course of the last few minutes, this business had just gotten a shit-ton more personal. I'd be damned if I was going to drag my friend into more danger, not knowing who or what was in her head with her.

"I don't suppose I have any idea what the Great Beast is," I asked myself as I ran, putting on speed as I headed to where the leprechauns were busy gnawing their way in.

Sadly, if Dr. Death had any insight, he wasn't in a sharing mood.

I doubted the sheet metal walls of Falcon's nest would stop the hungry teeth of those little troglodytes for more than a few seconds. Fortunately, I had a faster route, one not available to the two foot terrors.

A row of windows was situated about eight feet off the ground. They all appeared boarded up from the inside, but in the never-ending battle of vampire versus plywood, I knew who I'd put my money on.

"Coming through, you hungry little shits!"

If the leprechauns took offense, they gave no indication, laser-focused as they were on the task ahead – with no sign of their previous gleeful chaos.

Yeah, no doubt about it. Something was controlling these fuckers. Everything about them was too robotic. Don't get me wrong, these things alone had almost overrun Christy and me just the other day. So perhaps a bit less chaos in my life wasn't entirely a bad thing.

Still, the fact that there was a puppet master pulling their strings was not a warm fuzzy in my book, especially since whatever mojo was being used absolutely blew the shit out of a good old fashioned compulsion, enough to almost blow my freaking head off.

And then there was what had just happened to Sally. I had no clue what the fuck that was, but one thing was clear – these things, even with their marching orders, didn't want any piece of it.

Yeah, shit had rapidly gotten real again and then some. It was almost enough to make me miss the days when the worst I had to look forward to was dealing with Colin – almost.

Before I could worry about any of that, though, there was a baby bird in need of saving, one with a killer porno stache.

Hopefully he didn't have a readied action to blast whoever was first inside. Sadly, there wasn't time to stop and announce myself, even if I wanted to.

Though I was putting everything I had into it, I was slowing down nevertheless. My tank was nearly empty.

Fortunately, I was close enough that it didn't matter. I leapt, using whatever was left in my legs to propel me over the heads of the leprechauns, so I could ... totally misgauge the jump.

Fuck me!

I wasn't the most coordinated guy on the planet to begin with, and now – with floppy arms and a head full of cotton – I was about as adept as one might expect.

And it wasn't like it was a small window either. But no, I slammed right into the side of the building anyway, sliding down off it like a bug on a windshield.

I landed right in front of a group of those Lucky Charms eating assholes, their blocky teeth looking mighty terrifying this close up.

Had these dickheads been of their right mind, I'd have likely had just enough time to rue what a stupid idea this had been before becoming a pile of corned beef.

Thankfully, they were all still acting like good little puppets. So, I instead found myself next to an opening the little shitheads had just finished chewing through the wall, and with enough hesitation on their part to make good use of it.

It was a tight fit, but I was in no position to complain. It was either be killed or roll my ass in and try not to worry about the jagged metal as it ripped my arms to shreds.

On the upside, at least they were still partly numb from the poison.

Once inside, I got to my feet as quickly as I could, planning to kick the shit out of any of the little buggers who were hot on my tail...

And instead got to experience the less than wonderful sensation of something solid slamming into the back of my head.

"Ow! The fuck?" I cried, looking down at what had hit me and seeing, of course, a partially smashed potato.

I turned and found Falcon standing behind a makeshift barrier of broken furniture, a bag of spuds in hand.

"My apologies, Freewill," he said, still sounding annoyingly dapper. "I thought you were one of them."

"They're like two fucking feet tall."

"I know, but try listening to that infernal gnawing for more than a few minutes without going a tad batty."

Okay, I was willing to give him that one, especially once I felt tiny little hands grasping at my ankles as the leprechauns began forcing their way in after me.

"Shit!" I picked up the potato that had hit me and flung it at the grasping hands, watching it bounce harmlessly off the sheet metal as I missed. *Fuck!*

"Pop on over here and help me out, if you'd be so inclined. There's plenty of room for company."

I kicked one of the little demons in the face, leaving a footprint in its forehead. Sadly, that wouldn't slow it down for long.

Quickly, before any more of its buddies could follow, I hightailed it to where Falcon was entrenched. Truth of the matter was, he'd done pretty well with what he had to work with. It was like a defensible garbage fort, with an area around it cleared so as to not obstruct his aim. Fuck it, I wasn't too proud to share it with the guy.

I hopped over the barrier and landed on unsteady feet, listening to the crunch of metal as the leprechauns continued to widen the opening.

Falcon had been right. I could see how that could get maddening after a while. Still, it was probably a good thing. This close to him, I could smell the scent of his blood. Minus the incessant crunching, I had a feeling I'd be able to hear his heart pumping the sweet deliciousness through his veins.

Magi blood was full of all the vitamins and minerals a growing vamp needed for this nutritious breakfast. And it was right there for the taking. All I had to do was...

No, I reminded myself. No snacking on the wizard I was there to save. Focus, Bill!

"Seems like you've had a bit of a day since last I saw you," Falcon said, looking me over.

"It's getting there."

"I understand what you mean." He handed me a spud. "It's not exactly a pint, but right now it's probably the best I can offer."

I grabbed it in a shaky hand, then turned and lobbed it as a pair of leprechauns charged us.

The potato went flying off into the darkness, nowhere near its mark. Stupid poisoned arms.

Thankfully, Falcon was on the ball, lobbing two in quick succession, and leaving the leprechauns with mashed potato-filled holes where their faces used to be.

"Um, nice throw."

"Thanks. Used to play rugby. Handy skill to have."

"No doubt."

He glanced down at my still twitching arms. "I'm going to go out on a limb and assume you had a scrap with the apkallu out there."

"The apkallu?"

"Yes, indeed. Way back in the day they used to bugger around in ancient Babylonia, making right bastards of themselves to any unfortunate sailors they caught."

"Fascinating to know. So any idea why these alpaca..."

"Apkallu."

"Whatever the fuck. Any idea why they decided to ditch Mesopotamia in favor of Manhattan."

"That, friend, is the big question." He tossed the rest of the potatoes, five in total, into the air in the same moment he cast a spell. The spuds began to swirl around us in a circular pattern. Then, one shot out at lightning speed as another leprechaun got in and raced forward.

I let out a whistle of appreciation. "Motion detecting potato cannon spell. Handy."

"A little bit of homebrew sorcery on my part. Nothing but a party trick in any other circumstance, but handy as can be right now."

"Any port in a storm. Speaking of which, we know about these leprechaun assholes, but how do we deal with those fish fucks?"

Falcon shrugged uncomfortably. "Sad to say, but I was in the middle of looking that up when my shield unexpectedly fizzled. Damnedest thing."

"Yeah ... damnedest thing." I figured it might be best to not mention Sally, great beasts, or anything else potentially incriminating.

"Looks like we're in for a fight then. Lucky for me you chaps were in the area. By the way, what brings you out..."

"Oh, that? Um, well, we had a few questions about Sally's bracelet, but then you weren't picking up so we figured it was a nice night and all."

"What questions?"

Think fast, Bill. "You know, for the life of me, I can't remember right now. Getting the shit kicked out of me tends to do that."

"That it does, chum. How are you holding up, by the way, if I might ask?"

I lifted my hands. They were still shaking, but mostly controllable. "Getting there." Left unsaid was the fact that I was barely keeping myself from tearing his throat out. "How's things with you?"

"A bit knackered, but I'll make do."

"Hey, color me impressed, man. Holding up that shield for so long, I'm surprised you can even stand."

Thwppt! Another potato shot out, fucking up a leprechaun's day with a solid hit to the chest.

To my surprise, Falcon actually let out a laugh. "Oh, that wasn't me. No. If that were the case, I'd be positively legless. Had an Orb of Amun-Ra handy for just such an emergency."

"Orb of..."

"Think of it like a short-term magical battery, or back-up genny as you lot might call it."

Thwppt!

I couldn't help but notice our supply of potatoes was running low, and second shots were unlikely as the ones that hit home dissolved along with their targets. "I don't suppose you have any more of those orb thingies lying about."

He inclined his head, looking a wee bit embarrassed. "Sad to say, no. And somehow those blighters managed to deactivate all of my wards while I was out. I just barely managed to make it back inside before they caught me."

Oh yeah, no doubt about it. My karma was in the shitter as far as this guy went. On the flip side, it's not like biting him would really make things worse. Oh yeah. If anything, it would be a small mercy, saving him from a horrific death at the hands of... "No!"

"Excuse me?"

"Sorry, thinking out loud. What I meant to ask is, so what happens when we run out of potatoes?"

Thwppt!
Thwppt!

We glanced at each other as the last two shot out into the warehouse, taking down a pair of leprechauns. Too bad at least five more of the little fuckers had made it in before that last volley, with likely more on the way.

"Please tell me you have another bag somewhere."

"Fresh out," Falcon said, looking far less collected than I'd seen him up until now. "I don't suppose you'd care to make a run to the corner store for some more."

LUCKY HARMS

I kicked out at the nearest leprechaun, sending it flying off into the debris littering this place. Fuck me! It was like slamming my foot into a bag of wet cement. The goddamned things might be small, but they were built to last.

Next to me, Falcon shot a blast of fire into the remains of a couch, blowing it to bits and sending flaming debris into the horde of mini barbarians at our gates.

"I don't suppose you could maybe call your buddies down at the station?" I asked, picking up another of the hungry little shitheads by the scruff of its neck and giving it a good old-fashioned dwarf toss.

Sadly, all we were doing was scattering these guys. Their ability to resist both magic and injury meant they were back up and running toward us within seconds.

They're not here for us. They're here for him.

As was usual, lately anyway, Dr. Death was disturbingly apt. These things were mostly making a beeline for Falcon in their single-minded assault. I just sort of happened to be in the way. Truth of the matter was, I had a feeling that if I decided to, I dunno, take a piss break, they'd be happy to let me go.

But that wasn't my style.

I was no hero, don't get me wrong. I didn't have some Spider-Man complex about power and responsibility. And the only Uncle Ben I was aware of came from the rice aisle. I didn't sit around listening to the police scanner, hoping to hear about wrongs needing to be righted. If anything, I was happy to not have any part of that crap.

Yet, despite wanting to believe that, I found myself in situations like this time and time again.

Part of it was guilt. After all, I and my friends had played right into Gan's creepy little hands less than a month ago. As a result, magic was back and worse than ever. Sheila was gone, replaced by an Icon who, while my best friend, was about as well equipped for the job as a blind driving instructor. And Ed was still among the missing, albeit maybe that wasn't entirely bad as there was apparently a pack of psycho werewolves searching for his ass.

Yeah, guilt definitely played a part in it. The rest, call it a gamer's sense of balance. Though most of the campaigns I'd played with Dave had quickly gone off the rails, usually devolving into orgies in which my party ended up as the honorary dildos, they'd all mostly started with the same basic idea: evil was growing in the world and an opposing force was needed to keep it in check.

I think somewhere in my fucked-up mind I'd decided that me and my friends were the real life equivalent of that balance.

That said, I wouldn't have minded if some other gaming party took a turn from time to time.

"Sorry, no can do," Falcon replied, dragging me back to the here and now. He lobbed another indirect spell, ultimately doing little more than surrounding us with burning debris. "Sadly, this is beyond the ken of New York's finest. This is the reason they called me in, after all. Albeit, I didn't expect the a'chiad dé danann to hold such a grudge."

"This isn't their doing, even if they're still creepy little assholes. There's a ringleader calling the shots." I picked up a stool and smashed it over a leprechaun's head, knocking it to the floor. "Whoever it is, they're powerful. Oh, and before you ask, it isn't Char."

"Char?"

"That vamp vigilante I was telling you about."

"No offense, mate, but I kind of assumed that. The a'chiad seem to barely tolerate each other from what I've observed. I somehow don't see them rallying behind any banner but their own. Not to mention, they don't particularly care for water, so I sincerely doubt they'd go out of their way to become best mates with a bunch of bloody fish men."

Okay, maybe I was stating the obvious for anyone who wasn't a newb. Still, I wasn't sure whether it made me feel better or worse to know he'd concluded that there was something larger behind the scenes here.

Something larger like ... a Great Beast? "What?!"

"That's the question of the hour isn't it?" Falcon replied, no doubt thinking I was talking to him. "What exactly is controlling them?"

The unexpected suggestion from inside my own head caused me to pause in my defense. "Um ... yeah."

Talk about poor timing, as one of the little monsters picked that moment to launch itself at me, sinking its blocky teeth into my fucking crotch!

FUUUUUUUCK!

In the space of an instant, the crushing pain of a thousand cleated soccer players slammed into my balls.

All thoughts of any beast, minus the one between my legs, fled as I began to flail away at the leprechaun – punching, eye-gouging, doing whatever the hell I could to dislodge it.

All while screaming like a little bitch, of course, because there was no way I was taking this one like a man. Hell, I wasn't even sure that was possible.

I spun around, trying to pry this thing off me before it made a meal of my junk, but it was stuck tight like a taint-hungry tick.

And then it let go.

Sweet merciful God, it let go!

Oh, my poor aching dick. Even with vampire healing it was going to...

Hold on. Why did it let go?

I shouldn't have cared so long as it did but, blinking away the copious tears from my eyes, I instantly saw why. I'd been standing between this thing and Falcon. But in turning, I'd put him at this thing's flank, meaning the way to him was now free and clear.

Fuck it all. I didn't care who was calling the shots here or how evil they were. For that one small instant, I was simply grateful that they'd instilled into these creatures a single-minded purpose, one that didn't involve eating my dick for breakfast.

At the same time, I wasn't asshole enough to go and wrap my balls in gauze while these things chewed off parts of Falcon that didn't grow back.

I dropped to the floor, on legs that seemed no longer capable of doing anything more than curling up in a fetal position. However, I managed to reach out and snag the leprechaun by one of its stubby legs, tripping it face first onto the floor.

Not exactly a finishing move, but it was all I had in me at the moment.

Fortunately, rather than simply chomp off my fingers and be done with it, the creature continued trying to crawl toward Falcon's position.

"Are you all right?" he called to me from a few yards away, busy fending off four more of the leprechauns by himself and rapidly losing ground.

The only upside was there didn't appear to be more incoming at the moment. The tide from outside had begun to slake. No idea if it was my friends or something else, but I wasn't about to complain.

"J-just waiting for my dick to grow back."

"Take your time, Freewill. Nothing particularly interesting happening here."

Much as I didn't appreciate snark at the expense of my family jewels, he had a point. In a few minutes this would all be moot. With his magic useless against these things, and them pretty much invulnerable to anything not spud related, it was only a matter of time before he earned a one way ticket to their lower intestines.

And then what?

Yeah, it was possible that, their mission fulfilled, these fuckers would march off on some other errand. But it was equally likely they'd be freed from their spell only to eat everything they could get their grubby little teeth on, including me and my friends.

Shit! Maybe I should've saved those fries from earlier.

You're wrong. Potatoes are not their only weakness.

Once again, my subconscious decided to speak up. But at least this time nothing was in a position to chew off my favorite body parts.

The thing was, Dr. Death was right. He'd told me as much earlier. Hell, Falcon himself had confirmed it.

These things didn't like water. I wasn't sure if that was a wicked witch of the west thing or more like a cat getting pissed when you spritzed them in the face. But, with no potatoes in sight, it was all I had left to work with.

Fortunately, we were already at the docks, in a warehouse which jutted out to the edge of the pier.

"Falcon," I cried, hooking a thumb over my shoulder. "Get to the south end ... um, that way."

"I know which way is south."

"Then head that way as far as you can go. I have a plan."

"It's a bloody dead end."

"Not for a fucking wizard, idiot."

"Fair point."

He immediately made a run for it, heading past me and leaving the short-legged little gremlins in the dust. Less awesome was the fact that the one that had been crawling after him changed direction to follow ... once again putting me directly in its ball-chomping path.

Fuck me!

Under normal circumstances, I'd simply see how far I could toss the goddamned thing. But, as I tried to fend it off, I realized, with no small degree of horror, that I had nothing left. Hunger, injury, being on the go for hours on end, and healing from having my balls nearly eaten, had rendered me as weak as ... maybe not a baby, but not much better than one.

Case in point, this thing leapt at me, pure crazy in its eyes as it went for my face like this was nothing more than another shitty *Child's Play* sequel.

Unfortunately, I'd have had much more faith in my ability to win had the leprechaun been made of nothing but cheap plastic. Too bad it was more like fighting an angry miniature chimpanzee, as it grasped, clawed, and snapped at me.

"Goddamn it!" I tried to scramble away, but my body might as well have been moving in slow motion for all the progress I made.

"Not to be a pain, but what was that plan, Freewill?"

"Give me ... just a minute," I cried, now on my back doing everything I could to keep this thing from taking my nose off.

Hoping to keep its nasty yellow chompers at bay, I put a hand up to its face. "Chew on this, shithead!"

I extended my claws, driving my index and middle fingers deep into this thing's eye sockets, dousing my hand in thick, slimy, leprechaun blood.

Blood!

It wasn't human blood. Hell, it wasn't even vampire blood. But the sight of it caught my eyes, nevertheless. All at once, it was all I could focus on.

It's scent ... wasn't actually all that appealing really, both strange and alien, probably owing to the fact that I was dealing with a creature that time forgot. But, the nasty funk held just enough of that familiar coppery odor to make me salivate.

It was all I could do to not pull my fingers out and lick them clean.

Sadly, the creature, blinded as it was, apparently had the same idea. In my distracted state, I let my guard down, so mesmerized was I by the creature's unappealing yet absolutely enrapturing bodily fluids.

Before I could refocus, the leprechaun bit down with its heavy teeth, taking the tip of my thumb with it.

MOTHERFUCKER!!!

Jesus Christ. What was up with things either crushing, poisoning, or eating my fucking hands today? What was next, a spiked-gauntlet handjob?

Screw it! Two could play at this game.

Before I even realized what I was doing, I grabbed the leprechaun by the hair and yanked its head to the side. Teeth bared, I let the desire for blood take over as I sank my teeth deep into its thick rubbery neck.

Go figure, primitive leprechaun blood tasted about as good as I imagined it would. Think of cabbage but, instead of boiling it in water, use raw sewage instead.

The thing was, as vile as it tasted, I couldn't stop myself from slurping down more and more of it. It was like being back in college and experimenting with mixed drinks. Sometimes we'd find a winner, but more often than not we'd end up concocting something that tasted like it had come straight from Satan's asshole.

That didn't mean we let it go to waste, though. Besides, the more fucked up you were, the less taste really mattered.

It was kind of like that now, except instead of piss-drunk, I was starving – or at least it felt that way. And while a shit-encrusted cracker wasn't appealing to most, it was filet mignon to someone losing their mind to hunger.

The leprechaun began to convulse as I did my damnedest to drain it dry. I wasn't whether this would kill it or if it would be back to biting my ankles again in five minutes, but the truth was I didn't really care.

This was all about me.

And, amazingly enough, it seemed to be working. For all I knew, I'd end up puking rainbow-colored leprechaun chunks in the next five minutes, but for the moment the need to feed was starting to subside. Better yet, I felt my strength returning, at least enough to be functional.

The haze of hunger began to rise from my head and ... whoa!

Nope, scratch that. The haze wasn't actually lifting. If anything, it was simply grabbing a better seat, as a kaleidoscope of colors exploded behind my closed eyelids.

Da fuq?

I pulled my teeth out of the Leprechaun, then tossed its still twitching body to the side and opened my eyes.

"What the...?"

Becoming a vampire was a trippy sensation. Smells, sounds, and tastes were all enhanced to crazy levels. Sight, though, was a bit weirder. The rest were simply enhanced, but becoming a vampire was like cranking up the saturation levels on your eyeballs.

That said, it was fairly easy to adapt to. Everything was simply in sharper relief than it had been before.

This, though, was like someone had stepped into my head and fucked with the Photoshop settings of my mind.

Everything now glowed with an aura of its own, and I mean everything. There was a broken alarm clock a few feet away that was lit up like a chunk of Kryptonite.

I crawled over to look at it, then screamed when it sprouted arms and gave me the finger.

"Time to fuck off, asshole," it chittered before scurrying off like a clockwork cockroach.

Close by, a busted sofa grew a face and told me I'd better not even think of planting my ass there.

And it wasn't alone. In every direction I could see, inanimate objects came to life, most of them making rude gestures my way. And what didn't come to life was busy melting before my eyes, like some sort of fucked up Escher painting.

It was both wonderful and terrifying to behold, like being stuck in an R-rated Disney movie. That said, I'd smoked enough weed in my time to make it painfully obvious what was going on.

I was tripping balls on leprechaun blood.

Under different circumstances, I would've dug the shit out of this. Hell, I'd have parked my ass and enjoyed whatever shit the theater of my mind cared to show me, especially since it had been way too long since I'd gotten properly fucked up.

It was just one of many reasons why being an adult with responsibilities could really suck.

Sadly, now was not a good time to wander down that rabbit hole. I needed to focus. Falcon was waiting for me at the south end of the warehouse – whichever fucking way that was. And if I didn't get there soon, he'd end up being a smorgasbord to a bunch of midget cave trolls.

Interestingly enough, I could see at least three Falcons from my vantage point, all of them beckoning me in different directions, including one chummy fellow who was asking if I wanted to join him for some bangers, mash, and Doritos.

Truth be told, he was my favorite of the bunch, but I doubted he was real, not unless he'd inexplicably decided to break out his emergency stash and join me.

That would be so fucking cool.

"*Cool is all well and good, Freewill, but it won't save Mentor Falcon or stop these things.*"

"Huh?" I replied, replying to the familiar voice, one I hadn't heard in years.

Turning around, I realized another hallucinatory specter had joined the multiple Falcons putzing about – one I hadn't ever expected to see again.

"James?"

TRIPPING BILLS

James was as I remembered him, maybe minus the fact that he was glowing like someone had shoved a technicolor lightbulb up his ass. He was kind of like a leaner brown-haired version of Chris Evans' Captain America, with a bit more stubble. Of course, whereas a week's worth of facial hair would make people throw spare change my way, it gave him a rugged feel, the kind that would cause women to drop their panties in a heartbeat.

Not that I'd ever seen him abuse that superpower. He was the sort of guy who walked through life as if unaware he should be modeling underwear on the cover of GQ.

More important than his looks, though, had been the fact that he'd been unique among the elder vampires. Most of them had been humorless fucks, certain that their undead shit didn't stink. James, however, had been a good guy – smart, fair, and able to take a joke. Yeah, I'd seen him drink more espresso than was sane, but it's not like I could hold that against him. As far as vices went, that was a softball, especially for a guy around seven hundred years old.

Even his nickname had been cool. He wasn't James the Conqueror, or James the Bloody, as I'm sure plenty of other vamps would have preferred. Instead, he was simply known as the Wanderer. Apparently, at least from what Sally had told me, the guy talked the talk, in that he'd chosen to spend a good chunk of his long life actually out there living it.

In short, he was kind of like a real-life version of the adventurers I used to play in Dave's game, except infinitely cooler.

Sadly, he'd died back when the Source was destroyed. The spirit that had possessed him, making him a vampire, had been forced back to wherever it had come from, leaving his human half to rapidly age to match the long centuries he'd lived. However, even in that, he'd maintained his dignity.

Truth of the matter was, he was one of the only vamps I missed from those days, and not just because he'd pulled my ass from the fire on more than one occasion. If anything, these last few weeks had been even more terrifying because it felt like, without him, I was truly operating without a safety net.

Seeing him there now, staring at me with a bemused look upon his face, I really should've burst into tears and told him how much I missed him.

But I was high as fuck, so the best I was able to manage was, "Hey, man. What's up?"

"*What is up, Dr. Death,*" James replied, using his old nickname for me – which in turn had become my nickname for the beast inside of me. Goddamn, that made even less sense when I was tripping. "*...is that the a'chiad dé danann are still on the loose. And they shall soon make short work of the person you're supposedly here to save.*"

"Nah, it's cool, man. Falcon is right there chilling out."

James stepped up to where a semi-transparent Falcon sat smoking a fatty and waved a hand right through the wizard's head, dissipating him. Shit, one hallucination taking out another. That was meta as fuck.

"Dude, you just smoked his ass."

"*I need you to focus,*" he said, snapping his illusory fingers in front of my face. "*The blood of the a'chiad is apparently acting as a strong hallucinogenic right now. I need not tell you how unwise it was to ingest it, but what's done is done. Regardless, your healing should be able to compensate enough for you to complete your mission.*"

"I have no idea what the fuck you just said."

Illusion James stepped aside and pointed to the far end of the warehouse. Near the wall, I could see flashes of light as another Falcon was busy casting spells at a group of creepy circus midgets for whatever reason. "*That is the real Matthias Falcon, although I dare say he won't be real for much longer unless you implement your plan.*"

"Why doesn't he just ... what's the word, zap the fuck out of there?"

"*Have you not been paying attention? The a'chiad dé danann are magical parasites. They feed upon eldritch energy, enough so that certain spells are impossible with them in close quarters. And, even if he could escape, I sense a certain nobility within our dear Mentor Falcon. It's quite possible he understands that doing so could doom you and your friends.*"

"You could have just said he can't. Anyway, what was my plan again?"

Hallucinatory James raised a hand to the bridge of his nose and shook his head. "*Water. It's said these creatures have a weakness to it.*"

"*Oh yeah. Um ... what weakness?*" Little by little, I was noticing the weirdness around me starting to subside. No doubt my vamp healing was picking up steam. Even so, there was still a lot of weird going on, like the fact that Falcon didn't have any wings. Oh wait. That's the way he normally was.

"*Alas, I do not know,*" James replied. "*Our archives were vast, but my time spent studying them was ultimately limited compared to my exploration of this vast world. All I can recall is reading a quick mention of it.*"

Of course it couldn't be that easy. But I guess that would have to do. I tried to focus on where Falcon, the real one anyway, continued to battle the proto-leprechauns. I could do this. He was counting on me.

I prepared to launch myself that way before I could be distracted by anything else ... like, for instance, a nearby dresser that had suddenly grown several pairs of perfectly shaped tits. "Heh. They look like Christy's."

"*Focus, Dr. Death!*"

"Sorry." I ignored the busty dresser and narrowed my eyes in Falcon's direction.

"*Good luck, my friend.*"

A brief moment of clarity cut through the haze of being stoned outta my gourd, giving me a second to remember the loss I felt at James's death. A single tear slid down my cheek – either that or another piece of furniture had spit in my face. "Hey, James. I know this shit isn't real. But I wanted to let you know I really miss you."

"*Fret not, Dr. Death, for a part of me shall always be with you. Oh, and call me the Wanderer if you please. I always did rather favor that name.*"

I turned back to thank him, but he was gone – my vamp healing finally forcing reality to start asserting itself around me.

Break time was over. It was time to end this battle, one way or the other.

Tackling one person could be tricky enough, especially moving at vamp speed. Tackling a foursome of tiny little creeps all at once was closer to a pipe dream. Fortunately, whatever spell these things were under didn't make them the most perceptive fuckers on the planet.

That and I found a curtain rod that had somehow survived Sally's power. It wasn't all that sturdy, but I didn't need it to hold for long. The important thing was it was nice and wide.

Not a moment too soon, either, as Falcon's back was up against the wall. He looked absolutely exhausted, whereas the leprechauns advancing upon him looked good as new – which wasn't all that good, but it was still more than he could handle.

That was the problem with the Magi. They were walking artillery but had limited ammo before their load was spent. And Falcon looked spent. I could only hope he had a little bit left in him, because if not we were going to be utterly fucked.

"Heads up!" I cried, racing toward him, the bar held out before me.

He looked my way, confusion etched onto his face.

No real surprise there as I hadn't bothered to explain what I had planned, being busy getting stoned on leprechaun juice as I'd been.

"Go high!" was all I had time to scream before I closed in, lowering the bar enough that I was certain I was going to over-balance and face plant before I made it.

But somehow I managed to keep moving.

As for Falcon, he apparently got the hint – making a mad dive over me, the bar, and the heads of the leprechauns just as I slammed into them, pinning the evil little knuckle draggers to the wall.

Had I still been juiced up on vampire blood, I'd have likely had enough steam to plow straight through. As it was, though, I barely had enough to put a dent in the metal siding, much less hold the leprechauns in place for long.

"Blast us with whatever you've got left," I cried.

"Move out of the way, Freewill."

"There's no time." I wasn't lying either. The curtain rod was already deforming as the murderous little freaks tried to squirm free. "Now! Do it!"

I saw the flash from my periphery, casting our shadows against the wall. Knowing what it meant, I closed my eyes and braced myself for the end.

This was likely it. I was spent, done, finished. The only thing keeping me on my feet was a rapidly fading drug rush. No way was I going to survive a fireball, or any other killing magic for that matter.

What a way to go, I considered. All this time, I'd been making it a point to get the hell out of the way whenever a Magi opened fire. Yet here I was now, asking one to fry me at point blank range.

The hair on the back of my neck stood on end as I felt the tingle of power.

Here it comes.

In the next instant, it was as if the Giants' entire defensive lineup plowed into me from behind. There was no heat, no sensation of blowing up or being electrocuted. But goddamn if it wasn't like being hit by a truck.

And a big truck it apparently was, as both me and the leprechauns were instantly flattened against the side of the structure.

Ouch.

The outer wall let out a groan of tortured metal and then gave way, right as I was certain I was about to become a human pancake.

The next second found me in freefall, but only for a moment or two before I landed in the cold, not even remotely clean waters of the Hudson. Thank goodness vampires couldn't drown, because I was lucky to be able to dog paddle in my current shape.

But this wasn't about me.

It was all about the guests I'd brought along to this impromptu pool party.

Whatever spell or compulsion had been controlling the leprechauns seemed to have been instantly broken because, rather than accept their fate with quiet dignity, they all began to screech in panic as they desperately tried to clamber up onto the section of wall that had fallen in with us.

Too bad for them the heavy metal siding wasn't particularly buoyant. It went down quickly and so did they, desperate bubbles of air breaking the surface as they disappeared from sight.

Sadly, they weren't alone. Exhausted as I was, keeping my head above water was near impossible. After another moment, I slipped beneath the surface with them. It was ... unpleasant to say the least, and I made a mental note to try not to swallow any needles or used condoms that happened to float past.

The upside was that my night vision cut through the gloom a bit, enough for me to see what fate awaited the leprechauns.

Amazingly enough, the answer was far more mundane than I would've expected. They didn't dissolve or explode – which was good considering my close proximity. They simply sank, their squat bodies and short limbs effectively making them little more than angry little anchors.

But hey, that worked, provided they weren't like me and didn't have a particular need to breathe. If so, all I'd have done was piss them off, which seemed to be my unique specialty in the world of the supernatural.

One after another, the proto-leprechauns continued to sink until they were out of sight, leaving me alone in the dark waters.

There came a splash from above, making me wonder if I might have to duck some more debris, but then I saw another of the creatures – the one I'd bitten – flailing about as it sank. Guess Falcon was being thorough in his house cleaning. Smart. Now to figure out how to...

What the?

Just as the final leprechaun was busy sinking past me, the waters in the immediate area seemed to light up as if someone had turned on a high-powered beacon. Problem was, it was coming from below.

Wondering if maybe these fucking things exploded on a delay, I glanced downward and ... was suddenly glad I was in the water because my bladder instantly let go.

A massive pair of jaws rose up from beneath me, big enough to swallow a fucking car and full of teeth the size of saw blades. So large was it, that I couldn't get a good view of what it belonged to, except that it looked vaguely fishlike and was glowing an eerie electric blue ... like the granddaddy of those fish monsters up on the pier, except a magnitude more terrifying.

I could only watch in horror as the final leprechaun disappeared down the leviathan's gullet.

But, that was impossible. This thing, whatever it was, had to be the size of a freaking dinosaur – we're talking the aquarium scene from *Jurassic World* here. Yet I was pretty sure the water near the docks was no more than twenty feet deep – not enough for this Moby Dick-sized monstrosity to swim in, much less appear as if it were rising from the fucking Mariana Trench.

No way was this real. It had to be one last hallucination from that leprechaun blood. Yeah, that was it. It wasn't...

Get out of there, now!

Hallucination it might've been, but the voice in my subconscious was sure as shit convinced, although there was something different about it this time.

Sadly, this probably wasn't the ideal moment to analyze that particular nugget of insight.

The creature snapped its massive jaws shut, swallowing its meal whole and kicking my hallucination theory straight in the balls by the sheer amount of water it displaced – knocking me around in the churning surf like I was in a fucking washing machine.

I can't say for certain I wasn't still tripping balls, but it seemed like maybe a safe bet to at least pretend I wasn't. Needless to say, exhausted as I was, I somehow found the strength to paddle my tired ass back to the surface where I began to flail in panic, unsure of what to do next.

"Freewill!" Falcon's voice called from above. "Give me your hand."

I spat out a mouthful of water, wondering if he'd gone batty. The guy was standing at the edge of the hole he'd made in the warehouse wall, at least ten feet out of my reach. "How...?"

"Just do it!" he cried.

The water around me began to grow brighter.

Fuck it. I raised my hands out of the water, hoping Falcon had a rope trick spell handy.

Instead, a yellowish glow enveloped my arms, followed by the sensation of phantom hands closing over mine. A moment later, I was hoisted up out of the Hudson and back into the warehouse.

Landing on my feet, I looked back just in time to see the blue glow growing dimmer, as if whatever monstrosity it belonged to were returning to the nonexistent depths below us.

"I think there was something down there with you," Falcon said, breathing hard.

"No shit," I replied, my legs buckling and dropping me onto my ass. After a moment, I added, "Thanks, man. I appreciate the save."

"I figured it was the least I could do after hitting you with all that kinetic energy."

"Worked, though."

Falcon leaned against the nearest wall, looking almost as winded as I felt. "That it did, friend. Fair bit of insight there, by the way. If you don't mind me asking, how did you know they'd sink?"

"I didn't. But you said they didn't like water."

"I know, but that wasn't bloody much to go on."

"Seemed a better choice than letting them eat us."

"I'll give you that." He made a convoluted gesture and a flask appeared in his hands. Falcon unscrewed it, took a slug, then handed it to me.

Booze wasn't what I really wanted right then, but it would do in a pinch, especially if it kept me from murdering the shit out of this guy right after he'd saved my ass. A moment later, a belt of scotch hit my stomach, taking just enough of the edge off to let me speak again.

"Good stuff."

He nodded, taking it back. "Nothing tops off a fight to the death like a decent single malt."

I couldn't disagree with him. But what I could do was hopefully clear the air between us a bit, now while I was tired. Because later, when I had my wits about me again, I'd be just as likely to tell him to eat a dick.

"Listen, man. I need to apologize to you. I... I haven't been treating you very well."

It wasn't quite the confession he deserved, but I didn't think there was much to be gained by letting him know I was responsible for fucking up his defenses.

"Can't say I hadn't noticed," he replied with a grin. "If we're being truly honest with each other here, you've been a bit of a cunt."

I couldn't help but laugh. "Yeah, I guess I have been."

"Figured maybe it was a vampire thing, but I couldn't be sure. I can't pretend I've spent a lot of time in friendly quarters with your kind."

"It's not," I replied. "I mean, yeah, vampires in general tend to be dicks, but I was being one because..."

"Let me guess. It was that little misunderstanding the Academy had with the First Coven back in '07. Lot of bad blood came out of that one."

"I ... have no idea what that even is. No, it's nothing like that. It's just that ... Christy ... she and I ... she's ... shit! She's still out there!"

Goddamn, what an idiot I could be. Yes, Falcon was safe, for now anyway, but that wouldn't mean much if the rest of those things out there hurt my friends.

Despite wanting to do nothing more than lay there and wait for the sun to rise and put me out of my misery, I pushed myself to my feet. Falcon caught up to me a few steps later.

"Once more unto the breech, Freewill?"

"My friends..."

"Say no more. It would be my pleasure to join you."

My senses were still on the fritz. Between the residual drugs in my system, having taken a dip in the Hudson, and being about ready to drop, I would've been hard pressed to sniff out a pile of horse shit lying in the middle of my living room. Even so, it appeared to be quiet, the only sound seeming to be our footsteps as we navigated the mess that was now Falcon's warehouse.

"You were saying something about Mentor Fenton," Falcon said, as we made our way back toward the entrance.

"It's..." Oh, fuck it. They say confession is good for the soul. Guess it was time to test that theory. "I like her, I mean really like her. And it's difficult enough that her former boyfriend is back, not that I mind him being back, since he's my best friend and..."

"Not following, mate."

Yeah, I was rambling. It was so much easier to take an ass beating from murderous monsters than to discuss my feelings. At the same time, I'd fucked this guy over hard enough that, even if I couldn't make amends, I could at least clear the air between us. "Fine. I was jealous because you were hitting on her. Okay, happy now?"

"You think I was chatting her up? I did no such thing."

"You don't have to deny it, man. You were. And it was working, too." Fuck me! Why did I have to say that part? The last thing I needed was to let mustachioed Romeo here know that he had a shot. Still, it wasn't like I could take it back.

"I ... I'm flattered that you think so, Freewill," Falcon stammered, no doubt already scheming how to get his proper English mitts into her pants. "But I really wasn't."

Grrr! I knew I should've just killed the guy and been done with it.

We were nearing the entrance, slower than I would've preferred but, right then, staying upright was chore enough. There really wasn't time for this shit now, so I simply replied, "Yeah, you were. But it's ... *fine*, I guess. We can sort this out later."

To my surprise, Falcon grabbed hold of my shoulder and stopped me. "There's nothing to sort out."

"Listen, I get it, but..."

"I'm gay, mate."

"What?"

"Exactly what I just said. No offense to your female friend, but I already have a fine husband waiting back home at the estate."

There was definitely no time for this, but I found myself hesitating nevertheless. "So then what was up with all the compliments and politeness?"

Falcon made a haughty sound in his throat. "I'm British. It's what we do. I swear, one would think you yanks have never heard of proper manners."

"You're serious?"

"Absolutely."

And just like that, it was as if a weight of pure petty jealousy had lifted from my chest. Come tomorrow, once I'd had a chance to rest and fuel up, I had no doubt I was going to feel like quite the fucktard. For now, though, I was far too exhausted for such introspection. So, I simply said, "Okay then. How about we go save my friends? No, make that *our* friends."

YOU AIN'T THE BOSS OF ME

Turns out there wasn't much to save. Falcon was first out the door, glowing an angry red. However, he powered down almost immediately. At first, I thought he might've reached his limit, but then I saw his stance relax as I stumbled out behind him.

"Well, this is unexpected," he said, stepping aside.

I walked out to find my friends lined up near the wall of the warehouse, in front of the spot where the leprechauns had broken through. They'd formed a last line of defense between the creatures and us.

That explained why the incoming rush of creepy little fuckers had dried up, leaving us with only a handful to deal with. Albeit that handful had been more than enough.

All of them were alive, if somewhat worse for the wear. Christy looked dead on her feet. Sally was next to her, covered head to toe in blood and fish guts. As for Tom, he appeared somewhat distraught – staring down at a ninja turtle that was now missing an arm. Well, I'm sure that was traumatic for him anyway.

All around them lay piles of dust along with bodies of dead ... alpacas or whatever the hell Falcon had called them.

The apkallu.

"Thanks," I whispered beneath my breath, seriously weirded out to find my subconscious had adopted a new cadence, the same I'd heard while underwater. Strange, that he now sounded like...

The sound of feet hitting pavement caught my sensitive vampire ears, drawing me away from my thoughts.

I turned and saw a handful of tiny red-headed creatures running off in the direction of the city. A moment later, there came the sound of splashing from the opposite end of the pier, as if multiple somethings had decided to go for a nighttime swim.

"Yeah, that's right!" Tom shouted after them. "How do you like that shit, you fucking chum stains?"

I let out a laugh. He'd finally gotten a good one.

A scant moment later, I was nearly barreled off my feet as Christy threw herself into my arms.

"You're okay!"

"Mostly," I whispered back, returning the hug, "although, and I hate to say this, you might want to keep your distance until I can refill the tank."

"I'll take my chances."

That wasn't going to be an issue, though, as Tom stepped in – his aura lit up just enough to make me backpedal a few steps. "That's enough of that. Personal space, motherfucker. And no, you two should not get a room."

"Good to see you, too, man."

"Same, bro, although you look like you've been dipped in shit."

"Pretty close. I ended up in the Hudson."

Christy wrinkled her nose and laughed. "Next time tell me that before I hug you."

"You mean platonically, right?" Tom asked.

She sighed then, apparently tabling this discussion for later, stepped past us both. "I'm glad to see you're okay, Mentor Falcon."

"Thanks to you, Mentor Fenton," he replied, adding a cavalier bow.

Gah! Gay or not, this dude was still too smooth for my personal edification.

"Hey, it wasn't just her," Tom said. "You should have seen it when Sally..."

"Fought side by side with the Icon," Sally interrupted, the look on her face suggesting she was swallowing the equivalent of a shit sandwich. "Without him, we would've been screwed. Right, Christy?"

"Oh yes, definitely."

Tom smiled, no doubt enjoying the praise. "Much as I might agree, I was talking about how..."

"How you protected us with your invincible barrier of faith?" Sally once again cut in. "Yes, I agree it was ... impressive."

Their odd banter caught me by surprise for a moment, exhausted as I was. Then it hit me. They weren't kissing Tom's ass, so much as trying to deflect the idiot from spilling the beans about Sally.

Don't get me wrong. Falcon seemed to be okay, even if I wasn't quite ready to induct him into our inner circle yet. At the same time, dropping the whole great beast thing into his lap might not entirely be to our advantage.

Seeking to change the subject so as to keep Tom from flapping his gums, I turned to Christy and asked, "So what happened out here?"

She gestured to the area around us. "We tried to keep them off of you as long as possible. Not much else to it."

"Looks like you did a pretty good job."

She nodded, looking pleased. "We did okay. But this wasn't all on us."

"Yeah," Sally added, before Tom could open his mouth again. "A few minutes ago they simply stopped advancing. It was kind of like they all woke up. The vamps stood there looking confused, like the dumbasses they probably were. The others were a bit quicker to recover, and by that I mean they mostly went apeshit on each other."

"It was like a fucking battle royal," Tom said. "You should have seen it. All we had to do was stand back and watch while they kicked each other's asses. Wish I could've recorded it for Glen."

Sally rubbed her foot in a nearby pile of ash. "In case you're wondering, the vamps got the worst of it."

I nodded. "I'm not going to call that much of a loss."

"Me neither. As for the rest, I guess they finally got tired of murdering each other."

"Can't say I'm too..." I took a quick look around, realizing we were missing someone. "Hold on. Where's Char?"

Christy pointed back toward the city proper. "She took off right around the time the a'chiad dé danann did."

"She wasn't following them, was she?"

"I hope not."

I found myself hoping that wasn't the case, too. At the same time, there probably wasn't much we could do to track her if she had.

Besides, we were fresh out of potatoes.

Christy and Tom stayed behind with Falcon to make sure he was okay. Well, Christy did anyway. She tried to convince

Tom to go back to her place and relieve Glen, but he insisted on tagging along. Being that my best bud wasn't exactly renowned for his altruism, I had a feeling his motivations for sticking around were the same as mine had been, before I knew better anyway.

Fuck it. I could always clue him in later.

That left Sally and me to make our way back to her place to clean up. Fortunately, Falcon's warehouse wasn't far from where Village Coven's old safe house had once been, which meant easy access to the sewer tunnels – a good thing for me, as I really didn't want to end the night murdering random pedestrians on the street.

It was perhaps not the smartest move we could've made. The truth was, we had no way of knowing how safe the sewers were anymore, with all sorts of nasty things seemingly returning to this world. But at that moment, I was too tired to care.

"You look like shit," Sally said, matching step with me in the dark tunnel.

I glanced at her. "And you look like you just made a snuff film with the Gorton's fisherman."

That caught me an elbow to the ribs, probably not undeservedly.

"Maybe I should've borrowed a t-shirt from Falcon."

"That's assuming he could even find one after what you did to his place."

"True enough," she said with a laugh. "What can I say? I've still got it."

"That you do."

After a few more minutes of walking, the only sound thankfully being our footsteps and the ever-present drip of water, I asked, "So what really happened back there?"

"It wasn't all a lie. Tom actually was useful for a change."

"Oh?"

"In a dipshit sort of way, I guess. It also didn't hurt that those things continued giving me a wide berth, even though I didn't explode again. It was almost like..."

"You smelled like a rancid fish market?"

She glared sidelong at me. "I was going to say like I had a sign hanging around my neck that said off limits. But whatever. That gave Christy the idea for us to get in front of as many of those things as we could. It pretty much stopped them dead in their tracks. That gave Tom a chance to run through their ranks a couple of times, thinning the herd a bit."

"Then what?"

"Just like we said. They all kinda woke up and went back to being the assholes nature intended them to be."

"You think whoever was – I dunno – calling the shots gave up?"

"Hard to say. I mean, it seemed like they were all there to kill Falcon. But then why call off the dogs before the job was done? It doesn't make sense." She glanced at me, her eyes aglow. "Honestly, I thought it was something you did."

"Doubt it." I brought her up to speed on my portion of the fight, leaving out the parts that were obviously nothing more than drug-induced hallucination – as much as I might've wished James had actually been there.

"So you dumped them in the drink and that was it?"

"Mostly...," I trailed off, remembering the massive leprechaun-eating monstrosity that had appeared beneath me.

"Mostly?"

"I ... thought I saw something when I was underwater. Hard to say. I was high on leprechaun blood at the time."

"So glad to know you had time for a toke break while the rest of us were trying not to die."

"Don't judge me." Then, after a moment, I asked, "You don't happen to remember what this great beast thing looked like, do you?"

She shook her head. "Sorry, but I don't remember even saying it, much less getting a chance to check out its profile picture. It was like all of it happened in the time it took for me to blink my eyes."

"Nothing?"

"Not a word. It wasn't like being compelled, where you're like a puppet on a string but still aware. This was more like blacking out after a weekend binge."

"Can't say I have any shortage of experience with those."

"Oh? Did you ever wake up surrounded by dead bodies and covered in fish goo?"

"Hello? Are we forgetting about my Dr. Death-induced blackouts?"

"Oh, yeah. He was quite the murderous stud-boy."

"Not quite the word I'd use, but I'll give you the fish goo part. I did get the occasional dick drawn on my face, though."

"I have no doubt you deserved each and every one of them."

"Maybe, but I'm fairly certain none were drawn by fish monsters."

Sally shook her head, her expression turning serious in the dank tunnel. "Don't get me wrong, Bill. I'm happy something caused those things to back off. It's more the fact that *I* was that something which..."

"Scares you?"

"Pisses me off," she corrected. "For three decades, I was nothing more than a glorified slave to every vamp old enough to compel me. And now ... now I find myself right back where I started, just another puppet again."

"You're not a puppet."

"I don't know what I am right now. But what happened back there tells me one thing. Whatever it is that I got nailed with in place of that little bitch," she pointed to her head, "I'm not alone up here anymore."

Sadly, having seen what I had, I couldn't disagree. "We'll figure it out."

"I know."

I turned to her, surprised to not hear any sarcasm in her response.

"I mean it," she said, "crazy as it sounds. The game has changed, in ways we don't know yet. *I've* changed. But for everything I don't know, there's at least two things I'm one hundred percent certain of. I'm back in it again, whether or not I want to be..." She raised a hand as I opened my mouth. "I am. Let's not kid ourselves here. But I'm also in it with my friends ... including my partner, who I know would scour Heaven, Earth, and everywhere else he's clearly outmatched, if it meant helping me."

I raised an eyebrow. "This new optimistic Sally is going to take some getting used to."

"Don't get too comfortable with it. You're still a dumbass."

"Maybe, but I'm a dumbass who specifically told you to stay out of the fight back there. You had no way of knowing that those things would leave you alone, or whether or not something even weirder would happen."

"True enough. In fact, I only knew one thing for certain."

"What's that?"

"That you're not my coven master anymore. So, you can take your orders and shove them up your ass."

A moment later, the tunnels rang out with the sound of our laughter, somehow making the darkness a little less oppressive.

OF COURSE, THERE'S AN EPILOGUE ... DUH!

We made it back to Sally's place, only to find our wayward coven vamps had returned in the meantime. Turns out they'd left for nothing more important than to grab some pizzas for an all-night *Sharknado* marathon.

Because why the fuck not?

I was glad to see they were okay. But I was a lot gladder after I'd finished draining every last carton of pig blood they had on hand.

Once my head was clear again, realization set in as to what a shitty coven master I'd been as of late. Night Razor had been a true monster, a murderous asshole who ruled over his coven like a dictator – but in some ways I'd been just as bad. Ever since Sally had awoken, my hands-off approach had turned into something akin to full-on neglect.

After a quick shower, but before everyone could settle in for a night of mind-numbing B-movies, I sat down with them so we could talk – just that. I wasn't stupid enough to think it erased all of my sins of the past few days, but it gave us a chance to clear the air a bit.

It also served to remind me that there was a reason I was out there giving vamps a choice. Those who'd accepted didn't want to become monsters like those armband-wearing creeps, and part of making sure that didn't happen fell squarely onto my lap.

I needed to be better, and perhaps the first step on that long road was simply hanging out with them for some movie time.

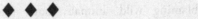

Amazingly enough, the rest of the night passed with no further incident – save me perhaps having my fill of fish stories for a while. I crashed on a spare couch and awoke sometime after noon the next day to find my hands and arms fully functional again. I went upstairs to check on Sally before heading out, but found a note waiting for me instead.

Alfonzo's flight got in early. Heading out for a hot date at the salon. Don't even think of interrupting us or I'll draw a dick on your face with a blowtorch.

PS: Talk to you soon, partner.

Oh well, guess it helped to have priorities.

That left me to bundle myself up against the sunlight and make my way back home to enjoy at least a day of relative normalcy.

One day turned into three, as it turned out, which I can't say I had any issue with.

During that time, there was no sign of explosive pulses, murderous leprechauns, or blind vampire vigilantes. Seems all the weirdness in the city had decided to retreat back to its own corner for the time being.

Tom met up with Kara again in that time, convincing her to help him raid his old storage box down in New Jersey – which his parents had refused to clean out after his death – returning with all sorts of useless shit to fuel his special sort of crazy as the new Icon.

We learned that Pop's house had been utterly trashed during the assault the night we'd been there. The police were blaming wild animals, both due to the damage the werewolves had caused as well as the fact that they'd found the place practically covered in wolf shit.

It was going to be a while before he could return home, not that he was in any rush. Now that he knew what was waiting for him there, he seemed pretty okay with taking an extended vacation down in Cape May.

Left unspoken was the feeling that those monsters weren't likely going to give up so easily, especially since we still weren't sure why they had a mad-on for Ed. That meant keeping close tabs on Pop, even if the idea of werewolves invading Cape May was kind of amusing. Left even more unsaid was still wondering who our unexpected savior had been and why they'd jumped in when they had. Were they looking to save us specifically, or had it simply been to fuck over Hobart and Myra, since they were kind of assholes?

At last, with most of us healed up, rested, and with things settling down to a dull roar, we gathered at Christy's place, or at least in the heavily warded apartment next door.

Even then, despite all the precautions she'd taken, Christy still asked Tom to take Tina to the park for a while. Considering the tyke's power and what we'd seen Sally do to Falcon's warehouse, it seemed a fair compromise.

That, and Tom was unlikely to add much to the conversation anyway.

"Love what you've done with the place," Sally remarked, eying some of the new wards etched into the walls. She was sporting a new do, courtesy of Alfonzo. Rather than going back to blond, like the old days, she'd done a one-eighty and gone dark – although I had a feeling it was more out of necessity than choice as I could still spy traces of green among her locks. A new pair of custom contacts completed the look, ensuring she could walk down the street without drawing stares – assuming, of course, she wasn't accosted by any Jenga enthusiasts.

"Hey, Dr. Strange has his Sanctum Sanctorum. Christy has her Sanctum Nextdoorum."

Sally glanced back at me. "I'm not even going to pretend that made sense."

"I believe I understood your reference, Freewill," Glen replied. "You're talking about the Marvel Comics character..."

"It's cool, man," I said, cutting him off. "Once you have to explain a joke, it isn't funny anymore."

He'd thankfully ditched the three-legged Irish Setter *disguise*. Sadly, he'd replaced it with a deceased tom cat he'd found in an alley somewhere. Unlike the dog, he didn't quite fit into this one, resulting in him looking like a disgusting cat zombie with a severe obesity problem.

Yeah, at some point we needed to have a talk about that.

But I figured I'd save bursting his enthusiastic little bubble for another day. For now, I could deal with him looking like *The Walking Dead* meets *Garfield*.

"Any word from Falcon?" I asked, turning to Christy.

"Aside from a courtesy text asking if everyone was behaving? Not much. I figure he might be busy for a while, repairing the damage we caused."

"You mean I caused."

She smiled. "Your heart was in the right place."

No, it really hadn't been, but I didn't see any reason to contradict her. If anything, she seemed pleased that I'd dropped the jealousy act. Why rock the boat? Either way, peace had been restored, even if the end result hadn't been any increase in our alone time together.

Yeah, that kind of sucked. But, much as I wanted to work on our relationship, I had to admit there were bigger fish to fry, at least for the moment.

"Any word on the stuff we asked him to look up?"

She shook her head.

Figured. We'd pretty much been responsible for turning his home into a shithole. So, I could see why we might not be at the top of his priority list. Still, hopefully he realized that helping solve our problems could potentially help with some of his own, at least regarding the weirdness in the city.

"Guess we're back to square one then," Sally remarked. "Knowing shit because Jack packed his bags and left town."

"Not entirely."

I glanced Christy's way from my spot on the couch, one of the few pieces of furniture left in the apartment. "Oh?"

"I haven't made much progress on this so-called great beast. Not surprisingly, it seems to be a fairly common nickname amongst ancient deities, and those are just the known pantheons. The name pops up numerous times across multiple different mythologies."

"Can't say I blame them. It's pretty badass."

"Maybe," she said. "But in terms of gods and demigods, it seems to be the equivalent of Robert or John."

"Or James?" I asked idly, not entirely sure why.

"I suppose. And that's not even considering other powerful entities, like elementals or dragons."

"Not sure I could handle going up against Bob the dragon," Sally replied.

"As I said, I'm still digging. However, I did have a bit of luck with another problem of ours."

"Which one?"

"Werewolves," Christy explained. "Lycanthropes, Hominus Lupinus, or however you want to call them. Much like great beast, they show up in myths and legends across multiple cultures."

"Nothing we already didn't know," I said, glancing Sally's way.

"Sometimes people see monsters," she replied with an eye-roll, "and sometimes they get high as balls and *think* they see monsters."

I raised an eyebrow, as that was disturbingly close to what I'd experienced while neck deep in the Hudson. Still, there was probably no point in running this discussion any further off the rails by bringing it up.

"True," Christy replied. "But it's interesting, nevertheless. Vampires and mages, for example, are fairly consistent in mythology. But tales of lupine shapeshifters, like the beast of Gévaudan, tend to be localized and short-lived. There'd be a spate of sightings over a relatively short span, but they all end just as quickly as they began. Over and over again, the pattern repeats across multiple cultures and myths, even up to recent urban legends like the beast of Bray Road."

I raised my arms and stretched. "That lines up pretty well with the old theory of people getting fucked up on wood alcohol, and then causing a panic until the local townsfolk threatened to kick their asses."

Christy nodded. "Which is consistent with what most of us have been led to believe."

"What do you mean led?"

"What if there's more to it than that? What if the reason these sightings all seemed to stop suddenly was because someone, or multiple someones, were working behind the scenes to put an end to them quickly and quietly?"

"So ... secret werewolf police?"

"I know how it sounds and, truth be told, I don't have anything to back it up."

"Too bad. That actually sounded kinda cool..."

"Except," Christy interrupted, "I did find one thing that might be important."

"Do tell us, Madam Witch," Glen bubbled before adding a quick, "Meow."

"You're here with us," I said. "No need to keep up the charade."

"Just getting in some practice, Freewill."

I was tempted to tell him to keep practicing. Maybe he'd get it right in another hundred years or so. But instead I turned my attention back to Christy. "Lay it on us."

"It's a short reference and a very old one at that. There's also a chance I might be translating it wrong. Enochian has gone through a few revisions over the centuries."

"How old are we talking?" Sally asked.

Christy grimaced. "Old. From roughly the same period when the ... White Mother is said to have ascended to the heavens."

"Pretty sure it wasn't actually heaven."

She threw me a pained smile. "Ditto. Anyway, I found a reference in an old scroll from that time. It's amazing I even noticed it. Nothing more than dumb luck really."

"What did it say?"

"Keep in mind, this could be nothing more than a metaphor, but roughly translated it reads: wherever Utu's shadow caressed the land, the wolves of men besieged the kingdom of Ib, seeking to lay them low."

"Wolves of men?" I repeated. "I suppose that could mean werewolves. Either that or there was a chihuahua uprising at some point."

"The kingdom of Ib?" Glen bubbled.

"Yes," Christy replied. "Again, assuming I translated it right. But it seems to suggest that in the early days of Ib's reign, there were rivals competing with vampires for supremacy."

"Yeah," Sally said. "They were called the Feet."

"I don't think so. The scroll specifically made mention of them as the Children of the Mountain, naming their domain as the forests and valleys. Why distinguish between the two if they meant the same thing?"

I shrugged. "Because ancient people were stupid?"

"Back up a second," Sally said. "You said this was a scroll dating back to the time of Ib? And you just happened to have it lying around in your personal library?"

She had a good point. I raised an eyebrow Christy's way. "Quite the eclectic collection you've got."

She grinned sheepishly. "I ... may have augmented my search a bit with ... the Falcon Archives."

I leaned forward, crossing my arms. "These wouldn't happen to be the same Falcon Archives you were declined access to, would they? And did Mr. Falcon suddenly change his mind?" Christy's silence on the matter was telling. "Uh huh, I see. So what happened to being disappointed with me for circumventing the so-called trust of the Magi?"

Her grin turned into a smile. "I thought about it for a bit, then realized I'd be remiss in helping my friends if I simply ignored the resources at hand."

"So, you pretty much said fuck it."

"More or less."

Sally clapped her hands and let out a laugh. "Look at you going all rebel witch. I love it."

Christy sat down next to me, snuggling into my arm. "Are you mad at me?"

I feigned annoyance ... for about two seconds anyway. "That depends. Am I going to get another lecture on what a bad vampire I am?"

"I guess you could say I've had a change of heart."

I leaned in and put my arm around her. "Then I think I can overlook you turning to the dark side."

She returned the motion and gave me a quick kiss on the lips.

"Get a room, you two."

I shot Sally a quick look, then turned back to Christy. "Technically, she's right. I mean, there is a room right over there, just a few feet away ... and Tom won't be back for a little..."

Almost like magic, we heard the front door of Christy's apartment open and him call out, "We're back."

"Of course he is."

Sally let out another bark of laughter as Christy and I scooted away from each other, lest we not hear the end of it. "Cock-blocked by the Icon. Someone oughta make that into a book."

The door between the apartments was still wide open – so of course Tina's voice came floating through a moment later.

"Daddy, what's cock-blocked mean?"

"I'll explain it to you later, Cheetara. Why don't you go play in your room?"

"Okay."

Tom stepped in a few seconds later.

"No, you will not explain it," Christy said almost immediately.

"What was I cockblocking?" He glared at me. "And it had better not be..."

"Relax, it wasn't," I replied, getting up. "She was just explaining to us how she gave Falcon the proverbial middle finger by accessing his precious archive."

"Really?" he asked. "Way to go, babe! Sticking it to the man."

"It's not quite like that," she replied, likewise rising.

"Hey, don't go downplaying this," I said. "You learned something about those werewolves. That's more than we had before."

"It's still not much. Nothing that can really help us. But, I did have one bit of actual good news I was saving for last. And, since everyone's here now..."

"Does it have to do with neutering those crazy ass-sniffers?"

"No," she told Tom. "This is about Ed."

"You figured out how to neuter Ed?"

Tempting as it was to reply, I chose to ignore him. "Do you know where he...?"

Christy held up a hand. "Not yet. Let me just preface what I'm about to say with that. But, I may have figured out a way to find him."

"How?"

"Every location spell I've tried has failed," she explained. "That means wherever he is, it's warded against detection."

I nodded. This was nothing we hadn't figured out already.

"But deep in the archives, I found mention of an old blood magic ritual, one I'd never heard of before.

Apparently, it was created by a long dead splinter sect, one accused of heresy against..."

"Let me guess. The White Mother?"

She nodded.

"I like these guys already."

"Can't say I disagree. Anyway, it's long, involved, and requires a lot of power. But if done correctly, we should be able to momentarily punch through even the strongest wards to get a sense of where he is."

"And once we know where his skinny ass is..." Tom said.

"We can rescue him," Sally finished.

"And that's a good thing, right?"

"Yes, Glen," I said. "That's a very good thing."

"Then let's do this! Meow!"

"It's not that easy," Christy explained. "There's components to gather, an incantation to translate and then re-translate to make sure I have it correct. And I'm going to need help."

"We'll help you," I replied, before realizing my stupidity. "You mean Magi help, right?"

"Yes. And even then, there's no guarantee. But if we can pull this off..."

Christy let the statement hang in the air, but that was okay. I could see a sense of renewed purpose both in her eyes and those of my friends. After weeks of spinning our wheels, we'd finally gotten a break.

Left unspoken was that, in addition to finding our friend, we could potentially find Gan, too – find her, force some answers from her, and hopefully put an end to whatever insane scheme she'd unleashed upon this world. It might not fix everything, but it would certainly be a step in the right direction.

All of them, even Sally, looked toward me – almost as if waiting to see what I'd say on the matter. Hah! As if I'd stand in the way of any effort to rescue one of our own.

"What Glen said. Let's do this!"

"Don't forget the meow, Freewill."

"Um, sure. Whatever."

I had no idea what this incantation involved, or what horrors would be thrown our way next, but none of that mattered at the moment. We finally had an opportunity to make our small group whole again.

Once that was done, maybe then we could finally see about bringing sanity back to this world rapidly going mad.

For now, though, we once again had hope and, so long as we had hope, we could face whatever came next.

THE END

Bill Ryder will return in
CARNAGE À TROIS (Bill of the Dead – 3)

BONUS CHAPTER

CARNAGE À TROIS

Bill of the Dead, Part 3

"Are you sure you want to do this? I mean, what if it all goes...?"

"What?" Sally asked, raising an eyebrow. "Tits up?"

"I was going to go with wrong."

"If it does, it does. Shit happens, Bill. That's simply a fact of life. Do you want to know the real difference between a good idea and a cataclysmically bad one?"

"Sure, why not," I replied.

"Glad to hear it, because I was going to tell you anyway. The difference is there is none. All ideas are just that, ideas. Good or bad are determined in hindsight. The best idea in the world doesn't mean shit if you fuck it up."

"So what you're saying is let's do this and not worry about it until such time as it bites us in the ass?"

"Exactly."

It was hard to argue with such impeccable logic as we headed downstairs to where the members of the new Village

Coven awaited us. No. That wasn't right. Village Coven was only their temporary name. Soon, they'd have a shiny new one.

I'd been wracking my brain to come up with something different, mostly failing until I realized there was a simpler method, something tried and true – having the members come up with suggestions and then tossing them in a hat. I'd briefly considered asking my friends to contribute as well but had quickly ixnayed that as, knowing my luck, we'd end up being known as the Bill Has No Dick Coven or something equally stupid.

Either way, I figured we'd save the naming ceremony for the end. I had a feeling the beginning of this little meet-up would likely be busy enough with everyone freaking the fuck out, as this was officially the first time Sally would be facing them since her little incident with Stewart – an unfortunate misunderstanding which had ended with him in about a million bite-sized pieces.

Ever since then, I'd done my fair share of talking the coven down, explaining that it had been an accident and that the supernatural world was a place where the phrase *shit happens* tended to apply more than usual. I'd been successful insofar as none of them had jumped ship yet but, needless to say, Sally hadn't been invited to anymore of their game nights.

I'd been debating how best to break the ice and get everyone back on talking terms again when the simplest of solutions had dropped into my lap. One of the new vamps had asked a question I didn't know the answer to. Sally, however, having once been a far more experienced vampire than I, could almost certainly provide some insight.

"You told these dipshits I was coming, right?" she asked once we'd stepped out of the stairwell and onto the floor the coven occupied.

"Shh. Keep it down. They can probably hear you."

"So?"

"So, I'm trying to smooth things over here, not hurt their feelings."

"Hurt their feelings?" she replied extra loud. "They're vampires, not the fucking Care Bears."

"I know. I'm just trying to be ... nicer about it." We stopped in front of apartment 2A, which had been designated as the coven's common space. I lifted my hand and rapped on the door.

"What the hell are you doing?"

"Knocking."

"Oh, for fuck's sake. Get out of the way. You're embarrassing me."

She elbowed past and shoved the door open.

In prior years and with a much different Village Coven, it was best to be prepared for anything, as it wasn't uncommon to barge in and see vamps fucking each other's brains out atop a pile of corpses. To say things had changed wasn't an understatement. The half dozen vamps who'd so far been recruited were all seated on the couch, fully clothed, and doing nothing more nefarious than watching TV.

A new day had truly dawned.

Whatever they'd been discussing immediately ceased as Sally stepped in, the only sounds to be heard that of whatever they'd been watching to pass the time, some banal sitcom if I was hearing right.

To their credit, none of the assembled vamps bolted or attacked, but there were certainly plenty of deer in the headlights stares going on, broken only once one of them took their eyes off us long enough to lower the volume on the TV.

Sally, never one for long hellos, jumped right in. "Your coven master asked me to come down here and..."

A thin, meek looking guy by the name of Craig raised his hand. "I'm not really comfortable with the word master."

Nods from the rest followed.

Oh boy.

I was instantly glad Sally hadn't come armed, because I had a feeling every single vamp here would be eating a bullet to the face.

But apparently she had a different take on things.

"Fine. Your coven *buddy* asked me to come down here and speak to you. Call him whatever you want but remember he's in charge. And in a vampire coven that means he has the final say over whether you live or fucking die!"

Okay, maybe not *that* different.

She stopped and took a deep breath. "But I'm not here to argue semantics. I've heard one of you had a question about feeding."

Another of the vamps, Jessica, said, "That was me." She had such a strong Velma vibe to her that I was surprised she didn't add jinkies to every sentence. "I wanted to know if it was possible to ... I guess, drink from someone without turning them into one of us."

"It's a smart question..."

"Even if you'll hopefully never have to," I interrupted. "Remember, our number one goal is to not hurt anyone."

"Which is nice but nothing more than a pipe dream," Sally continued, as if I hadn't spoken. "Bottom line is, you're vampires. You need blood to survive and it's the height of stupidity to imagine you'll never be in a situation where bagged or bottled blood is in short supply."

"I did pretty well." She raised an eyebrow at me. "For a while anyway."

"Exactly," she replied, turning back toward the others. "Feeding isn't exactly an art form, but it does involve learning to control your powers." She paused for a moment, her demeanor instantly changing from aggressive to something else. *What the*? "Because without control, bad things can happen, even if you don't mean them to. I ... lost control the other day and Stewart paid the price. I didn't mean it to happen, but it's something I can't take back. I need to be better than that. We all do."

Wow. That had totally come out of left field, mostly because I had a feeling if I'd asked her to apologize, she'd have told me to go fuck myself. But perhaps that was a good thing because it actually felt genuine – and not just to me.

"Thank you," Leslie, yet another of the vamps, whispered.

Sally threw her a curt nod then said, "Getting back to the point, it takes time to build up the control necessary to feed without turning. I think it was maybe four or five years before I could do it consistently."

"What did you do before then?" Bethany asked.

"Anything to make sure they didn't rise again. Usually a crushed skull will do the job nicely."

And so much for the touchy feely portion of our program.

"But you can work on that control with a few simple exercises..."

"How come you never told me any of this," I interrupted.

She glanced back my way. "Because I didn't expect you to make it four days, much less four years."

That led to a few chuckles at my expense, until Jessica said, "Hold on. If he's our coven master, how come you can talk to him that way?"

Before I could even flash her a smile of gratitude, Sally replied, "Because I'm an outside consultant. The rules don't apply to me. Now, as I was saying..."

"Holy shit!" another of the guys ... Oswald I think ... cried.

"Relax," Sally replied. "He's used to me saying..."

"Not that. Sorry, I meant on the TV."

I glanced that way, fully expecting to tell him to shut it off and pay the fuck attention, when I realized I recognized the place on the screen.

No doubt Sally noticed it as well, as she said, "Turn that up."

"City officials have so far refused to comment, but some are claiming this video, which has been circulating on social media, is proof positive that not only have the Strange Days returned, but that monsters now walk among us. We warn you in advance, what you are about to see may be disturbing to some viewers."

The video started innocently enough, someone filming a dark city street in Midtown. Then it panned up to reveal a familiar view – an out of focus chain link fence, and beyond it an abandoned pier and derelict warehouse.

"That's..."

"Falcon's place," Sally finished for me.

All at once, the air in front of the pier appeared to shimmer. In the next instant, the mundane imagery which had previously filled the screen was replaced with one of chaos. A purple energy dome appeared around the warehouse, for a moment anyway, before dissipating to nothingness. That was small beans, however, compared to the battle playing out on the ground around it.

It was a scene I knew well, being that we'd lived it barely a week ago. A flash of red off to one corner confirmed that. The only upside was that whoever had filmed this was too far away to capture Christy's face as she blasted a hole in the ground, sending several smaller figures flying.

The budding cinematographer apparently realized this, too, as they tried to zoom in on the battle, resulting in a still the newscast decided to pause on – a blurry closeup of a glowing fish monster, one of a race of beings called the apkallu.

"It was me, wasn't it?" Sally asked, as the news team continued to blather on, turning to a so-called expert to discuss the veracity of the film. "I caused that."

"Shit." There was no doubt, though. There was no way the timing was a coincidence. Sally had been swarmed during the battle, at least until the strange power inside of her had activated, sending out a pulse of energy that had not only blown the shit out of the creatures closest her, but had shorted out the force dome protecting Matthias Falcon's warehouse.

What apparently none of us realized at the time, though, was that the pulse had gone beyond that – frigging up the glamour surrounding the entire pier, the one that shielded the world from the weirdness going on inside.

And just our luck, one of the neighbors had been awake to capture it all.

I pulled out my phone and called up a few apps. *Son of a...* Sure enough, the video was trending on Twitter and already had millions of views on YouTube.

It wasn't the first time the weirdness had been filmed, but it might've been the first time it had gone viral, or been allowed to. In the past, such things had likely been squashed by the powers behind the curtain – the vampire nation, the Magi, et cetera. The vampire nation was gone, though. As for the rest, they were either asleep at the switch or no longer gave a damn.

"Double shit!"

"What do we do?" Craig asked, a tone of panic edging into his voice. "You said they can't know about us. You told us they'd hunt us down and..."

"I know what I told you," I replied, trying to think quickly. "But the situation has obviously changed. We..." *Come on, Bill, think!* "We ... need to get out in front of this."

"How so?" Sally asked, one eyebrow raised.

"I think it's time we finally do it."

"Do it?"

"Let the world know that vampires exist. That we walk among them, but we're not their enemies. We need to tell them everything before they can figure it out themselves, that way we control the narrative."

Sally inclined her head. "It sounds like you're talking about a..."

"Exactly. We need to hold a press conference about this, and we need to do it now."

To be continued in...

CARNAGE À TROIS
BILL OF THE DEAD – Book 3

AUTHOR'S NOTE

I won't lie to you. A small part of me is angry with myself for this book.

No, I'm not angry with how it turned out, the characters, plot etc. What I'm annoyed with is that it offers so many questions yet so few answers. Don't get me wrong. I was tempted to sprinkle some in here and there but, in the end, pacing of the story kept it from happening. There's also wanting to give certain plot points the details they deserve.

For instance, did you know that in the first few drafts of Strange Days (book 1 of Bill of the Dead), Sally actually woke up in the epilogue? No? Well, truthfully, why would you? I don't show my early drafts to many people. But there you have it. However, I ended up rewriting the epilogue completely, to remove those details and change up the character interactions because the original ending simply didn't feel fair to any of the characters.

It wasn't fair to Bill and Christy as it suddenly upended things and placed the spotlight on a character who was absent for a good chunk of the book. And it certainly wasn't fair to Sally as her miraculous resurrection deserved more than five hundred lines of text.

And I'll also admit, it allowed me to have some fun with it in this book as it was like "Here's the big mystery for book

2 ... which we shall now reveal in the very beginning of the story." I'll admit, I occasionally enjoy doing things like that – setting up a big plot point then, instead of drawing it out, being all, "Oh, hey. This shit's happening NOW!"

Because the truth of the matter is, life isn't always like a sitcom plot – where they can stretch out shit like this for seven seasons through a variety of bad timing and meet cutes. Life sometimes just happens, and my goal with every story I tell is to keep in mind the fact that reality doesn't always follow a script.

Anyway, my point is that sometimes questions are best left to build for a while, and I'm not just talking about the wait between one book and the next. And we're definitely in the building phase again. While I can't pretend to know exactly where Bill of the Dead will ultimately net out, I'm foreseeing a similar size to its predecessor – The Tome of Bill. In short, there's still plenty left to come. I can't promise it'll be a wonderful journey for our cast of characters or that all (or any) of them will survive it, but I can say that if you're still with me after this long, you may want to strap in because the ride's just getting started.

See you soon.

Rick G.

ABOUT THE AUTHOR

Rick Gualtieri lives alone in central New Jersey with only his
wife, three kids, and countless pets to both keep him
company and constantly plot against him. When he's not
busy monkey-clicking words, he can typically be found
jealously guarding his collection of vintage Transformers
from all who would seek to defile them.

Defilers beware!

Rick Gualtieri is the author of several books, including:

THE TOME OF BILL
 Bill the Vampire
 Scary Dead Things
 The Mourning Woods
 Holier Than Thou
 Sunset Strip
 Goddamned Freaky Monsters
 Half A Prayer
 The Wicked Dead
 Shining Fury
 The Last Coven

EVERYDAY HORRORS

THE HYBRID OF HIGH MOON
Get Bent!
Bent Outta Shape
Bent On Destruction

BILL OF THE DEAD
Strange Days
Everyday Horrors

TALES OF THE CRYPTO-HUNTER
Bigfoot Hunters
Devil Hunters

Second String Savior
Midnite's Daughter

Join Rick on Facebook:
www.facebook.com/RickGualtieriAuthor

Follow Bill the Vampire on Facebook:
www.facebook.com/BilltheVampire

CPSIA information can be obtained
at www.ICGtesting.com
Printed in the USA
LVHW030213191020
669134LV00005B/523